Swimming Naked

Laura Branchflower

LAURA BRANCHFLOWER

This novel is dedicated to Katie, Deighj, Tracie, Janet, and Ann (my blog sisters).

Chapter One

"Dadda...Dadda...up...up."

"Just a second, buddy." Phil was at the sink, screwing the top onto a baby bottle.

Lina watched Liam's small hands yank at Phil's pant leg, his demands to be picked up increasingly persistent. She rubbed her hand across her forehead. "I think I'm going to go upstairs."

"What?" Phil scooped up his son, handing him the bottle he'd just prepared as he turned to Lina.

"I have a headache. I'm going to go lie down for a minute." Her eyes were on the almost-one-year-old sucking on a bottle as his head rested on her husband's chest. She swallowed down the lump in her throat.

"Do you need me to get you anything?"

"No. I just...I can't," Lina whispered before rushing from the room.

"Katie?" Phil called out as he walked toward the family room. "Katie?"

"What?" Katie paused the television.

"I need you to watch Liam." He set him on the couch beside her.

"What?" Katie retreated to the corner of the couch, her eyes widening. "No way. I'm not watching him."

"I'm not asking."

"You said it wouldn't affect us if you brought him here. I don't want to be a babysitter. I don't even like kids."

"Watch him," he said firmly, pointing at Liam. "I'll be back in a few minutes."

Lina was sitting on the edge of the bed when she heard the bedroom door open. "I can't do it," she said. "I thought I could, but I can't. I'm sorry."

The mattress shifted as Phil sat down beside her. "It hasn't even been an hour."

"I can't look at him. I know it's not his fault, but he's the result of what you did—a living, breathing reminder."

"Lina." Phil stroked his hand up her back. "It'll get easier. Once you get to know him, you—"

"I don't want to know him." She came to her feet and headed toward her wardrobe. "I'll go to Adele's or my mom's for the night."

Phil cursed softly, leaning forward and resting his elbows on his knees as he gripped his head. "You said you would try. Forty-five minutes isn't trying."

Lina finished packing a small bag with pajamas and clothes for the following day before leaving the wardrobe and crossing to the bathroom. "I tried," she said when she felt Phil's presence in the doorway. "You have no idea how hard." She began to toss toiletries into the bag.

"One night. All I'm asking for is one night."

"I can't." Lina shook her head. She'd thought she could. She'd even picked out a crib and decorated a nursery for Phil's son, but the reality of him was so different from the imagined.

"I'll leave," he said, his voice sounding defeated. "I'll take him to a hotel."

"No. All his things are here. It'll be easier if I just go to Adele's." Lina lifted the bag and turned from the sink.

"You shouldn't be the one leaving."

"This is the best solution, Phil. I'll be back tomorrow."

Chapter Two

Six months earlier…

Phil Hunter stepped out of the shower and wrapped a towel around his waist. He was home. His wife was asleep in the next room. If he was dreaming, he didn't want to wake up.

"Phil?" Lina called out.

"Yeah, baby?"

"It's almost five." Lina was getting out of bed when he stepped out of the bathroom.

His gaze slowly traveled the length of her naked body, which, thanks to almost daily trips to the local yoga studio and her running routine, was still lean and fit at forty-one. "I could look at you forever."

"Stop." She didn't like being complimented for her physical appearance, even by him. It was one of the hundreds of things he'd missed about her. It was as if she was embarrassed by her beauty. And she was beautiful. Her thick brown hair, almost the exact shade as his, fell to her shoulders. Her chestnut-colored eyes were large and had an

4

almost imperceptible slant, giving her an exotic look. There was elegance to her, a refinement that enveloped her whether she was in the garden in cutoff jean shorts and a tank top or at a black-tie event in a floor-length gown with diamond earrings dangling from her ears.

"Stop staring at me," she laughed as she donned a robe.

"I can't help it." He slipped one of his hands inside her robe before she could close it, hauling her body into his. "I missed you. It was never right, us being apart."

"I know." She wrapped her arms around his neck as she tilted her head back, meeting his eyes.

He felt a stab of guilt for what he'd put her through. "Lina—"

"Don't," she interrupted. "You don't have to say anything. It's a fresh start. I forgive you."

"I want you to know, I would never—"

"I know," she again interrupted. "Last week when you took me to dinner, you asked me to consider something, remember?"

His eyes narrowed as he tried to recall what she was referring to. He'd said a lot of different things that night as he'd tried to convince her to take him back. "Are you talking about when I asked who you wanted to swim naked with when you were old and gray?"

"No, although it's the same thing. I'm referring to when you asked me to consider whether a flawed version of you is better for me than a perfect version of anyone else."

He felt humbled by the love he could see shining in her eyes as she stared up at him. "I remember."

"It is. I don't want to be with anyone else. Only you."

He covered her mouth with his, kissing her deeply as he led her back toward the bed.

"I need to go pick up some of my clothes," Phil said about thirty minutes later. He pressed his lips into Lina's shoulder. "I won't be long. I'll take Logan over later in the week to get whatever I can't carry tonight."

"We need to tell them," Lina said. She pushed herself up on her elbows, watching him as he began to dress.

"Don't you think they know? My car's in the driveway and my shoes and jacket are in the family room." He pulled up the zipper of his jeans.

"We still need to talk to them," Lina said.

"I think I left my shirt downstairs." They'd been in the family room when she'd told him she wanted him to come home, and they were already half undressed by the time they'd reached the bedroom."

"My clothes are down there." Lina scrambled from the bed. "You took all my clothes off down there. Oh my God. I'm sure they've seen them. What could they be thinking?"

"That I'm back." Phil headed toward the door. "I'm going to borrow one of Logan's shirts."

"No!" Lina cried. "You can't just go out there like that. It will confuse them. We need to talk to them first."

She was being ridiculous, but he wasn't going to argue with her, especially when she was wearing her worry frown. God he'd missed her expressions.

"I need a shirt," he said.

"Let me get dressed and then I'll get it."

He sat down on the edge of the bed, savoring the simple act of watching her put on a pair of jeans and a top. "You're so fucking beautiful."

"Stop it."

***

Lina took a deep breath as she left the master suite and headed down the hallway toward Logan's room. She was worried about his reaction to his father moving back in. Of their three children, he'd been the most unforgiving of Phil's infidelity. She found him in the den outside his room, sitting in front of the television playing a video game, his brow furrowed in concentration.

She felt like she was the child and he was the parent. "I need to borrow a T-shirt for your dad. Do you have something you think might fit him?" At six foot three, Phil was only an inch taller but considerably broader than his lanky son.

"You can look in my drawer," he answered absently, continuing to play his game.

She went into his room and crossed to his dresser, shuffling through the contents of his middle drawer, where she put his nicer T-shirts. She settled on one her oldest child, Megan, had brought him back from UVA when she came for her winter break from college.

"Is he back?" Logan asked when she began to walk past him. "I mean, is he moving back?" He pushed his wavy dark hair back from his eyes. He seemed to be changing more every day. At fifteen, her once cute boy with the ready smile and dimples was looking more like a man every day.

"He is. Are you okay with that?" It was an unfair question, considering his opinion had no bearing on her decision, but she wanted to know.

"I guess." He shrugged before returning his attention to the television screen.

Lina was headed back toward her bedroom when she was confronted by sixteen-year-old Katie who had just ascended the stairs. "You and Dad have been in your bedroom all day," Katie said in an accusatory tone. At barely five feet tall,

Katie definitely took after Lina's side of the family and in particular Lina's sister, Adele. Not only were they both petite, barely weighing one hundred pounds, but they had the same dark, straight hair and ivory complexion. If it weren't for Katie's light-blue eyes, the exact same color as Phil's, Lina would say she hadn't inherited any of the Hunters' physical traits.

Lina again felt like a child instead of the mother as her daughter looked suspiciously at her. "We were tired."

"Your clothes are all over the family room. I shouldn't have to come home to that."

"I have to get this to your father." Lina held up Logan's T-shirt.

"Dad knows things have changed, right? He can't expect to come back and start telling us what to do again."

"He is your father."

"But we've been fine without him living here, so he can't come back unless he agrees not to be so bossy."

Lina raised an eyebrow, listening to Katie recite her demands before she'd agree to her father returning home. They included not questioning her when she was leaving or arriving home, unlimited visits from her boyfriend, Matt, and no demands of any type. "Also, he can't control the remote. If we're downstairs watching something, he can't just come in and tell us to change the channel."

"That seems a little unreasonable, considering you have the den up here with a television."

"He has a television in his bedroom," Katie countered.

If she didn't look so serious, Lina would have laughed. "I'll take it under advisement," she said instead as she began to walk down the hall to her bedroom.

"The Matt part is nonnegotiable," Katie called after her.

"They know," Lina told Phil as she entered the bedroom.

"Good." Phil began to tug the UVA T-shirt over his head. It was snug, accentuating the width of his shoulders and the muscles in his upper arms. A former college lacrosse player, his hobby was now competing in triathlons, and his training was evident in his fit, athletic body.

Lina crossed to her dresser and took out a shirt she hadn't planned to admit she had. "His is too small for you."

He looked down at the faded T-shirt she'd handed him. It was the only original remaining from his time at Georgetown Law School. "I thought I lost it." He lifted his eyes to hers.

"No. You left it here." And I kept it, she thought but didn't say. On particularly lonely nights she would wear it so she could feel closer to him. Lina watched him peel off the tighter shirt, her eyes lingering on his muscled chest. She'd missed him so much.

"Should I keep it off?" he teased, catching her watching him.

"Don't be cocky."

"Come here."

"No." She shook her head. "It's late. I have to make dinner and you have to go to the Farside house to get clothes."

"Just one touch."

She couldn't resist him. She crossed to him, sliding her hands up his warm chest. "I need to get dinner ready."

"I know." He dropped his mouth to her neck and clasped her hips in his hands, dragging his lips over her sensitive skin. "But I need to be inside you one more time first."

***

An hour later, after picking up enough clothes from his rental house to last him a few days, Phil walked across the empty parking lot toward his church. The doors were unlocked, as he'd known they would be. He made his way to his familiar pew, knelt down, and brought his hands together. Instead of asking God to bring Lina back to him, as he had done daily for the past six months, he thanked Him for answering his prayers.

It was almost seven when Phil left the church and returned home. He came out of the mudroom, pausing just inside the kitchen. Lina's back was to him as she stood at the stove. He'd dreamed of the exact scene so many times over the past months, being home with his family for dinner. He crossed to her, cupping her hips as he pulled her back in to his body. "I love you," he whispered against her ear.

She leaned back in to him, sliding her hands over the top of one of his. "I didn't hear the garage door. Do you want a beer? Adele left some in the refrigerator the other day."

"I want you," he said.

"That will have to wait."

"I forgot how fucking good you smelled. I may spend the rest of the night just smelling you."

"Is dinner ready?"

The sound of Logan's voice had Lina slipping out of Phil's arms. "Yes. Grab yourself a drink and tell Katie it's time to eat."

Moments later Phil was twisting the cap off his beer as he watched Logan begin to take a seat at the head of the table. Logan caught himself before he sat down and shifted to the seat he used to occupy before Phil moved out.

"You don't have to pretend to be Dad anymore," Katie said.

"I didn't," Logan mumbled.

"Katie, don't tease him," Lina said.

"I'm not. He totally acted like he was Dad. He sat in his spot at the table. He sets the house alarm."

"Someone had to," Logan said.

"The only reason Matt isn't here is because he had band practice," Katie told Phil as he joined them at the table. "He comes for dinner a lot."

An image of Katie's tattooed boyfriend flashed in Phil's mind. He'd met him a few times. He was two years older than Katie and had no plans to go to college, instead focusing on making it as a musician. Phil wasn't impressed.

"Dig in, everyone," Lina said as she joined them.

Logan was uncharacteristically quiet at dinner, only speaking if he was asked a direct question. As soon as he finished eating, he excused himself and went upstairs.

Phil followed him. "Everything okay?" he asked, pausing in Logan's bedroom doorway.

"Yeah." Logan was sitting on the edge of his bed, staring down at his clasped hands.

"You don't seem okay. Is this about me moving home?"

Logan lifted his gaze to his father's. "I thought you were getting a divorce. It's kind of weird. I didn't know you were thinking about getting back together."

"I never wanted to move out. You knew that."

"Mom used to cry," Logan said. "At night, when she thought we were sleeping, I could hear her through her door. She'd pretend to be okay, but she wasn't."

Phil walked farther into the room, lowering himself down onto the bed beside Logan. "I hurt her. I know that. But she's forgiven me. I'm going to do everything in my power to make it up to her. Okay?"

"You'd never do it again, right?" He lifted his chin slightly. "Cheat on her."

"No," Phil answered, his heart aching at the pain in his son's eyes. "No, Logan."

"Good."

"I appreciate you looking after your mom and Katie when I wasn't here. I know you were trying to be the man of the house. I'm back now. You can relax, okay?"

"Yeah."

Knight, the boxer mix Lina had adopted shortly after Phil moved out, trotted into the room. "Where does he sleep?" Phil asked, scratching the dog's head. He had a vague memory of Lina saying the dog made her feel safe.

"With Mom."

"He can start sleeping with you," Phil said as he came to his feet.

"Really?" Logan's eyes widened. He looked happy for the first time that day.

"Yep. He's all yours."

Chapter Three

"Phil moved back home yesterday," Lina told her sister, Adele, the following morning. She was sitting in front of Adele's desk at Martins, the real-estate company where Adele worked as an agent and Lina worked as a stager.

Adele lifted her gaze from her laptop. "You don't expect that to come as a surprise to me, do you? You weren't even attempting to move on."

"I tried. I just. I didn't want to."

"So how is it going to work with the baby? Is he going to start bringing him to your house?"

"I don't know." Lina's stomach twisted at the thought of his child. "We haven't discussed it."

"You haven't discussed it?" Adele's already large eyes grew larger. "You've agreed to take him back without knowing how his son fits in to the equation?"

"It's not important. We'll make it work."

"I think it is important. Very important. And just for the record, I still think Phil's an asshole."

"I know what you think of him. You've told me repeatedly, but I would hope since I've decided to forgive him you could keep your negative opinions to yourself, at least around me."

"I can't make any promises." Adele came to her feet. "I need more coffee. Do you need more coffee?"

"No." Lina felt a wave of sadness as she watched Adele walk away, hating the estrangement between her sister and Phil. Lina knew that in addition to being outraged for her at Phil's infidelity, Adele felt personally betrayed. Because of their nonexistent father, Phil had been the most consistent male presence in all of their lives. From the moment he'd begun dating Lina at sixteen, he'd taken on the role of patriarch of Lina's family, warning other males to treat the Rayburn girls with respect, giving them life advice whether they wanted it or not, and handling the physical chores around the house, like shoveling their driveway during snowstorms and mowing their lawn.

He'd walked Adele down the aisle at her first wedding and offered a heartfelt toast at her second. He was there when Lina's younger sister, Shiloh, called him to come get her in the middle of the night after a fight with her husband or when she was stranded on the side of the road with a flat tire and no spare. For two and a half decades he'd been the most stable, reliable male presence in their lives.

***

Phil was in court all morning, so it was almost noon when he reached Hurte, Dunlop, and Smith, the Baltimore law office where he'd been practicing for eighteen years, the last thirteen as a full partner.

He'd barely made it out of the firm's plush lobby when he saw Wayne Hurte, one of the firm's founding partners and a close personal friend. As soon as he saw the smile on Wayne's face, he knew he'd heard he was back with Lina.

"The best fucking news I've heard in years," Wayne said before engulfing Phil in his arms. "It's fantastic." He kept his arm around Phil's shoulders as he ushered him into his office. "Diane cried when she called to tell me. She's been depressed since the two of you split. It will be nice to have my wife back." He was at the bar on the far end of his office.

"It's only noon," Phil pointed out.

"I wouldn't care if it were eight a.m. We're celebrating." Moments later he was handing Phil a glass of scotch. "To second chances," he said before tapping his glass.

Phil took a swallow of the scotch he hadn't intended to drink. "I don't know if I'm ever going to come down from this high."

"How did Kim react?"

"Thank you. That did it," Phil said dryly. "I haven't told her. It's been two days. I've got to get back to work." He finished the scotch and set his empty glass on the edge of Wayne's desk. "Thanks for the drink."

When he reached his office, his secretary, Anne, nodded toward the phone. "Kim's on the line," she whispered. She always whispered when she mentioned Kim, as if she were helping him keep a secret. Her hand was covering the mouthpiece of the phone.

"Put her through," he said, not slowing his stride. Moments later he was dropping down into the chair behind his desk and lifting the receiver to his ear. "Yes?"

"He just had his sixteen-week appointment with the pediatrician. One hundredth percentile for height and weight and excellent eye-hand coordination. The doctor said he's a big boy. He takes after his daddy."

"You couldn't have texted this?"

"I just took a chance you might be in."

"I told you to only call my cell."

"I tried. You didn't answer."

"That doesn't give you permission to call my office. I've got to go. I'll see him Wednesday night as planned." He ended the call. "Anne?" he called out. "Would you come in here?"

"Yes?" Anne asked after stepping into the room.

"Unless she's calling from a hospital, it's not important. Okay?"

She nodded, a blush settling over her face. "Sorry."

"There's nothing to be sorry about. I just wanted to make that clear. I don't want you to have to wonder if I want to take her call. I don't. And you don't have to bother to take a message. She has my cell number. She can leave a message directly with me. You don't need to be involved."

"Okay." She nodded. "So, I shouldn't even tell you that she's called?"

"No."

"Got it." She began to turn away.

"One more thing," he said, waiting for her to return her attention to him before continuing. "I'm back with my wife. Would you update my address information?"

"Yes." She smiled. "I'll do it right now. Congratulations. I mean, I know it's none of my business, but I'm very happy to hear that. It's wonderful news."

"It is," he agreed. He felt a stab of guilt as he watched her leave his office. He probably owed her an apology. She'd never mentioned it—she was too professional for that—but he had no doubt she'd known about the affair long before it became the main topic of gossip around the firm. She'd had a front-row seat to Kim's unfettered access to him. He could recall many evenings when she'd duck her head into his office to say good night and Kim would be sitting on the edge of his desk or on the couch, waiting for him to finish whatever work was in front of him.

***

Lina was in her bathroom putting on the final touches of her makeup later that evening when Phil appeared in the doorway. "What are you doing here?" she asked. "Did you forget about Logan's concert?"

"No." He slowly shook his head. "I'm here to pick up my wife." He stopped behind her, cupping her shoulders as he lowered his mouth to the side of her neck. "Are you ready?" He brushed his lips over her skin.

"You just drove forty minutes out of your way so you could turn around and drive back?" His office was ten minutes from Gilman, the all-boys high school Logan attended.

"I came home to pick up my wife."

"I'm capable of driving myself, you know." She was secretly pleased, not having relished the thought of navigating Baltimore's Beltway during rush hour.

"I know what you're capable of." He continued to run his mouth along her neck, the abrasiveness of his scruff rough against her skin.

She closed her eyes, leaning her body back in to his. "You're going to make us late."

"I think we can be a little late."

17

They were fifteen minutes late. Phil took a cursory glance through the window in the door, promptly opened it, and ushered Lina inside. The performance hadn't started. The headmaster was onstage, giving his usual spiel about the fine traditions of the school and the need for continued financial support from both current families and the alumni. If Lina had been alone, she would have quietly slipped into the closest seat, not wanting to draw attention to her late arrival.

Not Phil. He walked into the room the way he walked into every room, like he owned it. He was born believing the world was his for the taking. His confidence was effortless. Where Lina wasn't comfortable with a new situation until she had time to analyze her surroundings and figure out how she fit in, Phil never worried about fitting in. He expected others to adapt to him.

Lina felt the curious stares as they walked down the aisle, her hand held firmly in Phil's. They'd been estranged when Logan started at Gilman in the fall, so it was their first time attending a function together. She wasn't sure which parents knew their history, but she had no doubt there was going to be disappointment among the single mothers. Until his affair, she'd been oblivious to the attention he drew from the opposite sex. Now she couldn't stop herself from noticing the appreciative stares Phil was constantly receiving from other women.

Phil located two empty seats about ten rows back from the stage. They weren't next to each other—there were four occupied seats between them—but without Phil even having to make the request, people automatically shuffled around until the two empty seats were beside each other. They ended up in two of the best seats in the auditorium. The headmaster concluded his remarks as they sat down.

"Perfect timing," Phil said.

"Shh," Lina scolded.

He captured her hand in his, bringing it to rest on his thigh. "What is this again?"

"No talking," she whispered. "It's starting." It was hard to believe they'd been apart. It felt so natural to be sitting beside him with her hand on his thigh.

It was Gilman's annual talent show, which turned out to be surprisingly funny. Logan's act was the last of the evening. He'd barely mentioned it at home, so Lina was completely unprepared when her six-foot-two son stepped onstage dressed as a little girl, in a white leotard and a red-and-white polka-dot skirt, complete with black patent-leather shoes big enough to accommodate his size-thirteen feet and a red bow on top of his head. Beside him were Brian Drayton and Will Ellis, two of his closest friends, looking every bit as ridiculous.

The entire audience was roaring with laughter before they uttered a word. The boys stood side by side next to three evenly spaced microphones, looking completely serious until the laughter died down. Then they began to sing "I'm a Little Teapot." They sang the song in perfect harmony, even tilting their heads and swaying their hips at the same moments.

Like much of the audience, Lina laughed until she cried. The only person who laughed harder was Phil, who she knew would have fallen out of his chair if his size had allowed it. There just wasn't enough room.

As soon as the performance ended, Lina escaped to the restroom to touch up her makeup, having no doubt mascara was running down her cheeks. As she dabbed a wet towel beneath her eyes, a mother she knew from Logan's lacrosse team stopped beside her.

"I couldn't help notice you come in with Phil. Are you back together?"

"Yes," Lina answered. She could feel the curious glances from the other women waiting for open stalls. She had no desire to discuss her marriage in a bathroom filled with mothers of her son's classmates.

"Good for you. You're much more forgiving than I could ever be."

"I guess we're all different." Lina continued to touch up her makeup.

"What about the baby? Is he going to see it or—"

"Yes," Lina interrupted. "Excuse me." She stepped around her and left the bathroom, plowing directly into a hard body. "I'm so sorry," she began, "I didn't..." The words died in her throat when she looked up at Nick Drayton.

"Lina."

Lina's face heated. "Nick." It had been only two days since she'd see him, but it may as well have been a year, so much had changed.

"That was funny, wasn't it?" he asked.

"Oh my God." She pressed her hand into her chest. "I don't know if I've ever laughed that hard. I can already tell my stomach muscles are going to be sore tomorrow."

"I saw you arrive with your husband."

"Yes." She felt bad for not telling him beforehand. "I'm sorry. I meant to call you and let you know."

"It's okay. You don't owe me an explanation."

"I don't know if that's true." She'd been semi-dating him.

"How about our sons in dresses?"

***

Phil was near the punch bowl, conversing with several other fathers about the lacrosse team, when he spotted Lina across the lobby. She was laughing, and his first thought was how fucking beautiful she was. Then he realized she was talking to Nick Drayton. In an instant the lingering humor he'd been feeling since watching Logan dance and sing in a dress disappeared.

He navigated his way through the throng of people, willing himself to keep it together. Drayton saw him when he was still several yards away, the smile he'd been wearing fading from his face.

Phil came up behind Lina, capturing her hips with his hands and pulling her back in to the heat of his body. "Are you ready?" he asked against her ear, his eyes meeting Drayton's.

"Phil, you scared me." She glanced back at him.

He slid one of his hands over her stomach, pressing her back into him still farther. "Let's find Logan and go home."

"Lina, always a pleasure," Nick said politely, offering Lina a tight smile before walking off.

Phil was watching him walk away when Lina turned in his arms.

"Was that necessary?" she whispered.

"I don't like you talking to him."

"You don't? I couldn't tell," she said sarcastically. "I'm surprised you didn't throw me over your shoulder and carry me out of here."

"Can we go?" He didn't want to fight with her. He just needed to get away from Drayton.

"I'm mad at you," she told him as he led her toward the exit, his hand curved possessively around her waist.

"I know." He decided to let her cool off, not speaking to her again until they were in his car. "Did you text Logan?" he asked.

"Yes. He's on his way." She was staring out the window.

"Maybe we should move Logan to McDonogh, get a clean break from the guy."

Lina's eyes widened. "Move Logan from a school he loves because you don't want to have to see a man who at one time had feelings for me?"

"He was in love with you."

"You have a baby with another woman, Phil. Oh my God! I can't believe we're even having this conversation!"

"Calm down."

"No! I'm not going to calm down. This is insane. I never even slept with him. For the rest of my life I have to be in the same orbit as a woman you fucked for four months. I think you can handle having to run into Nick Drayton from time to time."

***

It wasn't quite six when Phil arrived at Kim's apartment on Wednesday evening. The nanny, a Hispanic woman in her early fifties, greeted him warmly. "Come in. Come in. I leave Mr. Liam in high chair. First time," she explained before hurrying back toward the kitchen.

Phil slowly followed, loosening his tie as he made his way to the kitchen located in the back of the two-bedroom condo. He felt a rush of feeling when he saw Liam sitting in a high chair, banging his fists on the tray.

"First time in high chair," Maria repeated. "Doctor say he strong enough."

"Hey there." Phil smiled when Liam's gaze focused on him.

Liam rewarded him with a smile of his own. "Baah, gaah, gaah," he babbled.

"Yes. Papa," Maria said. "Your papa."

"Hey, tough guy." Phil trailed his fingers back through Liam's silky, dark hair.

"You feed him." Maria pulled out a chair for Phil. "Eat real food. Formula no enough. Doctor say food too."

Moments later Phil was sitting at the table spooning a blend of rice, cereal, and applesauce into his son's eager mouth. "You like that?"

"He loves," Maria said. "Doctor say he good. Healthy."

"Did you take him to the doctor?" Phil asked. After Kim's phone call, he'd assumed Kim had.

"Sí. Yes." She nodded. "I take. Miss Kim working."

"I thought you didn't drive." He'd agreed to pay her subway fare as part of the employment agreement.

"We take bus."

"The bus?" Phil frowned. "You took him on a bus?"

"Sí. It fine."

"No." Phil shook his head. "I don't want him on a bus. You can take an Uber or cab. I'll pay, okay?"

"Yes." She nodded. "No more bus."

He continued to feed Liam while Maria cleaned the kitchen, smiling as Liam opened his mouth as wide as a little bird. "Easy, buddy," he chuckled when Liam grabbed the spoon and began trying to pry it away from him.

"I don't think that's a good idea." He was giving Liam another spoonful of food when he heard the sound of the front door, followed by the clicking of heels on the hardwood floor. He felt a bubbling of annoyance in his chest, knowing Kim was arriving home two hours earlier than normal on a night she knew he was visiting.

"Hello," she said, breezing into the room. In a slim-fitting skirt and a sleeveless top, her body was fit. There was no evidence that she'd had a baby four months earlier. "What a day." Her eyes lingered on Phil before shifting to Liam. "Hi." She touched Liam's cheek and he greeted her with a smile. "You can go, Maria." She crossed to the refrigerator. "Do you want something to drink, Phil? A beer? Scotch?"

"No."

She poured herself a glass of wine before leaning back against the counter, her gaze on Phil. With large green eyes and high cheekbones, her blonde hair falling in soft waves to her shoulders, she looked more like a model than a lawyer.

All Phil saw was the woman who'd almost succeeded in destroying his life.

"He slept through the night for the first time last night, thank God," Kim said.

"Good night," he said to Maria who had stopped beside the high chair to kiss Liam's cheek. "Thank you."

"I'm going to go change," Kim said. "Are you okay here?"

"Yep." Phil didn't look away from Liam.

"I think he's done," Kim said when she returned several minutes later. She'd changed into leggings and a loose T-shirt. Her hair was pulled up in a ponytail. "Do you want to take off your jacket before you hold him?" She unlatched Liam from his high chair and took him to the kitchen sink to clean off his hands and face.

The scene looked so familiar, and yet all of his other memories starred Lina, not Kim. Phil couldn't get used to the idea that this woman and not Lina had mothered his child. He came to his feet and shrugged off his jacket before placing it over the back of one of the kitchen chairs. Moments later, he was taking Liam in his arms.

"Baah," Liam said. He began to pat Phil's mouth.

"He's starting to really have control of his hands." Kim was standing close enough for him to make out the familiar scent of her perfume.

A smell that had at one time turned him on now had the opposite effect. "I'm going to take him into the other room. You can do whatever you need to do. I've got him for the next hour and a half or so."

Phil was sitting on the couch in the family room with Liam on his lap when Kim joined him less than an hour later, lowering herself onto the cushion beside them.

"You're a natural."

"I have experience." Phil didn't take his gaze from Liam who was fingering his watch. "He's getting tired."

"Are you coming on Saturday or Sunday this week?"

"Neither." He was taking Lina away for the weekend.

"You're going to skip two weekends in a row?"

"I'm here right now. He doesn't know the difference."

"I do. It's nice to have a break sometimes."

"Then why are you here?" he asked. "Why aren't you taking a break tonight?"

"I'm talking about the weekends."

"Maria was with him for ten hours last Saturday. I saw her invoice."

"I had to work and it makes me feel guilty leaving him with her so much. I don't feel guilty when he's with you. You're his father."

He didn't bother to point out that she barely left the room let alone her apartment during one of his visits. "I'm busy this weekend."

"Busy how?"

It was none of her business but he decided to tell her anyway, hoping it would end her ridiculous fantasy that they'd one day be a family. "I have plans with my wife both days."

Chapter Four

K im's eyes narrowed. "What do you mean, 'wife'? You're back with Lina?"

"I moved home this weekend."

She looked away from him for a moment, as if needing to gather her thoughts. "I thought—I thought you were getting divorced."

"No."

"What does this mean for Liam?"

"What do you mean? It changes nothing."

"But you're canceling two weekends in a row. You barely see him as it is, and now what?" Kim came to her feet. "You're going to see him even less?" She crossed her arms over her chest.

"I'm not going to be seeing less of him. I'm his father. I take that role seriously."

"Maybe for your other children."

"For *all* of my children," he corrected. "This can't be a surprise to you. I didn't leave her of my own volition."

27

Anger filled him at the memory of the birthday card Kim had sent Lina filled with pictures of them together. He knew it was time for him to leave. He didn't want to lose his temper in front of Liam.

"What are you doing?" she asked when he came to his feet. "It's only been an hour."

"I'm leaving. I'll see him next week."

"Just like that? You announce that you're getting back with *her* and now you're going to leave?"

He kissed Liam's forehead before holding him out to Kim. "Take him," he said when she made no move to do so.

"No."

He stepped around her and left the room, heading down the hall to Liam's nursery.

"What are you doing?" she asked, hurrying after him.

"Putting him down." He entered Liam's room and crossed to his crib. "Daddy has to leave," he told him before lowering him into his crib. Liam immediately began to cry.

"You're just going to leave him there crying?" Kim followed him out of the room and toward the front door. "Phil?" She clutched his arm when they reached the foyer. "We're not done talking."

"Get your fucking hands off me," he said coldly, wrenching his arm from her hold. "This conversation is over." He yanked open the door.

"I don't want him around *her* ever," she yelled after him.

He reached the bank of elevators at the end of the hall before he remembered he'd left his suit jacket hanging on her kitchen chair. There was no way he was going back to her apartment tonight. He pressed the down arrow.

***

Lina was coming out of the bathroom when Phil came into the bedroom less than an hour later. "I didn't expect you so early," she said before returning his kiss.

"Traffic was light." He gripped the material of her robe and kissed her again. "How was your day?"

"Good." She watched him disappear into his wardrobe. A knot formed in her stomach at the thought of where he'd been. "I'm going to go get a glass of wine. Do you want something?"

"Scotch."

Twenty minutes later Lina was on the couch in the sitting room off the bedroom, sipping from a glass of wine and staring unfocused into the gas flames of the fireplace. She hadn't discussed Liam with Phil since he'd moved back home and knew she needed to.

"I'm not going to be able to get used to this," Phil said, nodding at the fireplace as he joined her. His hair was damp from a shower and he was wearing only a pair of lounge pants, his chest bare.

"It's so much easier. I just push a button and we have a fire." She'd had the fireplace converted to gas a few months earlier.

"It's not real." He kneeled down before it, peering in at the flames. "It doesn't smell like a fire."

Lina watched the play of muscles in his upper back. Kim had probably admired those same muscles. "Did you see her today?"

He stilled before slowly coming to his feet and joining her on the couch. "Briefly." He stretched his arm along the back of the cushions behind her. "I interact with her as little as possible." He began to trail his fingers over the nape of her neck.

29

"When do you plan to see him again?"

"Next week."

"Do you see him every week?"

"Yes. Usually on the weekend but that didn't work out this week."

She didn't like the idea of losing him for a block of time every weekend. "Is there an agreement—like a custody agreement?"

"Yes. The custody agreement says that I have him every other weekend from Friday afternoon until Sunday evening. It's standard. Until he's a little older, I don't want to take him overnight."

His response wasn't a surprise. Lina had been the main caregiver for all their children. He'd never changed Megan's diaper and the other two only rarely. She couldn't imagine him caring for a baby on his own. "Does the agreement say anything about weeknights?"

"I have two but with my work schedule I can't commit to seeing him during the week. Especially considering he's an hour away.

"She's working?"

"She went back a couple of months ago."

"He's only four months old."

"I know. He really seems to like his nanny. She comes every day."

She and Kim were from different worlds. Lina couldn't imagine not staying home with her babies. "Who pays for that?"

"We both do. It's standard." He clasped the back of her neck. "I know this is hard for you."

Her gaze returned to the flames. "So, you're in Kim's house while she's home?" The thought of Kim interacting with him while he spent time with their son was almost too much to bear.

"Ideally she would go out while I'm visiting, but usually she's somewhere else in the apartment."

"I don't want to talk about what's already happened. But from now on I don't want you visiting him at her place if she's home."

"He's a baby. What do you—"

"Take him out. Take him for a walk. Do whatever you have to do. I don't want you breathing the same air as her."

***

The game was about to start when Phil approached the lacrosse field at Gilman the following afternoon. He had just finished a brief conversation with another father when he noticed Nick Drayton standing about fifteen yards to his right. He looked more like a surfer than a psychiatrist, with his overlong sandy-colored hair and golden tan. He'd treated Katie until Logan met his son, Brian, at a lacrosse tryout and the two boys became friends. He was staring down at his phone, paying no attention to the action getting underway on the field—not that Phil was paying attention, but it was a little different when your son was sitting on the bench. Unlike Logan, Brian Drayton had earned a coveted starting position.

Phil's gaze shifted to the field. Brian was in possession of the lacrosse ball, weaving his way past defenders so quickly it looked like they were cones instead of boys trying to stop him. Within seconds he was horizontal in the air, launching the ball past the goalie and into the back of the net.

Phil brought his hands together, joining the other Gilman parents in applauding the play. The boy was good. He was not only the best player at Gilman but the best player in the state, a state that bred the most elite players in the country.

His gaze returned to Brian's father, who was still messing with his phone, completely unaware that his son had just scored a goal. The anger that normally rose inside Phil when he saw Katie's former psychiatrist and the man who'd tried to turn Lina against him only reached a modest level, knowing after Lina's words Monday night that she'd never slept with him.

He forgot about Drayton when Logan came onto the field. He was a solid player, making good passes and getting open for his teammates, but unlike Brian Drayton, who created plays, Logan was more of a support player. He didn't play with enough confidence. He was too cautious. It was as if he was afraid of making a mistake. Phil took a deep breath, chastising himself for comparing Logan to Brian. Any player on the field would pale in comparison to Brian Drayton. Logan was a good player, and in time, with the proper coaching and encouragement, he'd gain confidence.

"Can we talk?"

Phil's entire body tensed up in response to Nick Drayton's voice. "About what?" He continued to watch the field.

"I think it's time to call a truce."

"A truce?" Phil turned to him. "Wouldn't that imply a battle was being waged?" The anger he'd thought he had a muzzle on reared to the surface as he met Nick's eyes.

"I don't want to fight with you." Nick's voice was low enough not to be overheard by the dozen or so other parents within close proximity. "I just want to talk."

As if by an unspoken agreement they began to walk, distancing themselves from the field. When they were about thirty yards away, they turned to face each other. "Talk," Phil said.

"For the sake of our sons," Nick began, "I think we need to draw a line in the sand and start fresh."

"Fresh?" Phil laughed aloud. "Are you asking to be my friend?"

"I think we can be civil."

"You tried to steal my wife, you hypocritical son of a bitch."

"I—"

"I want you to listen and listen carefully," Phil interrupted, the side of his jaw clenched. "You stay the fuck away from my wife. And I don't mean 'estranged wife,' because I'm back in my house. If you see her, you walk the other way. Is that clear? I am this close"—he held his index finger and thumb a quarter inch apart—"to suing you. You used your position as my daughter's psychiatrist to worm your way into my family. You should lose your fucking license. The only thing saving you is that I don't want to subject *my wife* to a drawn-out legal battle."

"I suppose your affair was my fault, too."

"Fuck you," Phil growled, stepping toward him.

"You don't deserve her."

"And yet I'm the man she wants."

"I know what happened to Lina as a teenager," Nick said, surprising Phil. "That two men broke into her house and raped her sister. That she believes if you hadn't arrived she would have suffered the same fate. I also know that trauma created the illusion in her mind that you're her protector—that she needs you."

"She does need me," Phil snarled. "That's what you don't get and you'll never get. I'm like her air."

"You've kept her in a cage. You've nurtured her dependence on you. That isn't love."

"You just can't handle that she's mine."

"She's working and gaining her independence. She is going to outgrow you."

"Is that the illusion you've created in your mind? Does that keep you warm at night?"

"Everything okay there?" the school's athletic director called out from several feet away.

"Yes," Phil answered, staring into Nick's eyes for a second longer. "We're done."

***

Lina stroked her hands down Phil's sweat-dampened back as they came down from their orgasms. She could feel the vibration of his heartbeat hard against her chest. He was like a man starving of thirst and she was his water. They'd had sex that morning and again when he'd first arrived home from Logan's game, and then as soon as they'd finished dinner, before she'd even cleaned the kitchen, he'd led her upstairs. She'd thought he'd wanted to discuss Logan, but instead he was pushing her back against the closed door and stripping off her clothes.

"I don't want you to talk to Drayton again," he said against her ear.

Lina's hands stilled on his back. He was still inside of her and he was talking about Nick.

"Lina?"

"I heard you," she said. "I just don't really want to talk about him at this moment."

He rolled off of her and onto his back, sighing deeply. "I just—I need to know that he's no longer in our lives."

34

"What happened?" she asked, knowing he must have run into him at the game.

"Did you have sex with him?"

"No," she rushed out. "I've already told you that."

He threw his arm over his eyes. "I'm sorry. I just—I don't trust him. He still wants you."

"What he wants is irrelevant. I don't want him."

"He's so fucking smug."

"Phil?" She tugged his arm away from his eyes. "You need to let this go. I'm not going to see him socially, but we can't avoid him. Brian is Logan's best friend. They play on the same lacrosse team. They go to the same school. We are going to run into him."

"You told him about Shiloh's rape?"

Her stomach dropped, as it always did when she was reminded of that night. "He said something to you about that?"

"He did. He took pleasure in telling me he knew about it. Why would you discuss that with him?"

"He's a psychiatrist."

"A child psychiatrist. He wasn't your psychiatrist."

"It just came out," she admitted, hurt that Nick would mention their private conversation to Phil.

"It didn't just come out. He manipulated you into opening up to him. That's what he's trained to do—get people to talk about themselves."

"I'm sorry I discussed it with him," she said. "Okay? Can we let this go?"

"Did he tell you that you developed an unhealthy dependence on me because of that night?"

He had but she wasn't going to admit that to Phil. He already hated him enough. "If he did, he's wrong. I was in love with you long before that night. I was already dependent on you. From the moment we met, I haven't wanted to be apart from you. If that's considered unhealthy, not wanting to be apart from the person you love, then I'm fine with being unhealthy."

"Baby—"

"It's always only been you, so please let go of this anger toward him."

"He tried to take you from me. I can't forget that."

"But he didn't. Just like she didn't take you from me."

***

"If you're calling so I can congratulate you for getting back with Lina, you're wasting your time," Adele said after answering Phil's call. "I knew it was inevitable. The two of you were pitiful apart, but I'm still mad at you."

"If I tell you I want to surprise Lina with a trip to Paris and I'm calling so you can clear her calendar for Monday and Tuesday, will that do anything to redeem me?"

"That depends. Can I go in your place?"

Phil chuckled. "Not exactly what I had in mind."

They stayed at the five-star Hôtel Plaza Athénée overlooking the avenue of Montaigne, with a view of the Eiffel Tower. They strolled along the Parisian streets hand in hand, ate at small cafés, and made love late into the night. It was the most romantic five days of Lina's life. It wasn't until they were on the plane flying home that she realized they'd had no serious discussions. They'd been officially back together for a week and two days and they'd yet to discuss how Liam would fit into her and their children's lives.

"Good," Katie responded when Lina asked how her weekend with her grandmother had gone. It was almost midnight and they'd arrived home to find Katie curled on the couch in the family room watching television. "Grandma is much cooler than the two of you. You should go away more often."

"We should," Phil agreed. "And you should go to bed. It's late and it's a school night."

"See." Katie sighed. "Not once did Grandma tell me to go to bed."

"That's because she isn't your parent," Lina said.

"Oh, Dad," Katie called out when Phil began to leave the room. "That woman—the one you had the baby with—she called."

Chapter Five

Lina's eyes widened. "She called our house phone?"

"You talked to her?" Phil set down their suitcases before retracing his steps to Katie.

"I answered the phone."

Lina couldn't believe the nerve of the woman. "What did you say?"

"That Dad wasn't home. What did you expect me to say?"

"If she ever calls again, don't talk to her," Phil said intensely, coming around the couch.

Katie frowned. "What was I supposed to do? Hang up on her?"

"Yes." Phil nodded. "Hang up on her. And that goes for you, too," he said to Logan, who had come into the room. "If Kim ever calls here, hang up the phone."

"I wouldn't talk to her," Logan said, frowning.

"It's not like I chose to," Katie said defensively. "I didn't even know who she was at first. I just answered the phone."

"It's okay," Lina said. "It's not your fault." She turned to Logan, running her hand down his back when he stopped beside her. "Why aren't you in bed? You have school tomorrow."

"I was hungry," Logan said. "Would you make me something?"

"Mom has been up for close to twenty-four hours," Phil began. "Have cereal or—"

"It's fine," Lina interrupted. "I slept on the plane. What would you like?"

Phil turned back to Katie as Lina followed Logan into the kitchen. "When did she call?"

"Today. Right after Grandma left. About seven. She sounded young. How old is she?"

"Don't worry about it." He picked up the suitcases and headed toward the front of the house.

"I'm not worried about it," Katie said, catching up to him as he began to ascend the stairs. "I was just wondering."

"Stop wondering. She has nothing to do with you. If she calls again, don't answer. We have caller ID for a reason."

"She could use a different phone," Katie pointed out.

"She could," he agreed. "And in that scenario you hang up on her." He continued to the master bedroom with Katie on his heels. "Is there something else you need?" he asked when she followed him into his room.

"I heard the baby. He was crying in the background. It was kind of weird knowing the baby crying was yours."

He set down the bags and turned to her. "Yeah, I guess it might be." He dragged a hand back through his hair. The stress that had taken a short hiatus during their time in Paris was back in full force.

"You never talk about him."

"He's a baby. There's not much to say. He doesn't really do anything besides sleep and eat."

"I hope you're not going to be a shitty father like Matt's, ignoring him because you have another family."

"I'm not going to ignore him."

"Matt acts like he doesn't care, but I know he does."

"I'm not going to ignore him, Katie."

"That isn't okay," Lina said as soon as she entered the bedroom. "I don't want her calling our house, *ever*." She walked past him and went into the bathroom, closing the door behind her.

"Fuck," he said aloud, dragging his hands down his face. He could kill Kim. He followed Lina into the bathroom. She was standing before the sink, brushing her teeth. "I'll take care of it."

She continued to brush her teeth, her movements more vigorous than usual. As soon as she finished, she was turning to him. "How?"

"She called because I was ignoring her. She's been calling and texting me for the past two days. If I'd responded she wouldn't have called the home phone." He could see her shoulders relax in response to his words.

"How often does she call you?" She leaned back against the counter.

"More than I'd like but not often. Usually only when I don't respond to her texts."

"I'm sorry for getting angry. It's just—I hate that she talked to Katie, that she felt she had a right to call our home."

"I know." He tucked a tendril of hair that was touching her cheek back behind her ear. "I'll take care of it."

"I don't want her manipulating you." She fisted his T-shirt. "You aren't hers to manipulate."

"Noted," he said dryly.

"We could get rid of the home phone."

"Completely?"

"We could give out my phone as the home number. I'm the only one who really uses it. The only time you talk on it is when your parents call."

"Are you sure?" He liked the idea, but he didn't want to cause her any inconvenience.

"Yes. It's mostly telemarketers anyway. And I don't want you to feel you have to answer her calls on your cell phone to keep her from calling our home phone. If it's disconnected it's a moot point."

***

"So? Are you going to tell me how it was?" Adele asked Lina the following morning. They were doing a final walk-through of a house scheduled to go on the market later that afternoon.

"You didn't ask," Lina said. They'd been together more than half an hour and it was the first Adele had mentioned the trip.

"That's because you look too happy. And although I like to see *you* happy, he doesn't deserve it. You've been glowing since you got back together. He's being rewarded for what he did."

"That's ridiculous. He is not being rewarded. His life is much more complicated now, believe me. And it was nice to get away from everything for a couple of days. This is what I want. Don't I deserve to be happy?"

"I just wish what made you happy didn't make him happy. So, Paris was everything you thought it would be?"

"It was," Lina answered with a sigh. "I wish we were still there. We need to get rid of these pictures," she said, nodding toward the pictures covering the top of a sideboard in the living room. "I missed them before. I love the black-and-whites though. They should stay." She lifted a framed portrait of a wheat field. "I wonder if it's a local photographer."

"It is," an attractive woman with wavy dark hair and a friendly smile answered as she breezed into the room. "Oh my God, you're gorgeous," she said, looking at Lina. "She's gorgeous," she repeated to Adele.

"I know. I hate her. She got the tall, beautiful genes. I'm the runt of the family."

"Oh, nonsense," the woman said, waving her off. "You're gorgeous, too. And you can always wear heels without towering over your date."

"Lina, meet Celeste Strahl."

"Your home is lovely," Lina said.

"I was telling Adele how talented you are. When I arrived home last week, I couldn't believe the transformation. I almost don't want to move now."

"Your home was beautiful to begin with," Lina said. "It's just when selling it, you want the minimalist look."

"We had it professionally decorated when we moved here three years ago, and I used that exact term then, 'minimalist look.' My husband doesn't like a lot of things around him. Clutter makes him nervous. I'd love to have you handle our new home. Do you have a card?"

"I'm flattered," Lina said, "but I'm just a stager. I'm not an interior decorator."

"Adele said you studied it in college."

"I did," Lina said. "But I never did it professionally. I started staging to help Adele, and then the next thing I knew they were offering me a job."

"And now I'm offering you a job," Celeste said. "I'd love for you to help me with my new home. Please say yes."

***

Phil arrived at Kim's condo a little before two o'clock on Saturday afternoon. His communication with her had been sparse since he'd told her to refrain from calling his home phone. She'd sent him one picture of Liam sitting in his high chair, stuffing a fistful of Cheerios into his mouth, and another of him in the bathtub, his hair slicked back from his face. The only other texts were a short exchange over the time of his visit that weekend.

He thought he was at the wrong door when instead of Kim an attractive, sophisticated-looking woman in her late forties or early fifties answered his knock. "I'm sorry," he began, his eyes narrowed in confusion. "I must have the wrong apartment." He pulled his head back enough to see the apartment number.

"No. You're at the right place. And you're definitely Phil. There aren't too many men that fit the bill of tall, dark, and movie-star handsome. Kim wasn't exaggerating. Please come in. I'm Evelyn, the grandmother."

He instantly saw her resemblance to Kim. They had the same green eyes and heart-shaped face. She was wearing a lavender pantsuit that reminded him of something his own mother would wear. "You had her young," he said, meaning it.

"Handsome and charming. I like you," she said with a wink. "I feel like we're almost related and yet we've never met." She curved her arm through his. "Come and meet my husband."

Not wanting to be rude, Phil had no choice but to let her lead him to the family room, where a man he assumed was Kim's father had come to his feet and was setting a newspaper on the coffee table. He was tall and lean with a full head of salt-and-pepper hair and looked to be about ten years older than his wife. He, too, had a sophisticated look, dressed in pressed tan slacks, a dark sweater, and loafers.

"He's definitely your son," Russel Ryan said after greeting Phil.

"Are you visiting from out of town or...?" He trailed off. He had no idea where her parents lived.

"We're down from New York for the weekend. We saw him over Christmas after he was born. He's growing like a weed."

"He is," Phil agreed.

"Kim says you have other children, too," Russel said.

"A boy and two girls," Phil answered.

"Are they local?"

"My oldest daughter is a freshman at UVA. My other two are still at home. We live in Maryland."

"Oh, I didn't realize you had custody of your other children," Evelyn said. "They must keep you busy."

"Here's Daddy," Kim announced as she entered the room, carrying Liam.

Liam smiled at Phil before immediately burying his face in Kim's neck. Within seconds he was lifting his head and giving Phil another smile before hiding his face once again.

"Why are you hiding from Daddy?"

"Hey." Phil took Liam from Kim, smiling down at him. "Are you shy today?"

"I assume everyone's met?" Kim asked.

"Yes. We were just learning that Phil has custody of his other children," her mother said. "You never mentioned that."

"It must have slipped my mind," Kim said. "Do you want to take him into his nursery? I left some toys out."

"Why are you sending him away?" Evelyn asked. "We'd like to get to know him a little."

"He's here to visit with Liam, not you," Kim said.

"He can't do both? I'm sure he's just as curious about us as we are about him. Our DNA is running through his son's blood."

"Mom," Kim said in warning. "He doesn't care about your DNA."

"Are you originally from Maryland?" Russel asked, ignoring his daughter.

"Yes. Born and raised."

"Do you have siblings?"

"Dad, he's here—"

"I can talk to your parents for a few minutes," Phil said, interrupting Kim. "And then I'd like to take Liam out for a little while."

"Out? Out where?" She frowned.

"For a walk. It's a nice day."

"That's a wonderful idea," Evelyn said, earning another glare from her daughter. "I worry about him not getting enough air, living in this high-rise. You don't live in a high-rise, do you, Phil?"

"No. I have a house." He lifted Liam high into the air, eliciting a gurgle of laughter.

"We're not really that familiar with Maryland," Evelyn said. "When Kim said she was leaving New York City to move to Baltimore, we were all shocked. She had always been a city girl—not that Baltimore isn't a city, but you know what I mean. Compared to New York it isn't exactly cosmopolitan."

"At the time we didn't know about you, so it was even more confusing," Russel added.

"Dad, please," Kim said. "We don't need to get into all of that. What's done is done."

"About me?" Phil asked, his brows pulled in confusion. "What am I missing?" He felt like he was in an alternate universe.

"Nothing," Kim said. "He's talking about your firm. I left New York to go to your firm."

"Why are you wearing a wedding band?" Russel asked, his gaze focused on the ring on Phil's left hand. "Are you married?"

Chapter Six

"Dad, can't you—"

"Yes, I'm married," Phil answered.

"Married?" Evelyn's eyes widened. "I thought you were divorced."

"I said he was getting a divorce," Kim said.

"No." Her father shook his head. "You said he was already divorced."

"You may have heard that, but that's not what I said. I told you—"

"That isn't a fact I would confuse," her father said. "And why are you wearing a wedding band if you're getting divorced?"

"I'm not getting a divorce," Phil said.

"Oh no," Evelyn whispered, gripping the collar of her jacket. "You had an affair with a married man?"

"He was separated," Kim lied.

"Look, I'm going to take him out for a walk," Phil said, having no desire to partake in Kim's family drama. "Would you get me the stroller?"

"What kind of man encourages his mistress to move closer to his wife and family?"

"I have no idea what we're talking about here," Phil said, looking between Kim and her father.

"You're the reason she left New York. She came to Baltimore to be with you."

"No." Phil shook his head. "We didn't know each other until she interviewed at my firm. She found us. It wasn't the other way around. Now if you'll excuse me, I'm here to visit my son."

Once Phil left Kim's apartment, he did his best to salvage his time with Liam, strolling him to a nearby park and stretching out on a blanket with him. Liam spent most of his time playing peekaboo or trying to pull off Phil's watch.

When he arrived back at the condominium it was again Evelyn opening the door. This time her greeting was lukewarm at best. "Kim ran out to get a haircut," she said. "She told me to give this to you." She was holding the suit jacket he had left behind on his last visit.

"I'm sorry if my marriage came as a surprise to you," Phil said. "There was no graceful way to tell you."

"It's okay." She forced a smile, but the strain on her face was obvious. "All that matters at this point is Liam. I hope that you'll play an active role in his life and he isn't kept in the shadows. A boy needs his father."

***

"You looked good out there," Phil told Logan as they walked toward his car.

"I almost scored. Coach said if I start shooting more, I'll get a chance to play up top. He said I'm passing when I should be taking a shot."

"So shoot more," Phil said.

"I'm going to. Brian said his dad was telling him about this book called *Outliers* or something like that. And if you do something ten thousand times you become, like, an expert

48

at it. How many times do think I've shot at goal? Not just in games but in practice, too."

"I don't know. You're almost fifteen and you've been playing since you were five. Maybe three thousand times."

"I was thinking twenty-five hundred," Logan said. They reached the car, and he tossed his gear and backpack into the back seat. "That means I only need to shoot it seventy-five hundred more times to become an expert," he continued when they were in the car. "If I start shooting it a hundred times a day, I'll be an expert in less than two and a half months. That's all it will take."

"Is that all?" Phil knew there was no way Logan was going to shoot the ball ten times a day, let alone one hundred. He hated practicing on his own.

"Yeah, isn't that cool?"

"I was thinking about taking Logan and a couple of his friends to see the college lacrosse championship on Memorial Day Weekend—just the championship game, not the whole tournament," Phil said to Lina when he arrived home with Logan.

"That's nice." She was at the counter, slicing vegetables.

"It's in Philadelphia this year." He leaned his hip against the counter as he watched her. "Do you want to come?"

"No."

"Come on. It will be fun. We could spend the night and check out the city."

She set down her knife and wiped her hands on a towel. She closed the small distance between them before framing his face with her cool hands. "No," she whispered before standing on her tiptoes and softly kissing his lips. "We've already seen the Liberty Bell."

He clasped the sides of her hips, pulling her lower body toward his. He knew she'd never really liked lacrosse. She thought it was too physical. When he'd spot her in the stands during his high school and college games, she'd more often than not have her hands covering her eyes. "Neither Logan nor I will be playing. You won't have to worry about us getting hurt."

"I never worried about you getting hurt. I was always worried you were going to hurt someone. I didn't want to have the memory of it in my mind." She linked her arms around his neck. "Take Logan and have fun. You don't need me there."

He let his gaze drift over her face. He knew every inch of it. Even the laugh lines around her eyes, which had come in the past couple of years, were etched in his memory. "I'm still making up for lost time."

"Gross—stop looking at each other like that," Katie said. "I shouldn't have to be afraid to come into my own kitchen."

Lina kissed him again before stepping away from him.

"Your kitchen?" Phil asked Katie. His gaze remained on Lina, watching the feminine sway of her hips as she crossed to the refrigerator.

"How old was I when we moved here?" she asked. "Dad?"

"What?" He reluctantly turned his attention to Katie. "Five or six. No, four."

"So it's been my kitchen for sixty-five percent of my life. The only person who it belongs to more is Logan. And I don't think he wants to see your PDAs either."

***

50

"You're radiant," Diane said when she met Lina for lunch a week later. "He so agrees with you."

"He does." Lina returned her warm hug.

"Things are good, aren't they?"

"They are." Lina smiled at the waiter as he set a glass of wine before her. "Thank you."

"I assumed you would want white."

"It's perfect," Lina said, lifting the glass to her lips.

"No, wait. We need to make a toast," Diane said. "To new beginnings."

"New beginnings," Lina repeated, raising her glass.

Of all Lina's friends, Diane was the staunchest Phil supporter. During the early days of her separation, when Lina was convinced she would never take Phil back, it had put a strain on their friendship because of Diane's constant pressure for Lina to move past the affair.

"You're in the honeymoon stage all over again, aren't you?"

Lina laughed. "There is no honeymoon stage with two teenagers in the house."

"I don't know if that's true. That healthy glow you're sporting doesn't just come from being happy. Oh my—are you blushing? You *are* blushing."

"Stop." Lina laughed, lifting her wineglass to hide the blush she knew was covering her face.

"Spill—he can't keep his hands off you, can he?"

He couldn't, but Lina wasn't about to share that with Diane. "Things are going well," Lina said instead. "Maybe all couples should take a six-month hiatus after twenty years or so. Keep things new."

"It wasn't quite six months. You had a bit of a rendezvous on Christmas if I recall."

"We did," she admitted, managing not to blush. She'd invited him to spend the night so the family could be together on Christmas morning and ended up crawling into bed with him in the middle of the night. She recalled his disappointment and surprise the next day when she told him it had been a momentary relapse and he wasn't allowed to come home.

"How are the kids adjusting?" Diane asked, bringing her back to the present. "I know you were a little nervous about Logan."

"Logan seems fine. They're both fine. It's like he never left. I thought there would be an adjustment period, you know, considering Phil is stricter than I am, but so far it's smooth sailing. Phil hasn't even complained about Matt's presence at the house."

"And Megan?"

"Megan is Megan," Lina said. She'd stopped trying to figure out her oldest child. "I guess she isn't mad at me anymore for making her father sad."

Diane laughed. "She just wanted her parents back together. I think that's normal."

"I'm not sure how normal it is to expect your mother to just get over an affair that resulted in a child. If the situation were reversed, I don't think she'd be so forgiving." In fact, she knew she wouldn't be, but in Megan's eyes Phil could do no wrong. The lectures she'd given Lina about how she was hurting their family by not letting Phil come home still stung.

"She's young," Diane said. "You can't hold it against her."

"I know." And she didn't, or at least she tried not to. "She's staying in Charlottesville for the summer, so we won't be seeing much of her." Lina went on to tell Diane about the internship Megan had secured with her business ethics professor. "She still plans to be a lawyer."

"Then I'm sure she will be," Diane said. "Speaking of careers, how did the interior decorating job go?"

"It's still going," Lina answered. "They're painting this week and finishing the kitchen. We've ordered most of the furniture. Now I'm concentrating on artwork and the window treatments. Our tastes are similar, so it's almost like I'm doing it all for myself."

"But you're being paid?"

"I am," Lina said. "Phil drew up the contract and insisted I charge at least one hundred and twenty-five an hour. He researched it and said that was a fair rate. She agreed without even blinking." Lina could hardly believe she was being paid so much to do something she loved.

"You're worth every penny," Diane said. "I'm sure you're a bit nervous about Saturday night, seeing everyone again, but I have to admit, I'm looking forward to having you back. Our get-togethers were so boring without you."

Lina's stomach dropped. "There's something this weekend?" She could feel the heat come back to her face.

"Yes, at Gina and Bob's. They're welcoming a new partner. Phil didn't tell you?"

"No, and I don't know if I'm ready to see everyone. No, strike that. I know I'm *not* ready to see everyone." She couldn't imagine having to endure the looks of pity on the other wives' faces. "None of them called me after the separation, not even Gina." She hadn't particularly wanted to talk, but their silence still hurt. These were women Lina had known since Phil started at the firm.

"You can't hold that against them," Diane said. "They didn't know what to say. It was awkward for everyone. They felt terrible about it."

"I thought they were my friends," Lina said, sounding naive even to her own ears. "I just…" She sighed. "I don't know if I'm ready to face them yet. I'm sure they'll think I'm pathetic for taking him back."

"When were you going to tell me about the dinner party at Gina and Bob's?" Lina asked Phil later that evening. She still felt knots in her stomach at the thought of it.

"I thought I had." He stifled a yawn as he pulled back the comforter.

"No." Lina began to fluff her pillow. "I would have remembered something like that."

"I looked at the calendar. There was no conflict."

"The conflict is in me. I'm not sure if I'm ready to be part of that crowd again."

His eyes narrowed in confusion. "I don't understand."

"You don't understand how it might be uncomfortable for me to be around all those couples, knowing that they know you fathered a son with an ex-associate at your firm?"

"It's none of their business."

"Oh, and that's how it works?" She tossed the pillow onto the mattress. "People only care about things that are their business?"

"Don't be sarcastic. I'm trying to understand what you're feeling."

"You had an affair with someone in the office, someone all those partners know and have no doubt talked about to their wives. I'm *feeling* like I don't want to see them."

He stared at her across the bed. "I can't just blow this off. We're welcoming a new partner."

"I don't expect you to blow it off. I just don't know if I can go."

"Are you saying you aren't going to accompany me to work-related functions anymore?"

"I don't know. I just feel very uncomfortable at the prospect. That's all I'm saying." She stretched out on the bed and lay back on her pillow.

"What can I do?" He came around the bed. "Tell me what I can do to make you feel more comfortable." The mattress shifted as he sat down beside her.

"There's nothing you can do. You can't keep people from talking about us. We'd be doing the same thing if one of them were in this situation."

He pressed his hand into the pillow beside her head, his eyebrows pulled together in concern as he looked down at her. "You won't be alone. I won't leave your side."

"You won't leave my side? You'll hang out with the wives all evening?"

"I'll do whatever it takes to get you to come. I flew solo for six months. I don't want to do that anymore. I need you with me."

"Who in the fuck cares what they think?" Adele asked the following morning as they sat side by side, getting pedicures.

"Shh." Lina gave her a sideways glare.

"Sorry." Adele held up her hands. "Are you worried about what *they* think, too?" She nodded toward the women working at their feet. "I don't think they give a fuck."

"Forget it," Lina said. "You don't understand."

"One of the perks of growing up is not having to spend your entire life in middle school. You already know these women aren't your friends. Friends wouldn't have gone six months without speaking to you, so why do you care what they think?"

"These are Phil's partners and their wives. They're not just anyone."

"But you could be," Adele said. "Anyone to them, I mean. I'm not talking about Diane, because I know she cares. Although I could never understand how she just expected you to get over what he did. She was like Mom with that 'boys will be boys' attitude, but at least she didn't abandon you. These other women that you're worried about dropped you. Think about that. Your ticket into their so-called friendship was Phil. Without him you were no longer in the club."

Adele was right. With the exception of Diane, none of the other wives had made any attempt to contact her after the breakup. She'd known some of them since Phil started at the firm years earlier. At first she'd been relieved, having no desire to discuss the affair, but as time passed with no word from any of them, she'd felt hurt, naively believing they'd been her friends.

"If Phil had ended up with Kim, they would have opened their doors and arms to her," Adele said. "Think about that."

***

"Are you okay?" Phil asked, taking his eyes off the road to look at Lina as he came to a stop at a red light. She was studying her reflection in the visor mirror.

"I wish you would stop asking me that." She closed the mirror and leaned back in the seat. "It's the third time since we left the house."

"Maybe that's because you haven't answered me." The car behind him beeped, and he brought his gaze back to the road. He was worried about her. She'd been out of sorts since they'd started getting ready to go out, trying on several outfits before settling on a simple black dress. Then she'd spent an exorbitant amount of time on her hair and makeup. He wasn't sure what she was thinking, but it was clear her physical appearance was more important than usual to her. "You're beautiful." He squeezed her thigh.

She had the visor open again and was peering at her reflection. "My eyes look tired."

"You're beautiful. Look at me. Baby?"

She looked away from the mirror. "Stop doting on me. You're making it worse." She shifted her gaze to the window.

When she began to finger her wedding band, he knew she was nervous. She wasn't normally fidgety. He shouldn't have pressured her to come. "Do you want me to take you out to dinner instead? I can call and cancel, make up an excuse."

"No." She released a breath. "I need to do this. I can't hide from it."

"She isn't going to break," Wayne said to Phil a couple of hours later as he came to stand beside him on the back deck of Bob Smith's massive Hunt Valley home. "I don't think you've taken your eyes off her for five minutes all evening."

"Probably not," Phil agreed, continuing to watch Lina, who was sitting with Diane and some of the other wives on an adjacent patio. "She was nervous about coming tonight. I hurt her confidence. I didn't get that until tonight. I was out half the day visiting Liam. I'm sure that didn't help. It's fresh in her mind."

"She's fine." He patted Phil's back. "The first time was going to be hard. Diane's taking care of her. Come on. Let's get you some scotch."

***

Shouts of laughter filled the air, drawing Lina's attention to the other side of the patio, where Phil was sitting around a table with the other men, smoking cigars and drinking scotch. The familiarity of the scene brought back warm memories of so many similar evenings.

"It's nice to have him back," Gina said from the chair beside Lina's.

"Back?" Lina pulled her gaze from the men.

"He was quieter without you. He's happy again."

"Me too," Lina said, because it was the truth. Regardless of what Phil had done, she was happier with him than without him.

"I'm so happy you're here," Gina said, sincerity shining in her eyes. "I feel awful that I didn't call you. I just—I didn't know what to say. I know that's no excuse, but it's the truth. It was such a shock, what happened. I mean if Phil could cheat on you, then none of us were safe. That's what it felt like."

"I hope that's not true."

"The way he looked at you—no, still looks at you. It boggles my—all of our minds," she said, confirming what Lina already knew. They'd discussed her and Phil's relationship, probably at length. "Do you know—"

"What are you two so serious about?" Diane asked as she, Carol Young, and the newest partner's wife, Amanda Knabb, came from the house.

"Nothing." Gina touched Lina's arm. "I'm sorry. I got carried away."

"No." Lina covered her hand with her own. "I'm glad you said something to me. I could feel the unspoken questions. It's a relief."

"What's a relief?" Carol asked.

"Gina and I were talking about Phil," Lina said.

Carol's eyes widened, swinging from Lina to Gina and then finally to Diane.

"It just came out," Gina said defensively. She, too, was looking at Diane.

Lina laughed for the first time that evening. "It's okay, Diane."

"You and Phil seem so normal," Carol said, taking the empty chair beside Lina's. "You're doing well?"

Again, Lina was touched by the sincerity in the other woman's eyes. Adele was wrong. They were her friends, maybe not Diane level but friends nonetheless. "We are." Her gaze traveled back to Phil. Their eyes met across the patio, and he lifted his chin, asking her without words if she was okay. She smiled.

"There it is," Gina said, witnessing the exchange. "How could someone possibly get between that?"

"Gina!" Diane warned. "I think you've had too much to drink."

"No, it's okay," Lina said. "It's a question I've asked myself so many times over the past year. It's a cliché, but the truth is we stopped communicating. It was just a brief time when we were dealing with issues with the kids." She couldn't just say Katie. It would feel too much like she was blaming her.

"Enough. This is supposed to be a celebration," Diane said. "More wine," she called out. "And turn up the music. Phil?" She waved at him. "Come over here and dance with your wife."

"What?" He put his hand to his ear.

"Come dance with Lina—make the world right again."

***

Something had changed. It was as if a switch had flipped and Lina was happy again. He'd known when he met her eyes across the patio. Phil came to his feet as Diane beckoned him over to them. "Bob." He paused beside his chair. "Could you play something on the stereo for me?"

"Dance with me," he said to Lina seconds later, stopping beside her chair.

"There's no music," she protested as she let him draw her to her feet.

He slid his palm over hers, entwining their fingers. "There will be." As if choreographed, Michael Bolton's rendition of "When a Man Loves a Woman" began streaming from stereo speakers as Phil took her into his arms. They swayed more than danced, his body flush against hers as the song played, and when it ended Phil dipped her back over his arm and kissed her to the delight of their friends, who whistled and clapped their approval.

Chapter Seven

Lina awoke the following morning to a text from Diane. That dance last night was like something out of a romantic movie. We all could feel the love. So happy to have our golden couple back. Picture perfect! A picture of them dancing was attached to the text. Lina stared at the image. Her back was to the camera. One of her hands was clasped in Phil's and the other was curved around his neck. He had one hand splayed on her lower back. The expression on his face as he stared down into her eyes was one of pure, unadulterated love.

The image of another picture flashed in her mind, of Phil holding Kim in his arms in a similar pose. The picture had haunted her for months. It was one of four photographs Kim had sent Lina on her forty-first birthday. They say a picture speaks a thousand words. In Lina's case they brought Phil's betrayal into stark reality. Seeing him with Kim, smiling at Kim, dancing with Kim had been impossible to erase from her mind.

Now, as she looked at the image of herself in her husband's arms, she was transported once again back to that picture. Her stomach turned at the memory of how she'd felt when she'd seen him holding Kim in his arms, looking down at her with an expression she believed was reserved for her.

"Aren't you going to get up?" Phil had come out of the bathroom without her realizing it and was at his bureau, opening a drawer. "We have less than half an hour if we want to make the nine thirty service."

"I'm skipping today," she said, darkening the display on her phone. "You can go with the kids."

"Why?"

"I'm tired." She lay back against her pillow. "I'm going to go back to sleep."

"That's not a good enough excuse. Come on." He stepped into his boxer briefs. "We'll go to brunch after."

"Why did you take her dancing?" The words were out of her mouth before she could stop them.

He didn't respond at first, staring at her from across the room. "Lina?" he finally asked, his eyes narrowed in confusion. "I don't—"

"Dancing is ours. Why would you dance with Kim?"

"No." He shook his head, his lips turned down. "I never danced with her."

"The pictures Kim sent me. One of them is of the two of you dancing."

"I don't remember dancing with her."

"You were dancing." She'd looked at the copies of the photos enough times to have them permanently burned into her memory. "You were in a bar or something."

"Then it was only a moment. Maybe a song came on at the bar and we danced for a second. I honestly have no memory of it."

62

Annoyance rushed to her chest. How could he not recall something that caused her so much heartache? She sat up on the bed, frowning across the room at him. "Did you look at the pictures she sent me that day? I left them in your robe pocket so you could see them."

"Why do you want to talk about this?"

"Probably because we never did. I created stories around those pictures, stories that probably aren't even true. Like believing you took her dancing."

"I never took her dancing."

"Where did you take her?"

He dragged his hand down his face. "How is this moving forward? A new beginning, remember?"

"I don't think that's possible until we've fully dealt with the past." She felt the truth in the words as she said them.

"It's eight thirty on Sunday morning. Do you really want to do this right now?"

"Yes." She nodded. "I do. I want to put her behind us as much as you do, but I need to know the truth about the pictures first."

"Can we wait until after church?"

"No." She slowly shook her head. It was as if now that she'd decided to discuss the pictures, she had to do it at that moment, before she put her head back in the sand about them.

"Let me tell the kids we're going to a later Mass," he said, reaching for a pair of sweatpants.

***

It was fifteen minutes before Phil returned to the bedroom, balancing two mugs of coffee as he carefully closed the bedroom door. Lina was still in bed, sitting cross-legged on the center of the mattress, nervously twisting her wedding band. She'd slipped on a silk nightgown.

"I don't think this is a good idea," he said after lowering himself onto the mattress beside her and setting the coffee on the nightstand. "What if it reopens everything?" *And you want me to leave again*, he thought but didn't say.

"It won't," she said. "Not talking about it is keeping it alive in my head."

"What do you want to know?"

"Where you took her."

"I didn't take her anywhere."

"You weren't in your office in those pictures, Phil."

He thought back to the pictures. He'd come home from a night in the ER after punching the brick wall in front of Nick Drayton's town house instead of his face as intended. He was exhausted, in pain, and vacillating between rage and devastation at the knowledge that Lina had spent the night with Drayton. He'd been wrongly convinced at the time they'd had sex. He'd found the photos in the pocket of his robe, where Lina told him she'd left them. The only one he could clearly remember was the one from Steamboat. The other photos had seemed insignificant in comparison. He had a vague memory of one from Kim's bedroom, taken while he was sleeping. The others, like the one Lina was now talking about, he couldn't recall.

"I never took her anywhere that wasn't somehow an extension of business. We ate out when we were traveling for work, never locally."

"You were wearing casual clothes in the photos."

He racked his brain. She'd clearly spent time analyzing the pictures, which he'd literally lit on fire minutes after finding them, wanting no reminder of his time with Kim.

"Maybe in New York. Sometimes the trips went into the weekend. I didn't wear a suit to the office on weekends."

"You didn't look at them, did you?" she asked. "You don't remember the pictures."

He rubbed his hand over his forehead. "No. Not really."

"Those pictures destroyed me," she whispered. "How could you not even bother to look at what she sent me?"

The pain in her eyes was like a punch to his gut. "Baby, don't." He stroked his hand around her shoulder, gripping her gently. "Don't read anything into it. I knew what I had done. I didn't need to see the evidence."

"You looked at her like you loved her."

"No." He pulled his head back, shaking his head in denial. "That isn't true. I didn't love her."

Tears came to her eyes. He knew she was recalling all the details he had no way of remembering. He should have looked at the pictures. "It was one of the looks you give me. I thought it was only for me."

"Oh, baby." He pulled her into his arms and was relieved when she didn't fight him. He could feel the press of her face in the crook of his neck. He tightened his arms around her, wanting to take her pain away. "I don't know what you think you saw, but I promise you it wasn't love—I only love you. I've only ever loved you."

"I have the pictures," she said after a minute, pulling back slightly. "I want to show you."

He could feel his pulse increasing. "How?"

"I took pictures of them with my cell phone." She brushed a few stray tears from beneath her eyes.

He had no fucking desire to see those pictures. "Delete them. You're keeping this alive. You forgave me, remember? I don't want to fucking do this."

"But I need to understand them."

65

"Understand what? I had an affair. I admitted it. There's nothing I can say to justify it or make it go away. You have to let it go."

"I thought I had, but then Diane sent me a picture of the two of us from last night. It's a beautiful picture, frame-worthy beautiful. But when I saw it, instead of appreciating it, loving it, I thought of you and Kim. It took my mind back to the picture of the two of you dancing."

He fell back on the mattress, covering his face with his hands. "I don't want to relive it. Don't you get that? It's the lowest point of my life."

"I just need to understand them and then I can let them go. I'll delete them after."

It was a nightmare. He'd woken to a nightmare. After making it through the evening at Gina and Bob's he'd thought they were in a better place. This felt like they were moving backward. "Okay." He sat up. "Where are they? Let's get this over with." He plowed his fingers back through his hair.

"This isn't about punishing you. It's something I need to heal."

"What if it doesn't help you heal? What if they make you angry all over again? What then?" It was his greatest fear, that she'd decide she couldn't forgive him after all.

"It won't." She crawled across the mattress and into his lap, cupping his face in her hands. "I don't want to be without you. I love you."

They were side by side on the couch in the sitting room, their bodies touching from thigh to shoulder, as if each needing the contact for emotional support. Phil watched Lina tapping the display on her phone, and then just like that he was looking at the first of the four pictures Kim had sent her that day. He was lying in Kim's bed asleep when he should have been home with his wife and family.

"Her apartment," he said. "It was one of the Sunday nights I spent there before an early flight to New York."

"How many times did you do that?"

He rubbed the back of his neck. "Two, maybe three."

She deleted the picture from her phone.

He released a breath. One down, three to go.

The next photo was harder to stomach. He was with Kim, touching Kim. She was sitting on a barstool and he was standing beside her with his hand resting on her upper thigh while he chatted with an associate from the firm she'd worked for in New York. He had no idea who had taken the picture. She'd clearly asked someone to. "This is a pub near our office in New York. We went there on a Saturday after working most of the day. There were a few people there Kim knew from her time working in the city. He's one of them."

"He thought you were a couple?"

His chest hurt at the pain he could hear in Lina's voice. "Probably. I don't know. Lina, are you sure—"

"Yes." She deleted the picture.

He felt like he'd been physically punched when he saw the next picture. It was the picture she'd already asked him about. He was indeed dancing, and he had his hands on Kim's ass. Lina's hand was shaking slightly as she held the phone.

He took the phone, fighting the urge to launch it toward the wall, wanting nothing more than to destroy the moment captured in the photograph. He couldn't fathom the pain she must have experienced having to see the photo of him grasping the ass of another woman.

Instead of pulling away from him like he'd expected, Lina's hand slid over his stomach as she snuggled closer into his side, resting her cheek against his chest. He lifted his arm and curved it around her shoulders. "This picture wasn't about her," he said. "It isn't what it looks like."

"What is it then?" Her voice was a whisper.

"I'd just gotten word Braxton had agreed to settle."

"Braxton?"

"The dispute over the property in New York—the shopping centers," he reminded her. "It was the reason I was traveling to New York so much." When she didn't say anything, he knew she had no idea which case he was talking about. Had he really never discussed the biggest case of his career with her? "I'd just learned that it wouldn't be going to trial," he continued. "That they'd agreed to our settlement demand. It was the largest settlement in the firm's history, and it was my win. I was celebrating. It had nothing to do with Kim. She was just there."

"The largest in the firm's history?" She lifted her head from his chest and was looking at him. "Like, monetarily?"

"Yes."

"You never told me that."

"Most of our discussions centered around Katie back then." She'd been a few months into her therapy with Drayton at that point.

"I should have known. How could you not share something so important with me?"

"Katie was living in her room," he said, the guilt he always felt at the memory coming back in full force. "You resented my time away. What was I supposed to say? I may be failing as a father, but look what a great success I am at work?"

"You never failed as a father. You're a wonderful father. We were both struggling with how to handle her. And this was your career. It had nothing to do with Katie. You should have shared it with me."

"It didn't feel right, not at that time."

"But it did with her? To share a pinnacle moment of your career with another woman?"

"It wasn't like that. She was involved in the case and was there." He again looked down at the photo. "At that moment, I was feeling euphoric after winning a big case and I was celebrating."

"With her," she said, her voice filled with hurt.

"I wish I could undo it."

"Delete it," she said. "I don't want to ever see it again."

He lifted the phone and was preparing to delete it when he remembered her comment from earlier about the photo from Diane. He quickly located it on her phone. "That's love," he said, looking down at the image. He flipped back to the photo with Kim. "That's not." He turned the display to Lina, switching back and forth between them. "There's no comparison. Do you see the difference in my eyes?" he asked.

"I do, but I still hate that you celebrated something so important with her. We can never have that moment back. She shared it with you."

"I don't associate her with that win." He deleted the picture from her phone.

"There's one more," she said. Once again she was coming closer, pressing herself into his side as she reached for the phone.

"I don't need to see it," he said. "I remember it." It was the picture from Steamboat. Kim had photographed him asleep with a picture of him and Lina displayed on the nightstand.

"That was the picture I couldn't reconcile in my mind," she began, speaking so softly he had to concentrate to hear her. "It's the one that made me leave that day and kept me from letting you come back home. You let her in our bed."

"No." He tightened his arm around her. "I never let her in our bed. I let her in our home."

"Don't lie to me. I don't want you to lie. You canceled our spring break and took her there."

"No. Lina, you're wrong," he said intensely. "I canceled spring break because of the Braxton case. I was in New York working. I didn't take her on a vacation. We spent the night in Steamboat—one night. We were going to Denver for the Property Conference in April. Our connection from Chicago to Denver was canceled due to a storm. Instead of spending the night in Chicago, I decided to fly into Hayden and drive to Denver. It was about seven in the evening when we landed. I'd planned to drive to Denver that night, but when we were renting the car, I found out I-40 was closed because of an accident. We'd stopped for food and it was getting late. I tried two hotels, but they were sold out. I should have kept looking. Instead I took her…" He trailed off. "As soon as we stepped into the foyer, I knew it was a mistake. You were everywhere. It was our house. She didn't belong. I should have left. She convinced me it would be okay, that she'd just sleep in one of the kids' rooms and we'd leave first thing in the morning. It was already late, so I figured since we were already there…" He again trailed off. He could feel Lina's nails sinking into his shoulder.

"She came to you, though."

"Yes." He'd woken to Kim giving him a blow job. It had taken his mind a moment to process what was happening, but when it had he'd shoved her away. He'd been so angry at Kim. Two weeks later the affair was over. He couldn't

70

look at her without thinking about Lina. "I didn't fuck her in our bed. I swear to you I didn't."

"Okay."

He could hear the doubt in her voice. She didn't believe him. "I have no reason to lie to you now. You've forgiven me."

"Did you have oral sex?"

Fuck. He hadn't wanted to go there. "I didn't. She tried. I stopped her."

"I don't want to hear any more," Lina said, pulling back from him.

"Lina, don't." He gripped her hand when she tried to pull farther away. "I swear on our children's lives, I'm telling you the truth."

"You should never have let her in our house. That was our home. Our children's home," she said, her voice shaking with emotion. "That was my favorite place, and now I can never go back."

His gut twisted at the raw pain he could see in her eyes. "I'm sorry, baby." His hold on her hand tightened. "I was a fucking idiot." Tears began to slide down her cheeks. "Come here." He could see the hesitation in her eyes. "Please." He released a breath when she let him pull her into his arms. He could feel the wetness from her tears on his neck. "I'm so sorry."

"How—how could you have cheated on me? How? I can't get my mind to understand. It's not you. It's not the you I'm with right now."

"It wasn't me. I was escaping. I was a fucking coward. I failed you, and I'll never forgive myself, but I promise you nothing like that will ever happen again.

***

Lina felt closer to Phil after going through the pictures. It was as if they'd been through a private hell together. They were in church. She was beside him, her hand clasped firmly in his as they rested on his thigh. She thought back to the first time she'd gone to church with him. It had been after she'd witnessed her sister, Shiloh's, rape. She'd been only sixteen at the time. Phil had sat beside her, holding her hand like he was now. She'd found solace in both Phil and the church. She felt the same solace now, twenty-six years later.

It was a day of healing, or at least that's what it felt like to Lina. They spent the afternoon spreading mulch in Lina's flower beds, and then Phil and Logan grilled steaks for dinner. When Lina sat down beside Phil in the family room later that evening, she realized they had barely spent a minute apart all day. They hadn't spoken any more about the photographs—there was nothing to say—but she knew they were experiencing the same emotional hangover. He had felt her pain that morning, seeing the photographs through her eyes for the first time.

It was sometime in the middle of the night when Lina awoke. Phil was sitting on the edge of the bed, leaning forward with his elbows braced on his knees, breathing in and out deeply.

"What's the matter?" she asked, pushing herself up on her elbows. "Phil?"

"Nothing, I just—I had a nightmare."

"A nightmare?" She couldn't recall him ever having a nightmare, or at least not one he shared with her. "Do you remember it?"

"Unfortunately."

"It was that bad?"

He fell back onto the mattress beside her, tossing his forearm over his eyes. "Yes." He let out a deep sigh. "It felt real."

"What was it about?"

"Us. I dreamed this was all a dream and that I was still living in that house in Farside," he said, referring to the house he'd lived in when they were separated.

"It was a dream." She pressed her lips to his shoulder.

"I used to have the exact opposite dream when we were separated. I would dream we were together and I would be so relieved, but then I'd wake up and I'd still be in that house. God, I hate that fucking house. I can't even drive by it without feeling this tightness in my chest."

"Stop talking about it." She tugged his arm from his eyes.

"I was so fucking lost without you."

"It was just a dream," she whispered, curving her body around the back of his as he rolled onto his side.

"I couldn't go through that again."

"You'll never have to." She stroked her hand up and down his arm. "Just go back to sleep." She pressed her cheek against his back. Within a few minutes his breathing changed, and she realized he'd fallen asleep. She'd been with him more than twenty-six years and this was the first time she could recall him expressing any type of vulnerability.

Chapter Eight

"You're late," Lina said when Phil stepped out of the mudroom and into the kitchen.

"I am?" He paused to meet her lips for a kiss.

"Katie." She tugged on the lapels of his suit jacket. "Your daughter's seventeenth birthday. Our reservation is for seven. I tried to call you, but your phone kept going straight to voice mail. Everyone else is already at the restaurant."

He'd completely forgotten about Katie's birthday. "I turned it off earlier and forgot to turn it back on. Do I have time to change?"

"No." She took his arm, turning him back into the mudroom. "We're already going to be ten minutes late."

In addition to Katie and Logan, Matt, Lina's parents, and Adele were already seated at the restaurant when Lina and Phil arrived. "Is this place new?" Phil asked Lina after they sat down, taking in the brightly lit restaurant with light-stained hardwood floors and modern art decorating the walls.

"No. It's been here for years."

"I'll just have a steak," he said, closing the menu.

"That should be interesting," Adele said from across the table. "I suppose they could give you a big slab of tofu. Maybe you wouldn't notice."

"Are you looking for suggestions, Phil?" Lina's father, Drew Rayburn, asked, looking at him over the rims of his reading glasses. "They've really mastered the art of imitating the actual flavors of meat and cheese in recent years. You barely notice the difference."

"What is he talking about?" Phil asked Lina, ignoring her father as he opened his menu again.

"This is a vegan restaurant," she said, rubbing her hand on his thigh.

"Vegan?"

"Why don't you try a pizza?" Lina suggested.

"I thought vegans didn't eat dairy."

"They don't. The cheese is made from soybean."

"Wait—they have chicken quesadillas. I'll just get that."

"Do you see the quotes around 'chicken'?" Lina asked, touching the word "chicken" on his menu. "That means it isn't actually chicken. It's probably good though."

"How about the crab cake? Is it crab?"

"No. Look at the quotes around 'crab.'"

"Christ." He closed his menu. "You can order for me." What in the hell was the point? Every item on the menu was a fraud.

"The beer's not bad," Adele said, holding up her glass. "It's an IPA—organic, of course."

"Pinot?" Phil asked Lina when a waitress arrived to take their drink order. "And I'll have one of those." He nodded across the table to Adele.

"The origins of the organic food movement aren't new," Drew said to no one in particular. "They began in Europe in the 1920s. Of course, they didn't gain traction in the United States until the late 1960s and early '70s. In this country it was due to some high-profile cases regarding pesticides."

Phil stopped listening as Drew continued with his history lesson. He could barely stomach Lina's father. The man had basically packed a bag and left his family thirty years ago, providing not much more than monetary support, as he had a prestigious career as a professor at the University of Chicago. In the past year he had divorced his second wife and returned to claim the family he'd abandoned. For reasons inconceivable to Phil, Lina's mother had taken him back with open arms, as if the previous thirty years hadn't occurred.

The rest of the family seemed to be doing the same. Until the prior fall, Lina hadn't spoken to him in twenty years, and their children had never met him. Now he was being invited to every family get-together. With a wedding planned for July, it looked like Drew Rayburn was back to stay.

"How can you forgive him?" Phil asked Lina as soon as they were in the privacy of their car. "He chose to skip your entire childhood."

"It's not about forgiving him. He's marrying my mother. What do you expect me to do? Disown her, the woman who raised me on her own? Plus, the kids like him."

"I don't," Phil said. "At all."

"I know. Everyone knows. You're not doing a very good job of hiding that fact."

"I'm not trying to," Phil said.

"Well, try," Lina said. "What are you doing?" she asked when he turned into the Wendy's parking lot.

"Getting something to eat."

"Phil—" She was cut off by the ringing of her cell phone. "It's Logan," she said, bringing it to her ear. "What's wrong...? No. Your dad just wanted something...We're going to have cake and ice cream...Okay...I heard you." She ended the call. "Your son would like a double cheeseburger."

"Of course he would," Phil said smugly. "How about Matt?"

"He didn't mention Matt."

"I'm sure he wants one, too. He just didn't want to admit it in front of the birthday girl."

***

Lina was at the kitchen island with her mother and Adele, placing candles on Katie's cake, while Matt and Logan sat at the table, wolfing down burgers and French fries as if they hadn't just eaten. Katie handled it all good-naturedly, spouting off the nutritional facts of the food they were putting into their bodies.

Phil came into the room, freshly changed into shorts and a T-shirt, and sat down at his usual spot at the end of the table and began to eat his own hamburger.

"Katie said we're eating cartilage, tissues and...what was the last thing you just said?" Logan asked.

"Peripheral nerves," Katie answered.

"Yeah. They taste pretty good, don't they, Dad?" he asked with a smirk before biting into his hamburger.

"Tell them what you were telling me about the meat-processing places, Grandpa," Katie said.

"I was reading a—"

"No," Phil said, cutting Drew off midsentence. "I don't want to hear about a meat-processing facility while I eat a goddamn hamburger."

"Phil," Lina chastised, not liking the tone he was using.

"I'm eating," he pointed out. "If Logan and Matt want to hear about it, they can go out on the deck with him."

Both Matt and Logan quickly seconded that they didn't want to hear about a meat-processing facility. Drew shrugged and crossed into the kitchen to look at the cake.

"Did you know that birthday cakes date back to the ancient Greeks and were a special way to pay tribute to the Greek moon goddess, Selene?"

"No," Lina answered. "I never actually thought about it." She met Adele's eyes, trying not to laugh. She was beginning to wonder if Drew spent his spare time reading random entries in Wikipedia.

"Of course, the origin can also be traced back to the Germans, the Swiss, and even pagans," he continued, before launching into a history of each.

"Does he ever stop talking?" Phil whispered in Lina's ear as he gripped her hips from behind. She was standing at the counter, dishing ice cream onto the plates Adele was passing out.

"Be nice." She bit her lip to keep from laughing.

"I've been meaning to ask you if you would give me away at my wedding," Lina's mom said, coming to stand beside them. At sixty-seven, Alice Rayburn had the youthful vibe and disposition of someone half her age.

Lina could feel Phil's hands tighten on her hips. "Mom, don't you think you're a little old to be given away?" she asked. "I mean, you're not really anyone's to give away." There was no way Phil would agree to walk her mother down the aisle, not when it was Drew Rayburn he was walking her to.

"It's a tradition."

"Since when are you into tradition?"

"No," Phil said. "That's not going to happen."

"Who else am I going to ask?" Alice frowned as Phil walked away.

"No one," Lina said. She was still having a hard time fathoming why her free-spirited mother wanted to have a wedding. "Why don't you just elope?"

"Why would I do that? I want my family to share in our happiness. How many children get to watch their parents get married?"

"None, because it's not normal," Lina answered.

"Oh, don't be such a fuddy-duddy. You're too young to be so stuck in your ways. When am I going to meet my new grandson?"

Lina almost dropped the plate in her hand. "What are you talking about?" she whispered, looking around to make sure no one was listening to their conversation.

"The baby."

"I know what you're talking about," Lina whispered.

"Then why did you ask me what I was talking about?"

"Because I don't want to talk about it."

"You haven't met him yet?" Alice asked, her eyes widening. "You don't plan to ignore him, do you?"

"Mom," Lina hissed. "Katie's birthday isn't the time to discuss this."

"Well, when is the time then? He's Phil's son. You can't very well ignore him. He's going to be part of your life."

Alice's words replayed in Lina's mind as she prepared for bed. Her mother was right. She couldn't just ignore Liam's

79

existence. Eventually she was going to have to meet him and accept him into the family. She just wasn't ready yet.

The ringing of the phone interrupted her thoughts, and she answered without checking the caller ID.

"I need to speak with Phil," came the distinctly female voice.

Lina's hand tightened on the receiver. She'd heard her voice only once before, but she was almost certain it was Kim. "Who is this?"

"Just put him on the phone."

"You have no business calling our home at this hour or ever."

"I don't?" Kim laughed softly. "I'm calling the home of my son's father. I think I can call at any hour I want."

"This is *our* home. If you'd like to speak to him, use his cell phone." Lina disconnected the call. The phone immediately began to ring again. She clicked the phone on and off again, effectively disconnecting the incoming call. When it rang a third time she did the same thing.

"Who in the hell keeps calling?" Phil asked as he came out of the bathroom, shirtless with his toothbrush in his hand. "It's after eleven."

"Kim," Lina answered. "She clearly didn't get the message about not calling our home. According to her she's allowed to call at any hour she would like."

He crossed to his bureau to retrieve his cell phone. "What did she want?"

"You," Lina answered as she yanked down the comforter.

"I thought you were going to disconnect the line."

"And I thought you were going to keep her from calling here ever again," she countered, annoyance in her voice.

"I'm not the enemy." He came to the bed with his phone in his hand. "I forgot the cell was off." He was looking down at his phone as it powered on.

"It couldn't be too serious, whatever she wanted. She laughed at me when I told her not to call here." She went to lie down but immediately changed her mind, knowing she was never going to fall asleep. "Just the sound of her voice is…" She trailed off as Phil brought his phone to his ear.

"What?" he bit out, his jaw shaking with anger. He turned away from the bed and Lina, walking toward the windows overlooking the backyard. "I told you never to call my house…No…It's eleven thirty. This could have waited until tomorrow. I'm not at your beck and call…Our communication can be done via text…Unless he's on his way to a hospital, you are never to fucking call me again…Calling my house, my wife, is harassment…Don't push me, Kim. I will get a restraining order." He ended the call.

"What did she want?" Lina asked as he headed back toward the bathroom.

"Nothing that couldn't have waited until tomorrow." He disappeared into the bathroom.

Lina's heart rate was still elevated when Phil joined her in bed a few minutes later, smelling of a mixture of spearmint toothpaste and soap. She could feel the tension radiating off of him.

"I should have disconnected the line," she said.

"This isn't on you," he said. "I brought her into our fucking lives." He reached over her and turned out the bedside light, blanketing the room in darkness. "She wants me to stay until ten tomorrow night. She has a work dinner and the nanny has a conflict."

"Are you going to?"

He sighed. "Do you mind? If you do, I could ask the nanny to figure something out."

"No. It's okay. I don't mind you being there without her." Lina curved her body into the side of his, resting her cheek on his warm chest. "It will be nice for you to have a little extra time with him."

Chapter Nine

It took Phil less than two hours to realize he was in over his head. He may have fathered three other children, but it was Lina who'd fed them, bathed them, and changed their diapers. His role with baby rearing had consisted of him handing them over to Lina whenever they needed something more than a toss in the air or a game of peekaboo.

He was at the sink, running a wet cloth over a carrot stain on his dress shirt, when Liam, who was in his high chair, decided to put applesauce in his hair. "Jesus Christ." Phil sighed, crossing to him. "Why are you doing that?"

"Gaah, gaah," Liam shouted, continuing to rub his hands through his hair.

"It's for eating." Phil removed the tray from the high chair before unstrapping Liam. "You're a mess." He carried him to the sink.

Liam slapped one of his applesauce-covered hands against his father's head as he gurgled with laughter. "Baah." Liam's other hand gripped Phil's tie.

"Are you always this bad?"

Liam's answer was another slap to Phil's head.

Phil turned on the faucet and managed to clean off Liam's hands and get most of the applesauce from his hair. In the process he drenched his own shirt and Liam's outfit. "I think you need a bath."

He carried him to the nursery and set him in his crib. Liam immediately began to wail in protest. "I'm not putting you to bed," Phil reassured him as he tugged at the knot of his tie. "Just a second, buddy. Daddy needs to take off his shirt." He finished removing his tie and wet shirt before stripping off Liam's clothes.

He realized when they reached the bathroom that he'd never given one of his children a bath. He couldn't recall ever even changing a diaper. He pulled back the shower curtain and noticed a blue plastic tub. He vaguely remembered Lina using something similar to bathe their kids.

Thirty minutes, several towels, and three diapers later, Phil had bathed, diapered, and dressed Liam in a long-sleeved onesie. "You're a good boy, aren't you?" Phil asked him as he heated his bottle.

Liam fingered the sleeve of Phil's undershirt, staring up at him with sleep-filled eyes.

"It's almost ready, buddy." Phil brushed his lips over Liam's forehead.

Phil was on the couch in the family room, watching a twenty-four-hour news channel, with Liam asleep on his chest. Despite their limited time together, he felt the same pulsating connection to him that he'd felt for his other children. It was as if something deeper than just his conscious mind knew that he was his father.

He carefully transported Liam from the family room to his nursery, placing him in his crib before quietly leaving his room. It was after ten. He sent Kim a quick text asking when she'd be home. Ten minutes later there was still no response.

It was after midnight when Phil heard the sound of the front door opening. He was off the couch and halfway down the hall before Kim stepped into the foyer. "Where the fuck have you been?" he bit out. "You said ten o'clock."

"You scared me," she said, bringing her hand to her chest.

"It's after midnight."

"Sorry. The meeting went longer than I expected." Her gaze dropped to his undershirt. "Is that an invitation?"

"You're two hours late," he snarled.

"I was in a meeting." She pressed her hand against the wall as she slipped off her shoes. "I could make it up to you if you'd like."

"Don't play with me."

"I'm not playing," she said, meeting his eyes. "You can take me right here."

"Next time you tell me you're going to be home at a certain time, you better fucking be home," he warned before slamming out of her apartment.

"Phil?" Lina's sleep-filled voice greeted him when he stepped into the kitchen from the mudroom.

He crossed to the family room, where she was lying on the couch under a comforter. "What are you doing down here?"

"I fell asleep." She pushed herself up to a sitting position. "Where's your shirt?"

He looked down at his undershirt. "It got wet when I was rinsing applesauce off of him."

"You took it off in her apartment."

"Yes."

"And then you left it there?"

"Not intentionally. I was in a hurry to get out of there."

"She saw you like that?"

"I was drenched. Would you prefer I spend the evening in a wet shirt?"

"Yes. I think I would." She got up from the couch and headed for the front of the house.

"Lina?" He jogged to catch up with her. "Come on." He caught her arm as they reached the stairs. "Don't be like this."

"Like what?" She crossed her arms over her chest. "Upset that you took your shirt off at another woman's house or that you left your shirt at another woman's house?"

"Do you really think if I took off my shirt to fuck her, I'd leave it there?" He regretted the words as soon as he said them. The pain in her eyes was like a knife in his heart. "I'm sorry."

"Don't follow me," she said before fleeing up the stairs.

He gripped the banister, staring down at the floor as he mentally berated himself for his insensitivity. "Fuck."

"Dad?"

He lifted his eyes to find Logan, looking half asleep, standing at the top of the staircase. "What are you doing up?"

"What happened?"

"Nothing."

"Why was Mom upset?"

"We just had a misunderstanding. It's nothing for you to worry about." He began to ascend the stairs. "It's late," he said when he reached the top. "Why don't you go back to bed?"

"She told you not to follow her," Logan said, shifting slightly so he blocked his path.

"Go to bed, Logan."

Logan shook his head, a blush staining his cheeks. "She said—"

"This is between me and your mother," Phil interrupted, trying to keep a rein on his temper. "Get out of my way. I'm not going to tell you again."

"It's okay, Logan," Lina called out from down the hall. "I'm fine."

Phil waited for her to go back into their bedroom before returning his attention to Logan. "I know you mean well," he said, "but don't *ever* try to block my path again. Is that clear?" His eyes widened as he stared into Logan's eyes. "Is it?"

"Yeah," Logan answered, dropping his gaze.

Lina was in their bed, curled onto her side facing away from the door, when Phil entered their bedroom. "I'm sorry. That was insensitive and thoughtless."

"I just want to go to sleep."

"Baby—"

"It's one o'clock in the morning. We can talk about it tomorrow."

When he stretched out beside her ten minutes later, he knew she was still awake. She was holding her body too stiffly. "I didn't mean to hurt you," he said as he curved his body into the back of hers. "The thought of her—of being with her—repulses me. I forget that you aren't in my head, knowing how I feel. Forgive me." He felt her body relax back into his.

"It's just—the way you said it. It made me think about the times you were with her and then you got dressed and came home to me."

"I'm sorry."

"I hate that you have to see her—that you talk to her."

"I know." He tightened his hold around her. "I don't like seeing her either. You know that, right?"

"Yes."

***

By the time Lina got herself out of bed and into the shower the following morning it was almost eleven, so she took the day off, deciding to catch up on errands before the long holiday weekend. She was in Phil's wardrobe, gathering his suits to take to the dry cleaner, when she felt a slip of paper in the interior pocket of one of his jackets. Her heart began to pound when she realized it was a receipt from Victoria's Secret. She let the jacket fall to the floor as she left his wardrobe, her eyes glued to the paper in her hand. He'd spent three hundred and eighty dollars at a women's lingerie store.

She sat down on the end of the bed, her hand shaking slightly as she continued to stare at the receipt. It was a memento from his time with Kim. There was no other explanation. A wave of nausea hit her at the thought of him choosing sexy lingerie for his mistress. She crinkled the paper up in her hand. It was over. She wasn't going to let her mind go back there. Forward. Phil had said they would move forward together. She would throw it away and not give it another moment of her energy.

The receipt was still clenched in her fist when she stepped out into the garage. Her mind became her enemy, suddenly desiring to know what Phil had bought Kim. She opened her hand, staring at the crumpled ball of paper in her palm. Instead of tossing it into the trash can, she carefully opened the receipt.

He'd bought her three items, but Lina couldn't make out what they were from the abbreviations. The receipt was from the Victoria's Secret in the Inner Harbor. It was walking distance from his office. The time stamp on the receipt was twelve thirty in the afternoon. He'd left his office and gone to a lingerie store in the middle of a workday. Anger bubbled in her chest at the thought of him carrying a bag of gifts for Kim into his law office. The purchases had been made in April. A little more than a year ago. No. She caught her breath when her eyes zeroed in on the date. The receipt wasn't a year old. It was a month old.

Chapter Ten

He'd bought the lingerie a month earlier. He'd been living with her at the time. Her mind searched for an explanation. A lump formed in her throat. Maybe it was for her. But if that were the case, why hadn't he given it to her yet? Her mind spun with endless possibilities. Anxiety clawed at her insides. No. He wasn't having an affair. She knew it, and yet the unease wouldn't let up. She recalled the look of concern in his eyes that morning when he asked her if they were okay. They were okay. She knew that with every fiber of her being. Their connection was strong.

She took the receipt back into the house, did her best to flatten out the wrinkles, and took a picture of it with her cell phone. Seconds later she was sending a copy of it to Phil. *What is this?*

She stared at her phone, gripping it between her hands. After ten minutes with no response she called his office. "Hi, Anne. It's Lina Hunter. Is he in?" Her heart was beating so hard she felt like it could burst through her chest.

"Hi, Mrs. Hunter. He is, but he's in a meeting with a client."

"Would you give him a message for me please? It's—it's urgent."

"Oh, if it's urgent I can interrupt—"

"No. I don't need to talk to him. Just tell him to read the message I sent him and that I'm waiting for his reply. Thanks."

***

Phil was in the conference room, going through the terms of a real-estate contract with one of the firm's largest clients, when his secretary poked her head into the room. "Can it wait thirty minutes?" he asked, annoyed at the interruption. She knew better than to disturb him when he was with a client.

"I'm sorry, but your wife said it was urgent."

"Continue without me," he told one of his associates before excusing himself and following Anne out into the hallway. "What's going on?"

"I don't know. She just said it was urgent that you read her text and send her a reply." She held out his cell phone, which he had left on his desk.

He tapped in his passcode before opening Lina's message. His eyes narrowed in confusion as he looked at the receipt from Victoria's Secret. He lifted his gaze back to Anne, who was nervously watching him. "She told you this was urgent?"

"Yes." She nodded.

"Could you have misunderstood her?"

"No. I don't think so. She seemed upset."

He gripped his chin, once again staring at the picture. He had no idea what he was supposed to make of it. "What did she say exactly?"

"That it was urgent you read her message, and she's awaiting your reply."

"That's it?"

"Yes."

"Thank you." He was torn between getting back to his meeting and finding out what in the hell was going on with Lina. It seemed like a joke, but he couldn't be sure.

I'm in the middle of a meeting, baby. I think I'm missing a text or two. I have no idea what that receipt means.

Her reply took less than five seconds. *It was in the interior pocket of your charcoal suit jacket.*

You must be mistaken. I've never been in that store. Could we talk about this later? I need to get back to my meeting.

He watched the blinking bubbles alerting him she was drafting her reply. *I found it in your pocket. The store is near your office. How did it get in your pocket if it isn't yours?*

It hit him then that she believed he'd been shopping at a women's lingerie store. He rubbed the back of his neck. *I have no idea, but it's not mine. I've got to get back to my meeting. I'll call you as soon as I'm done.*

***

Lina stripped off her gardening gloves as she watched Phil's BMW disappear into the garage. Since their brief flurry of text messages, she'd managed to push the receipt from her mind and lose herself in her gardens, pruning and planting flowers and taking advantage of a beautiful spring day. As she watched Phil emerge from the garage, her anxiety over what the receipt meant came back in full force.

"You're early."

"Why didn't you answer your phone? I've been trying to reach you for two hours."

"I was gardening." She wiped the back of her hand over her forehead. "I still have more to do."

"What's going on?" He hooked his finger into the belt loop of her cutoff jean shorts when she began to turn away. "I don't get a kiss?"

"I'll get you dirty," she said, pressing her hands against his chest as she attempted to keep him at bay.

"I don't care." He tugged her closer, curving his free hand around her jaw. "I don't know what you're thinking, but you're wrong. That receipt is not mine."

"Then what was it doing in your pocket?" She wanted to believe him, but the evidence didn't support what he was saying.

"Did you look at the date on it? We were in Paris. We didn't come home until the following day."

"Paris," she repeated. It wasn't his receipt. She could feel the tension leave her body. "How did it get in your pocket?"

"I don't know, but it's not mine."

She slipped her hands beneath his suit jacket and wrapped her arms around him as she pressed her cheek into his upper chest, no longer concerned with soiling his suit. "I didn't think it was," she whispered, "but then I was afraid I was being naive."

"No." He engulfed her in his arms. "I've never stepped into one of those stores. And if I did, it would only be for you." He brushed his lips over her temple. "Someone is messing with us."

"Who?" She pulled back enough to look up at him. "It's not even funny. It ruined my day."

"I don't know. But someone put it there."

93

As soon as Phil saw the jacket lying on the end of the bed, his jaw tightened and his hands clenched at his sides. "It was Kim. It's the jacket I left at her place."

"Kim?" Lina repeated.

He yanked off his tie as he headed for his wardrobe. He fumbled with the buttons on his shirt, finally just ripping it open.

"What are you doing?" Lina asked from the doorway, her eyes on the buttons that had fallen to the floor.

"This isn't okay." He began to unclasp his belt. "She's not getting away with it." He was out of his pants and stepping into khaki shorts. His eyes were hard and his jaw firm. "She's pushed me too far." He crouched down to put on his running shoes, quickly lacing them.

"You need to calm down."

He brushed past her as he left the wardrobe, shrugging into a T-shirt as he headed for the door.

"Phil, stop," Lina called out, rushing after him. "You have to talk to me."

"We'll talk when I get back." he said, not slowing his stride as he descended the stairs. He was in the mudroom and pulling open the door to the garage before Lina caught up to him.

"Stop!" she cried.

"I have to do this," he said, pausing in the doorway. "First the late call, then last night, and now this. I'm putting a fucking end to it."

"Any time she gets you to come to her and leave me, she's winning."

"She isn't—"

"You're not leaving your family at three thirty on a Friday afternoon for God knows how long to confront her about something that's already happened. She's stolen last night from us and most of today. She's not taking another minute of my weekend."

"Lina—"

"No." She pressed her hands into his chest. "You're not leaving."

He released a breath and she could almost see the anger draining from him. "I don't want her to get away with this."

"She isn't. We figured it out. And next time I will automatically assume she's trying to hurt me and I won't let her."

The sound of a car had them both looking to the driveway. Lina felt Phil's body tense under her hands when Nick Drayton's Porsche came into view. "Fuck me," he growled.

"Don't," Lina whispered. "He's just dropping off Brian."

The passenger door opened and Brian emerged, and then to Lina's dread the driver's door opened and Nick emerged. He looked tan and relaxed in jeans and a short-sleeved black crewneck, sunglasses concealing his eyes. He gave Brian a quick hug and seemed to be about to get back into his car when he spotted them.

"Hey, Hunters," Brian said, coming into the garage.

"Hi, sweetie, Logan's in the pool." Lina forced a smile.

As soon as Brian was in the house, Phil was disentangling himself from Lina and stalking out of the garage. "Get back in your fucking car and get out of here," he barked, rounding Nick's car and stopping within feet of him.

"Phil! Stop!" Lina rushed to his side, wedging herself between them. "Don't take your mood out on him."

"Get out of here!" Phil snarled. "And next time stay in your fucking car."

"I'm sorry," Lina managed to say to Nick before gripping Phil's arm and propelling him back toward the house. She sagged with relief when she heard the engine of Nick's car.

***

Phil feigned left, sending Brian diving into the grass before swinging to the right and launching the lacrosse ball into the back of the net. "Game," he shouted, swiping his hand down his sweat-drenched face as he headed toward the sideline of the quarter-size lacrosse field in their backyard and the pitcher of lemonade Lina had delivered earlier.

"Great shot, Dad," Logan said, jogging up beside him. "You schooled him."

"Yeah," Phil agreed, knowing his days of schooling Brian Drayton were quickly drawing to an end. The kid was too good. Pairing him with Mike for their two-on-two scrimmage had basically been a handicap. "Why don't you go see if your uncle is okay," Phil said, looking back over his shoulder at his brother, who was lying flat on his back in the middle of the field.

"I want a rematch," Brian said, joining them. He took the cup of lemonade Phil handed him, bringing it to his mouth and finishing it in several long swallows. "You only beat me by three."

"Maybe tomorrow," Phil said. "When you're my age you need a recovery period."

"No way," Brian said. "You're more fit than anyone. You'd probably still be the best player on a college team."

"I doubt that," Phil said. "But I appreciate the vote of confidence."

He raised his eyebrows at his brother, who had finally come to his feet. "You're forty-four, not eighty-four," he called out as Mike lumbered over toward them. Like Phil, Mike had played D1 lacrosse in college, but unlike Phil, who had carved out the time to exercise in the ensuing years, Mike only exercised sporadically and carried a few extra pounds around his middle.

"I didn't eat enough this morning," Mike complained.

"Are you sure?" Phil asked dryly. "You don't look like someone who would miss a meal."

"All I had was a cinnamon roll," he said, either not hearing Phil's unsubtle insult or choosing to ignore it.

Phil's attention shifted from Mike when he noticed Lina walking across the grass toward them wearing cutoff jean shorts and a tank top. His gaze lingered on her long tan legs, remembering how they'd been wrapped around him that morning. His body instantly came to attention.

"Are you staying for lunch, Mike?" Lina asked, reaching for the empty pitcher. "We have plenty."

Phil caught her around the middle and pulled her back against him.

"Stop. You're sweaty."

"I know." He pulled her closer instead of releasing her. "I don't mind." He dropped a kiss on the side of her neck.

"I do," she laughed, slipping out of his reach. "Mike?"

"No, thanks. I just came over to get some much-needed exercise. Jeanie has a long list of chores I have to get done."

"Next time." She turned back to Phil, standing on her tiptoes to brush her lips over his cheek. "Lunch is ready."

"Things appear to be back on track," Mike said as Phil walked with him toward his car. "I mean with you and Lina."

"Yes," Phil agreed. "Now I need to figure out how to deal with Kim." He proceeded to confide in him about the receipt

Kim had left in his pocket. "If Lina hadn't stopped me, I don't know what in the hell I would have done."

"Jesus," Mike said, stopping as they reached the driveway. "Is she certifiable? Are you going to find a rabbit boiling on the stove?"

"No. She isn't crazy. Just delusional. The idea of a man not wanting her is apparently alien to her. I think she actually believed I'd eventually come back to her. And 'come back' is a generous term because I was never with her—not in more than a physical sense. It's always been Lina."

"You know I never said anything to you after you moved out because I didn't want to kick you while you were down, but what the fuck were you thinking? I mean *Lina*? You cheated on Lina?"

"I don't need a lecture, Mike," he said, annoyance shooting through him. "I'm more aware than anyone how much I fucked up my life."

"Sorry," Mike said. "It's just…" He trailed off. "It's just hard to believe." He looked down at his phone. "Just a second. It's Jeanie," he said as he brought his phone to his ear.

Phil clasped the back of his neck, looking out at the woods that flanked his property. Mike was right. It was even hard for him to believe he'd cheated on Lina. He'd been temporarily insane. He thought back to the night it started. He'd been in New York City on business and he'd returned Lina's call after returning to his hotel room. She'd told him she was giving Katie back her cell phone. He'd taken it away months earlier when he'd caught her doing drugs.

"What in the fuck, Lina? I don't have a say anymore? This doctor is now making the decisions?"

"He's the professional. What do you want to do? Ignore the advice we're paying for?"

"No, not ignore it. We can take it under advisement, but you're acting like he's some god—like we have to blindly follow everything he says."

"What he's saying is working. She actually talked to me today. And yesterday she came down for dinner without being called. She's getting better!"

"Don't raise your voice at me!"

"Why not? Are you the only one who's allowed to yell?"

"I'm her father. You should be discussing things with me."

"We are discussing it," Lina snapped. "We are on the phone right now discussing it. Even though I didn't want to call you because I knew you would be completely unreasonable about it, I called to discuss it with you."

"Oh, is that right? You don't want to talk to me?" His hand tightened on the phone.

"Not about Katie. Because you just can't accept that you have no idea how to parent her."

"You won't let me parent her!"

"I did let you! I let you sever her Internet access and take away her phone. I agreed to that. I didn't want to, but I did, and look what happened."

"So now what? It's my fault? Is that what the good doctor said? That I'm the reason she cut herself?"

Seconds went by before she responded. "Losing access to her friends was probably a contributing factor to her depression."

"Do whatever the fuck you want with her. I'll just work and pay the bills." He hurled his phone across the hotel room, shattering it on the wall. "Fuck!"

"What?" Phil asked, pulling his mind back to the present when he realized Mike was speaking to him.

"I was asking about Kim. Is she actively pursuing you?"

"Actively pursuing me?" Phil repeated, lifting an eyebrow. "Let's just say she isn't subtle in letting me know she'd like me to fuck her."

"Jesus."

"Yeah," Phil agreed. "It doesn't matter how many times I rebuff her. Her tenacity is boundless. As an attorney it serves her well. But in this case, I'm seriously considering a restraining order."

"Wouldn't that get her disbarred?"

"Probably, but I'm not going to stand by while she torments my wife. Lina has been through enough."

"She's just trying to create a rift between the two of you."

"I realize that, Mike."

"Driving from Virginia to Baltimore on a weekday to go to that particular store, that took effort. Why give her the satisfaction of thinking it even remotely succeeded? She's probably waiting for you to show up or call. Let her keep waiting. That receipt could have easily gone undetected. Let her believe it was all for naught. Don't play into her game."

Chapter Eleven

"Oh my God," Adele said the next afternoon after meeting Brian Drayton for the first time. "He looks so much like his father."

"I know," Lina said.

They were stretched out on lounge chairs beside the pool, enjoying another picture-perfect day with temperatures hovering in the low eighties. Logan, Brian, and a few of Logan's other friends had just cut through the pool area on their way to the lacrosse field.

"I thought Phil was taking them to Philadelphia this weekend."

"He decided to drive up Monday for the championship game," Lina said. She knew it was because he hadn't wanted to leave her overnight.

"Have you seen Nick lately?"

"He dropped Brian off yesterday." Lina felt a flash of anxiety at the memory of the way Phil had treated him. "I wish Phil would stop harboring this hostility toward him."

"What do you expect? You dated him."

"It's not like I slept with him," Lina said. "He could at least be civil."

Adele laughed. "Do you know your husband? He's never going to be civil to Nick Drayton. He's jealous of him."

Lina had come to the same conclusion herself. "But there's no reason for him to be jealous."

"Nick saved Katie. You say it all the time. Following his advice is what pulled Katie out of her depression. Don't you think that eats at Phil a little, knowing that another man had to step into your family and help his daughter?"

"Nick is a trained professional. What we were doing wasn't working. We had no choice but to take her to a psychiatrist."

"I know. But put yourself in Phil's shoes for a second. He loves control, and during that time he lost it. Nick was calling the shots when it came to parenting Katie. It bothered him that another man could get through to his daughter when he couldn't."

Lina thought of Phil's words the morning they went through the pictures. He'd said he failed as a father. Her stomach twisted at the memory of the pain she'd seen in his eyes. "We didn't have a choice," she repeated, more to herself than to Adele. "He wanted her to get better, too."

"Of course he did. And I'm sure his ego could have handled the bruising if all Nick did was save Katie. But then he came after you."

"He wasn't after me." She could feel her face heating.

"He told you he had feelings for you when you were still with Phil."

"He knew we were having problems," Lina said defensively. "He knew about Kim."

"That actually makes it worse. And as much as I think Phil is being a hypocrite, I can see why he doesn't want Nick anywhere near you."

Adele's words played in Lina's head for the remainder of the day. When Phil joined her in their bedroom later that night, she decided to broach the subject. "I need to ask you something, and I want you to answer me honestly regardless of whether or not you think it will make me angry."

He was standing before his bureau, taking off his watch. "Are you sure you want to chance getting angry at eleven o'clock at night?"

"It's bothering me, and I won't be able to sleep if I keep thinking about it."

"What is it?"

"Do you feel like I cheated on you emotionally with Nick Drayton?"

He curved his hand around the back of his neck. "Cheated on," he repeated, his eyes narrowed. "No, I don't feel that you cheated on me. I think you confided in him too much. Sought out his counsel instead of mine at times. But it wasn't intentional. He lulled you into doing it. He asked you inappropriate questions about our marriage under the guise of treating Katie. He knew you were desperate to help her and took advantage of the situation because he had feelings for you. He's the one who crossed the line, not you."

"Do you think that caused the distance between us?"

"I know he did."

"And that made room for Kim?"

"If you're asking if Drayton is responsible for my affair, the answer is no. I'm responsible. We were struggling. Yes, in part it was because of him, but I should have made different choices."

"But what if he'd never come into our lives?"

"He did come into our lives." Phil sat down on the edge of the bed. "And I did cheat. Why are we going backward?"

"I was just wondering if the anger you feel toward him is because you blame him for everything."

"I feel anger toward him because he likes to sit in judgment over me while the truth is he pursued the married mother of one of his patients. He would have had an affair with you if you were willing. You know that, right?"

She hesitated before answering, considering his question. "Not while we were together."

"You're not that naive. I saw the way he looked at you. The first time I met him, at Megan's graduation, I could see his interest."

She couldn't deny it. She had noticed the way he'd looked at her that day, too. "He never said anything inappropriate, though, not while we were together." As soon as she said the words, she remembered Nick had told her both that he was attracted to her and loved her before she separated from Phil.

"That isn't true." Phil was watching her closely. "Is it?"

"I'm not interested in him in that way."

"That isn't what I asked. But you don't have to answer because the truth was all over your face."

Over the next several days, Lina struggled with what to do about Nick. She hadn't texted him since she got back with Phil, but knowing she had the option brought her comfort. He'd brought Katie back to her, and he had been her counselor and friend during her separation from Phil. It couldn't remain that way. It wasn't fair to Nick or to Phil to continue the relationship. She knew that, but severing ties with him filled her with anxiety. He'd been her crutch. She drafted and deleted dozens of texts before finally settling on one.

Nick—I know this message is overdue, and I apologize. It took me longer than it should have to articulate my thoughts. You came into my life at a very difficult time, and your counsel and friendship during that time is something I will always cherish. You brought Katie back to us, and for that I will never be able to thank you enough. I shudder to think where we would be now if you hadn't agreed to take her on as your patient. Thank you. I also want to apologize for the way Phil has treated you and continues to treat you. He is a complicated man. I know you believe that I have an unhealthy dependence on him, but you're wrong. He is the love of my life. From the moment I saw him, before words were even spoken, I knew he was my person. Unless you have experienced that kind of connection, I don't think you can understand what it means. I suppose I'm telling you this so that you'll understand that there isn't a doubt in my mind that I'm where I'm supposed to be. For that reason, I have to end our friendship. I don't expect a response to this message. I wish you the best.

Lina wiped a few tears from her eyes before pressing the send button.

Chapter Twelve

There were more than one hundred and fifty guests gathered to witness the nuptials between Alice and Drew Rayburn. It was an eclectic group, with people dressed in everything from tuxedos and dresses to shorts and jeans. It was like a window into Lina's childhood, where people from all walks of life, from poets to dishwashers, would have equal access to the Rayburn house. What they did have in common was a belief in the occult and a love for Alice Rayburn, who shared her vast knowledge of astrology with anyone who was interested. And often those who weren't, spouting out her unorthodox beliefs without filter.

Phil could still remember the first time his parents met Alice Rayburn. His mother had insisted she and his father needed to see where their son was spending so much of his time. Alice agreed that it was time to meet Lina's future in-laws. She'd done Phil's astrological chart months earlier and determined, according to her, that they were cosmic soul mates destined to be together not only in their current lifetime but for all lifetimes.

His mother baked a cake, and she, along with Phil and his father, stopped over early on a Sunday afternoon. The first thing Alice said after greeting them was that their son possessed a gold aura, indicating the highest spiritual level a person could attain. At that point the Hunters' eyes had glossed over and opinions had been formed. Alice Rayburn was eccentric.

Phil's parents had been noticeably absent from the wedding invitation list. Alice had finally showed her cards, saying without words what Phil had known for years: Alice didn't like his parents. She'd resented them since they'd taken Lina in when she was sixteen. It didn't matter that it was Lina's idea, that she didn't feel safe after the home invasion unless she was with Phil. Alice felt that the Hunters should have encouraged her to go home. When they didn't, instead embracing Lina and treating her like one of their own, Alice considered it an affront to her role as Lina's mother. Normally free-loving and nonjudgmental, Alice had shown up at the Hunter household the day before Lina's seventeenth birthday and accused them of trying to steal her daughter. Lina, who was present for her mother's tirade, told Alice she belonged with Phil and was never going to live apart from him again.

Alice left without her daughter that day. It was never spoken of again. Over the ensuing decades, through college graduations, births, and holidays, Alice appeared outwardly friendly to his parents, but it never felt authentic to Phil. Lina reprimanded her mother on more than a few occasions, especially when the children were younger, because Alice would literally pluck the children from Susan's arms as if she had more rights to them than Susan.

"They're more mine than hers," Alice would say. "Everyone knows grandchildren are connected more to their maternal grandparents. It's just natural. They came from the mother's body, after all."

"She's beautiful," Lina whispered, pulling Phil's thoughts back to the wedding.

"She is," Phil agreed, watching a tuxedo-clad Logan lead his grandmother down the aisle. Alice Rayburn, in a white cocktail-length wedding dress, her hair swept up in a chignon, looked radiant. Today, Alice was a bride.

His thoughts drifted to Lina and how he'd felt twenty-one years earlier, when his father walked her down the aisle to him. He remembered the lump in his throat and how he'd prayed he'd be able to say his vows without crying. He'd somehow managed. He took a deep breath. The twenty-two-year-old him wouldn't have believed him capable of being with another woman. The forty-three-year-old him could barely conceive it. And yet the proof of his infidelity was now seven months old.

He felt Lina's fingers slide over his palm before entwining with his. Her lips were turned up in a soft smile as she watched Logan deliver her mother to her father. "You're actually enjoying this," he whispered in her ear.

"Shhh," she chastised him, squeezing his hand.

"Are you sure you don't want my handkerchief?" he teased.

"Yes."

"Good, because I really think I might cry. The thought of having to endure him at every family function—"

"Phil—stop," she whispered. She was attempting to frown at him, but he could tell from the twitching at the corners of her lips that she was trying not to laugh.

His focus shifted to Shiloh who was sitting with her husband, Julian, on the groom's side of the aisle. Julian was an improvement over Shiloh's first husband, who'd physically abused her, but not by much. Phil had banned him from his house after Julian yelled at Shiloh in a drunken rage at a party. The rest of the family had since forgiven him. Shiloh had been in a car accident a few months earlier and Julian had patiently nursed her back to health. It was enough to redeem him in Alice and Adele's eyes. Phil wasn't as forgiving.

***

"Apparently, I'm next," Adele said after slipping into the chair beside Lina's at one of several tables surrounding the makeshift dance floor in Alice's backyard. "According to my solar return, anyway."

"Next?" Lina pulled her gaze from the dance floor.

"For marriage. Mom said he's so close she's surprised I haven't met him yet." She lifted her wineglass to her lips.

"Nice." Lina nodded.

"I'm not getting married again," Adele said dryly.

"You never know. The right guy could come along and sweep you off your feet."

"I just wish I could find someone to fuck."

"Adele!" Lina frowned at her.

"What?" Adele's eye's widened. "I do. We both know what you're doing every night. You've been smiling since you got back with him. Why should you be the only one getting action? Do you know how long it's been for me?"

"No, but I'm sure you're going to tell me."

"Six weeks. And after today it's going to be six weeks and one day, because there is absolutely no one fuckable here." She looked around at the other guests, who were spread out between the dance area, the tables, and the patio. "I find myself wanting to believe in astrology. I want—no, strike that—I *need* to find someone. Doesn't Phil know anyone?"

"You know that's not going to happen," Lina said. Phil had set Adele up twice, and both times she'd dated the men just long enough for them to fall in love with her and then promptly dumped them. Phil was convinced Adele's special talent was breaking men's hearts, and he was no longer willing to provide the victims.

"He can't hold those two against me forever. It's been more than three years."

"I think he can," Lina said. Her gaze shifted to the dance floor, where Phil was dancing with her mother, smiling down at her and looking amused as she talked nonstop.

"Do you think we should start calling Drew Dad again?"

"No." Lina's gaze shifted from Phil and her mother to Katie and Drew. "I stopped thinking of him as a dad so long ago, I don't think I could switch back."

"He's starting to grow on me. I could do without his diarrhea of the mouth, but he makes Mom happy. I like the idea of her having someone to grow old with."

"Me too." Lina's gaze returned to her mother and Phil. He whispered something in Alice's ear, and she slapped his chest. Lina smiled. As much as her mom could get frustrated with what she considered Phil's controlling personality, she adored him. He was the son she'd never had.

"Do you have to look so happy?" Adele asked. "You're making it hard for me to continue to hate him."

"I love him."

"Obviously."

"This may sound odd, but I think we may be closer now than we were before Kim."

"It does sound odd," Adele said. "Especially considering you have yet to meet the baby."

Lina's stomach dropped at the mention of Liam. "I plan to meet him," she insisted. "I just—Phil and I are still getting used to being together again."

Adele quirked an eyebrow. "Are you believing yourself right now? You've been with him practically your entire life. You didn't get used to *not* being with him when you were apart. Do you want to know what I think?"

"No," Lina answered.

"I think you're trying to pretend Liam doesn't exist."

"You're wrong. It's impossible to pretend he doesn't exist when Phil disappears once a week to visit him. I don't really want to talk about this right now."

"Is she still leaving random receipts in his pockets?"

"No," Lina answered. "It was just the one time. He never mentioned it, so she probably assumes it was never found. Things have been quiet since." For the most part she barely thought about Kim except on the days Phil was with Liam.

"Maybe she's met someone else to stick her claws in."

"I can only hope," Lina said.

Chapter Thirteen

"Where are you going?" Phil asked a few Saturdays later, pushing himself up on his elbows and squinting across the bedroom at Lina, who was dressed and at the door.

"Sorry. I was trying not to wake you. I have a breakfast appointment. Another potential client."

"It's Saturday."

"I know. It was the only time that worked for both of us over the next month, and I know you're going to see Liam today so it seemed like a good time." She was back at the bed, leaning down and meeting his lips. "I have to go. I'll see you when you get back."

"Wait—wait." He clasped her wrist. "It's only eight. Don't we have time for—"

"No." She kissed him again before pulling from his grasp. "My meeting's in Bethesda. I have to leave now, or I'll be late."

"Bethesda?" That was more than forty-five minutes away.

"Yes. They have homes there, too," she teased.

Phil watched her walk toward the door, her hips swaying beneath her skirt. "No more Saturday meetings," he called out. "Saturday mornings are mine."

"I'll make it up to you tonight." She threw him a kiss before leaving the room.

He fell back on the bed, sighing deeply. He was all about her having a career if that's what she wanted, but not one that interfered with their life.

"Where's Mom?" Logan asked an hour later, following Knight into the house. He set the newspaper he'd retrieved from the end of the driveway onto the table in front of Phil.

"She had an appointment."

Logan poured himself a bowl of cereal before sitting across from Phil at the table. "When will she be home?"

"I'm not sure. Probably noon or so."

"Could you take me to Will's at eleven thirty if she's not back?"

"Your sister can take you," Phil said.

"No," Katie said. She was standing near the sink pouring herself a cup of coffee. "He can take an Uber."

"I'm not paying for an Uber when you can drive him."

"Why should I have to drive him? I'm not his parent. It's like you and Mom expect me to be his personal chauffeur. I drive him more places than I drive myself."

"Consider it your job," Phil said dryly.

"I'm Matt's social media person. That's my job."

"Consider it your job that pays for your gas and clothes and—"

113

"I can pay for my own. I have over five thousand dollars in my account."

It was money she'd saved from his parents' birthday and holiday gifts. She wasn't like Megan and Logan who would immediately go out and buy themselves something. Katie prided herself in being a minimalist, refusing to partake in what she referred to as the rabid materialism of her generation.

"Stop arguing with me. I want you to drive your brother to Will's. This isn't a discussion. I have to be in Chevy Chase at eleven. I can't take him."

"Would you at least pay me?" Katie joined them at the table. "You're the reason I don't have a paying job."

It was true. When she'd talked about getting a job, he'd insisted her only job was school. "You just told me you have five thousand dollars."

"Are you going to punish me for being responsible?"

He took out his wallet, extracted a twenty-dollar bill, and held it out to her, pulling it back when she reached for it. "This is only because I'm feeling generous."

"Whatever." Katie snagged the money from his hand. "Mom always makes pancakes on Saturdays."

"And your point?"

"You could make them."

He lifted an eyebrow. "How likely do you think that is?" Besides grilling, he had no skills in the food prep area.

"With Mom working more you should learn."

He chuckled. "I have a better idea."

"No way." She stole a piece of toast from his plate. "So you're going to see Liam?"

"Yes."

"Grandma said he looks like Logan."

Phil's gaze shifted to Logan who was staring down at his cereal. "He does."

Logan roughly pushed back his chair, toppling it over onto the hardwood floor. "He doesn't look like me!"

"Hey, get back here! Logan!" Phil was out of his chair and following him toward the front of the house. "Don't you walk away from me!" He grabbed his arm. "Get back in there and fix the chair."

Logan squared his shoulders, marching back into the kitchen and righting the chair. When he attempted to leave the kitchen, Phil stepped in his path.

"Look at me," Phil demanded. "Logan, look at me," he repeated when Logan didn't instantly comply. "This isn't about you. I know you're having a hard time with it but having a temper tantrum serves no purpose."

"I just want to go to my room."

"What do you expect me to do? Ignore him? I'm his father."

Logan lowered his eyes. "Can I go to my room, please?"

"Lo—"

"Please," he whispered. His chin had begun to quiver.

"Go ahead," Phil said, realizing he was about to cry. He dragged his hand down his face. He had no idea how to get through to him.

"You really don't have a choice," Katie said. "You're his dad."

"I am," Phil agreed. Who would have guessed Katie would be the one to understand?

"Do you have his picture?"

Phil brought up a recent picture Kim had sent him of Liam. He was standing in his crib, holding onto the rails, a wide smile on his face. "That's him." He handed the phone to Katie.

He watched her eyes drift over the image, her brows pulled together in concentration. "He's so big."

"Eight months on the twenty-third," Phil said.

"He does look like Logan," she said. "Does he talk yet?"

"Not really. He babbles mostly."

"I should probably meet him sometime. He is my brother."

"You should," Phil agreed.

Later that evening Phil decided to broach the subject with Lina. It had been four months since he'd moved back home and she'd shown no interest in meeting Liam. He was beginning to wonder if she ever would. "I understand if you're not ready but I'd like to introduce him to the kids, well at least Katie. She wants to meet him."

"Katie?"

"She mentioned it this morning. I could take her with me next week."

"No. I don't want her anywhere near Kim."

Phil followed her into the master bath. "She asked to meet him."

"I know. I know. It's just…I'd prefer that we wait and all do it together. You know, when he's older and comes for a visit."

He watched her begin to wash her face, trying to gauge what she was feeling. He didn't want to push her into a meeting but he also was tired of keeping Liam separate from the rest of his family. Not even Mike or his parents had met him. It was as if he only existed in four-hour increments once a week. "I like the idea of everyone meeting him as a family."

"Good." She finished washing her face and began patting her face dry with a wash cloth.

"Any idea when that might take place?"

She paused, meeting Phil's eyes in the mirror. "I guess I should start converting the upstairs guestroom into a nursery for him. When that's done, we can start figuring out dates."

***

It was the last Friday in August. Phil was in his office, finishing up some work before heading to the beach with Lina and the kids for a week-long vacation, when he received a phone call from Tom Hendrix, a former law-school classmate and a partner in another Baltimore firm.

After they shared pleasantries for a couple of minutes, the other man got to the point of the call. "I thought I should give you the courtesy of letting you know, in case you didn't already, Kim is coming to our Baltimore office."

Phil, who had been leaning back in his chair with his legs perched up on the desk, slowly dropped his feet to the ground. He wasn't naive. He'd assumed most of his colleagues knew about the affair—the legal community in Baltimore was small—but this was the first time someone was blatantly alluding to it. "Coming as in permanently?" he asked, failing to keep the intensity from his voice.

"So, she didn't tell you?"

"No, she didn't tell me. I helped her get that job, Tom— to get her out of this fucking city."

"You know her résumé. She would have her pick of local firms if we weren't willing to accommodate her. She's not happy at our Washington office, and we didn't want to lose her. She wants to be in Baltimore."

"Why? Why does she want to be in Baltimore?"

"Honestly? She said she wanted her son closer to you."

117

Phil waited until he was in his car and on his way home before calling Kim. "When were you going to tell me?" he asked as soon as she answered his call.

"It didn't become official until today," Kim answered. "I tried to call you earlier but as usual you didn't answer."

"We agreed you would leave Baltimore—that's why I helped you find that job."

"No, you convinced me to leave. But I'm not happy so I'm coming back."

Phil's hand tightened on the steering wheel. "What about Maria?"

"What about her?" she laughed. "She's a babysitter, Phil. Do you expect me to not move because of his babysitter?"

"She's been watching him since he was a month old. He likes her. She's reliable."

"I'm more concerned with him seeing his father. I thought it would be nice for him to be closer to you. Maybe you'll be able to see him for more than four hours a week."

"You should have talked to me," he said. "You should have told me what you were planning."

"Why? So you could talk me out of moving? I want Liam closer to you. It's what's best for him."

***

When Lina opened her eyes, it took her a moment to remember that she wasn't at home but in the beachfront house they'd rented in Bethany Beach, Delaware. She could hear the distant sound of waves crashing against the shore. As her eyes adjusted to the darkened room, she noted the sliding doors leading off the bedroom to their private deck were open. She found Phil there, in shorts but no shirt, his hands resting on the deck rail as he stared out at the ocean.

She stroked her hands up his warm back. He'd been quiet all day, even passing on Logan and Brian's request to play lacrosse with them on the beach. When she'd confronted him earlier, he'd denied anything was wrong. "What are you thinking about?"

"I couldn't sleep."

She wrapped her arms around him from behind, laying her cheek against his back. "Talk to me." She could feel the tension in him. "I know you. Is something going on at work? You're not going to tell me you have to go back early, are you?" It had happened once when the kids were still young. Phil was so focused on making partner he'd wanted to drive back to Baltimore for what he'd deemed an important client. Lina had put her foot down, telling him he wasn't leaving her alone during their family vacation. He'd stayed, but as a precaution for the next several years, she'd made sure their vacation destinations were too far away to simply drive home.

"Kim is transferring to Hendrix, Wolff, and Pearson's Baltimore office. She's moving back."

Lina let her arms drop to her sides. A knot formed in the pit of her stomach. "Why didn't you tell me? We agreed on full disclosure when it came to her."

"I was going to. I didn't want it to ruin this week."

"Ruin this week? You barely spoke today. You were already letting it ruin our week."

"I'm sorry, baby." The half of his face illuminated by the full moon looked exhausted, like the weight of the world was on him. "I guess I'm just trying to come to terms with it myself."

"Why would she do that?" she asked, knowing the answer. Kim wanted to be closer to Phil.

"I don't know what motivates her. She wasn't even the one to tell me. Tom Hendrix called as a courtesy."

"He knows about the two of you?" She crossed her arms over her chest, nauseous at the realization that most of Phil's colleagues in the legal community knew.

"I'm sorry."

"Stop telling me you're sorry—it doesn't help."

"But I am." He cupped the side of her face. "I know how hard this is for you."

"No, you don't. You have no idea what it feels like to be me." She shrugged off his hand and went back to the bedroom. She knew she was being unfair. She'd taken him back knowing about Kim, but it was late, and the thought of Kim being in her orbit was too much to take in at three o'clock in the morning. "I'm sure she'll be broadcasting that you're Liam's father all over town," she said when she felt Phil's presence in the room. "It's only a matter of time before somebody in their school hears about it from their parent. How many lawyers do you know whose children go to Gilman or McDonogh?"

"What do you want me to do?"

"Stop her," she answered. "Make her stay where she is." She was slipping on a sundress while she spoke.

"I would if I could."

She hated the anger she was feeling, hated how much power she was giving Kim.

"What are you doing? Why are you getting dressed?"

"I'm going to the beach." She headed toward the door.

"Not alone you're not," Phil said. "It's the middle of the night."

***

It took fifteen minutes for Lina to let go of the anger. She was on a blanket beside Phil, staring out at the ocean. He'd given her space, sitting silently beside her.

"I've been trying to put her out of my mind, you know—pretend she doesn't exist." She'd done it with Liam, too, but she wasn't ready to admit that aloud. "But I don't think that's going to work because she's here to stay."

"I'm sorry." He began to caress her back.

"I know you're not responsible for what she does."

"I'm responsible for bringing her into our lives. I brought a stranger into our lives."

"She is a stranger, isn't she?"

"Yes." He brushed his lips over her temple. His arm tightened around her. "She's no one. She's never been anything to me. My duty is only to Liam. I'm not going to let her interfere with our life. You are my priority—only you."

Lina stared out at the ocean for a moment longer and then she was coming to her feet. "Let's go for a swim."

"Baby, it's the middle of the night."

"I don't care."

"Someone could see," he said when she began to peel off her dress.

"No, they can't. It's too dark." She tossed her dress at him. "Come on."

"What if the kids are still up? Lina," he called out when she began to walk toward the water.

"No one can see us. Their bedroom is on the other side of the house." She walked a few more steps before turning back to him. "You're not going to make me swim alone, are you?" She smiled. "Come on. I want to swim naked with you."

Phil glanced back at the darkened house. "Fuck it," he said before jumping to his feet and stripping off his clothes.

Chapter Fourteen

With the start of the school year and a flurry of new decorating requests, Lina felt like she barely had a free moment over the next couple of weeks, and although she wasn't actively thinking about Liam, he was always there, lingering in the back of her mind and creating an underlying anxiety she couldn't seem to shake. After spending an afternoon wandering through children's furniture stores and picking out items for a client who wanted assistance with a nursery, decorating ideas for Liam's room began to take shape in her mind.

"What are you doing?" Logan asked after dinner one evening when he found her on a ladder in the upstairs guest room. "Do you need help?"

"No, thanks. I just finished taking measurements."

"For what?"

"New window treatments." She came down from the ladder. "Did you finish your homework?"

"What's this?" He picked up a baby furniture catalog that was on the bed. "Why do you have this?" His eyes were narrowed in confusion.

There was no easy way to tell him, so she just settled on the truth. "I'm converting the room into a nursery."

His eyes widened. "You're pregnant?"

"No." Her hand came to her chest. "No, Logan." The thought was so far from her reality it took her a moment to recover from it. "No."

He let the catalog fall from his hand. "You're going to let him come here?" His lips were turned down.

"Eventually. Not right away. We'll talk about it as a family first."

"I don't want him here," he rushed out.

"It's not that simple."

"Why? Because Dad's already decided?" He crossed his arms over his chest. "Don't you get a say? Don't I get a say?"

"It's not a matter of what you want, honey. It's a matter of what is right."

"Having him here isn't right! I don't want to know him."

"Logan." Lina tried to touch his arm, but he backed out of her reach.

"Dad is making you do this, isn't he?"

"No." She shook her head. "He isn't making me do anything. This was my idea."

"You're lying!"

"Hey!" Phil exclaimed, coming into the room. "What is going on?" His gaze swung from Lina to Logan.

"I don't want him here," Logan said, avoiding Phil's eyes as he headed for the door. "I don't want him in our house!"

"Who?" Phil asked.

"Liam," Lina answered, gripping her forehead. "I told him about the nursery."

Realization came to Phil's face. "I'll talk to him."

"No. Let me. I want him to know it was my idea. I think that's important."

Logan was donning his headphones and preparing to start a video game when Lina found him in the upstairs den a few minutes later. "Can we talk?"

"No," he said, continuing to push buttons to begin his game.

"Please." She nodded toward his bedroom.

He let out an audible sigh before yanking off his headphones. "Fine," he grumbled before preceding her into his room.

"I'm sorry for breaking it to you like that," she said as soon as they were both sitting, Logan on his bed and Lina in his desk chair. "We should have discussed it as a family before I started doing anything in the room."

"Why would we need to discuss it? It doesn't matter. I still wouldn't want him here and you'd still bring him here anyway."

"This isn't easy for any of us, but we can't pretend he doesn't exist."

"Why not?"

"Because your father is his father."

"So? What does that have to do with me?"

"We're a family—and…" She trailed off. She wanted to say Liam was part of their family now, too, but she couldn't. She couldn't voice the words. "We need to learn to accept him. That's the right thing to do."

"What's wrong with the way he's doing it now?" Logan asked. "Why does he have to bring him here?"

"It's not enough taking him out for a couple of hours a week. As he gets older, he'll be spending more time with him."

"He can spend more time with him without bringing him here."

"This is your father's home, too. And eventually he's going to have him overnight. That's why I'm setting up the room."

"I'm not going to be here if he's here," Logan said. "I'll stay with Brian or Will."

"Don't say that."

"I will. I don't want to ever see him. I hate him."

"Logan—no." She felt an ache at the pain radiating from him. "He's a baby."

"I don't care. I hate him! I don't want to talk anymore."

Lina racked her brain, trying to think of something to say to lessen his pain. Nothing came. She finally stood up and left his room. She pulled his door closed, leaning her forehead against it as she breathed in and out deeply, willing herself not to cry.

"Everything okay?" Phil asked from behind her.

"He just—he needs some time." She turned to face him, tears glistening in her eyes.

"What in the hell did he say to you?" He reached for the doorknob.

"No—don't." She pressed her hands into his chest. "He didn't say anything. He's just upset."

"You're crying."

"I'm upset that he's upset."

The anger left him in an instant. "Should I talk to him?"

"No." She took his arm, propelling him away from Logan's room. "He's too upset right now. He'll come around. He has a big heart."

Lina was still worried about Logan when she arrived at the office the following morning. He'd been quieter than normal on the drive to his bus stop. When she'd asked him if he was okay, he'd mumbled something about his history teacher giving him too much homework.

"He's upset," Adele said when Lina shared her concerns. "He's coming to terms with the fact that his father is a selfish prick."

"Seriously?" Lina tilted her head to the side. "That doesn't help."

"Don't be so sensitive. You know what I mean. Logan idolized him. If he wasn't upset, I'd be more concerned. That would mean he didn't think there was anything wrong with what Phil did."

"I just wish I could talk to Nick about it. He'd—"

"No," Adele interrupted, shaking her head. "Don't even go there."

"I said I wish, not that I was going to."

"Don't you think it's ironic that Nick accused you of being too dependent on Phil when you were completely dependent on him for parenting advice?"

"That's not true," Lina said irritably. "He was treating Katie."

"He was counseling you about all of them. I was with you during some of the calls. You even discussed Megan with him."

"He's a professional," Lina defended.

"I don't think you need a professional to tell you how often to reach out to your daughter when she goes away to college. That seems like something you could have figured out on your own."

SWIMMING NAKED

"Fine." Lina sighed, knowing she was right. "Why are we even talking about this?"

"Because you mentioned Nick."

"I know why. Let's just stop."

"I have to go anyway," Adele said, gathering up some files on her desk. "I have a new client." She began to walk away. "Oh, wait." She turned back to Lina. "When were you going to tell me about Dolmar Enterprises?"

"Dolmar Enterprises?" Lina frowned.

"Damien Rouse. I ran into Celeste last night. She said she passed his number to you and that he called you."

"William Rouse called me," Lina corrected.

"That's his younger brother. He's the VP."

"I have a lunch meeting with him tomorrow. What is Dolmar Enterprises?"

"They're one of the largest real-estate-development companies in Maryland. Damien Rouse started it. They have properties in northern Virginia as well."

"I don't think he mentioned his company. He just said he was interested in talking to me about my work." She'd been in the grocery store at the time of his call and had answered the unfamiliar number in case it had to do with one of her children. She could barely remember what he'd said.

"Celeste said he's interested in talking to you about being their creative lead."

"What?" Lina's eyes widened. "Are you sure?" She tried to recall the conversation.

"That was Celeste's understanding."

"I'm not looking for a new job. I should call and cancel."

"It won't hurt you to hear what he has to say. There's no pressure on you. Just go."

127

Nerves churned in Lina's stomach when she entered the upscale lobby of the Hay Adams Hotel in Washington, DC. She was thankful she'd decided to wear a skirt suit. She could at least look like she belonged among the other bustling professionals. It wasn't that she hadn't been to her share of upscale hotels and restaurants, but it had always been as Phil's wife.

After giving her name to the maître d', she was directed to a table on the far end of the restaurant along the windows. A man who looked to be in his late forties came to his feet as she approached. He was tall and classically handsome, with dark hair and equally dark eyes. His hair was cut close to his scalp. He looked Italian or Mediterranean, with a smooth olive complexion. His dark-blue suit was custom tailored. She detected a subtle scent of an expensive cologne when she returned his handshake. "Lina." He smiled.

"Hi." Her mind went blank. She couldn't recall his name.

"I'm William Rouse," he said, saving her. "Thanks for taking my meeting."

There was a warmth to him that put her at ease. "You're welcome."

"My brother's a big fan of your work," William began without preamble after they had taken their seats.

"That's flattering," Lina said. "I really haven't done much."

"That would probably explain the lack of an online presence. Did you bring a résumé with you?"

Heat came to her face. This was a job interview. She should have prepared a résumé. "No. I'm sorry. I—I don't have one. I wasn't really looking for a job. I…" She trailed off, not sure how much to reveal. "I misunderstood you on the phone. I assumed you were interested in hiring me as an interior decorator for your house. It wasn't until yesterday that my sister told me about your company."

"That's not off the table. It could probably use a face-lift. Did you bring your portfolio?"

"No." She cringed. "I'm sorry. I'm wasting your time." She may have looked the part of a professional woman, but it was becoming painfully obvious she was in over her head. "I'm just a home stager who moonlights as an interior decorator."

"You're not wasting my time," he reassured her. "I'm here because my brother has seen two of the homes you've decorated and he thinks you're talented."

"Two? I thought he just saw Celeste Strahl's."

"And the Harrises'," he said, referring to the home she'd recently done in Bethesda. "He has an eye for talent, and you apparently have it. I'll have to trust him, since you don't have a portfolio," he teased, giving her a wink. "How do you get interior decorator clients without a portfolio?"

"Word of mouth and I guess my phone. I have some pictures I've taken."

"That sounds like a portfolio to me. May I see?"

She tapped on her display, bringing up some pictures of a recent job. "I did their kitchen, family room, and bathroom," she said, handing him her phone.

He took his time, slowly scanning the twenty or so pictures she'd taken. "Is he a model, or is this your bathroom?" He turned the phone to reveal a picture she'd taken of Phil, standing before the vanity, shaving in nothing but a towel.

"Oh my God." She snatched the phone, heat staining her cheeks. "That's my husband." She'd thought he'd looked particularly sexy and had taken the photo.

"You're blushing."

"I'm embarrassed," she said, reaching for her water glass. "Could I get any more unprofessional?"

He chuckled. "Probably."

Some of her embarrassment left when she realized he was teasing her. "I'm sorry."

"Don't be. I saw enough to know my brother's right. You're very talented."

"Thank you."

"And your husband has impressive lats."

Lina's hand shook with excitement when she called Phil. "I think I'm about to get a new job," she said.

"Another one? That's great, baby. Maybe it's time to start thinking about doing that exclusively. It's starting to consume so much of your time."

"No, I mean a real job, not a side job. I just had an interview with a place called Dolmar Enterprises. They—"

"I know what they do," Phil interrupted. "What are you talking about, an interview?"

Lina briefly told him how the lunch meeting had come to be. "It's like destiny or something."

"Lina—"

"I'd be their creative lead," she interrupted. "Can you imagine? They'd pay me to design the interiors of their model homes. The position would require me to stay up on the latest trends, which I do on my own already. He said eventually I could be a trendsetter. Nothing's definite yet, but I could tell he liked me. He's taking me to New York with him next week to attend the Interior Design Expo. If—"

"Wait—wait," Phil interrupted. "You can't just go off to New York with some guy you don't even know."

"It's a job interview. Since I don't have a long work history, he wants to get an idea of how my mind works."

"Who is this guy? Is he married?"

"I have no idea if he's married. This was a job interview. His name is William Rouse."

"Does he know you're married?"

If anyone else asked that, Lina would have assumed he was joking. "This was a job interview, Phil. Not a date. Are you listening to yourself?"

"I don't want you going away with him."

"I'm not going away *with* him. I'm attending a design expo."

"Whatever. I don't want you going."

She could feel her face heating. "I'm going. If you don't *trust* me, you can come with me."

"I have court next week, and you're not the one I don't trust. What is the point anyway? They're out of Bethesda, aren't they? That's an hour commute in traffic each way. We still have two children in the house who depend on you."

"They're fifteen and seventeen. I think they can handle me being out of the house a little more." She didn't want to argue with him about it, especially when she was feeling so good.

"You can't just make a unilateral decision without discussing it with me."

"I haven't made a decision. There's no decision to make yet."

"You said you were going to New York."

"That's because I am," Lina said. "You don't ask my permission before you go on a business trip. You just tell me, so I'm telling you. I'm going to New York next Thursday."

"I have to go into a meeting. We can talk about this tonight."

"Fine but I'm going."

The following Thursday Lina was sitting beside Adele on the train on her way to New York.

"Yep, it's definitely nice," Adele said, handing Lina back her phone.

"Wait. Did you flip through them? There's more than one."

Adele held up her hands, refusing to take the phone. "It's a nursery, Lina. It's beautiful, really. I don't need to see a dozen more pictures to know that."

"I just wanted to show you what it was going to look like."

"You need to put that away, literally and figuratively," Adele said. "You're on your way to New York City for the most important interview of your life and all you want to talk about is the nursery you're designing for Phil's son. You need to take off the wife-slash-mommy hat for a couple of days. You're just Lina Hunter, the interior designer, until we get back Saturday."

"Why can't I be both?" Lina asked. "I am both, you know." She looked down at her phone, tapping through the colors and pictures she'd chosen for Liam's nursery. The more she worked on it, the more she began to picture welcoming him into her home. It was centered around a Noah's ark theme. She was going to have several pairs of animals painted on the walls. It was intentionally different from the sports themes she'd used in Logan's rooms over the years. She didn't want any comparisons.

"You're hopeless," Adele said.

Lina ignored her, continuing to flip through the photos on her phone. She stopped on the one she'd taken of Phil shaving. It was the picture William Rouse had seen. She knew she should probably delete it before someone else accidentally came upon it, but she didn't want to. He looked too good. He was standing before the bathroom mirror, naked except for a towel tied loosely around his waist, beads of water visible on his chest and back. She'd taken the picture from behind him. His chin was covered with shaving gel and he was mid-stroke with the razor. He'd paused when she'd stepped into the bathroom, meeting her eyes in the mirror. She'd taken her phone out to capture the moment. He'd puckered his lips a second before she'd taken the picture. She ran her finger over the sexy image of him. Suddenly she wished she wasn't staying in New York an extra night.

"Seriously?"

Lina jumped at the sound of Adele's voice. "What?" She darkened the display on her phone.

"You're pathetic. We haven't even passed Philadelphia and you're already pining away for him."

"No, I'm not," she lied. "I was looking at a picture."

"Of him," Adele said. "Do you seriously think on his way to Chicago last month he sat on the plane flipping through pictures of you?"

"I don't know what he was doing."

"I do. He was preparing for whatever kind of business he had up there, just like everyone on this train is doing right now, except for you."

"I'm meeting William for lunch, and then we're going to the expo. There's nothing for me to study. Are you trying to make me nervous?"

"No. I'm trying to get you to separate yourself from the role of Phil's wife for a couple of days. You may surprise yourself and actually have a good time without him."

William stood when Lina approached his table at Majorelle in the Lowell Hotel on the Upper East Side. He looked the part of a New York businessman in a dark custom-cut suit. "I see your style sense includes clothes as well," he said, taking in her black dress and knee-high boots.

"Thank you." She returned his smile, feeling completely at ease with him, as she had the last time they'd met.

"How's your room?"

"Beautiful. I've never stayed in this hotel. My husband likes the Carlyle."

"I like that one, too."

They talked about the train ride up, and Lina confessed she'd brought her sister along. "She loves to shop, and I thought it would be fun to stay an extra night."

"Excellent. I hope to meet her," William said before shifting their conversation to design.

"I can't believe it's already six," Lina said as she and William left the convention center. "That was fun."

William smiled. "This really isn't work to you at all, is it?"

"No," she said honestly. "I've enjoyed decorating since I was a little girl. I did study it in school, but it was always my hobby. I've had a subscription to both *Architectural Digest* and *Better Homes and Gardens* since I was about ten—wow, more than thirty years. I've always loved beautiful homes."

"Gardens, too?"

"Yes." She smiled. "I have flower gardens. That passion I inherited from my mother. I miss them in the winter."

William held up his hand to hail a cab and moments later was following her into the back seat. After giving the hotel name to the driver, he settled into the seat beside her. "I don't need to spend another day with you to know we want you at

Dolmar, Lina. I'll talk to HR tomorrow, but expect an offer soon."

"I thought you wanted to spend two days with me."

"I do. It's a pleasure watching your mind work. Damien was ready to hire you without even a face-to-face after seeing your work. I was the cautious one. But you've sold me, too. You have a gift, and we'd love to exploit it."

"They want me." Lina called Phil as soon as she reached the privacy of her hotel room. "Adele said people work their entire careers for jobs like these and it just fell into my lap. I can't believe someone offered me a job."

"Why can't you believe it? You have a job."

"This is different. Adele got me that job. This was all me."

"You've already accepted the position?"

"No. I told you I wouldn't without discussing it with you. But I want to. They're going to send me an official offer."

"How many hours do they expect you to put in a week? Is this a full-time position?"

"I don't know. All the details will be in the offer letter." She took off her jacket, cradling the phone against her shoulder as she used both hands to hang it in the closet. "Are you still there?"

"Yes, I'm here. I think we need to see the offer letter before you let yourself get too excited. We need to balance the needs of our family with the position."

"This is the first time in my life I've been really excited about the possibility of a career. Can't you just be happy for me?"

It was a few moments before he responded. "I am happy for you. And I'm proud of you. I just—I don't want you to take on more than you can handle. We depend on you. I depend on you. You're the glue that holds us together."

"If it's too much I can quit. I really want this."

"I'm not going to stand in your way from doing something you want. But let's see what the offer letter says. There's always room for negotiation."

"Thank you," she said. "I love you."

"Is this guy married?"

Lina laughed. "I don't know." She began to look through the clothes she'd hung in the closet earlier. "It hasn't come up."

"Does he know you're married?"

"Why are you suddenly so jealous?"

"It's not sudden. I've never trusted other men around you."

"You can trust me." She held a dress up before her, looking at her reflection in the mirror. "And he does know I'm married. For one, I'm wearing your diamond on my finger. And for another, I can't seem to not bring you up. Aren't you supposed to be in court? I was planning to leave you a message."

"The case was postponed. I'm on my way home. Katie's picking up pizza."

"What about a vegetable? Is she picking up a salad, too? Logan's stomach bothers him if he doesn't get vegetables. There's broccoli in the freezer."

"I'm sure he'll be fine without vegetables for one day," Phil said.

"It's easy to boil broccoli."

"Then if he wants it, he can make it. What are your plans tonight?"

"William is taking us to dinner. When he found out Adele was here, he invited her, too."

"Don't drink too much, and call me when you get back from dinner."

"I don't know how late it will be."

"It doesn't matter. I won't be able to sleep until I know you're back in your room."

***

Phil arrived home in a bad mood, the idea of Lina working full time weighing on his mind. "Logan?" he barked out when he stumbled on his lacrosse stick in the mudroom.

"Yeah?" Logan padded in from the family room, stifling a yawn.

"Pick up your lacrosse stuff."

"There's no orange juice," Katie complained, peering into the refrigerator. "I told Mom Tuesday we were out. Now we're not going to get any until Saturday. What time is she getting back?"

"Late. You have a car. You could have bought some." Phil reached around her for a beer.

"That's Mom's job," Katie said. "If I started picking things up, too, it would get confusing."

"Where's the pizza?"

"It's coming. I just ordered it."

"Where's the mail?" he asked, scanning the counter, which was littered with the remnants of breakfast, half-full cups and plates scattered around. Lina had been gone less than twelve hours and the house was already a wreck.

"I don't know. In the mailbox, I guess. Mom brings it in."

He plowed his fingers through his hair. "Why don't you clean up in here?" he said to Katie.

"Why should I clean up? It isn't all mine. Why don't you ask Logan? He never has to do anything."

"Because I asked you. And I didn't see you offering to help him carry all those branches to the curb," he said, referring to the yard work Logan had done the day before.

"Matt helped him do yard work last week. That counts as me."

"Just clean it up."

"You treat him differently because he's a boy," Katie grumbled. "It's not fair."

"Would you run out and get the mail?" he asked Logan, who had returned from the garage.

"I'd rather get the mail," Katie said.

"Don't argue with me tonight, Katie," he said.

"You're completely sexist."

"You're right, so stop arguing and clean up the kitchen," he demanded, pointing at her. "Now!"

Phil took his bad mood out on his body, running five miles in under thirty minutes before doing push-ups and sit-ups to exhaustion. He was dripping with sweat when he came up from the basement, too spent to even care that Matt had come over.

***

Lina followed Adele down the hallway to the bank of elevators. They were supposed to meet William in the hotel bar before dinner.

"Ladies," a handsome man of about fifty greeted them as they entered the elevator.

Lina offered him a friendly smile before shifting her gaze to the display indicating the floor number. She could feel him staring at her during the forty-floor descent.

"That man was consuming you with his eyes," Adele whispered as they left the elevator. "He wasn't even attempting to be subtle."

"I didn't notice," Lina lied. He'd been studying her like she was a piece of art instead of a person. "William said to meet him in the bar."

"I'm definitely a fan of this hotel," Adele said after they were seated. "I didn't realize that I had a thing for men in suits. Or maybe it's just rich men, but I've definitely found my heaven," Adele said. "To you," she said, holding up her martini, "for going more than thirty minutes without mentioning Phil. I think it's a record."

"Ha ha," Lina said dryly, tapping her glass to Adele's. "I talked to him earlier."

"That's okay. Baby steps."

"This is straight alcohol," Lina said after trying her drink.

"It has vermouth in it. Are you going to judge me if I don't come back to the room with you tonight?"

"Yes."

"Ladies." A man nodded to them as he walked past.

"Why aren't there men like this at home?" Adele whispered. "He was hot."

"I'm sure most of these men are married," Lina said. "They're just here on business." Her thoughts shifted to Phil, who'd been on a business trip in this exact city the first time he was with Kim. Her stomach sank at the memory. He'd been one of these men walking around in a suit while women like Adele lusted after him. She took another sip of her drink.

"Don't think about that," Adele said.

"What?" Lina asked.

"You don't exactly have a poker face. I know where your..." She trailed off as her eyes focused on something behind Lina.

"Good. You started without me," William said, joining them. "You must be the sister." He held his hand out to Adele.

"Adele," she said, her eyes twinkling with amusement when he lifted her hand to his mouth, brushing his lips over the back of it. "You seriously just kissed my hand?"

"I did." He kissed it again. "Twice."

"Does your wife know that you kiss random women's hands?"

"You're not a random woman and I'm not married." He looked past her to the bartender and ordered a scotch.

"You're wearing a wedding band," Adele said, looking pointedly at his hand.

"You noticed that, did you?" He winked at Lina before returning his attention to Adele.

"Why are you wearing it if you're not married?"

"To keep the good girls away," he said.

Adele shook her head. "I knew you were an asshole. I'm shocked I'm not attracted to you. You're completely my type."

He threw back his head and laughed aloud. "A beautiful liar."

"Have you always been so full of yourself?"

"I have."

The chemistry between them was potent. Adele's face was flushed, and William was staring at her like she was going to be his next meal.

"Seriously, why are you wearing a wedding band if you aren't married?" Adele asked.

"It was my father's. My parents were killed in a car crash when I was seventeen," he said, suddenly somber.

"Fuck," Adele whispered. "I'm sorry."

"It's been a long time. There he is." He held up his hand to someone behind Lina. "It turns out my brother is in town as well."

Damien Rouse was an older, more serious version of William, with an intensity Lina found intimidating. He immediately turned the conversation to business. "I've been hiring and firing creative leads for my commercial properties for years. They've come from the best schools. New York School of Interior Design, the Savannah College of Art and Design—you name it. Nothing ever feels original. And then I walked into the Strahls' house and I knew within five minutes that you were what I was looking for."

"That's very flattering," Lina said. "But as I've explained to your brother, it's been more of a hobby than a career. I don't want to project myself as something I'm not. My degree is twenty years old."

"Modest, too." He smiled for the first time. "You're refreshing. Your lack of formalized training is probably what drew me to you. Your work isn't regurgitated versions of what everyone else is doing. You're not a rule follower. I could see that in the Strahls' house. The colors you chose for their kitchen shouldn't have worked—the slate gray with the white granite—but it did. It was brilliant."

It was almost midnight when Lina returned to her hotel room, still on a high from the whirlwind day. They'd had dinner at Gramercy Tavern, a favorite of Damien's, before going across town to a jazz club, a first for Lina. Adele and William had stopped at the bar for a nightcap, but Lina had wanted to get back to the room to call Phil.

"It's a surreal feeling. I just—I never imagined this happening to me. I feel like pinching myself."

"I've always known you were talented," Phil said. "As soon as you put yourself out there, this was inevitable."

"Really?" She rolled onto her side. "You're not just saying that because I'm your wife?"

"No, baby."

"There's an interior design conference in Paris in May he said they wanted to send me to. You could come with me."

It took him seconds to respond. "I have a job. And we have kids."

"I know. But you also get vacation, and my mom or your mom could watch them. Wouldn't you like to go back?"

"I could take you back. Anytime you want. You don't have to take this job to get back to Paris."

"I know. I was just...Are you okay?"

"I miss my wife," he said deeply. "What are you wearing?"

She smiled. "You're bad."

"Answer me," he ordered. "I need to picture you."

"My red silk pajamas. What are you wearing?"

"What do you think?"

She closed her eyes, imagining him stretched out beneath the sheets completely naked. "Nothing."

"Now tell me what I wish I was wearing."

Saturday was definitely too far away. "Me."

"Come home tomorrow?"

"I can't do that to Adele. We already have tickets to a show. I promised her."

"What about me?"

"I think you can survive one more day without me."

Lina woke with a start. "Phil?"

"No, not Phil," Adele said.

"What time is it?"

142

"Three. I promised you I'd sleep here, and here I am. Ow," Adele yelped. "I just stubbed my toe."

Lina pushed herself up on her elbows. "Were you at the bar all this time?"

"No," Adele answered. "But don't worry. You asked me not to sleep with him, and I didn't."

"Thank you," Lina said, falling back against the pillows with a relieved sigh.

"I just gave him a blow job."

Chapter Fifteen

"I can't believe you did that," Lina said the following morning, pacing back and forth in front of the bed Adele was trying to sleep in. "Do you know how awkward that makes things for me? He's going to be my boss."

"Please stop." Adele moaned, pulling a pillow over her head.

"No, I'm not going to stop." Lina ripped the pillow from her, tossing it across the bed. "When you asked if I minded if you went for a drink with him, I specifically asked if you could control yourself and you said you could."

"I did. He wanted to fuck me, and I wouldn't let him. That took a lot of self-restraint."

"Controlling yourself meant not giving him a blow job."

"No, it didn't," Adele said. "I never would have agreed to that."

"Oh. My. God," Lina said, staring down at her with her hands on her hips. "You sound like Mom. Completely crazy."

"Yeah." Adele pushed herself up on her elbows, returning Lina's glare. "Well, you sound like Phil. And that isn't a compliment."

"I'm having breakfast with him. How am I supposed to look at him knowing what happened between the two of you last night?"

"I have to look at Phil. I'm sure you give him blow jobs occasionally."

"That is completely different. He's my husband."

"You are such a prude," Adele said. "Just go." She waved at the door. "I need sleep."

"Was this a one-time thing, or are you planning to see him again?"

"I have no idea."

"Do you like him?"

"I gave him a blow job, Lina. Yes, I kind of like him."

William was a few minutes late to the restaurant, for which Lina was thankful because it gave her a chance to have a cup of coffee and settle her nerves. Adele was right. She was being a prude. So what if her sister had seen her boss naked?

"Good morning." She forced a smile as he joined her.

"Is it?" He took the seat across from her. "Sorry I'm late. I overslept. Coffee, please," he said to a passing waiter. "So," he began, looking across the table at Lina, "should we tackle the elephant in the room or ignore it?"

"I think ignore it," Lina said.

"Works for me." He dragged his hands down his face as he leaned back in his chair. "I'm going to be useless until I get my coffee."

"I'm afraid she'll hurt you," Lina rushed out.

"Hurt me?" A slow smile came to his face.

"I feel like since I introduced you, I'm responsible. You must think I'm an awful sister, but I just—I just don't want things to get awkward for us when she undoubtedly dumps you. Every guy she dates falls for her. And they end up with a broken heart."

He laughed aloud at that. "Duly noted, Lina, but I promise you my heart is safe."

Lina's face heated when she realized how naive she sounded. He was a handsome, forty-seven-year-old man who had a one-night thing with her sister, and she was acting like he was already thinking about marriage. "I'm sorry. Just ignore me. I've been with the same man since I was fifteen. I have no idea what the dating world is like."

"Fifteen? Impressive. How many children?"

Liam popped into her head. "Um—three."

He smiled. "You're sure?"

"Yes." Lina nodded.

***

Phil noted Matt's Mustang in the driveway when he returned home from an early run. It wasn't quite ten a.m. The kid definitely spent more time at their home than his own. Katie's voice drifted to him from the back of the house as he closed the front door. He found them on the family-room couch, Katie leaning against Matt's side with his arm stretched around her shoulders as she read from a book of poetry.

"I need you to clean up the house before Mom gets back tonight," he said. "I don't want her coming home to this mess."

"What?" Katie closed the book as she sat up. "It's not my mess. I'm not picking up after Logan. And that's yours," she said, looking pointedly at the empty beer bottle on the coffee table.

"Whose shoes are those?" Phil pointed at a pair of shoes on the floor. "Whose dishes?" He nodded at the half-full cup and plate on the coffee table. "Whose book bag?"

"I'm using it all. The rest of the stuff in here is Logan's and *yours*."

"I want everything cleaned up, including the kitchen. That includes vacuuming."

"That's not—"

"I'll give you forty dollars."

She relaxed back into Matt. "Fifty."

"Forty-five and you're making my bed, too." He left the room, looking down at his cell phone as he headed toward the front of the house. He was scheduled to visit with Liam at noon and had texted Kim saying he would like to stretch his two-hour visit into four. Lina wasn't scheduled to arrive home until late in the evening and Logan was going to a high school football game, so he figured he should take advantage of his free afternoon.

There was a new text from Lina, replying to the good-morning text he'd sent her an hour earlier. *I miss you.*

He was preparing to respond when another text arrived, this one from Kim.

Noon to four is fine. We're at our new place. Moments later he received a second message with her address. Phil paused halfway up the stairs, his eyes narrowed. She'd moved to his neighborhood.

147

Chapter Sixteen

P hil arrived at the address Kim provided thirty minutes earlier than scheduled, slamming his car door before jogging up the walk to a three-story town house. He pressed the button for the doorbell and then began slapping his hand on the door, too riled up to stay still.

When thirty seconds passed without a response, he tried the knob and found the door unlocked. He stepped into the two-story foyer. A large crystal chandelier hung from the ceiling. There were boxes stacked in a room to the left. It was obvious a move was in progress. Kim was a talented attorney, but with her limited experience there was no way she could have afforded the house on her associate's salary. His child support was footing a large portion of her rent or mortgage.

"Kim?" he called out. "Kim?" His running shoes cushioned the sounds of his steps on the hardwood as he made his way through the foyer, into a living room, and then to a large gourmet kitchen with granite countertops and stainless-steel appliances. It wasn't as high-end as the kitchen in his own home, which Lina had updated a few years prior, but it was definitely constructed with top-of-the-line materials.

He continued through the kitchen to a family room, which was set in the back of the house. There was a playpen set up in front of the fireplace. Lina had never used one for their children. He heard Liam a moment before he saw him. He was sitting in the center of the playpen, babbling at the stuffed bear in his hands.

His eyes widened when he saw Phil. "Dadda."

Phil's anger dropped a notch as he lifted Liam into his arms. "Hey, buddy." He brushed his lips over his son's soft cheek.

"Dadda!" Liam squealed, patting Phil's face.

Phil felt the usual mixture of guilt and love in response to Liam's enthusiastic greeting. "That's right, buddy. I'm your daddy." He couldn't know for sure because he hadn't paid close attention with his other children, but he felt like Liam used the word "daddy" more than they had. It was as if he was unconsciously reminding Phil that he was his son.

"Dadda."

Phil pressed his lips into his forehead. "I love you, too." He thought of how Logan's eyes used to light up whenever he came into the room when he was Liam's age. Of course, with him it had been daily. With Liam it was only once a week.

"Phil?"

His entire body tensed up in response to Kim's voice.

"What are you doing here?"

He slowly turned to find Kim standing just inside the room. The smell of her perfume wafted in the air. "What am *I* doing here?" His eyes narrowed in anger. "What in the *fuck* are you doing here?" he exploded, the veins in his neck and temples bulging.

She took a step backward. "I—I told you I was coming back to Baltimore."

"*Baltimore* is thirty fucking minutes away! This is *my* home!"

Liam burst into tears.

"Fuck," Phil whispered.

"I was trying to make it convenient for you to see your son," she said.

"You should have checked with me," he said, keeping his voice low as he attempted to soothe Liam, rubbing his hand over his back. "Closer to the office would have been convenient."

"Maybe if you had answered my phone calls you could have told me how you felt."

"You could have texted me," he bit out. "Did you buy this place?"

She lifted her chin. "Yes."

"Fuck!"

Liam began to wail.

Phil turned from Kim, jiggling Liam in his arms as he crossed to the French doors leading onto the back deck. He stepped outside, breathing in the cool autumn air as he attempted to calm down. "I'm sorry," he whispered against the top of Liam's head. "Daddy's sorry." It was a nightmare. He couldn't imagine how Lina was going to react. They'd have to move. With Logan and Katie in private school, they could live anywhere.

It took minutes, but eventually Liam's tears stopped and he fell asleep against his father's chest. Kim was in the kitchen, putting dishes away, when Phil came back into the house. "I need his stroller and diaper bag."

"Where are you taking him?"

He took a deep breath. Just the sound of her voice made him want to punch a wall. "Just get me his stuff," he said through gritted teeth, walking past her, toward the front of the house. "I'll have him back at four."

"I moved here because I thought it was what was best for Liam." Kim joined Phil in the foyer with the stroller and the diaper bag. "I'm not trying to cause problems for you. That's the last thing I want to do."

"Is it?" He slung the diaper bag over his shoulder. "You don't want to cause me trouble?"

"No, of course not."

He lifted the stroller and opened the front door, pausing before he stepped outside. "Then why did you put a Victoria's Secret receipt in my suit jacket for my wife to find?"

Her eyes widened in surprise before she quickly masked it. "I have no idea what you're talking about."

"You're not a very good liar."

***

"Asshole," Adele said, looking down at her phone.

"What?" Lina asked. They were on the train, less than an hour from home.

"William. He sent me his address."

"His address?" Lina frowned. "Why would he do that?"

"Why do you think? He wants me to come over."

"Oh." Lina's gaze returned to the magazine she'd been flipping through. She'd been relieved after her conversation with William, assuming, incorrectly obviously, that the relationship wasn't going anywhere.

"Nice." Adele held out her phone.

Lina's eyes narrowed as she took in the large modern home. "Is that his house?"

"Yep. He lives in Potomac. Two-point-nine million, according to Zillow."

"I didn't need to know that," Lina said.

"Do you mind taking an Uber home?"

"What? Why? You're not going to actually go there, are you? We're not getting back until ten. You wouldn't even get to his house until eleven. You just called him an asshole."

"I happen to like this asshole."

An hour later, Adele followed Lina off the train and down the platform toward the front of the station. "We'll just use my phone to get your Uber. You really need to download the app though. If you start traveling more, you're going to want to use it sometimes."

"I don't know. Can't anyone be an Uber driver? Phil will probably have a fit if I show up in one of those. Maybe I should just take a cab."

"I use them all the time," Adele said, tapping on her phone as they walked down the platform. "Phil probably does, too, when he's traveling. Everyone does. There's…" She trailed off. "Never mind. Your Uber is here."

"Already?"

"Yes. Your driver has a BMW."

Lina smiled when she saw Phil striding toward them looking ruggedly handsome in jeans and a dark sweater, a couple of days' scruff on his face.

"Ladies." He cupped the side of Lina's jaw as he brushed his lips over hers. "Hi, baby," he whispered before kissing her again.

"*Ciao*," Adele said.

"Wait—wait," Phil said. "Where are you going?"

"To my car. I drove, remember?"

SWIMMING NAKED

"We'll take you." He took her suitcase in one hand and Lina's in the other, leaving them with their shopping bags. "It's late."

"Give me my bag back, Phil. I walk to my car alone all the time," Adele said.

"Not when I'm around, you don't."

"Caveman," Adele grumbled, rolling her eyes.

After seeing Adele safely to her car, Phil wrapped his arm around Lina's shoulders as they made their way out of the parking garage. When they reached his BMW, he opened her door and waited until she was safely inside before putting her suitcase in the trunk.

"My feet are killing me," Lina said once the car was in motion and they were headed home. "We must have walked ten miles." She slipped off her shoes, sighing with relief.

"Here." He patted his thigh. "Give them to me."

Lina turned sideways in her seat, lifting up her legs and placing her feet on Phil's thighs as she leaned back against the door. She moaned aloud when he began to massage the sole of one of her feet. "God, I love you."

"Enough to not leave me alone again?"

"As little as possible. That feels so good." She closed her eyes. "How are the kids?" It felt like a week instead of two days since she'd seen them.

"Logan had a date last night."

"What?" She pulled her feet back, sitting up straighter on the seat. "How come you didn't tell me?"

"I just told you."

"I mean before—before the date. Who is she?" She'd been gone two days and missed something significant.

"Tiffany something. I don't remember. She's a senior at River Hill."

153

"A senior? He's a sophomore. What do we know about this girl?"

"I just told you what we know about her."

"Why does he always date older girls?" The girl he had dated the year before had been two years older as well. "That's not normal, is it?"

"He likes them more experienced."

"That's not even funny. You're kidding, right?"

"Right," he answered.

"Are you? Or are you just saying that because you think that's what I want to hear?"

"I don't know why he likes older girls."

"It's not like he's mature for his age," Lina continued. "I don't like the idea of it. She could manipulate him."

"Let it go. It was one date."

"Did you meet her?"

"No. He was going with a group. I dropped him at Will's."

"Why didn't he mention it to me before I left? He used to talk to me more."

"Be happy you had him as long as you did. I never shared with my mom like he shared with you. What you're getting from him now is more normal."

"What are you saying? That this is how it's going to be from now on?" Lina frowned at him. "That he's not going to talk to me anymore?" She felt sick at the thought.

He took her hand and brought it to his mouth, brushing his lips over the inside of her wrist. "Don't be sad."

"I am sad. Logan has always been the open one, and he didn't share this with me."

"He's turning into a man. He couldn't be a mama's boy forever. But you'll always be his first love. And you'll always be the love of my life."

"I want to be the love of both of your lives."

He smiled. "Now you're just being greedy." He kissed her hand again before bringing it to rest on his thigh.

"What else did I miss?" In an instant she could feel the mood in the car shift. "What?"

"We'll talk when we get home."

"Did something happen? Is Katie—"

"Katie's fine. We'll talk at home."

It was something to do with Kim. Lina could see it in the set of his jaw. "She took the job and moved to Baltimore, didn't she?"

"Lina—"

"Just tell me." She sighed. "I know it's about her."

"We have to move."

"What? What are you talking about? Why would we have to move?" He loved their home as much as she did. They'd lived in it more than thirteen years. They'd never even talked about the possibility of moving.

"Kim."

"Kim," she repeated, her stomach dropping. "What did she do?"

"Can we—"

"Tell me," Lina said.

"She bought a town house in River Hill."

"You mean our River Hill?" she asked in disbelief. "She bought a house five minutes from us?"

"Yes."

"Oh my God." Lina brought her hands up to cover her face. "Our grocery store is right there. My yoga studio." She felt nauseous.

"I'm sorry, baby." He slid his hand over her upper back.

"She's trying to ruin our lives," Lina whispered.

"We can move."

155

"No!" Lina shook her head. "She's not driving us out of our home. This is our children's home. I already lost Steamboat because of her. Oh my God. I can't believe this. I can't believe this." She felt the pressure of tears behind her eyes. "Oh my God. We're going to run into her when we go out. I could see her at the grocery store. Oh my God." It was like a nightmare.

"I'm sorry."

"Everyone is going to know. Everyone in the legal community and now everyone in our neighborhood. This is my fault."

"No. No. How could this be your fault?"

"Because I haven't even met him. It's been six months since you came back. I've been living as if it didn't happen. My mom says that when you resist something it comes at you harder."

"Your mother says a lot of crazy things."

"No, she's right. I should have met him by now. I've been putting it off too long."

"Lina, baby, this has nothing to do with you not meeting him. This is Kim trying to upset our lives. That's it. That's all it is."

"Well, if that's all it is, it's working."

Chapter Seventeen

O ver the ensuing days Lina threw herself into Liam's nursery, ordering the furniture and peripherals, painting the walls, and getting Phil and Matt to move the existing furniture into their shed. She'd made a point of not asking for Logan's help and insisted Phil do the same, so she was thankful that Matt was around to assist with the heavy lifting.

The following Wednesday, ten days after Lina's New York interview, Dolmar Enterprises sent her an official job offer. It was three pages and full of information on 401(k)s and health benefits, but the section her eyes kept going back to was her title. She was the creative director of their residential property division, responsible for the conception, planning, and execution of their interior spaces. At forty-one she was receiving her first official offer letter. She felt silly when tears came to her eyes.

She called Phil first, but when there was no answer she called Adele. "I received the offer," she said.

"How much?" Adele asked.

"I don't know."

"It's in the offer. That's the whole point of the letter."

"Oh." She began to scan the letter.

"It will be in the first paragraph. Maybe the first line."

Lina's eyes widened when she saw the amount. She had been so overwhelmed by the title she had completely missed the salary figure. "One hundred and twenty-five thousand," she said.

"Not bad," Adele said.

She heard a beep on the line and saw that Phil was calling. "I'll call you back," she said to Adele before switching to Phil. "I got my letter," she rushed out. "I'm their creative director, and they're paying me one hundred and twenty-five thousand. Plus a 401(k) and all these other things I can't remember right now. And they want me to start ASAP. I can't believe it."

"Wait. Wait. Slow down, baby. Take a deep breath and repeat everything you just said. I couldn't understand you."

Lina slowly repeated what she'd told him. "I feel like I'm dreaming."

"Would you forward me the letter? I'd like to read it."

She nodded. "Okay. And what do I do about Martins? Do I just call and quit, or—"

"No. You send them a letter of resignation. I'll help you draft that tonight. I've got to go into a meeting, but we'll go out tonight to celebrate. Make reservations at Clyde's. And make sure you forward me the letter. I'm proud of you."

***

Phil didn't like it. It was too much of a commitment. The new position required her to go into an office in Bethesda two days a week. The other days she could work remotely from home. They expected her to travel to trade shows and conventions. Three residential properties were in the works. The first would be opening the following year in Columbia, Maryland, then another in Bethesda a few months later, and the last in New York City. She would be expected to spend time at all three sites.

The only upside Phil could see was that it made Lina happy. That knowledge alone provided enough motivation for him to try to keep his negative thoughts to himself, at least through the celebratory dinner.

"Wait. What did you just say?" he asked, pausing with his beer bottle at his mouth. They were at Clyde's, one of Lina's favorite local restaurants, with Logan, Katie, and Matt. He'd intentionally chosen one that was a little out of the way, not wanting any chance of running into Kim.

"I start the first week in November," Lina said. "Adele said I should give Martins at least two weeks."

He set the bottle on the table without taking a sip. "You've already accepted the position?"

"Of course. Right after I talked to you. Why wouldn't I accept it?"

"We haven't discussed it."

"What's there to discuss? I want the job. You know that."

"That was their offer. You're supposed to take a few days to think about it and then come back with a counteroffer. It's a negotiation."

"I don't need to negotiate. I liked their offer."

"That offer," he began, trying to keep his emotions in check, "states that you're going to spend two days a week in Bethesda. That's probably an hour commute each way in rush hour. Add that to a nine-and-a-half- to ten-hour workday and you're talking about being away from the house for twelve hours twice a week."

"You're always working," Katie piped in. "Why shouldn't she?"

"You're not part of this discussion," Phil said.

"Why not? I—"

"Katie," he warned, frowning across the table at her.

"Who's going to take me to the bus stop?" Logan asked.

"We'll figure it out," Lina said.

"I don't want Mrs. Ellis driving me. She never stops talking. It's so annoying," he complained.

Phil felt a stab of guilt when he saw the sadness overcome Lina's expression. "We'll figure out the logistics later. What matters is that Mom has found a job she's excited about." He held out his beer. "To Mom, the newest creative director at Dolmar Enterprises."

Everyone picked up their glasses. Phil was relieved to see the smile return to Lina's face as they toasted her. "We're proud of you," Phil said.

***

"I know it's going to be an adjustment for you and the kids, but I want to do this," Lina told Phil after the kids went up to bed later that evening. She was curled into his side on the family-room couch. The television was tuned to a national news channel.

"I know you do." His arm around her shoulders tightened, and she felt the press of his lips on top of her head. "And you should, but it needs to be three-quarters time at first, at least until Logan has his license. He still depends on you for transportation."

"I only have to go in twice a week. In a couple of months he'll be playing lacrosse again, so he'll come home on the late bus. I can drive in after dropping him off, and then Katie can pick him up."

"What about when you travel? What if our trips overlap? I'm a partner. My schedule is unpredictable. Knowing you're home, taking care of everything, that's a lot off my plate."

"I have my mom and Adele. Brian's mom said she's always available. She doesn't work."

"She isn't their mother. I've worked hard so we don't have to rely on other people to raise our kids. You can start out at three-fourths and we'll see how it goes."

Lina's stomach sank at the thought of calling William and telling him she could only work thirty hours a week. "I don't even think that's an option. How would you respond if a lawyer told you they could only work three-quarters of the time? Would you hire them?"

"That's a little different."

"How?" She pulled back from him so she could see his face. "How is it different?"

"They're not my wife. They didn't agree to stay home and raise my children."

"Phil, I'm trying to be serious."

"I am being serious. This staging position worked because it was part time and flexible. You have to be available for the kids."

"I will be. I'll be working from home most of the time. I think they can handle me going in to an office twice a week. They're teenagers."

"Teenagers probably need as much parenting as toddlers. I don't want them home alone all the time."

"It's two days! You're being completely ridiculous."

"Am I?" he asked, his voice getting more intense. "What happened to interior decorating? You told me your plan was to build that up. What changed?"

"Me. I changed my mind. I want this job. And as my husband you should be supporting me, not trying to hold me back."

"I'm not trying to hold you back. I'm trying to be realistic. You have no idea what kind of commitment you're agreeing to."

"Maybe not, but I'm going to find out."

"He's unreasonable," Lina complained to Adele the following day. "Katie is almost out of the house, and Logan gets his license this summer. Why shouldn't I work?"

"He'll be fine once he gets used to it," Adele said. "He probably feels like he's losing control of you."

"We went to bed mad. I hate that. When we got back together, I promised myself I wouldn't do that again, but we couldn't agree. Can you imagine if I called and told them I could only work part time? Or that my husband said I can't commute?"

"I can imagine, but I don't think you'd have a job."

Lina frowned. "Don't repeat any of this to William. I assume you're still talking to him?"

"He sent me a picture of his dick last night. I don't know if that constitutes talking."

Lina scrunched up her face in disgust. "That's so crude."

"I know." Adele laughed. "He's such an asshole."

Lina decided to make a nice dinner as a kind of peace offering. Phil hadn't called or texted all day, which was unusual, and she assumed he was still upset with her.

"I found a ride to the bus stop on the days you work," Logan said after arriving home and going straight to the refrigerator. "So you don't have to ask Will or Brian's moms."

"Who is the ride with?"

"A girl I know. She goes to River Hill. She passes my bus stop on her way to school. We're not that much out of her way."

He still hadn't mentioned his date to her and clammed up when Lina asked about it. "Is it Tiffany? The one you went to the dance with?"

"Yeah." He turned from the refrigerator with a carton of milk.

"Is she your girlfriend or—"

"We're friends," he interrupted.

"That was nice of her to offer, but I think I'll be able to do it. I'll just go to work after dropping you."

"She doesn't mind," Logan said. "She wants to take me."

"It's a nice option," Lina said. "But I think we'll be fine." She watched him pour himself a glass of milk. He looked more like Phil with his shorter haircut. "Why don't you have her over?"

"Maybe." He plopped down into a chair at the kitchen island. "I need you to sign something. It isn't a big deal, but you have to sign it." He dug into his backpack and pulled out a sheet of paper. "I've already pulled it up."

Lina's eyes narrowed as she looked at the progress report. He was getting a D in history. He'd always been a good student, maybe not straight As like Katie and Megan but never anything below a B. "Logan—"

"You don't have to say anything."

"I think I do. It's kind of my role as your mother. What's going on? This isn't like you."

"I know. I'm already doing better. Can you just sign it?"

Lina took the pen he was holding out and began to sign the slip. "You need—"

"I will," he interrupted. "Can you just sign it and not tell Dad? He'll make it bigger than it is."

"What will I make bigger than it is?" Phil asked, stepping out of the mudroom.

"You're early," Lina said.

"What's going on?"

Logan's back was to his father and he was begging Lina with his eyes not to tell him. Of course, it was too late. The paper was in her hand. "He received a progress report."

Phil was beside them, taking the paper from Lina's hand. "History? You have a D in history?"

"Phil." Lina touched his arm. "I've already talked to him."

"I haven't," he said, not taking his eyes from Logan. "It's history. You just have to do the reading and memorize facts."

"He's boring. He's the worst teacher I've ever had."

"I don't care if he's boring. School is your job. A D is failing at your job."

"He gives us twice as much work as the other history teacher," Logan said defensively. "He acts like we don't have any other classes."

"Don't make excuses. This grade," he said, shaking the paper, "is a result of you not doing your job."

"I'm not the only one. Like half the class got—"

"Go get your Xbox and bring it to me."

"What?" Logan's eyes widened. "Why?"

"Because you clearly need to spend more time doing your schoolwork."

"I'm going to bring it up."

"Good. And when you do you can have it back." Phil crossed to the refrigerator, opened the door, and reached for a beer.

"That's not fair," Logan said to Lina. "I bought it with my own money!"

"Watch your tone," Phil bit out, turning back to him. "We spend thirty thousand dollars a year on your education. A D in history is unacceptable. You have lost your privilege to play that game until you prove to me that you can handle your job. Now, stop arguing with me and get the goddamn gaming system, or I'll take it away from you permanently."

"Don't you think that was a little extreme?" Lina asked after Logan left the kitchen. "It's his first progress report."

"No." He shook his head. "I don't think it was extreme at all. A D in history is pure laziness. He spends too much time playing video games. He's up there all the time."

"How about if we just take it away on weeknights and he can have it back Friday to Sunday? It's not even his report card."

"Would you have even told me if I hadn't walked in when I did?"

"What?"

"You heard me." He leaned back against the counter as he watched her.

"Yes, I would have told you," she said, not sure whether or not that was true.

"I don't believe you. You baby him too much. We have to hold him accountable. Sophomore and junior years are the most important when he's applying to college."

"I know. I just think it's too much for a first offense. And with everything going on with the nursery and planning Liam's first visit, I don't think we should be so hard on him."

"Are you saying his grade is because of Liam—"

"No." She shook her head. "Definitely not. But I think his gaming is his way of relaxing, and I don't think we should completely strip it from him. I think the weeknights are enough."

"Lina—"

"Please." She crossed to where he was standing, sliding her hands beneath his suit jacket. "I may baby him, but you're too hard on him."

"I am not too hard on him. My father would have taken away my weekends if I brought home a D."

"You're not your father." She brushed her lips over his. "Just the weeknights. It's enough."

He took a moment before he conceded, sighing deeply. "Okay, just the weeknights."

"What are you doing?" Lina asked when she awoke in the middle of the night to find Phil sitting on the edge of the bed.

"I can't sleep. I was going to get up and do some work instead of just lie here."

"Why can't you sleep?" She propped herself up on her elbow.

"I don't know."

"Is it about Logan?"

"No. I just…I don't think it's the right time for you to take on this job."

Of course. He was still upset about the job. "If it doesn't work with our family, I'll quit. I just want to try."

"Why?" He looked back at her. His face was barely discernible in the darkened bedroom. "You used to be happy staying home and taking care of me and the kids. Why isn't that enough anymore?"

"It is enough, but why can't I have more? The kids are growing up. Logan will have his license next fall. And I like working. I didn't know I would, but I do. Why is that wrong?"

"It's not. It's just *this* job. The commute, the travel. Katie may need help applying to colleges, and with Logan's grades he needs us around more, not less."

"Katie isn't going to let me help her, and Logan just had one bad mark. He'll pull it up. It's not like I watch him study."

"Maybe you need to."

"I really want to do this. How about a three-month trial? At the end of January we'll reassess."

"What about the nursery? Are we just going to put that on hold?"

There was almost a resigned quality to his voice, as if he was beginning to believe she was never going to meet Liam. She felt guilty for waiting so long. "No, of course not." She crawled across the bed to him, wrapping her arms around him from behind and pressing her cheek against the side of his. "It will be done by the end of the month. I was planning to talk to you tomorrow about when to schedule his first overnight."

"Overnight?"

"Yes. A couple of hours isn't enough. We should start getting him used to coming here." She dropped her mouth to his neck, running her lips over his warm skin. "I love you."

He let her pull him backward until he was lying flat on his back. "I know this isn't easy for you."

"Shh," she whispered, positioning herself on top of him, her thighs straddling his hips. "I love you and he's part of you, so I'll love him, too." She could feel the truth of her words as she said them.

He framed her face with his hands, pulling her head down until her forehead was pressed into his. "I love you so fucking much. You know that?"

"I count on it," she whispered before meeting his lips.

Chapter Eighteen

The following week, after staging a home down the street from her parents' house, Lina stopped by for a quick visit. "Where's Drew?"

"He's a guest lecturer at Hopkins today. I really wish you'd stop calling him Drew. He's your father. It's disrespectful."

"I went more than twenty years without seeing him," Lina reminded her. "It's hard to think of him as my father."

"You call Phil's father 'Dad,' and he's not your father."

"True, but he acted like my father."

"But he's not your father," Alice said. "You have a father."

"Okay. Let's just drop this. I have enough stress in my life. This is so unimportant."

"To you maybe, but I know it hurts your father's feelings."

Lina didn't believe that for a second. She doubted Drew even noticed what she called him. "I'm meeting Liam next

169

week." Just saying it aloud increased her anxiety level. "He's going to spend Friday night with us."

"You haven't met him yet?" Alice joined her at the kitchen table, setting a cup of tea before her.

"No, Mom. I would have told you if I'd met him. It's just been hard with the kids and—"

"I'd like to meet him. Why don't we have a family dinner? I'm sure your father and—"

"No," Lina interrupted. "Not the first visit. After we're used to him, I'll invite everyone."

"I don't understand why you have to make such a big deal out of this," Alice said.

"Because it is a big deal. Most normal people would think their husband having a baby with another woman is a big deal. So, can we just agree to disagree on whether or not it's a big deal?" she asked, annoyance creeping into her voice.

"Fine. I'm just trying to save you pain."

"It's too late for that."

"Adele said they'd moved to the area."

"Yes."

"I know you're upset about it, but my recommendation to you is to reach out and bury the hatchet. It isn't good for you to hold on to this inner resentment."

"I have zero desire to bury anything. I never want to see her," Lina fumed. "She slept with my husband. She tried to destroy my marriage. And now she's moved into my neighborhood."

Lina's first thoughts on the morning of her birthday were of Kim and the pictures Kim had sent her exactly one year ago. They would forever be associated with her birthday. She knew she would never be able to enjoy the day in the same way again. Phil had wanted to take her away for a couple of days, but with Liam's upcoming visit that weekend and her new job starting the following Monday, she had too many loose ends to wrap up.

"You didn't have to take the day off," Lina told Phil when she found him in his study dressed in jeans and a sweater. He'd taken Logan to the bus stop earlier and woke her up with coffee and her favorite pastry. "I'm not even going to be here most of the day."

"I will be," he said, lifting his gaze from his computer display. "I need to finish putting the crib together and hang those shelves you bought."

"I'm not afraid of her," she said, knowing why he'd chosen to take the day off.

"Good." He slid the chair back from his desk as she came up beside him, tugging her down into his lap.

"Did you talk to Megan about Liam?" She began to play with the hair at his nape.

"I did. She has too much going on to come up for the weekend. She'll just meet him over Thanksgiving or when she's home for Christmas. We need to talk to Logan and Katie."

"We will tonight. Don't expect a lot from Logan. He's already said he isn't going to be home when Liam comes over. I don't think we should push—not at first, anyway." She could see he wanted to argue, but he remained silent, probably because it was her birthday. "You're getting grayer," she said, her fingers trailing through the splattering of gray hair at his temples. "There's a lot right around here."

"I'm getting old."

"You wear it well," she said, thinking of how handsome he looked.

"I wear you well." He curved his hand around the back of her head.

***

It was after nine when they arrived home from Lina's birthday dinner. To Phil's relief, Kim had been silent. Although Lina had claimed not to be afraid of Kim, Phil knew the memory of her previous birthday had weighed on her mind. He'd felt anger at Kim in waves throughout the day as he, too, relived the nightmare from the previous year. It was the anniversary of the night Lina had spent with Nick Drayton, and while he believed her that nothing had happened, the memory of her walking into Drayton's town house while he stood on the porch still felt like a punch to his stomach.

"Don't go anywhere," Phil said to Logan and Katie when they all came into the house from the garage. "Your mom and I need to talk to the two of you."

"You're not going to tell us you're getting a divorce again, are you?" Katie asked.

"No!" Phil and Lina said in unison.

"Good, because Mom's birthday would be a really weird time to tell us. Last year it was the day after and—"

"Katie, enough!" Phil said. "We're not getting a divorce."

"Fine. You don't have to get angry about it." She dropped down in a chair beside Logan at the kitchen table. "It wasn't like it was an unreasonable conclusion."

Katie was right. They'd sat them down in the exact same spot a year ago to tell them they were separating. "Let's do this in the living room," he said, touching Lina's arm before she sat down.

"Wait," she whispered to him when he began to follow the kids toward the front of the house. "Let me tell them. I think it's important that they know it's my idea."

"I'm sure you've both noticed that your dad and I have been transforming the guest room upstairs into a nursery," she began. "Dad finished putting the crib together today, which was the final piece. We're planning to have Liam spend the night this Friday."

"I'm not going to be here," Logan said, getting to his feet.

"Sit down," Phil said shortly, anger rushing to his chest.

Logan hesitated for a fraction of a second before dropping back down onto the couch beside Katie. He was leaning forward with his knees spread wide and his elbows resting on his thighs.

"He'll be here from about six Friday until five on Saturday. Nothing is expected of either of you. It would be nice if you could be here, but if you're not ready that's your prerogative."

"You're not going to expect me to babysit, are you?" Katie asked. "I want to meet him, but I'm—"

"No," Lina interrupted. "No one is asking you to babysit. Dad has a limited time with him, and—"

"Can I go?" Logan interrupted.

"Let her finish, Logan," Phil said.

Lina touched Phil's thigh, giving him a reassuring squeeze. "I'm done."

Logan jumped up and left the room.

Phil had to fight the urge to follow him. He was acting like a spoiled child.

"It's okay," Lina said, patting his thigh. "Baby steps."

"I think he's jealous," Katie said. "He likes being your only son."

"I think it may be a little more complicated than that," Lina said.

"I don't," Katie continued. "If Liam was a girl he'd be fine."

"I don't like that we're letting him leave," Phil said to Lina as they got ready for bed. "He's part of this family. You can't just pick what parts you like."

"I think this situation is a little out of the ordinary, don't you?"

"We're still his family. You're letting him abandon the family. I'm not sure what kind of message that's sending him. You don't just bail when you don't like a situation. He shouldn't think it's an option. We're teaching him to be man, not a boy."

"He's upset. And I think Katie's partially right. He feels threatened by Liam's existence."

"That's ridiculous." He yanked back the comforter.

"It doesn't matter if you think it's ridiculous," Lina said, slipping off her robe before getting into bed. "It's what he's feeling."

"I told him a year ago that no one could ever replace him."

"Maybe you need to tell him again. He's sensitive. You seem to keep forgetting that."

"I think you babied him too much."

"Now you're being ridiculous. He isn't you. Stop expecting him to act the way you think he should act. He's his own person and a pretty extraordinary person at that." She rolled over on her side, away from him.

"Hey. Don't get mad at me." He gently cupped her shoulder and tugged her backward. "We're just talking."

"He needs time, Phil," she said. "It doesn't have to be a rush. Liam isn't going anywhere."

"How much time?"

"I don't know. We'll just take it one visit at a time. But he has a big heart. He'll eventually come around."

Chapter Nineteen

Lina spent most of Friday in a heightened state of anxiety, unable to think of anything but Liam's impending visit. She filled out some employment paperwork for Dolmar Enterprises, went to the grocery store and bought way too much baby food, vacuumed the entire house even though the cleaning service had been out the day before, and then attended a midday yoga session, hoping that would calm her nerves. It didn't. When five o'clock came around, approximately an hour before Phil and Liam were due to arrive, she poured herself a large glass of wine and settled down at the table with a magazine.

Thirty minutes later her heart began to pound in her chest when she heard the sound of the garage door opening. When it turned out to be Katie instead of Phil, her shoulders sagged with relief.

"What time are they coming?" Katie asked.

"Your dad is supposed to pick him up at six, but it could be earlier. So anytime."

"Tell me when they get here," Katie said before heading toward the front of the house.

"Wait. Where are you going?" Lina asked. She'd been desperate for a distraction and was hoping Katie would provide it.

"To change out of my uniform," Katie responded over her shoulder.

Lina was again flipping through the magazine when the mudroom door opened. This time it was Phil entering with Liam clutched in one arm. "Hi." She came to her feet. Her gaze zeroed in on the little boy swallowed up in a coat and hat. "Isn't he hot?"

"Probably." Phil tugged the knit cap off his head, revealing a full head of dark silky hair. "The nanny dressed him."

She took a tentative step toward them, thankful for the wine in her system. "He's beautiful," she whispered as her eyes traveled over his face. Her first thought was that he was a Hunter, with his dark hair and blue eyes, but as she continued to study him she realized how extraordinary his likeness was to Phil. From the shape of his nose and eyes to the curve of his lips and the small cleft in his chin, he was all Phil.

"Hi, Liam," she managed over the lump in her throat.

Liam reached for her.

She took a step back from him, folding her arms over her chest. "You should probably take his coat off. His cheeks are red." She crossed to the table and picked up her almost empty wineglass.

"You were supposed to tell me when he arrived," Katie said as she came into the kitchen. "Oh my God. He looks just like Logan."

"Gaah," Liam said, giving her a smile.

"Hi. Hi, Liam," Katie said in a higher-than-normal pitch. "He's so cute. He only has six teeth."

"Here, help me get off his coat," Phil said.

Lina finished the wine in her glass, stealing glances at them as Katie stripped off Liam's coat. "What time does he normally eat?" Lina asked.

"He's squeezing my finger," Katie said. "Look how little his nails are."

"Soon," Phil said to Lina. "I'm going to take him upstairs with me while I change. When I get back, I'll feed him."

"I'll come with you," Katie said, following Phil from the room.

Lina collapsed into a chair, closing her eyes as pain rocketed through her. It was real. He had a baby with another woman. She covered her mouth, stifling a sob. She needed to get ahold of herself. She considered having another glass of wine to settle the churning in her stomach but decided getting drunk wasn't a good solution. Instead she threw herself into making dinner.

***

"Dadda...Dadda...up...up." Liam had pulled himself to a standing position, his arm hooked around Phil's leg for support. His free hand was yanking on Phil's pants.

"Just a second, buddy." Phil was at the sink, screwing the top onto Liam's bottle.

"Dadda!" Liam yelled. "Dadda!" He tugged harder on Phil's lounge pants. "Up! Up!

"I think I'm going to go upstairs," Lina said from behind him.

Phil scooped Liam up into his arms, handing him his bottle. "What?" he asked Lina.

"I have a headache. I'm going to go lie down for a minute."

"Do you need me to get you anything?"

"No. I just…I can't," Lina whispered before rushing from the room.

"Katie?" Phil called out as he walked toward the family room. "Katie?"

"What?" Katie paused the television screen.

"I need you to watch Liam." He set him on the couch beside her.

"What?" Katie retreated to the corner of the couch, her blue eyes opening wider. "No way. I'm not watching him."

"I'm not asking."

"You said it wouldn't affect us if you brought him here. I don't want to be a babysitter. I don't even like kids."

"Watch him," he said firmly, pointing at Liam. "I'll be back in a few minutes."

Lina had been quiet during dinner, but he'd thought it was going well. He found her sitting on the edge of their bed. "I can't do it," she said. "I thought I could, but I can't. I'm sorry."

"It hasn't even been an hour," he said after lowering himself beside her.

"I can't look at him. I know it's not his fault, but he's the result of what you did—a living, breathing reminder."

"Lina." Phil stroked his hand up her back. "It'll get easier. Once you get to know him, you—"

"I don't want to know him." Her words were like a knife in his heart. She came to her feet and headed toward her wardrobe. "I'll go to Adele's or my mom's for the night."

"Fuck." Phil leaned forward, resting his elbows on his knees as he gripped his head. "You said you would try. Forty-five minutes isn't trying." He could hear her walking around the room as she tossed things into a bag, and then she disappeared into the bathroom. He slowly came to his feet, following. He leaned against the doorframe, watching her continue to pack, his stomach sinking.

"I tried," she said, not looking at him. "You have no idea how hard."

"One night. All I'm asking for is one night."

"I can't." Lina shook her head.

"I'll leave," he said deeply. "I'll take him to a hotel."

"No. All his things are here. It'll be easier if I just go to Adele's." Lina lifted the bag and turned from the sink.

"You shouldn't be the one leaving."

"This is the best solution, Phil. I'll be back tomorrow."

He watched her leave the room, his hand clasping the back of his neck. He dropped his head forward, closing his eyes and praying for strength.

***

"I didn't expect to feel this way," Lina said. She was at Adele's, sitting beside her on her family-room couch, sharing a bottle of wine. "It was surreal watching them together. I mean, Liam knows Phil's his father. He calls him Dadda."

"What did you expect? I mean, no offense, but he is his daddy."

"I don't know what I was expecting. Nothing, I guess. Maybe I was living in denial."

"Does he look like Phil?"

Lina grimaced as a vision of Liam flashed in her mind. "Yes. He looks like one of our kids. He reminds me of Logan at that age." She made a pained expression at the thought of

Logan. "I'm such a hypocrite, expecting him to accept Liam when I can't even handle it."

"You left Logan there?"

"No. He's at a friend's. It's just Phil and Katie. How is this real? How can he have a son that isn't mine?"

"He cheated on you."

"That was a rhetorical question," Lina said dryly. "But thanks for the reminder."

"I'm not going to say 'I told you so' because we both know I did, but seriously, how could you not have a hard time with this?"

"I thought I'd be bigger. It's not Liam's fault. He's just a baby. I thought when I saw him I would just love him, knowing he's Phil's." She leaned back into the couch. "I couldn't stop thinking of her. What am I going to do? Phil has him every other weekend."

"That's Phil's problem."

"I don't want to lose my husband every other weekend."

"Well, then you'll just have to try again. It was the first time. Don't be so hard on yourself. It will get easier."

***

Phil rang the doorbell at Kim's house just before five the following afternoon, Liam cradled in one arm, a diaper bag flung over the shoulder of the other. "He fell asleep on the drive over," he said as soon as Kim opened the door. "Where do you want him?" he asked coolly, stepping around her and into the foyer.

"The nursery," she answered, closing the door. "It's upstairs. Second door on the right."

Moments later Phil was carefully lowering his son into his crib. The nursery, like the rest of the house, was decorated impeccably, whales and dolphins gracing the walls in what was clearly a nautical theme. He leaned in and brushed his lips against Liam's forehead.

"He looks more like you every minute," Kim said as Phil turned from the crib.

"He was hungry, so I fed him some applesauce at two," he said, not pausing as he strode out of the room and toward the staircase. "He had a bottle an hour later. I changed his diaper before I left my house, so he should be okay."

"How did it go last night?"

"Fine," Phil answered, continuing down the stairs.

"Phil. Wait." She placed her hand on his arm as they reached the door. "I think you can give me a little more than 'fine.'"

"He was safe and happy. That's all you have a right to know." He opened the door.

"I'm your son's mother. I would think that would garner me a measure of respect," she said, her tone matching the coolness of his.

"Respect?" He paused in the open doorway, turning his head slightly to meet her eyes. "I don't think you're in a position to talk to me about respect. You bought a house in my neighborhood despite the fact that you know I don't want you near my family."

"Isn't Liam your family?" she asked. "This neighborhood is where you chose to raise your other children. Are they more important than him?"

"This isn't about Liam. It's about you. I don't want *you* near my wife. She's been through enough."

"*She's* been through enough?" Kim laughed. "I'm the single mother with an almost-one-year-old, and it wasn't due to artificial insemination."

"I'm not doing this," he said, continuing out the door.

"Wait," Kim called after him. "I need to talk to you about something."

"What?" He swung back around. "What now?"

"I don't want to fight with you. Can't we be civil to one another? I'm not the enemy. I just want what's best for Liam. The two of us arguing isn't what's best for him."

"Is this what you need to talk about?" he asked.

"I wanted to discuss the holidays."

"What about them? We agreed that you would have him for all holidays this year. The alternating doesn't start until next year."

"I was just thinking about it and realized I had him for Christmas last year. It just seems unfair that I get two years in a row. This should be your year."

"No."

"No?" Kim repeated, her eyes widening. "You don't want to spend Christmas with your son?"

"I want to follow the agreement."

***

Lina picked Logan up on her way home from Adele's. "What did you do?" she asked after several seconds of silence.

Logan shrugged, continuing to look out the passenger-side window. "You didn't let him in my room, did you? I don't want him touching my stuff."

"He's a baby, Logan, and your dad was with him. I'm sure he didn't go in your room."

"I'm going to get a lock for my door."

"This isn't easy on any of us, including your dad."

"It's his fault," Logan grumbled.

182

"That's true," Lina conceded. "But it isn't Liam's." She knew she was talking to herself as much as to Logan. "We just need to make the best of a difficult situation."

"It's fucked up."

"Logan!" Her gaze flew in his direction.

"Sorry," he said, his face heating. "But it is."

"That's no excuse for that language." She'd never heard him curse.

"Sorry," he repeated.

Katie was alone in the kitchen, opening boxes of Chinese takeout, when Lina preceded Logan into the kitchen a short time later. "Oh good," Lina said. It was after six, and she hadn't considered what to make for dinner.

"Dad made me pick it up," Katie said. "I wanted pizza."

"Where is he?"

"I don't know, but he's in a bad mood. He wouldn't let Matt come over tonight. Why did you leave without telling me yesterday?"

"I'm sorry," Lina said, realizing she hadn't even considered Katie when she'd fled the house. "I should have said something."

"Was it because of Liam? I thought you wanted him to come here."

"You left?" Logan asked.

Lina's guilt at abandoning Phil returned in full force, knowing if any of Logan's resistance to accepting Liam was due to loyalty to her it would further solidify it. "I decided to spend the evening with Adele," she said, turning to pull plates from the cabinet. "It was a last-minute thing."

"Because you didn't want to be around Liam?" Katie asked.

"No. I just wanted to give your Dad time alone with him," she lied. "Are you ready to eat?" She turned to Logan, holding out a plate.

"Why did you try to get me to stay home if you were just going to leave?" Logan asked.

"I thought it would be good for you to get to know him," Lina said.

"He's our brother," Katie added.

"Shut up!" Logan snapped.

"Logan!" Lina frowned at him.

"I don't want her calling him that." He took the plate from Lina and began roughly spooning food onto his plate, seemingly intent on taking his frustration out on the Chinese food.

"Fine. I won't call him that," Katie said. "But that's what he is," she continued. "Even Grandma and Grandpa think of him as their grandson, and he isn't related to them by blood."

"Katie, please," Lina said, and then Katie's words penetrated into her mind. "Did they come over?"

"Yes. Liam really liked Grandma, didn't he, Dad?" Katie asked.

Lina turned to see Phil coming into the kitchen. "My parents?" She raised her eyebrows.

"Not my idea," Phil said, pausing beside her to lean in and brush his lips over hers. "They just showed up."

"She asked me the other day if she could stop by to meet him this weekend and I said no."

"When has 'no' ever stopped your mother? I'm surprised she bothered to ask." He stepped around her to take a beer from the refrigerator.

"She said Liam is basically her grandson," Katie said.

"He isn't Mom's son," Logan fumed, "so he can't be her grandson."

"He's Mom's stepson," Katie said. "So at a minimum he's her step-grandson."

"Katie, let it go," Phil said.

"What? You said we were supposed to give him a chance, and Logan isn't."

"Enough," Phil said more firmly. "No more."

"What did I do?" She frowned at him.

"You continue to talk, and I've asked you to stop. Why don't the two of you take your food to the table? We're all here. We can eat as a family." As they gathered their plates, Phil returned his attention to Lina. "Do you want a glass of wine, or I could make you a drink?"

"Water." She cringed at the thought of alcohol, still suffering the effects of overindulging with Adele the night before. "I'll stick with water."

"Are we okay?" he asked, in a tone low enough for only her ears.

"Of course." She clasped his hand, giving it a reassuring squeeze in response to the concern in his eyes. "I'm just a little tired. I didn't sleep well. I missed my husband."

"Yeah?" He placed his beer on the island behind her, his eyes never leaving hers as he curved his hands around her hips. "I missed you." He brushed his lips over hers. "I love you," he said, his breath warm against her lips.

"I know." Lina fisted the front of his shirt.

"Stop it!" Katie called out. "No one wants to see their parents kissing."

Phil lifted his head slightly, pressing his forehead against Lina's. "Remember when we wanted her to talk more?"

"Shh." Lina tugged on his shirt. "Be nice."

It was close to ten when Lina said good night to Katie and Logan and made her way to her bedroom. Phil, who had spent the evening in the upstairs rec room playing video games with Logan, joined her in the master bath as she finished washing her face.

"How is he? Did he talk about Liam?"

Phil paused behind her, cupping her shoulders as he dropped his mouth to the side of her neck. "No, but he's fine. You smell nice."

"It's Adele's body wash."

"It's you."

"How was last night? Did you get any sleep?"

"Once I brought him into bed with me."

"You let him sleep with you?" She met his gaze in the mirror. He'd always been adamant that he didn't want the kids in bed with them. She remembered walking around with them in her arms in the middle of the night, sometimes for more than an hour, until they fell back to sleep.

"It was his first time with me. Strange crib. Strange house. I didn't want to make it harder on him than it already was. He settled down as soon as he lay down with me."

She hated the thought. It was as if a piece of Kim was in their bed. She tried to pull away from him, but Phil's hold on her arms tightened. "What's that look?"

"Nothing. I just…I'm surprised. We never did that."

"The circumstances are a little different. You weren't here. I was alone in the bed. I didn't know it would be a big deal to you or I wouldn't have brought him in with me."

She was being ridiculous. She was making him feel guilty for comforting a baby. "It's fine." She slipped from his hold, continuing out into the bedroom. "Just ignore me."

"I'm not going to ignore you," he said, following her. "If you're saying you don't want him in our bed, I won't bring him in our bed."

"No—I don't know what I'm saying. It's late and I'm tired. We can talk about it tomorrow."

"I don't want you to go to sleep upset."

"I'm not upset," she lied. "It's just been a long couple of days. I don't even know what there is to talk about. I knew this wasn't going to be easy, and it's not, but it's our life now. It's just going to take some mental adjustments."

Lina lay back against the pillows, her thoughts drifting to Kim. "How long were you there when you dropped him off?" she asked when Phil reappeared a few minutes later.

"Just long enough to pass him off. Maybe three minutes." He stepped out of his briefs before lowering himself onto the bed beside her.

"Did she try to talk to you?"

He propped himself up on one elbow as he looked down at her. "Baby—"

"She did. I can see it in your eyes."

"She offered to let me have Liam for Christmas. That was all we talked about."

"Christmas?" Lina repeated, a knot twisting in her stomach. She didn't want to have Liam for Christmas.

"I said no," Phil said.

A wave of relief rushed through Lina. "Why would she want to give him up for Christmas?"

"I have no idea."

"Do you think she did it to make you feel guilty, assuming you'd say no?"

"I don't know what motivates her, and I'm not going to expend energy trying to figure her out. She offered and I said no."

"Or maybe she hoped it would cause stress for me. If you said yes, I mean."

"I never would have said yes without consulting you. I told you if you took me back, you would come first. Those weren't just words, Lina. This family—our family—will always come first. I know it's too soon for Logan and for you. I would never even suggest it."

"Okay." The unease bubbling within her dissipated in response to his words.

"If it's too soon for me to bring him here, that's okay, too. I'll figure something out."

"No." She curved her hand around his neck. "I want you to keep bringing him here."

"You do?" His eyes were narrowed in confusion.

"Yes." She nodded.

"If you change your mind—"

"I won't," she interrupted. "This is going to work." She could see the relief in his eyes at her words.

"Why are you wearing this?" He tugged at the hem of her silk nightgown.

"It's cold." She breathed in as his hand stroked a path up her thigh.

"Panties, too?"

"I thought you'd be too tired after last night." She lifted her hips as he began to ease her panties down.

"No." He slowly shook his head. "I'm not too tired." He pushed her back into the mattress as he shifted his body over hers. "Are you too tired?" He began to rub himself against her, his body completely hard. "I can stop."

"No, you can't." Lina linked both arms around his neck. "And I don't want you to."

***

"Kim Ryan is sitting in our conference room," Mark Dwyer, one of the senior partners in Phil's firm, announced after entering his office the following Monday.

"What?" Phil came to his feet, a frown marring his features.

"She's here with her son—your son. She stopped by to say hello."

"Fuck." Phil dragged his hand down his face.

Mark gave him a sympathetic smile before heading toward the door. "I thought you'd want to know."

Phil's first instinct was to go out to the conference room and escort Kim from the building, but realizing that would create more of a scene than she was already creating, he decided to do nothing, instead closing his office door and trying to concentrate on the brief he'd been working on all morning.

Thirty minutes passed before a knock preceded the entrance of Anne. As soon as he saw her flushed cheeks, he knew Kim had arrived. "Send them in," he said before she uttered a word, pushing back his chair.

Liam squealed in delight at the sight of his father, bouncing up and down against Kim's side. "Dadda!"

Phil walked around his desk and took Liam from Kim. "Hi, buddy."

"Dadda." Liam patted Phil's chin.

"What are you doing here?" Phil asked Kim.

"I was in the area, so I stopped by to show everyone Liam. I used to work here, remember? I didn't think you'd want me to leave without letting you see your son." She extracted a framed eight-by-ten photograph of Liam from the diaper bag. "I also brought you this. It's a black-and-white like your others." She stepped around him and placed the picture on top of the bookshelf behind his desk, directly next to a photo of Logan. "They look alike."

"I'm capable of getting my own pictures. You can take that with you. You are not welcome here." His words were short and measured.

"Your *son's* not welcome here?"

"Not when he's accompanied by you. I need to get back to work." He pressed his lips against Liam's forehead. When he attempted to give Liam back to Kim, Liam protested, clinging to Phil's neck.

"I need to use the ladies' room. Could you watch him for a minute?"

Phil glared at her, the side of his jaw clenched. "I'm working," he bit out. "Take him with you."

"You can't spare five minutes?"

Phil pried Liam's fingers from around his neck. "Take him," he growled, holding him out to her.

Liam sucked in his bottom lip and began to cry.

"Fuck," Phil muttered under his breath, pulling Liam back into his chest. "It's okay, buddy." He began to jiggle him in his arms. "Go," he said to Kim, nodding toward the door. "Five minutes." As soon as she left, he began pacing across his office, continuing to shake Liam in his arms. "I'm sorry," he whispered against his head. "Daddy's sorry he scared you. It's okay."

It took a few minutes for Liam to stop crying and then a few more for Phil to coach a smile from him. Kim returned as he opened his office door with the intention of asking Anne to go find her.

"Never again," Phil said as he stepped out into his lobby. "You are not welcome in these offices. Do you understand?" he asked, unconcerned with the fact Anne could hear their conversation.

"Come on, Liam." Kim began prying a protesting Liam from Phil's arms. "Daddy's busy."

"Tell them in the main lobby if she shows up again to call security," he told Anne.

"You don't have to be such an asshole," Kim said, her face heated.

"Never again," he repeated before walking back into his office.

"I hear you had a visitor," Wayne said later that afternoon. "Well, two actually."

"Unfortunately," Phil said, not looking away from his computer screen. "How was court?"

"They took the deal." Wayne crossed to the bar and poured two glasses of scotch. "She just showed up?"

"It's not going to happen again."

"Is that him?" Wayne was looking past Phil to the photograph on the bookshelf.

Phil turned in his chair, studying the picture for the first time. It was clearly professionally done. Liam was outside, sitting beside a tree along a river, smiling at the camera. "That's him."

"Handsome boy."

"He is," Phil agreed. "His mother I could do without." He joined Wayne at the conference room table on the far end of the office. "I've given her zero encouragement for over a year and a half and she still acts like something's going to change. What in the fuck do I have to do to get through to her?"

"Even with your kid in tow, half the male population in the office was panting over her, according to Rick. She'll be someone else's problem soon enough."

"I hope so."

"How's Lina doing with her living so close?"

"She doesn't like it. I'm sure she's worried about running into her, but she wouldn't even consider moving. It's a lot, though. All of it. Liam. Kim. It's a lot."

Chapter Twenty

It was Wednesday, five days since Lina's failed attempt at spending an evening with Liam. She'd told Phil she was ready to try again, but all day she vacillated over whether or not to escape to Adele's, Diane's, or her mother's. When five o'clock came around, she was almost surprised to find herself home preparing dinner as she sipped Chardonnay.

Thanks to a glass and a half of wine, the sound of the garage door opening didn't set off the dread Lina expected, just a flutter of unease in her tummy. She was surprised when Logan, instead of Phil, came into the house. "I thought you had the SAT prep tonight." Phil was supposed to pick him up at nine p.m., after dropping Liam off.

"It was canceled. The instructor's sick. Mrs. Ellis offered to drive me home. Hey, boy," he greeted Knight, who was wagging his tail enthusiastically. "What are you making?"

He dropped his book bag on the kitchen island before pulling open the refrigerator.

"Lasagna."

"Cool." He turned from the refrigerator with the container of milk in his hand. "Can I play my computer game?"

"It's a school night."

"I know, but I finished all my homework because I thought I had the SAT prep. If the tutor hadn't gotten sick, I'd be there, not studying for school."

"You're convincing the wrong person. It's Dad's rule. You can talk to him when..." She trailed off, remembering that he'd be showing up any minute with Liam in tow. "Your dad is bringing Liam here for a couple of hours tonight. I thought you'd be in class or I would have told you earlier."

Logan's entire body stiffened. With his shorter hair and serious expression, she was struck by how handsome and mature he looked. Phil was right. He was turning into a man. "When?"

"Any minute."

"Tell me when he's gone." He set the milk container on the island, yanked up his book bag, and left the room, Knight at his heels.

She was still processing Logan's sudden departure when the door opened again. This time it was Phil and Liam coming into the room.

"Gaah," Liam said as soon as he saw her.

Lina's heart jumped. "Hi, Liam." She watched Phil remove his coat and hat. "It's really not cold enough for all those clothes."

"I kept the car cold," Phil said. He crossed to her, kissing her softly. "Okay?"

"Yes." She smiled at Liam, who was reaching out toward her. "Hi." She held out her own hand.

He gripped two of her fingers with his hand, a hand that was a small version of Phil's. His wrists were almost as large as hers.

A baby giant, Lina thought. Logan had been smaller. He'd inherited Phil's height but not his bulk. Liam had clearly inherited both. "He's strong," Lina said when Liam continued to hold her fingers in his viselike grip.

"He's smart. He doesn't want to let you go." He leaned in, kissing her again. "Are we alone?"

"Logan's upstairs. The SAT class was canceled. Has he eaten?"

"Not yet. The nanny gave me something for him. It's in the diaper bag. Where's Katie?"

"She went to a yoga class. She should be back soon."

"Yoga?" Phil raised his eyebrows.

"She thinks she'll like it. I hope she does. Are you going to change?" Her gaze shifted back to Liam, who was staring at her like he was trying to memorize her face.

"I'll...uh...take him with me," Phil said.

Lina knew he was waiting for her to offer to watch him, but she couldn't, not yet. "Okay. I'll set the table and make the salad. Does his food need to be heated?"

"I don't think so." He looked down at the diaper bag. "I usually just serve it to him cold."

"I'll check." Lina took the diaper bag from his shoulder. "You go." She watched them leave the room, releasing a breath when they were out of sight. Baby steps.

***

Phil hesitated at the top of the staircase, debating whether or not to take Liam to Logan's room. The door was closed, which wasn't unusual, but he wasn't sure that forcing a meeting was a good idea. "Not today, buddy," he said aloud to Liam before continuing to the master suite. Before they reached it, Logan's door opened just enough to let Knight out. The dog rushed to greet them, his tail wagging.

"Daw!" Liam yelled excitedly. "Daw!"

"That's right. Dog." Phil crouched down, maintaining his hold on Liam, who began to half slap, half pat Knight. "Be gentle," Phil said, gripping his hand and running it down Knight's coat. "See? Gentle."

Liam let out a squeal of laughter when Knight licked his face.

"He likes you," Phil said, smiling in reaction to Liam's obvious delight. "Come on," he said after a few minutes. "Daddy has to change." As he came to his feet, he saw Logan's door close. He'd obviously been watching them. He took Liam's hand. "Let's go meet your brother."

"It's Dad," Phil said moments later, tapping the back of his hand on Logan's door.

Seconds passed with no response. Phil was about to knock again when Logan's voice came through the door. "I'm busy."

"Open the door."

Another pause. "No."

Annoyance bubbled in Phil's chest. "It wasn't a request."

The door opened. "What do you want?" Logan snapped.

Phil was taken aback by the anger and defiance radiating from his son. "Excuse me?" He took a step closer to Logan, staring into his eyes. "What did you just say to me?"

Logan dropped his eyes. "I was doing something," he mumbled.

"Look at me," Phil said, waiting for him to raise his eyes before continuing. "Don't ever talk to me with that tone of voice again. Do you understand me?"

"Yes," Logan answered.

"You don't always have to like me, but you will show me respect. Is that clear?"

"Yeah," he mumbled.

"Excuse me?"

"I said yes," Logan answered.

A movement against Phil's leg reminded him he wasn't alone. He scooped up Liam from the floor. "This is Liam."

Logan's gaze shifted to the baby, no discernible expression on his face.

Liam rested his head against Phil's chest as he took in his brother for the first time.

"You can hate what I did. You can even hate me, but you can't hate him. He's as innocent as you are in all of this."

Logan's gaze returned to Phil. "May I go back to my homework now?"

"Yes, but I expect you at dinner."

***

Katie returned home with Matt, bursting into the kitchen uncharacteristically excited after her first yoga class. "All those stupid sports teams you and Dad forced me to join and the whole time that was waiting for me. I can't believe you never took me or even suggested I go."

"Hi, Matt." Lina touched his arm.

"Lasagna?" he asked, his eyes lighting up when he saw the lasagna cooling on the stove. "Your food is the reason I stick around."

"Yeah right," Katie said, shoving him in his side. "Seriously, Mom, that was, like, amazing. I'm going to be an instructor."

"After one session you think you're qualified for that?" Lina teased.

"I meant eventually. I'm going to go every day. It's only two hundred a month for unlimited. I can join online. I just need your credit card."

"I bought you a two-week pass. If you still want to join at the end of it, we'll talk about it."

"I'll want to. And what do you mean talk about it? What's there to talk about?"

"Whether or not you need to go every day for one. Two hundred dollars isn't cheap."

"I bet you spend a lot more on Logan's lacrosse. And Megan's, too, when she played. This is the first thing I've found that I like. Why do you only worry about money when it comes to me?"

"I'm not worried about the money," Lina assured her. "If this is something you really want to do, you can do it. But you may find three or five times a week is enough."

"It won't be."

"All I'm asking for is a week," Lina said. "If you still want the unlimited after two weeks, we'll do it."

"I will." She rewarded Lina with a rare hug. "I loved it. Now I understand why you and Grandma do it all the time. Is that a diaper bag?" Katie asked, spotting Liam's diaper bag on the counter. "Is Liam here?"

"He's upstairs with your dad." She'd barely gotten the words out before Katie grabbed Matt's hand and led him from the room.

To Lina's surprise, Logan appeared a few minutes later. It was clear from his downtrodden expression something was wrong. "I was going to bring you a plate."

"Dad said I have to eat down here," he said, avoiding her eyes.

"What?" She was at his side, running her hand down his arm. "When did he say that?" Just like that, her little boy was back.

"A few minutes ago." He brushed a tear from beneath his eye with the back of his hand.

A surge of protectiveness flowed through her. "No." She shook her head. She normally tried to support Phil's decisions, wanting to provide a united front to their children, but not this time. She wasn't forcing Logan to be around Liam until he was ready. "You don't have to stay down here unless you want to."

"Dad said—"

"Don't worry about your father. I'll deal with him."

It was apparent when Katie returned to the kitchen, still wearing yoga leggings and a baggy sweatshirt, Liam perched on her hip, she no longer had an aversion to babies, or at least not one baby in particular. For his part, Liam seemed equally infatuated, babbling away as he smiled adoringly at her.

"Looks like you have some competition," Lina said to Matt, who was trailing a few feet behind them.

"He's so cute. I just want to squeeze him," Katie said. "Aren't you?" She nuzzled his neck, eliciting gurgles of deep baby laughter.

Lina's annoyance at Phil took a temporary reprieve as she witnessed Liam and Katie's obvious bond. "He really likes you."

"He loves me," Katie said. "Don't you, Liam? Don't you?"

"Ay, Ay," he said, fisting her hair.

Katie's eyes widened. "He's trying to say my name. Did you hear that? Say Katie, Liam. Katie."

"Ay, Ay," Liam repeated.

"Is he trying to say my name?" she asked excitedly.

199

"I think so," Lina said. He was smart. She could see the intelligence in his eyes.

"He said my name," Katie told Phil as he came into the kitchen holding the high chair Lina had bought earlier in the week. "He can't say K, so he just calls me Ay."

"Dadda," Liam shrieked, pointing at his father.

"That's right. That's Daddy. I'm Katie, and that's Matt." She turned him to Matt. "Do you want to hold him?"

"No. I'm good." Matt held up his hands, taking a step backward.

"He doesn't bite," Katie said. "Just hold him. I want to take a picture."

Lina stepped beside Phil, who was setting the high chair beside his chair at the head of the table. "Did you tell Logan he had to eat with us?" she whispered, not wanting to be overheard by Katie and Matt.

"Yes."

"Well, I told him he didn't."

"Why would you do that?"

"Because we agreed we wouldn't force this on him. Telling him he has to come to dinner is *forcing* it on him."

"You weren't there for the conversation that led to that decision."

"I know I wasn't, because if I had been, that *decision* wouldn't have been made," she fumed.

"Fine," he bit back.

Katie monopolized Liam's attention and the conversation during dinner, allowing Lina to stay virtually silent. Phil hadn't said a word to her since their exchange, and although he was interacting with the other three at the table, she could tell he was upset. He hadn't looked at her once. They'd had disagreements in the seven months since they'd reconciled, but until tonight none that reminded her of their fights about Katie, when she'd felt such anger toward him.

Lina was in the midst of cleaning the kitchen when Phil told her he was taking Liam home. "I'll be back in twenty minutes."

"Phil?" Lina called as he disappeared into the mudroom.

"Yes?" He stepped back out into the kitchen. Liam was straddling his side, once again bundled in his coat.

"You're going to leave without letting me say goodbye to him?"

"I didn't think you cared."

"Of course I care." She squeezed Liam's hand. A vision of Kim came to Lina's mind. "I'm coming with you," she said, deciding in that moment that she didn't want Phil alone with Kim when he was clearly still upset with her.

"What?" Phil frowned. "Why?"

"Because I want to. I want to see where they live."

"Lina—"

"I'm coming with you," she insisted.

"He's asleep," Lina said less than a minute into their drive.

"Katie wore him out," Phil said.

Lina's gaze shifted from Liam to Phil as she settled back in her seat. "I'm sorry for snapping at you earlier. He was upset, and I think I internalized some of his feelings."

"It's fine." His hands tightened on the steering wheel.

"No. It's not fine. I don't like the distance I felt between us tonight. I don't want to go back there."

He placed one of his hands on her thigh. "We're not going back anywhere."

She slid her palm over the back of his hand. "You were mad at me during dinner."

"No. I was frustrated at the situation. I wasn't mad at you."

"Logan will eventually come around. Liam has a charm to him that pulls you in."

"Does he?"

"He's endearing," Lina said. "Logan won't be immune to it. Look at Katie. She's crazy about him."

"I didn't see that one coming." He squeezed her thigh. "Thanks for sticking around tonight."

"It was better. The first time was more of a shock. It's hard knowing…" She trailed off, not wanting to mention Kim.

"I know."

He turned off the highway onto a winding road leading back through the luxury town house community. For the first time since leaving their house, Lina regretted her decision to accompany him. She didn't want to be anywhere near Kim.

"Are you okay?" Phil asked.

"I asked to come."

"That's her place on the end. The one with the red bricks. I'll just be a minute," he said as he put the car in park.

There was a tree in the front yard, but with the branches bare of leaves, Lina had a clear view of the front door. Her heartbeat accelerated as he reached the porch. She hadn't seen Kim since she'd run into her at the wedding of one of Phil's associates. She'd been pregnant with Phil's child at the time. The door opened before he knocked. Lina's stomach clenched as soon as Kim came into view. Despite the winter temperatures, she was wearing compression shorts and a tank top, her lean body on full display. She'd clearly lost all her baby weight. She looked incredibly fit and more beautiful than Lina remembered. It was going to take a long time to erase this image of Kim from her mind.

"What a skank!" Adele said the following day.

"Shh." Lina frowned across the table at Adele. "We're in a restaurant."

"Does she think she's in a movie? Tell me where she lives. I'd love to go over and smack the shit out of her."

"Adele," Lina warned. "I'm going to have to censor what I tell you in public if you can't control your responses."

"Did Phil call her out on it? He better have."

"When I commented on it, he just said she was probably running. He seemed completely unfazed by the whole thing. I honestly don't even think he noticed what she was wearing."

"He noticed."

"No, I really don't think he did. He was intent on giving her Liam and getting back to the car. He knew I was waiting."

"You know what this means, don't you? It means you're going to go with him from now on. You should probably go up to the door with him, too. She'll open the door in lingerie and you'll be standing there beside him. Can you imagine?"

"Unfortunately, I can," Lina said, an image of Kim in her shorts and tank top flashing in her mind. "She looks like she spends all of her free time in a gym."

Adele raised an eyebrow. "Oh please. You *do* spend all your free time at the gym. You have an amazing body. There is no forty-two-year-old that has a better body."

"I *do not* spend all my free time at the gym. I do yoga at the yoga studio and run outside, unless it's raining and then I use the treadmill in the basement. I don't even belong to a gym."

"You are sooo literal—just like Phil. My point, if you'll let me make it, is you're probably fitter than ninety-nine percent of the female population."

"I'm fit—I realize that—but a fit forty-two-year-old can't really compete with a fit thirty-two-year-old. That's the point I'm trying to make."

"You don't have to compete with her. Phil could have had her, but he chose you, remember? You're the one wearing his obscenely large rock on the third finger of your left hand."

"It's not obscenely big." Lina frowned as she studied the one-carat diamond on her finger. "It's not even big."

"Oh my God. I'm kidding. Have you completely lost your sense of humor? You used to get my dry wit."

"Sorry, but I'm not really in a joking mood when I'm discussing my husband's ex-mistress." Just saying the word "mistress" made her stomach churn.

"I realized the other day that I've finally forgiven Phil," Adele said. "I no longer have the urge to punch him in the face when I see him."

"That's good to hear." Lina checked the time on her phone. "I need to get home. I shouldn't have even met you. I have hours' worth of work left today."

"Relax. William said you're doing well."

"He did? He said that?"

"His exact words were 'she's doing great.'"

Lina didn't feel like she was doing great. She felt completely overwhelmed.

***

Phil, flanked by his clients and two of his associates, stepped out of the elevator into the lobby of Hendrix, Wolff, and

Pearson LLP late that morning. "Phil." Tom Hendrix greeted him immediately before leading them to their conference room, where several of their lawyers were already assembled.

The case involved a property dispute between a real-estate developer, Phil's client, and a homeowner association. Both sides were hoping for a resolution before their court date the following week. They had just taken their seats when Kim swept into the room.

"Sorry I'm late," she said breathlessly, setting her things in an empty chair. "Babysitter issues." She slipped off her jacket, revealing a formfitting cream dress. The scent of her perfume filled the air. Phil was the only male present whose eyes didn't linger on her.

"I picked the wrong law firm," one of his clients whispered beside him.

"Oh, Phil," she said, pinpointing him with her stare. "I forgot to give you this when you were over the other day." She lifted a shirt enclosed in a dry cleaner's plastic. "I had it cleaned." It was the shirt he'd left at her house after the applesauce incident with Liam.

Chapter Twenty-one

The room was suddenly quiet as all eyes shifted between Phil and Kim. "Let's get started," Phil said, lifting the top page of the documents in front of him. Kim wasn't the lead attorney and she spoke very little over the course of the two-hour meeting, so Phil was able to ignore her for the most part. When they wrapped up right before lunch with a tentative agreement, he took one of his associates aside, advised him where to take the clients for lunch, and told him he'd meet them there shortly.

"Let's talk," he said to Kim, disregarding the curious stares. The damage had been done. After her stunt he had no doubt every person in the room assumed they were still having an affair. He followed her down a short hall to her office, his hands balled into fists at his sides.

She perched herself on the edge of her desk once they were in her office with the door closed. "What's up?"

He let his gaze travel up and down the length of her. "My dick isn't interested anymore."

She parted her legs slightly. "I don't believe you."

He smiled, but his eyes were stone cold. "You really think it was you, don't you? That I couldn't resist *you*. The truth is you could have been anyone. You just happened to be the one there that night. And then I kept fucking you because it was easy. You were an easy fuck. And that's all I see when I look at you—an easy fuck."

Kim's face heated. "You're lying."

"No." He slowly shook his head. "I was always honest with you. You just lived in a fucking illusion." His gaze again traveled over her. "There is only one woman I want, and she carries my name." He walked past her and out of her office.

"Everything okay?" Tom Hendrix fell into step beside Phil as he walked down the hall toward the lobby.

"Yes," Phil answered. He'd intentionally kept his voice low while he was in Kim's office, so he knew no one had overheard him.

"Do you have a second?"

Phil glanced at his watch. "One."

"I'm still having a hard time wrapping my head around the fact that she has your son. You're still with Lina?"

"Yes."

"And she knows about the boy?"

"What do you think?" Phil asked, frowning in irritation. "Half the city knows. Do you really think I'm going to try to keep it from my wife?"

"No. No. Of course not. Look, when I assigned Kim to this case, I didn't realize you still had her on the side."

"I don't," Phil snapped. "Jesus, Tom, is this really what you brought me in here to discuss? What are we, fucking women?"

"Sorry. I just assumed. Sorry. The whole thing is just hard to comprehend. You would have been the last person I'd expect to stray. I mean…don't get me wrong…I'd have a hard time resisting Kim if she came at me, but you have Lina. Lina's—"

Phil held up a silencing hand. "I know what my wife is. You don't have to sell her to me. And frankly this is none of your fucking business. And if you care at all about our working relationship, you'll take her off this case and any others that involve my firm." He wanted to punch him in the mouth, but instead he left his office.

*   *   *

The following week, Lina went into Dolmar Enterprises on Friday instead of her scheduled Thursday so she could attend an afternoon meeting. It was after five before it wrapped up, and she was gathering up her purse and computer when one of the women who worked in the sales office poked her head in her office and invited her to join her and several of the other employees for happy hour.

"Come on," the woman implored when Lina hesitated. "Everyone's coming. We're a fun group. I promise."

An hour and two drinks later, Lina was in the midst of a conversation with a group from the marketing department when a man sidled up to her and asked if he could buy her a drink. She politely declined but was instantly transported back to the few times during her separation from Phil when Adele convinced her to join her for happy hour and men would approach to talk to her or buy her a drink. Those were the nights that had her crying herself to sleep, knowing any other man would just be a substitute for Phil. Tonight, with the knowledge she'd be going home to Phil, she was actually enjoying herself. When the others in her group decided to go on to dinner, Lina said her goodbyes. It wasn't until she was in her car and looking at her phone that she realized she'd neglected to tell Phil she was going to be late. She had two missed calls and four text messages.

At 5:00 *Leaving work*

At 5:45 *I just picked up Liam. Should I order in? No one's home so I assume it's just us?*

At 6:00 *I ordered from the new tavern down the street*

At 7:00 *Call me*

"I'm sorry," she said as soon as he answered. "I went out with some of the people from work and I lost track of time. Are you mad?"

"No. I was just worried." He sounded tired. "I guess Logan's away for the weekend?"

"Yes." She felt guilty for not being there to see Liam. By the time she arrived home, he'd probably be down for the night. "I'll be home soon. Thanks for ordering dinner."

The sound of the television greeted Lina when she came into the kitchen. She found Phil in the family room, leaned back on the couch with his knees spread wide and a beer in his hand watching a college football game. He shifted his gaze away from the television when she came around the couch, his eyes roaming over her.

"Come here," he said deeply. He set his beer on the end table before holding his hand out to her.

"How long has he been asleep?" She let him pull her between his legs, clasping his shoulders when he pressed his face into her stomach. She kissed the top of his head, stroking her hands down his back. "I'm sorry I missed him.

I didn't realize how late it was." She breathed in when she felt his warm palms sliding up the back of her thighs.

"How many men came on to you?"

"None."

"Liar." He cupped her butt.

"I'm not lying. One asked to buy me a drink. That was it." She slipped off her shoes and straddled his lap when he leaned back into the couch. "You're the only one I want."

"Yeah." He pushed up with his hips.

"When did you get so hard?" She sunk her fingers into his shoulders as she began to rotate her hips.

"As soon as I saw you in that dress."

"Let's go upstairs. Katie could come home."

"She's at a concert." He lifted himself up just enough to push his lounge pants down around his thighs. "And I can't wait."

"Phil, what if—"

He covered her mouth with his before she could say more, his tongue stroking over hers. She moaned into his mouth when he continued to rub against her. She felt a small tug before her panties came loose and then he was clasping her hips and lifting her over him. She wrapped her arms around his neck, her tongue tangling with his as she sunk down onto him, his body filling hers completely.

A few hours later Lina was on the verge of another climax, her fingers sinking into Phil's muscled back when she heard Liam's cry over the monitor. "Phil, stop," she whispered. "Liam—"

"Ignore him," he said, thrusting into her.

"I can't. He's crying."

"He's fine," he growled.

"No. Go get him."

"Fuck." He turned his face into her neck, breathing in and out deeply, his body stilled over hers. "He can wait five minutes."

"No." She gripped his shoulders. "I can't with him crying. Go take care of him."

He groaned in frustration.

"Go," she insisted. Moments later she heard his voice over the monitor.

"You have terrible timing, buddy…Come on…shh… What's the matter?"

Lina rolled onto her side, listening to Phil comfort his son. It was a new dimension to him. He'd never gotten up with their kids. It was always Lina soothing them back to sleep.

"Do you want a bottle?" he asked before the monitor went quiet.

Lina couldn't remember the last time one of the kids interrupted them during sex. She decided it was when Logan had the stomach flu in seventh grade. Megan had knocked on their door because Logan hadn't made it to the bathroom and there was vomit on the family-room couch. In a minute Lina had gone from being entwined with Phil's warm body to scrubbing vomit off their leather couch. She'd thought those days were behind them. With Liam in the picture they had another decade and a half to go.

"Dadda," Liam's voice came over the monitor a few minutes later.

"Shh…Go to sleep."

"Dadda!" Liam shrieked. "Dadda!" He began to cry.

Lina was slipping on her robe with the intention of going to help calm Liam when the crying stopped. Seconds later the bedroom door opened. Phil entered with Liam in his arms.

"He won't stay down," Phil complained, frustration in his voice. "I changed him and gave him a bottle. As soon as I put him in the crib he starts to cry. I don't know what the hell he wants."

"First you need to calm down," Lina said, stepping up beside them. "He's sensitive." She trailed her fingers through the back of Liam's hair. "He thinks you're upset with him."

"I am upset with him. I want to fuck you and he won't shut up."

"Phil, stop," she scolded before taking Liam from him. "It's okay," she whispered, jiggling him against her body. "Shhh." It took about a minute for him to stop crying.

Phil followed her back to the nursery, standing in the doorway while she continued to rock Liam in her arms. Ten minutes later she was carefully laying a sleeping Liam back into his crib.

"You're like a baby whisperer," he said as he pulled the nursery door closed.

"No, I just have patience, something you could use a little more of. He's a baby. He can't help it."

"I can't either." He swung her up into his arms.

"Phil," she laughed, wrapping her arms around his neck.

"What are you doing?" Katie asked. She was standing at the top of the stairs.

"Carrying Mom to bed," Phil said, striding toward their bedroom. "Good night."

***

The following Thursday the Ravens were hosting the Steelers at M&T Stadium in Baltimore. With temperatures projected to be in the twenties at the eight p.m. kickoff, Lina

212

opted out, so Phil invited his brother to join him and Logan. After the first quarter with the Ravens up ten to three, Logan went off to get some more food.

"How's Lina's new job?" Mike asked.

"She likes it." Phil took a swallow from the beer in his hand.

"And you?"

Phil shrugged. "I don't know. I wish she didn't have the commute. The days she goes in she's out of the house before I'm even out of bed. It's an adjustment. I'm used to having her around. But she's happy, so that's what I'm concentrating on."

"Remember when Mom tried to work?"

Phil had a vague memory of his mother getting a job at the local library when he was in high school. "That didn't last long."

"No. Dad didn't like having to fix his own breakfast in the morning. Jeanie's idea of fixing my breakfast is setting the cereal box on the table next to a bowl."

Phil chuckled.

"Funny to you. Your wife treats you like a king."

"I'm not going to argue with that." Phil took another swallow of beer.

"Have you brought Liam over again?"

"He was over last weekend. It went well. She's a little reserved with him but she's starting to warm up. She held him a few times. Logan's the one I'm worried about. He won't even look at him."

"Give him time. How would you have felt if Dad brought home a son from another woman? I doubt we would have accepted him right away."

The thought of his conservative, Catholic father having an affair was inconceivable to Phil. "That would never have happened." Picking up the phone and calling his parents to tell them he had cheated on Lina was one of the most difficult things he'd ever done. And it was every bit as painful as he knew it would be. His mother cried and his father could barely speak. They'd raised him to be a better man.

***

"I feel like I haven't seen you in months," Diane said when they met for a pedicure the Saturday before Thanksgiving. "Oh wait, I haven't seen you in months."

Lina laughed. "It hasn't been that long."

"We met for lunch in September," Diane said. "That was the last time."

"You're right," Lina said, stunned it had been that long.

"I know I'm right, and I'm really starting to resent this career of yours."

Hearing Diane say she had a career sounded so odd, and yet it was true. She had a career. "I'll do better. It's just been so hectic with the new job. Phil was right. Driving into Bethesda is a nightmare during rush hour, but I think I've finally figured it out. If I leave the house by seven, I beat most of the traffic and then I'm home before Phil in the evening. And it's just two days a week."

"What about Logan?"

"His girlfriend takes him to the stop on the mornings I go in. I'm back in time in the evenings to get him."

"A girlfriend?"

"He doesn't actually call her that and we haven't met her yet, but I think that's what she is. He's suddenly attached to his phone, always texting, and he's just different. I used to have to tell him to shower. Now he's taking two a day."

"That's just the age—teenage boys love their showers."

"No." Lina grimaced. "I didn't mean it like that. I just meant he likes to be clean for her."

"Right. That's what he's doing," Diane teased. "I raised two boys. They were extra clean at that age, too."

"Let's change the subject," Lina begged, not wanting to think of Logan doing anything to himself in the shower.

"Is Katie still with Matt?"

"Yes. I don't see that ending anytime soon, if ever. They remind me of me and Phil at that age—always together. She has zero interest in looking at colleges. She hasn't said it, but I'm sure she's planning to go to Maryland or Towson. I can't see her leaving him. I'm sure Phil is going to have a fit. He likes Matt, but liking him and wanting him as a son-in-law are entirely different things. I know he's hoping she'll go away and the relationship will just fizzle out. I don't see that happening."

They went on to other subjects, talking about Diane's upcoming trip to visit her son and his wife in California for Thanksgiving and the firm's plan to have the holiday party at the Four Seasons Hotel. "Where did we have it last year again?" Diane asked. "I must be getting old that I can't even remember."

"I wasn't there," Lina reminded her. "A year ago Phil and I were separated."

"Sorry." Diane gave her thigh a reassuring squeeze. "I sometimes forget that the two of you were ever apart."

"Me too."

"Are you still looking over your shoulder everywhere you go? I can't believe she lives around here. I always search for her when I go out." She unconsciously looked around the small shop.

"To tell you the truth, I haven't been. At first I was, but with the new job I've just had too many other things on my mind. And the convenience of having Liam closer means we're no longer losing Phil one night a week. He just brings Liam to the house. I think she's finally given up, thank God. I'm actually starting to believe she moved closer for Liam and not to wreak havoc in our lives. Things have been quiet since she left the receipt in his pocket."

"I wouldn't call them quiet exactly," Diane said. "Not with the stunts she's pulled on Phil."

Lina's heart dropped. "What stunts?"

Phil was using the leaf blower to clear off the front walk when Lina arrived home.

"Why didn't you tell me about Kim coming to the office?" she asked, stalking up to him. "I shouldn't have to find these things out from Diane."

He turned off the leaf blower. "Calm down."

"No. I'm not going to calm down. I told you when we were at the beach that I wanted full disclosure when it came to her. And here we are less than three months later having the exact same conversation."

"It was nothing. I knew it would upset you, and I didn't want to ruin an evening by having to discuss it."

"You shouldn't base what you tell me on whether it will upset me or not," she fumed, her hands propped on her hips as she glared at him.

"I was trying to protect you."

"It's too late! You already brought her into our lives. You can't undo it! I'm your wife, Phil, not your child. I don't want you to pick and choose what you share with me based on what you think will or won't upset me, especially when it comes to her. I had let my guard down, assuming incorrectly, obviously, that she wasn't still trying to steal my husband. You trying to protect me makes me more vulnerable, not less."

Chapter Twenty-two

"**D**ad!" Megan launched herself into Phil's arms when he arrived home from work the day before Thanksgiving. Tall and striking, Megan was a female version of Phil. Her chestnut eyes were the only physical attribute she'd inherited from Lina.

Phil returned her hug, pressing his lips into her cheek. "Hi, sweetie. Traffic okay?"

"Yes. It took a little under four hours."

"Dad!" Katie screeched, mimicking Megan's greeting. "What are you, like, ten?"

"Katie," Phil warned.

"What? She hurts my ears. Where's Liam? It's Wednesday."

"His mother has him for the Thanksgiving holiday, which includes today." He had no idea what Kim's plans were but assumed she'd go up to New York to visit her parents.

"I thought I was going to get to meet him," Megan said.

"You're home for almost a month for Christmas. You'll meet him then. Where's Mom?"

"She hasn't gotten home from work yet," Katie answered, not looking up from the book she was reading at the table.

"Do you want to go for a run before it gets dark?" Megan asked. "I've been training for a 10K. It's for autism awareness. Maybe your firm could sponsor me."

"Sure, or Mom and I could. Let me change into my running clothes. I'll meet you down here in ten minutes. How about you?" he asked as he paused behind Katie's chair. "Why don't you run with us?" He tugged on her ponytail.

"Stop." She swatted at his hand. "Do you really think I'd willingly spend time with either of you?"

He gave her ponytail another tug. "I love you, too."

"If you loved me, you'd let Matt come to Thanksgiving."

"He has a grandmother." He'd said no when she asked him days earlier if she could bring Matt to the family Thanksgiving at his brother's.

"She's working at five. He won't leave her until—"

"We're not rehashing this," he interrupted. "I told you just family."

"Grandma said you and Mom spent every Thanksgiving together from the time you met—that you'd go from her house to your house."

"That's because your grandparents are nicer than I am," he said.

Lina still wasn't home when Phil and Megan returned from their six-mile run, not an hour later when he came up from the basement after lifting weights, nor when he joined the kids in the family room fresh from a shower.

"She's stuck in traffic," Logan said. "She said to tell you to order in. She still needs to go by the grocery store to get stuff to make pies for tomorrow."

Phil plowed his fingers through his damp hair. He'd told her traffic would be heavier on the Wednesday before Thanksgiving and that she shouldn't go in, but she'd insisted she'd be fine, that she was going in for an early meeting and would be on the road before noon. Now it was almost seven and there was no sign of her.

"What time is she going to be home?"

"It sounded like a while. She was still in Virginia."

"Virginia?" Phil frowned. "What is she doing in Virginia?"

"I don't know. She tried to call you, but you didn't answer. Her phone was dying, and she couldn't find her charger."

It was only Wednesday, and it was the second night that week they were ordering in. She'd worked late Monday as well. "Katie, why don't you take Logan and go pick up Chinese?"

"Ask Megan. I'm not the only one here with a license."

"I'm not asking Megan. I'm telling you."

"I don't mind, Dad," Megan said. "It will give me a chance to catch up with my little brother."

They were halfway through dinner when Lina arrived home balancing several bags of groceries, a briefcase, and her purse as she came out of the mudroom into the kitchen. Both Phil and Logan sprang to their feet to help her.

"What a day. I'm sorry." She gave Phil a quick kiss as he removed the groceries from her arms. "I had no idea that they had this entire Thanksgiving luncheon planned at our northern Virginia office." She let Logan take her briefcase and purse. "Thanks, honey."

"Hi, Mom." Megan came from the table to give her a warm hug. "Wow, you look like a real businesswoman."

She is a real businesswoman, Phil thought. She had the work schedule and paycheck to prove it. As he poured her a glass of wine, he thought of all the times she'd handed him a beer or a glass of scotch when he returned home from work over the years.

"Here you go, baby." He touched her back as he came up beside her with the glass.

"That is just what I need. Thank you." She leaned back into him.

"Hungry?" He stroked his hand over her hip.

"No, but I'll sit with everyone while you finish."

"How much do you make?" Megan asked after they were seated at the table.

"That's not an appropriate question," Phil said.

"One hundred and twenty-five thousand," Katie answered. "What?" She looked from her dad to her mom. "You shouldn't have left your offer letter lying around if you didn't want people to read it."

"That sounds like a lot," Megan said. "A guy I know who graduated from the engineering school is starting at eighty thousand."

"It is a lot," Phil said. "Mom has a unique talent."

"It's decorating," Megan scoffed. "Anyone can do that."

"That's true," Lina said with an amused smile. "I'm as dumbfounded as you, Megan."

"I'm not," Phil said, frowning at Megan. "Your mom has a degree in interior design, and she's good at it."

"I was just saying that it's not hard, like engineering or being a lawyer."

221

"It takes talent and hard work to be the best at anything," Phil said. "Someone recognized your mother's talent and is willing to pay for it. Don't belittle it."

Phil was still annoyed by Megan's comment when dinner was over, so he took her into the dining room to speak to her alone. "Don't do that again."

"What?" Her eyes widened.

"Demean your mother's accomplishments."

"I wasn't," she said, her face heating.

"Yes, that's exactly what you were doing. Your mother has been studying decorating trends for the past twenty years. Positions like this don't just happen. She's good at what she does. You should be congratulating her."

"Sorry."

"Don't do it again."

"I won't. I'm sorry."

"Okay." He pulled her in for a hug. "I'm not mad. I just want you to be supportive of your mom." He kissed the top of her head. "Let's go into the family room. I think Logan wants to watch a movie."

Three hours later, as the credits rolled up on the television screen, Phil discovered that he was the only one in the family room still awake. He'd told them they wouldn't be able to make it through a second movie, but Logan had insisted and the rest of them had given in. Now they were all asleep. Logan and Katie were under a blanket on the love seat, Lina was curled into the corner of the oversized chair, and Megan was beside him. His eyes lingered on Lina. Her head was tilted to the side, resting on her hands, which were pressed together as if she were praying. She looked graceful and classy even in sleep. They'd officially been back together longer than they'd been apart. He thanked God every day for bringing her back to him.

They'd spent last Thanksgiving apart. Lina had insisted he take the kids to his brother's because that was their tradition and she wanted to give the children as much normalcy as she could, knowing their lives were in an uproar due to the separation. The only problem was that Lina was central to that tradition. Phil's memory of that day was one of gut-wrenching sadness. He'd missed her to the point of physical pain. He'd thought of her as they played their annual touch-football game, remembering how he'd always made her play on the opposing team so he had an excuse to touch her, playfully tackling her to the ground whenever she had the ball. He'd thought of her as they watched the Macy's Thanksgiving Day Parade, remembering how she'd scold him when he inevitably complained because it was so fucking boring. He'd passed on the traditional family-versus-family game of charades, unable to even attempt to go through the motions without Lina. But the worst part of the day had been when his sister-in-law, Jeanie, had handed him an empty dinner plate. Lina had been preparing his Thanksgiving plate since he was sixteen and she'd witnessed him eating his turkey, stuffing, and cranberry sauce separately. She'd said there was an art to layering the three on your plate and insisted on doing it for him. She'd done it for him that first year and the next twenty-five. When he'd held the empty plate the year before, he'd been consumed by a profound loss. He couldn't bring himself to fill it. He'd told Jeanie his stomach was bothering him and inwardly knew that if Lina didn't take him back, he'd never be able to partake in a Thanksgiving feast again.

Phil's phone lit up on the coffee table with a new text message. He carefully shifted Megan's head from his chest so he could lean forward to retrieve it. He knew before he lifted the phone it was going to be Kim. No one else would be texting him at 1:45 in the morning.

Kim: *I'm at the pediatric emergency room at Howard General Hospital. He has a fever of over 105.*

Phil's hand tightened on the phone. A high fever wasn't always serious. His gaze shifted back to Lina. He wasn't leaving her, not on Thanksgiving. *Let me know how it goes,* he texted back.

As he knew it would, his phone lit up with an incoming call. He immediately declined it. Within seconds he received another text.

Kim: *Your son is in the emergency room. You told me to contact you if this ever happened. I would think you'd want to be there.*

Phil: *I'm sure you have it under control. Let me know what the doctor says*

He darkened the screen and slipped the phone into his pocket, ignoring the vibration of new text messages as he woke Megan, Logan, and Katie, quietly ushering them out of the room so they wouldn't disturb Lina.

He pulled his coat from the hall closet, opened the front door, and followed Knight outside. He walked twenty yards down the driveway before taking his phone from his pocket. There were two missed calls and several text messages. He began to swipe his thumb over the display, scanning the messages. She was waiting to see a doctor. Liam's temperature was 105.5. When the phone vibrated in his hand, he glanced toward the front of the house before bringing it to his ear.

"Yes?"

"Your son is in the hospital and you're ignoring my calls?"

"Has he seen a doctor?"

"No. I'm in a waiting room."

"Then why are you calling me? I told you to let me know what the doctor says."

"I'm calling you because you're his father and I'm sick with worry. Your son is almost lethargic he's so sick and you're what? Too busy to be bothered?"

"There's nothing I can do."

"You're his father. He's scared and upset. You should be here."

"If he's scared and upset," he bit out, "you should be comforting him instead of talking to me. My presence isn't necessary. Let me know what the doctor says." He ended the call, stuffing the cell phone into his pocket, where it immediately began vibrating again.

He took a deep breath, staring up at the star-filled sky. It had been ten minutes since her first text and they still hadn't examined him. The triage nurse clearly didn't believe he was in any type of danger.

***

Lina was alone in the family room when she woke up. It took her a moment to remember they'd been watching a movie. After turning off the television, she padded down the hall toward the front of the house.

She was preparing to go upstairs when she noticed the floodlights illuminating the front yard and Phil and Knight midway down the drive. She stepped out onto the front porch, wrapping her arms around herself when she was hit by a gust of cold air. It took her only a moment to realize Phil was on the phone, his deep voice penetrating the night air.

"My presence isn't necessary. Let me know what the doctor says," was all she heard before he ended the call.

She watched him slip his hand into his pocket and tilt his head slightly back. She had no doubt that it had been Kim on the other end of the line, trying to insert herself into their Thanksgiving. "Phil?" she called out after a full minute passed.

He turned at the sound of her voice. "Baby, it's freezing out here." He began to walk toward her, his long athletic strides quickly covering the ground. "You shouldn't be outside without a coat." He stepped around her and opened the front door. "Come on." He placed his hand on the small of her back and followed her and Knight inside.

"What did she want? What's the emergency?" She could see the strain in his face.

"I took care of it. Let's just go to bed." He turned away from her to shrug out of his coat. "It's almost two thirty."

"Tell me." She took his hand when he turned from the closet, cupping it between both of hers to warm his cold skin. "How long were you out there?"

"Not long."

"Come on." She led him into the living room and pulled him down onto the love seat. "No secrets, remember?"

"It's Thanksgiving, Lina." He squeezed her hand. "I don't want her to be part of our Thanksgiving."

"She already is. You're upset. Tell me what she said."

Lina listened as he recounted the details of the earlier text messages and the phone conversation, trailing her fingers over the back of his hand as she processed his words.

"Did the doctor tell her to go to the emergency room? It sounds kind of drastic. Katie used to get fevers that high all the time until we had tubes put in her ears, remember?"

"Vaguely. You think it's an ear infection?"

226

"Probably. I wonder if she gave him Motrin or Tylenol for the fever. I wouldn't put it past her to leave it untreated so she could take him to the hospital."

"Jesus." He made a pained expression. "I hope she wouldn't do that to him."

"Call her and tell her you want to talk to the doctor."

"The doctor?" He frowned.

"We can't take her at her word. It's a reasonable request. If she won't let you it's because she's bluffing and trying to manipulate you. Call her." She wasn't letting Kim manipulate him.

When he began to stand up, Lina gripped his hand. "No, here." She could see his internal struggle. "It's not going to upset me to hear you talk to her."

Phil lifted his cell phone to his ear, his gaze fixed forward. "Has the doctor seen him yet...? Well, when he gets there, I'd like you to call me...because I want to talk to him...or her. Jesus." He dragged his hand down his face. "Just call me so I can talk to the doctor...No, no, I'm not coming there unless a doctor tells me I need to...That's your choice." The side of his jaw began to clench and unclench as he listened to whatever Kim was saying. "I'm not debating this with you. If it's as serious as you're telling me, I want to hear it from a doctor...Then that's your decision." He ended the call.

"She's not going to let you talk to him," Lina guessed.

"I could hear Liam crying in the background. She should have been comforting him, not talking to me."

"She's trying to upset you."

He pressed his hands into his thighs, pushing himself to his feet. "It's late. I'm going to lock up and set the alarm."

"We can go if you want, to the hospital. I don't want you to worry about him all night."

227

"No. I think he's fine. Let's just go to bed."

Lina was almost asleep when Phil rolled over for what seemed like the tenth time since they'd gotten into bed an hour earlier. It was now three thirty. They were due at Jeanie and Mike's at ten. At this rate they weren't going to get any sleep.

"Call the hospital," she whispered, stroking her hand down his arm. "You're his father. They'll tell you what's going on." She wished she had thought of it earlier.

"Ear infection," he said, turning off the light five minutes later. "They sent him home with an antibiotic thirty minutes ago."

"Good." She curved her body into the side of his as he lay back on the bed. "He'll be fine." She pressed her lips into his shoulder.

"Katie used to get them?"

"Yes, at the same age. He'll be okay. I promise."

Twelve hours later, Lina was beside Phil at the dining room table at Mike and Jeanie's. Where Christmas was a joint holiday shared with Lina's family as well as Phil's, the tradition was to have a Hunter-only Thanksgiving at Phil's brother's house. After Mike finished saying Grace, Lina took Phil's plate to the buffet of food set up along the wall.

When Lina set the full plate in front of Phil moments later, he took her hand before she could walk away. "What's wrong?"

"Nothing."

She smiled. "Are you going to let my hand go so I can get something to eat?"

"Thank you for making my plate."

"Don't I always make your plate?"

"I want you to know I don't take it for granted."

The love coming from his eyes warmed her heart. He was talking about her, that he didn't take her for granted. "I know you don't." She leaned in and met his lips for a soft kiss.

As she dished up her own food her thoughts drifted to the Thanksgiving the year before. She hadn't celebrated it. She'd been alone, too sad to go to her mother's place. She gave a silent prayer of thanks for having her family back.

On the day after Thanksgiving Lina was up early. She wanted to get in an early yoga session. Megan, who was alone in the kitchen when Lina came downstairs, asked to join her.

"Of course," Lina said, feeling a stab of guilt for not thinking to invite her on her own.

While Lina was drinking coffee and waiting for Megan to change, Katie appeared dressed in leggings and a loose T-shirt. "I'm going to yoga."

"So are we," Lina said. "We can all drive together. Megan's just changing."

"I don't want to go with her," Katie said.

"Be nice," Lina said in a voice low enough not to be overheard. "She's home for less than four days."

"I'll just drive myself."

"That's silly," Lina said. "We're not taking two cars."

"Fine," Katie grumbled, walking toward the mudroom. "I get the front seat."

If Megan sensed Katie wasn't pleased with her presence, she didn't show it, chatting enthusiastically the entire five-minute drive about her classes, her sorority, and her overall college experience. "You're going to love it," she told Katie. "It's like being a real adult."

"Except you're not paying any of your own bills," Katie said. "Real adults support themselves."

229

"I have a scholarship. That pays a big portion of my expenses," Megan said. "Where are you applying?" she asked Katie as they got out of the car.

Katie shrugged. "I haven't decided."

"Do you know what you want to major in?"

"Philosophy."

"Have you looked at UVA?"

"I don't think I want to go that far away."

"It's only, like, four hours."

To Lina's delight they continued to talk as they made their way to the entrance of the yoga studio, sounding more like friends than the combatants that they normally resembled. She was disappointed but not surprised when Megan decided to do Power Yoga instead of the regular yoga she and Katie preferred.

"It's not enough of a workout," Megan said, sounding like Phil, who claimed yoga wasn't exercise. "If I do yours, I'll have to run later."

"She doesn't get that it's for your mind as much as your body," Katie complained as she rolled out her mat beside Lina's. "It isn't supposed to be a competition."

An hour later Lina followed Katie back out into the lobby, encompassed by the sense of well-being she almost always experienced after yoga. Megan, who indeed looked like she'd had a more intense workout, her face red from exertion, was chatting with a woman near the front doors.

"Can you sign me up for the full membership since you're here?" Katie asked.

"Yes, but are you sure you need the unlimited?" she asked as they headed to the front desk.

"Yes. I come every day."

"I know you do, but are you going to continue to when…?" Lina trailed off as her gaze focused on the woman standing beside Megan. It was Kim.

Chapter Twenty-three

"Let's go," Lina said to Katie.

"You just said you'd sign me up."

"I'll do it tomorrow."

"That doesn't make any sense. We're here now," Katie said, following her toward the entrance.

Megan noticed them when they were several yards away. "Mom, this is—"

"We have to get home," Lina interrupted, ignoring Kim completely as she reached for the door.

"Mom, she's friends with Dad. She recognized me from my picture in his office."

"She isn't friends with your father," Lina said in a surprisingly composed voice, considering her heart felt like it was beating at an alarming rate.

Megan frowned as she lifted the drink in her hand. "She bought me a smoothie. I owe her five dollars."

Lina stepped to Megan, took the smoothie from her hand, and shoved it into a nearby trash can. "Come on." She gripped Megan's arm, propelling her toward the door. "We have to get home to your father."

"What is wrong with you?" Megan asked as soon as they were all outside. "Why did you do that? I barely drank any of it."

Lina walked hurriedly through the parking lot, ignoring Megan's barrage of questions until they were in the car. "That was her."

"Who?" Megan asked.

"Liam's mother." She released a breath as she started the car.

"Liam's mother," Megan repeated in confusion. "Who's Liam?"

"Dad's Liam?" Katie asked from the back seat.

"Yes."

"But she's so young," Megan said.

Lina closed her eyes.

"She seemed nice," Megan continued.

"She isn't nice," Katie said. "She had an affair with Dad. She isn't nice."

"I didn't say she *was* nice. I said she *seemed* nice. What was she doing here anyway? Why was she at our yoga place?"

"I don't know." Lina put the car into drive and began maneuvering out of the parking spot.

"Are you okay to drive?" Megan asked. "Your hands are shaking."

"I'm fine. I was just—I was a little surprised to see you talking to her."

"I didn't know who she was," Megan said defensively. "I wouldn't have talked—"

"I know," Lina interrupted her, covering her hand. "It's not your fault."

***

Phil looked up from the newspaper when Logan shuffled into the kitchen, his eyes puffy with sleep.

"Can we get the tree today? Will's family puts theirs up the day after Thanksgiving every year."

"What's the rush?"

"We can have it longer. We can decorate the outside of the house today, too." He took a box of cereal from the pantry. "I can bring everything out of the basement. I'll do most of the work."

The sound of the garage door opening preceded the entrance of Megan, followed by Katie.

"We're going to get the tree today," Logan announced. "Do you want to come?"

"No," Megan answered, not pausing as she continued out of the room.

"Is she okay?" Phil asked Katie.

Katie shrugged, avoiding his eyes as she crossed to the pantry.

His attention turned to Lina as she entered the kitchen. "What's going on? Megan looked upset."

Lina's gaze shifted to Logan.

"What's wrong?" Phil asked as soon as they were in the mudroom with the door closed.

"Kim was there. At yoga. She was in Megan's class. She apparently recognized Megan from the pictures in your office."

Blood surged to his head. "She spoke to her?"

"Yes. I don't know—"

Phil snatched his keys from a hook beside the door and slammed into the garage, ignoring Lina's pleas to stop as he got in his car, started the engine, and drove away.

His anger only grew during the five-minute drive to Kim's. Both her assigned spots were taken, so he parked behind her Lexus, boxing her in. He was out of his car and jogging toward her door, completely immune to the fact that he was in shorts and a T-shirt when the air temperature was below thirty.

He was momentarily surprised when instead of Kim, a woman in her early thirties with blonde hair and a petite build answered the door. "Get Kim," he bit out, gripping the doorframe and putting his foot just inside the house so she couldn't close the door.

She held up her hands, taking a step backward. "I think you need to take a few deep breaths."

"Get. Kim," he repeated as he came into the house. "Now!"

"I don't know what she did, but you need to calm the fuck down because you're scaring the shit out of me. You're Phil, right?"

"This isn't a social call."

She held up her cell phone. "I don't want to, but I will call the police if you take another step."

A ball came rolling down the hallway, followed by the pitter-patter of feet and Liam's voice. "Ba...ba...ba."

"I'm Cammie, Kim's older sister. I'm not the enemy."

Liam came barreling into the foyer after the ball. His eyes widened when he saw Phil. "Dadda!" he squealed, ignoring the ball in favor of his father. "Dadda!" He wrapped his little arms around Phil's leg.

"Hey, buddy." Phil forced a smile he didn't feel as he lifted Liam into his arms.

"Dadda!" Liam said, looking at his aunt as he patted Phil's face.

"Yes, that's your daddy. I can see that."

"Ba," Liam said, pointing at the ball, which had stopped rolling and was resting near the door. He struggled to get down.

Phil set him on his feet, watching him scamper across the foyer to the ball. "Where's Kim?" he asked, doing his best to keep his anger in check.

"What did she do?"

Phil watched Liam pick up the ball and launch it haphazardly back down the hallway. "Ba," he shouted before chasing after it.

"Phil?" Kim halted halfway down the stairs. She was dressed in dark running tights and a hoodie, gloves dangling from one hand. "What are you doing here?"

The anger that had taken a minute hiatus was back in an instant. "You know exactly why I'm here." He launched himself up the stairs, taking them two at a time until he was in front of her, pointing his finger in her face. "You stay the fuck away from my wife," he snarled, spit spewing from his mouth. "You stay the fuck away from my children. You stay the fuck away from my house."

"Mama!" Liam's high-pitched wail penetrated Phil's ears and subconscious. Liam was climbing up the stairs, tears streaming from his eyes. "Mama!" He held his hand toward her.

"Oh my God." Cammie scooped him into her arms. "I didn't realize he was in here." She pulled him into her chest. "It's okay, Liam. Mommy's okay." She rushed him out of the foyer.

"I didn't know they went to that yoga studio."

"Stay. Away," he bit out.

236

"Believe it or not, I didn't choose to fall in love with you," Kim said, brushing a few stray tears from her cheek with the back of her hand. "It just happened."

"You don't know me enough to love me. We fucked for a few months, Kim. Get over it!" He turned and began descending the stairs.

"I bet your other children have never had to witness you talk to their mother like that."

"You're right," he agreed. "Because I respect their mother." He opened the door and left the house.

"You are such an asshole!" Kim cried as she ran out of the house behind him.

"You have no idea what an asshole I can be." He stopped when they reached his car, pointing his finger in her face once more. "Stay the fuck away from my wife!"

She met his eyes, her own swimming with tears. "I think I might hate you."

"Thank. God," he snarled. "You are *nothing* to me. Do you understand that? And I will do whatever it takes to protect my family. If that means destroying your career, I will. If you speak to them again, I'm filing a restraining order, and Hendrix, Wolff, and Pearson will know. Don't mess with me."

"I hate you," she whispered before jogging away.

As Phil lowered himself into the driver's seat of his car, his eyes focused on Kim's house. Guilt rocketed through him at the memory of Liam's distraught cry. Lina would never have left one of their children when they were in such a state. Kim had gone running.

When Phil stepped back into the foyer, he heard Liam's muffled cries coming from the back of the house. He found him in the kitchen, cradled in his aunt's arms, crying so hard he was hyperventilating, his little body jerking every few seconds. "Hey, buddy," he said softly, stroking his hand over Liam's sweat-drenched hair.

"Mama," Liam whimpered.

"It's okay." He took Liam from Cammie, pulling him into his body. "I'm sorry," he whispered against the side of his head, jiggling him as he crossed to the French doors overlooking a wooded lot. "Shh, shh." After a minute he felt Liam calming, the tears drying, but his body continued to jerk every few seconds, the aftermath of his hard cry. "Where's your ball? Do you want to show Daddy how hard you can throw it?"

"Ba," Liam said.

"Yeah, where's your ball?"

"Here." Cammie was beside them, holding out the ball.

"Ba," Liam said, his hand gripping the small red ball. He smiled.

Phil's heart tugged as he looked at his son's tear-swollen eyes. It was the second time in the past month he'd scared him. He wasn't going to let it happen again. "You want to show me how you can throw it?" He bent down to a knee, setting Liam on the floor beside him. "Go ahead. Throw it."

Liam threw it more up than out. Phil picked up the ball and placed his hand around the back of Liam's as he showed him the motion of a throw. "Like this. Throw it like this," he said, demonstrating again.

Liam launched the ball across the room.

"Wow!" Cammie clapped her hands. "That was awesome, Liam."

Liam smiled and clapped for himself before running after the ball.

Phil came to his feet. He rubbed his hand over the back of his neck, kneading the tight muscles. "I'm sorry. I could have handled that better."

"You're right. You could have. The intensity you came in here with would be scary coming from a small man. You're not a small man."

"No," he agreed.

"Dadda!" Liam yelled, his arm held back.

"I'm watching, buddy. Go ahead." He smiled when Liam again made a perfectly executed throw. "Good job."

"Where's Kim?" Cammie asked.

"Running," Phil answered. "Tell me something. Are there mental issues in your family I should be aware of?"

"No." Cammie laughed. "She isn't crazy, but she is used to getting what she wants. She wanted and still wants you. You're definitely the first guy to ever break up with her."

"Breaking up with implies a relationship. I had a fling with your sister."

"In your mind maybe, but in hers it was a relationship. Before she even started working at your firm, she told me you were the man she was going to marry."

"Before?" He frowned in confusion. "I wasn't even the partner interviewing her. I barely spoke to her."

"She watched you give a closing argument up in New York. You were defending a pharmaceutical executive, I think she said. She thought you were mesmerizing. She updated her résumé and sent it to your firm within a week. She took a significant salary cut leaving her firm in New York to go down to Baltimore. We were all shocked. She graduated first in her law class at Columbia. She was on the fast track to make partner."

"Are you saying your sister came to Baltimore for me?"

"Yes."

She'd come to Baltimore for him. Phil's hands tightened on the steering wheel on his drive home. He had no doubt now that she'd gotten pregnant on purpose. For someone who prided himself on his ability to read others, he'd certainly missed all the ques with Kim. He'd even believed her when she'd told him it was a coincidence that she'd joined the same Saturday morning running group. They'd had limited interactions there, but he'd left with her when they were done. Fuck. No wonder people from the running group started assuming they were a couple. Everything was so clear now. He'd been a fucking idiot. He had no one to blame but himself.

Chapter Twenty-four

The kitchen was in breakfast mode when Phil returned home. Katie was pouring herself a cup of coffee, Lina was at the stove, and Logan was sitting at the kitchen island.

"I brought up the Christmas boxes," Logan said. "I wasn't sure which lights were for the outside of the house. Do you want to come look so I can get started?"

Phil didn't. He wanted to talk to Lina, who was watching him with an equal mixture of annoyance and relief in her eyes. "Let me just grab a slice of bacon first." He crossed to Lina, cupping the side of her hip with one hand while he reached around her with the other to snatch a piece of bacon from a plate beside the stove. "I'm sorry," he whispered in her ear. "I couldn't just ignore what she did."

"You could have long enough to talk to me," she said, continuing to poke at the bacon in the skillet.

"I was angry."

"Which is exactly why you should have waited a few minutes. You were in no condition to drive. You could have—"

"Dad?" Logan interrupted. "Are you coming?"

"Yes," Lina answered for him. "And make sure you go talk to Megan when you're done," she whispered for his ears only.

Phil lightly tapped his knuckles against Megan's door a short time later. "Sweetheart, it's Dad. May I come in?"

The click of the lock releasing preceded a light "okay." Phil entered the room to find Megan lying on her bed, still in her yoga attire, curled on her side, facing the wall. "Hey." He sat down on the edge of her mattress. "Are you okay?"

"Yes. I'm just tired."

"Megan?" He gently squeezed her shoulder. "Talk to me, sweetheart. Are you upset? Mom told me what happened."

"I don't think I really want to talk about it, Dad."

"I need to know what she said to you."

"Nothing. It was just a normal conversation. She said she was a lawyer and that she had worked with you and that you were brilliant or mesmerizing or something like that. I don't remember exactly."

"What did she say to upset you?"

"Nothing."

"She must have said something. You're clearly upset."

"I just...I...I didn't expect her to look like that...to be so much younger than Mom." She turned her face into her pillow.

He hadn't seen her cry since she was thirteen and her team lost the middle school lacrosse championship. She was never a child that cried easily. "Megan? Look at me. Tell me what's going on." He clasped her shoulder and slowly rolled her onto her back. The pain in the tear-filled eyes looking up at him tore at his heart. "Sweetheart?"

"It wasn't real," she whispered. "Until I saw her, what you did wasn't real." She wiped at her eyes. "How could you do that? How could you be with someone besides Mom?"

He hesitated, trying to think of a sufficient answer, but of course there wasn't one. "I messed up," he finally said.

"Like Carrie's dad," she whispered, referring to one of her friends whose father left her mother for a younger woman. "I remember thinking you would never do something like that, and now you have."

"No. I didn't leave. I would never leave Mom."

"But you were with that Kim! You got her pregnant and she had your baby." She slapped her hands over her eyes. "How could you have done that?" she cried. "How?"

Phil squeezed his forehead. "There's no excuse, no way to justify what I did. And I have to live with that knowledge, that I hurt your mother and you kids. It kills me that I've disappointed you. But I will tell you this. For the rest of my life I'm going to try to make it up to your mother. That's all I can do—atone for my sins."

***

Lina was in the living room in the front of the house, sorting through the Christmas boxes with Logan, when Phil came down the stairs. As soon as she saw the stern expression on his face, she knew something was wrong.

"What happened?"

"She's just upset. You should talk to her."

"Hey, Dad? Look." Logan held up a five-foot grinch. "It's to put in the front yard next to one of the trees. Mom bought this last year. We haven't used it yet."

"That's great, buddy," Phil said, barely glancing at Logan. "I need to exercise. Then I can help you."

243

"Phil—wait." Lina followed him to the door leading down to the basement. "What did she say?"

"Nothing I didn't deserve. Don't worry about me. Worry about her."

"Honey, are you okay?" Lina asked moments later, stepping into Megan's room.

"No," Megan whispered before collapsing in Lina's arms.

"Oh, sweetie." Lina led her to her bed, her heart aching for Megan, who had always been a daddy's girl. Almost from the day Lina stopped nursing her, Megan had preferred Phil. If he was home, he was the parent Megan sought out to fix a booboo, read her a bedtime story, or make her feel safe after a bad dream. Lina used to worry she was somehow deficient in the nurturing department until Katie came along. Katie loved Phil, but like most young children, she preferred her mother. Over the years Lina came to accept that Megan just shared a special bond with Phil.

Now with that same daughter crying in her arms, Lina wasn't sure what to do, so she settled on what felt the most natural, stroking her hand up and down Megan's back and assuring her that everything was going to be okay.

"I'm sorry," Megan whispered after several minutes.

"I'm your mother. You don't have to apologize for being emotional."

"No. I don't mean about that. I mean about not being there for you, not understanding what you were feeling."

She was talking about her reaction to Phil's affair more than a year ago. "No." Lina shook her head. "Megan, no. You're just a girl. It isn't your job to comfort me. You didn't do anything wrong." She pulled her in for a hug, squeezing her tightly. "You're not supposed to know how to handle a situation like this. I hate that you have to even think about it."

"I just didn't understand until I saw her," Megan whispered. "How could he have done that to you?"

"It was wrong. There's nothing that can justify it. But I know how sorry he is, how much he loves all of us."

"I wouldn't have talked to her if I had known who she was. I hate that I was nice to her."

Lina framed her face with her hands. "It wasn't your fault. You had no way of knowing who she was."

Lina felt like an actress, playing the part of a happy mother as she finished going through the boxes with Logan, unable to shake the sadness that enveloped her after her words with Megan. Megan seemed to have recovered, announcing that she was meeting friends for lunch and even giving her father a hug when he came downstairs after his shower. It was as if Megan's sadness had been a cloak that she'd passed to Lina.

"Are you okay, Mom?"

Lina spun around, her hand touching her chest. "Logan. I didn't hear you come in. Are you already done putting up the lights?"

"No." He shook his head. "I came in to get a heavier coat. Are you okay?"

"Yes." She forced a smile. "Just a little tired. Someone made me stay up and watch *Christmas Vacation* last night," she teased.

"Katie just told me that woman was there—at yoga. Liam's mom."

"She was." She turned back to the bowl of cookie dough she was mixing.

"Do you need a hug?"

The unexpected question brought tears to her eyes. She blinked them away, forcing a smile to her face as she turned from her task and let her fifteen-year-old son wrap her in his arms, offering her a dose of much-needed comfort. "I could never turn down a hug from you," she whispered.

"I lost it when I went over there today. It was in front of Liam. He was pretty shaken up," Phil told Lina later that evening as they sat alone in the family room discussing what had occurred with Kim.

Lina's stomach sank, imagining how scary an enraged Phil would be to a baby. She couldn't remember him ever yelling around their children when they were young. "Was he okay?"

"Eventually. She never went to him. She just left him for her sister to deal with. He was calling out for her. I can't get that fucking vision of him out of my head, his face distraught and his little hands reaching out to her. And she just left." He shook his head. "What in the fuck did I do, Lina? That's his mother. She didn't even seem to care."

"She was upset," she said, more to soothe Phil's obvious distress than to defend Kim. "It may not have even registered in her mind."

"It would have registered in your mind. It registered in mine." He leaned his head back, pushing the heels of his hands into his eyes. "I can't do that to him again. I don't want to scar him."

"You won't." She rubbed his arm. "One time isn't going to scar him. He'll be okay." Her thoughts turned to Kim, wondering what kind of person wouldn't immediately comfort their child.

Chapter Twenty-five

O ver the next few weeks, Phil saw nothing of Kim. The nanny was there to handle both his pickups and drop offs. Kim seemed to finally understand that he had no interest in any type of relationship with her. The result seemed to be that she was spending less time with Liam. The nanny had billed him over seventy hours each of the past two weeks.

He was also no longer receiving daily pictures or occasional updates about Liam. Now with no contact between visits, Phil found himself missing Liam more. He'd decided after the holidays he was going to speak to Lina about bringing Liam to the house two nights a week instead of the current one-night schedule. He needed more time with him.

When he arrived to pick him up for his usual Wednesday night visit, he was surprised when Kim answered his knock. He'd sent both her and the babysitter a text, as was his habit, giving her a ten-minute warning of his impending arrival. The nanny normally had him at the door and ready.

"Come on in," she said, stepping back.

"Where is he?"

"In the family room."

He brushed past her and into the foyer. "You knew what time I was coming. You should have had him ready."

"I'm Liam's mother, Phil," Kim said, practically running to keep up with him as his long strides took him in the direction of the family room at the back of the house. "You can at least be civil to me."

"Maybe if you started acting like his mother and didn't leave him with a fucking babysitter eighty hours a week, I'd treat you civilly. Hey, buddy." He smiled as soon as he saw Liam who was lying on his back in the middle of the playpen, twirling a plastic pony in his hands.

Liam immediately lost interest in the toy when he saw his father, grabbing the side of the playpen as he scampered to his feet. "Dadda!"

Phil could smell the dirty diaper even before he lifted Liam from the playpen. He held him out to Kim. "Christ," he said under his breath. "Just hurry. I only have two hours. I don't want to spend it here."

"Why are you so stuck on time? I'm not. Keep him for three if you'd like." She laid out a changing pad on the floor and took Liam.

"Dadda!" Liam protested, holding his arms out to Phil.

"Daddy isn't leaving. I just need to change your diaper." Kim said. "There's a cute video I took of him yesterday if you want to watch it. It's on my phone, right there." She nodded toward her phone on the coffee table.

"I'm good." He shoved his hands into his coat pockets.

"It's just a video, Phil."

"Just change his fucking diaper so I can get out of here," he bit out.

Her whole body tensed up. "I don't know why you have to be so hostile."

"I told you I was picking him up at six ten. It's now six fifteen and you seem in no hurry to get him ready. I'm not here to interact with you."

She changed the diaper, put Liam in his winter coat, and silently handed him to Phil.

***

The venue for the holiday party was the ballroom at the Four Seasons in Baltimore. Phil wanted to make a day of it, getting down there early to stroll through shops and walk around the Inner Harbor. At first Lina resisted, not wanting to leave Megan, who had arrived home from college the evening before, but Phil was insistent, pointing out how seldom they had the opportunity to be alone.

When they arrived in their suite they were greeted by champagne and chocolate-covered strawberries. "Are you sure you want to leave the hotel?" Lina asked. She loved the Inner Harbor, but she couldn't imagine leaving the luxurious room to walk around outside on a cold December day.

"No." He was behind her, wrapping his arms around her. "Let's order room service."

Lina's entire body hummed with the aftermath of sex. They'd spent the entire afternoon in bed or in the large bathtub in their suite. It wasn't until she was dressed and applying the final touches to her makeup that nerves began to flutter around her stomach. She and Phil may have been back together for eight months, but it was the first time they were making an appearance in front of his entire firm since they'd reconciled. There was no doubt in her mind that every associate at the firm knew Phil had fathered a child with Kim.

"Okay?" Phil raised an eyebrow after coming out of the bathroom to find her making herself a drink at the minibar.

"I'm just thirsty." She lifted the gin and tonic to her lips and took several long swallows. "Very thirsty," she added before downing the rest of the drink.

"What's going on?"

"Nerves. I don't like the thought of people talking about us."

His eyes registered understanding. "We're old news. Josh Keating left his wife for the nanny. He's bringing her tonight."

"No!" Lina gasped. "He left Helen?" Josh Keating had been at the firm almost as long as Phil, and they'd attended his and Helen's wedding a decade earlier.

"He did."

"And he's bringing the nanny? That's awful."

"And that's what everyone's talking about." He took the empty glass from her hand, setting it on the minibar. "Ready?"

"Did you hear about Josh and Helen?" Diane snagged Lina almost as soon as they arrived. "He actually brought the other woman with him tonight. Wayne told me on the way over. It's been less than a month."

"I just heard," Lina said. "Poor Helen." As soon as the words left her mouth her thoughts shifted inward, knowing a year ago everyone was feeling the same pity toward her. She hated the thought. "Where's Wayne?"

"Oh, who knows? Probably talking the ear off of some terribly important client." She paused to take a crab ball appetizer from a passing waiter. "I shouldn't eat this. I promised myself I'd be good tonight."

"Why would you choose tonight to be good? Wait until after the New Year."

"Easy for you to say. I'd be eating more than one of these if I had your slim figure. You look fabulous, by the way. When you and Phil walked in every head turned in your direction."

"That's probably because they were feeling sorry for me." Lina finished the champagne in her glass. "I'm last year's Helen."

"Nonsense. You're too beautiful to be pitied. You could have any man you want. Let's find you another glass of champagne."

***

Phil looked up from his newspaper at the sound of Lina stirring in the hotel bed. It was almost noon. She was going to have a nasty hangover. She couldn't mix alcohols, especially when champagne was involved, and she'd done exactly that the night before. The last time was a New Year's Eve when the kids were all young. She'd been in bed for two days, severely hungover, swearing she'd never drink again.

"What is that noise?" She groaned.

"I don't hear a noise."

"It's your newspaper. Why can't you read on your cell phone?"

He folded the paper and set it on the table next to the remnants of the breakfast he'd ordered from room service three hours earlier. "There are two aspirin and a glass of water on the nightstand."

"Shh…Why are you yelling?"

"I didn't realize I was." He came to his feet. "Would you like some coffee?"

"No. Would you mind whispering? I don't think you know how to talk in a low voice."

"I'm sorry."

"You're not whispering. Please tell me I didn't embarrass us last night."

"You didn't embarrass us," he whispered.

"What?"

He crossed to the bed. The mattress shifted as he sat down beside her. "You didn't embarrass us," he whispered.

"I didn't?"

"No." He gently pushed her hair back from her face. She looked pale, nothing like the woman who'd danced until the wee hours of the morning. "You were the life of the party."

"I feel terrible. I'm never drinking again."

"Take the aspirin. They'll make you feel better. I arranged for late checkout, so there's no rush." He'd stopped whispering, but she didn't seem to notice.

"Did we leave the hotel last night?"

"We did. When the party ended at midnight, you joined several of the associates who knew all the hot nightspots. Luckily, you let me tag along."

"Oh God. We went barhopping with your associates?"

"Is that a question, or are you starting to remember?"

"I'm remembering. I'm sorry." She'd gone from irritable to remorseful.

"There's nothing to be sorry about. You're allowed to have fun."

"But your clients were there, and I know you see these things more as business events. I was a liability last night."

"No. You were happy. And you didn't really get started until after we left the hotel."

"Did I get on a stage at some point?"

"You did." He smiled at the memory of her joining the band at one of the bars.

She rolled away from him, groaning aloud. "I acted like Adele."

"No, it was all you. It reminded me of that time you got up onstage at Rehoboth Beach, remember?" They'd been watching a concert as part of a Fourth of July celebration and she'd decided to join in, managing to skirt security and climb on the stage in her black bikini. He remembered thinking he was the luckiest guy in the world as he watched her dancing with the band.

"I was a sixteen-year-old girl, not a forty-two-year-old mother of three. And in front of your associates—it's so embarrassing. I can't imagine what they're thinking today."

"They're thinking I have a smoking-hot wife. That's what they're thinking." He stretched out on the bed beside her, curling his body to the back of hers. "You have nothing to be embarrassed about. You were letting off steam. You were incredible." He brushed his lips over the back of her shoulder. "I couldn't wait to get you back here."

"I don't remember—"

"We didn't. You fell asleep on me."

"What are you doing?" she asked when he began to push himself against her butt.

Phil smiled against her shoulder. "I'll do all the work."

"No!" She scooted across the bed to get away from him. "I feel like I might throw up and you're talking about having sex with me."

"Come back here. I'm teasing you." He again situated himself behind her.

"It's not funny."

"I'm sorry."

***

Lina felt like the worst mother and daughter-in-law on the face of the earth. Instead of spending time with her daughter who had just arrived home from college or her in-laws, who were visiting for the first time in a year, she'd been in bed recovering from the worst hangover of her life. What made matters worse was that she'd let everyone believe she was suffering from the stomach flu, which resulted in her mother-in-law fussing over her and lavishing her with attention she didn't want or deserve.

"Here's a fresh cup of ice chips," Susan Hunter said as she came into the master suite for the third time that afternoon. "I've also brought some Gatorade. I know you said you didn't want any, but it's important to stay hydrated. You'll feel better if you just take a little sip every five minutes or so. I found some crackers in the pantry. I used to give the boys saltines, but all you had was this whole wheat brand. It may be a little harder on your stomach—"

"Mom? What are you doing in here?" Phil asked, coming through the doorway.

"I was bringing her a few things."

"What she needs is sleep."

"It's important she stay hydrated. A lot of people end up in the emergency room with the stomach flu because of dehydration. You look very pale. Have you taken your temperature?"

"No, because I'm actually feeling better," Lina lied.

"I've scrubbed down all the bathrooms and the kitchen with Clorox. These flus are quite contagious. It would be awful for the children to come down with it on Christmas."

"I wish you had let Phil do that," Lina said, looking pointedly at him.

"I didn't mind. It's not like anything is dirty. Your house is always so—"

"Mom," Phil interrupted, curving his arm around her shoulders. "Let's let Lina sleep. Come on." He steered her toward the door.

"Mom? Mom, are you awake? Mom?"

Lina awoke with a start, looking up at Logan, who was standing beside the bed. "Logan?"

"Are you awake?"

If it weren't for her headache and the fact that he looked so serious she may have laughed at the absurdity of his question. "Yes. What's wrong?" She held out her hand.

He jumped back before she touched him. "Grandma said you're contagious."

"No. I promise you I'm not contagious." She patted the mattress. "Come and sit. I don't want to have to look up that far."

He sat down beside her but kept his hands firmly in his lap. "Do you think it would be weird if I gave Tiffany a Christmas gift? Brian and Will said I'll look lame if I give her something since we aren't, like, official or anything."

"I don't think that's true. If you want to give her something, give her something. You really like this girl?"

He nodded. "Yeah."

"Nothing too expensive, but something small would be fine."

"Like a necklace?"

"A necklace sounds nice. You could check with your sisters. I'm sure they would help you pick something out."

"I already picked it out. I just wanted to make sure it was okay to give her something."

"Do you have a picture of it?"

He stood up and removed his phone from his pocket. "If I order it by five o'clock today, they'll deliver it to her on Christmas Eve. For ten extra dollars they'll gift wrap it."

Lina looked at the image of a silver wire heart pendant hanging from a simple chain. "Oh, I like it."

"I thought it was better than the lockets or the ones with the fake diamonds."

"It's beautiful. She's obviously very special."

"Do you want to see her picture?"

"I do." Moments later she was looking at a picture of the girl who seemed to be capturing her son's heart. There was no question she was attractive with her heart-shaped face and large green eyes, but she wasn't as innocent looking as Lina had expected. The pose in the photo, from her head tilt to the slight pucker to her lips, was obviously perfected in a mirror.

"What's the matter?"

Lina replaced her frown with a smile. "Nothing. I'm just having a hard time focusing. She's very pretty."

"Yeah," he agreed, smiling down at his phone.

"I don't like her," Lina told Phil when he came into their bedroom in the early evening. "She's too old for him and she looks"—she paused as she tried to think of the right word—"shallow. Like one of those girls who giggle just to get attention."

He raised an eyebrow. "All this from a picture?"

"Yes." She knew she sounded shallow herself, but she didn't care.

"Imagine how you're going to feel when you come home one day to find her groping him in the pool, tattoos covering one of her arms. Oh wait." He smirked. "I think I'm getting confused. That was me meeting Matt for the first time."

"It's not funny."

"Oh, I know. Believe me."

"You like Matt."

"I tolerate him," Phil corrected. "Because you make me."

"That's not true. You like him. You just won't let yourself admit it because you're too pig-headed."

"How come you always resort to name calling when you're losing an argument?" He approached the bed.

"I resort to name calling because you're frustrating to talk to sometimes. And I'm not losing this argument. That's your overinflated ego talking, because it can't handle losing."

He pressed his knee onto the mattress as he leaned over her, placing his hands on the pillow on either side of her head. "There you go again."

"Are you trying to intimidate me?" she asked, looking up into his eyes, which were inches from hers.

"Why? Am I?"

"No." She laid her palms flat on his chest. "I still feel sick."

"Are you trying to tell me you're unwilling to fulfill your wifely duties?"

"Phillip," his mother scolded, surprising them both with her sudden presence. "She's sick and in all likelihood contagious."

"Mom, do you mind?" he asked, continuing to stare down at Lina. "We're not teenagers."

"You're certainly acting like one." She paused beside the bed, balancing a tray. "I made Lina some broth."

Phil pushed off the bed, coming to his feet. "Happy?" he asked his mother.

"I will be after you wash your hands." She nodded toward the bathroom.

Lina stifled a smile as she watched him follow his mother's orders. It was as if they were sixteen and seventeen again and living in his parents' house. His parents had allowed them to share a room—Lina had been too afraid to be alone—but they'd insisted on having unfettered access, regularly entering their room without warning to deter them from engaging in what his Catholic parents referred to as immoral behavior.

"How are you feeling, dear?"

"Better. Just a little tired."

"Do you think you can keep down some broth?"

"I think so."

Phil emerged from the bathroom. "All clean." He walked over to the bed, leaned down, and dropped a hard kiss on Lina's mouth before winking at his stunned mother and leaving the room.

"Why does he want to be sick?" Mrs. Hunter asked.

"I don't have the flu," Lina said. "It was something I ate or drank. Several people from the party are feeling the same way I am." It wasn't exactly a lie, Lina decided, figuring at least a few others had to have hangovers.

"That's awful. You'd think a hotel of that caliber would be more careful."

"You can just set that on the dresser," Lina said. "I'm not quite ready for it yet."

Mrs. Hunter complied, and then instead of leaving, she lingered. "Oh, would you look at that." She picked up the photo on the nightstand of Lina and Phil as teenagers. It was taken at the beach. Lina was sitting on his lap and he had his arms wrapped loosely around her with his chin resting on her shoulder. "The two of you haven't changed a bit."

"I think we've changed a little."

"Not really." She stared at the photograph for several more seconds before replacing it. "I'm so happy you were able to find it in your heart to forgive him. He was lost without you. A big part of who he is is tied into you. He thinks of himself as your protector. It's been that way since he saved you and Shiloh. Anything other than the two of you together felt so wrong."

"I know."

"Are you happy? I mean, I know you're not feeling well right now, but otherwise, are you happy?" She sat down on the edge of the bed, her eyes full of concern. "You seem happy, the two of you."

"We are. It's challenging sometimes dealing with—with Liam's mother, but I think it's just going to take some time."

"Jeanie told me about the awful things she did to you, sending you those pictures and…" She seemed to struggle to find the right words. "I've been praying for her because there's clearly something dark inside a person who would go to such lengths to hurt you like that."

"There is," Lina agreed.

"You know if you ever need anything, Bruce and I are always here for you. We love you and Phil and the kids so much," she whispered, her voice breaking.

"I know." Lina squeezed her hand. "We love you, too. And please don't worry about us. We're fine. We're going to be fine."

***

Later that evening, while Phil was watching a movie in the family room with his parents, Logan, and Megan he received a text from Kim. It was a picture of Liam smiling as he sat in front of a cake with one burning candle, a birthday hat propped atop his head. Phil felt a tug in his heart as he looked at the joy in Liam's eyes. Memories of Logan's, Megan's, and Katie's first birthdays flooded Phil's mind. He remembered them all, their attempts to blow out the candle, Logan's beaming smile when Lina brought in a dozen helium-filled balloons, Megan's delight at all the attention, and Katie ignoring the guests in favor of her enormous pile of gifts. It hit him that he'd never have those memories of Liam.

"Oh my God!" Megan cried from beside him. "I got straight As again! My chem grade just came in."

Phil darkened the display, setting the phone back on the coffee table as he turned to Megan, joining his parents in their words of praise. "Excellent, sweetheart." He wrapped his arm around her shoulders and pressed his lips against her forehead. "I'm proud of you."

Chapter Twenty-six

When Phil entered the kitchen the following morning, his mother was at the stove making pancakes and bacon, his father was at the table reading the newspaper, Katie was hunched over a bowl of cereal, staring down at her cell phone, and Megan was at the kitchen island eating a yogurt.

He glanced down at his cell phone to confirm the time, but instead his attention was caught by the date. It was December twenty-third, Liam's birthday. A year ago to the hour he'd received a text from Kim telling him her water broke and she was on her way to the hospital. She'd asked him to come. He hadn't. Instead he'd waited until the following morning.

It was Christmas Eve. Phil arrived at the hospital early, hoping to catch a glimpse of the baby in the nursery without having to see Kim. He stood before a wall of windows, his eyes narrowed as he scanned the dozen or so newborns.

"Which baby are you looking for?" A young nurse with a friendly smile came to stand beside him.

"Ryan. Kim Ryan," he answered.

"He's with his mom. Room 211. I can show you."

He hesitated, not wanting to see Kim, but his desire to meet his son was powerful. "Thanks."

Kim was alone in her room, feeding the baby from a bottle. She looked up when Phil paused in the doorway. "Hi." She gave him a tired smile. "Do you want to meet your son?"

He took a deep breath. "I do." He thought of Lina as he approached the bed. It should have been Lina, not Kim, holding his baby. "May I?"

"Of course." She shifted slightly, so he could pick up the baby.

Phil was overcome with the same sense of wonder that had hit him when he'd met Megan, Katie, and Logan for the first time. The little person he was holding in his arms was his child. He felt a surge of protectiveness at the knowledge.

"He was over ten pounds," Kim said. "I had to have a C-section."

"Big boy," he said, continuing to stare down at his son.

"He takes after his father. I was thinking of naming him Phillip Jr."

"No." He shook his head. "Logan has my middle name." He wouldn't do that to Logan or to Lina.

"Do you have any ideas? I want him to have your last name. He'll carry it his whole life."

Phil thought of his favorite uncle. "Liam. Liam Michael Hunter."

"Have a seat and I'll bring you some coffee," his mother said, breaking into his thoughts.

"Why is everyone up so early?" He wrapped his arm around Megan, who'd crossed the kitchen to give him a hug, dropping a kiss on top of her head.

"I wanted to make sure I got to the kitchen before Lina," his mother answered. "I know how she loves to wait on everyone, and she's in no condition to do so."

"No worries on that front. She woke me up and told me to go to the bakery down the street and pick up breakfast." He joined his father and Katie at the table.

"That isn't necessary. I've got it under control. She's still feeling bad then?"

"She's on the mend," he answered. "Fifty percent better than yesterday." He frowned at Katie, who was wearing earbuds. "You know those aren't allowed at the table." It had been months since he'd had to remind her. "Take them out."

She tugged them from her ears. "It was too noisy in here."

"Families are noisy. You can handle it for a few days."

"Dad?" Megan called out. "I was one of only ten As in chem from my professor, and he has over a hundred students."

"Maybe you should be a chemist," Bruce Hunter said.

"No. I'm going to be a lawyer like Dad."

"You could be a patent attorney," Phil said. "Get your undergrad in chemistry or engineering."

"I didn't really like chemistry. It was just easy for me. I think I'm going to get my degree in political science. That's what yours is in, right?" she asked Phil.

"Yes."

"Are you making pancakes?" Logan asked, looking only half awake as he came into the kitchen.

"Yes," Mrs. Hunter answered as she placed a cup of coffee before Phil. "They'll be ready in a few minutes. What would you like to drink?"

"I can get it," Logan answered, stifling a yawn. "Is Mom still sick?"

"She's better." Phil was staring down at his phone, looking at the picture of Liam Kim had sent him the night before.

"How come you're allowed to have a cell phone at the table when you get on me for having one?" Katie asked.

"Excuse me?" Phil lifted his gaze from his phone, staring across the table at her.

"It's a double standard. You should be acting like you want us to act."

"He's the parent," Megan said. "He makes the rules. When you're a parent, you—"

"I wasn't talking to you," Katie said, frowning at Megan.

"I'm just giving my opinion."

"No one asked for your opinion."

"No one asked for your opinion about Dad looking at his phone at the table, but you gave it."

"If I stand with my cereal can I put my earbuds back in?" Katie asked Phil.

"No. For my Christmas gift, I'd like you to be nice to your sister regardless of how you're actually feeling inside."

"I've already bought your gift. I'm not giving you two."

***

Lina put on her running clothes, determined to go down to the basement and sweat the lingering hangover out of her body. She was lacing her shoes when Phil joined her in the master suite.

"What are our plans today?" he asked.

"My plans are to go grocery shopping, bake, and finish wrapping the gifts in the basement. I'm overwhelmed just thinking about everything I have to do."

"Do you need anything from me?"

"You said you'd make a run to the liquor store. We need wine for Christmas dinner and whatever else you think."

"Is that it?"

"I think so."

"I was going to go out to buy Liam a birthday and Christmas gift and then swing by to drop them off. I thought I'd ask my parents if they wanted to join me. Maybe take him out for an hour or so if Kim's agreeable."

"Oh." His announcement surprised her. She'd put Liam out of her mind, assuming they wouldn't see him again until after Christmas.

"They haven't met him. I'd like them to. It's his birthday."

"His birthday," she repeated. She'd completely forgotten about his birthday. "Of course. Of course they should. I already bought him gifts. You don't have to get him more. They're wrapped and in the closet in his nursey."

"You bought them?"

"Yes." She stopped beside him, pressing her hand into his stomach as she kissed his cheek. "Of course I bought them. Don't I always buy the kids their gifts?"

He snagged her hand before she could walk away. "Thank you."

"You don't have to thank me. I wanted to."

Thirty minutes later Lina dropped down on Phil's weight-lifting bench, feeling almost faint. She removed her earbuds and was just bringing a water bottle to her lips when she heard the sound of someone coming down the basement steps.

"Oh, Lina," Susan said when she came into view. "I couldn't believe it when Phil told me you were exercising."

"I just felt like I needed to cleanse the toxins from my body," she explained before taking another sip of water.

"But you barely ate yesterday."

"I just did a light workout," she assured her. "I can already tell I'm better."

"Do you need me to bring you some Gatorade? You look a little shaky."

"I promise you, I'm fine."

Susan nodded. "Honey, are you sure you're okay with us going to meet Liam? Of course I want to meet him, but with Christmas only two days away, I don't want to do anything that will bring you pain."

"I told Phil I was okay with it."

"I know you did, but I wanted to check with you myself. We could wait until the spring."

"No." Lina shook her head. "He's already a year old. You should meet him. He's your grandson."

When Lina returned home from the grocery store, she was surprised to find Susan in the kitchen. "What are you doing here? I thought you were going with Phil."

"He's at the liquor store with Bruce. Phil couldn't get ahold of Kim. We drove by and her car was there, but there was no sign of them. I suppose it will have to wait until spring after all."

***

The sound of Frank Sinatra's rendition of "I'll Be Home for Christmas" grew louder as Phil descended the stairs. Logan was kneeling on the floor in front of the Christmas tree, wearing pajamas covered in elves and assembling the tracks for their electric train.

"I think I'm going to get it myself this year," Logan told Phil. For the past three years he'd attempted to put the tracks together himself, but he could never get the connections quite right and he'd have to ask for help.

"Good." Phil squeezed his shoulder before continuing to the kitchen.

"Are you going running in that?" Mrs. Hunter asked, taking in Phil's shorts and Georgetown T-shirt. "It's only twenty-five degrees outside."

"I am, but inside." He stepped around her to pour himself a mug of coffee. "Where's Dad?"

"He's still sleeping. He isn't used to this nonstop activity anymore. We aren't getting any younger, you know."

"Neither am I." He glanced down at his cell phone as it buzzed with a new text message. It was Kim finally responding to his text from the day before.

I'm not home. I offered him to you for Christmas a month ago and you said no.

He frowned as he reread her text. *I wasn't asking for him for Christmas. I was asking to see him on his birthday. Any chance of me bringing my parents around today to meet him?* It would be inconvenient, but he'd make it work.

No. We're away for Christmas.

He'd assumed she was staying local, but that didn't appear to be accurate. *Thanks. Tell him Merry Christmas for me. I'll see him Friday.*

Friday? Her response was almost immediate.

Yes. It's my weekend.

"Do we have to do this?" Phil asked Lina. He came out of his wardrobe in only black boxer briefs. "It's midnight and we still have to put all the gifts under the tree. I'm tired." They'd just returned home from Christmas Eve Mass, and Logan was insisting they come down to watch *Elf*.

"It's a tradition," Lina said.

"Last year I was the only one awake at the end of the movie. And one year doesn't make a tradition."

"Don't be a Scrooge. Here." She paused beside him, holding out a pair of elf pajamas, the exact replica of the ones Logan was wearing earlier.

"What in the hell are those?" he asked, making no move to take them from her outstretched hand.

"I bought us all a pair for Christmas."

"I'm not wearing them."

"Come on. It will be fun. It will make the kids laugh."

"No." He crossed to his bureau.

"For me?" She watched him step into a pair of dark-blue lounge pants, the muscles in his upper arms and back rippling beneath his skin. "Just wear them long enough for a picture. Do you know how hard it was to get a pair large enough for you?"

"That's because there's no market for them." He tugged a long-sleeved dark T-shirt over his head. "If I put those on I'll lose my man card, and neither of us wants that, do we?"

"I'm willing to chance it," she said dryly.

"Well, lucky for you, I'm not." He stopped before her and dropped a soft kiss on her lips. "My wife isn't going to have a memory of me in those."

She tossed them onto the end of the bed, knowing he wasn't going to change his mind. "You're no fun."

Phil wasn't the only one not wearing the elf pajamas when they made their way down to the family room. Katie, too, was in her normal sleeping apparel, loose cotton lounge pants and an oversized sweatshirt. "No one is taking a picture of me in those."

"I think they're cute," Megan said, curling up on the couch beside Logan. "I already have fifty-three likes on insta, and it's only been five minutes."

Phil dropped down on the other side of Megan, stretching his arm out along the couch behind her. His request to watch *It's a Wonderful Life* or *A Christmas Story* instead of *Elf* was greeted by a chorus of no's.

An hour and a half later, Phil was the only one awake. His gaze traveled over Lina and then over each of his children. His family. His thoughts shifted to Liam, as they had been doing on and off all day. He wasn't sure if it was due to guilt because he hadn't shared his birthday with him or just the unease associated with not knowing where he was, but something felt off.

Chapter Twenty-seven

The aroma of fresh-brewed coffee penetrated Lina's subconscious a moment before she heard Phil's deep voice. "Time to wake up, beautiful. It's nine o'clock."

She smiled, opening her eyes to find Phil sitting on the edge of the bed beside her with a mug of steaming coffee. "You brought me coffee in bed."

"I did." He leaned down and gave her a soft kiss. "Merry Christmas, baby."

"Merry Christmas." She'd forgotten. "How long have you been up?" He was already showered and dressed.

"A while. I worked out." He helped her sit up, propping a pillow behind her before handing her the coffee.

"You didn't shave."

"No." He scrubbed his hand down over his scruff, which after five days of not shaving was almost thick enough to be considered a beard. "Do you want me to?"

"No. I think it's sexy." She scraped her fingers through it. "How much time do we have?" She trailed her fingers down to the first button of his shirt.

"Not enough for that." He stilled her hand with his, bringing it up to his mouth and kissing her palm. "I'll let you unwrap me later. Alice is downstairs. You need to go referee."

"Why?" She groaned. "I talked to her yesterday. She said she wasn't coming until noon."

"And you believed her?"

Without fail, if Phil's parents were staying at their house, Lina's mother showed up bright and early Christmas morning. If Susan Hunter was going to share in the memory of her grandchildren opening their Christmas presents, Alice was going to be there also.

"I thought maybe it would be different this year since she has Drew."

"She brought him," Phil said.

"You were nice to him, right? Please tell me you were nice to him."

"I let him in, didn't I?" He came to his feet. "Instead of pretending she isn't going to show up when my parents are here, why don't we just invite her? That way she'll arrive at a normal time, like nine. She was here at seven thirty."

"I can't do that to your mother."

"She's here," he said, his eyes widening. "I know you're trying to protect my mother, but it's not working. Alice is coming."

"Is she cooking?"

"Yes, and my mom is at the table letting her run the show."

Although she was too nice to ever say an ill word against Alice, Lina knew Susan Hunter wasn't comfortable in her presence. For one, they were complete opposites. Susan was conservative and Catholic, while Alice was ultra-liberal and nonreligious. But the main reason—at least Lina assumed it was the main reason—was because Susan could sense Alice's desire to usurp her role as a grandmother. Alice wanted to be the one serving them breakfast on Christmas morning and having an up-front view of the gift opening. Susan did everything she could to stay out of Alice's way, not wanting any part of a competition.

"I'd better get down there." She took a couple swallows of coffee before forcing herself out of bed.

As Lina observed Drew conversing with Bruce and Susan, she realized it was the first time Phil's parents were meeting her father. It was a surreal moment witnessing her biological father, who she barely knew, interacting with the couple who had been like parents to her from the time she was a teenager.

"I think your father may be the most boring person I've ever met," Phil whispered in her ear as he curved his hand around her waist. "If I were a good son, I'd go rescue my parents."

"They seem fine."

"They're being nice. He's teaching them about the programming language they use in robotics. I doubt they understand a word he's saying."

"Shhh. He'll hear you."

"No, he won't. That would require him to stop talking."

"Phil," she warned.

When Shiloh and Julian arrived midafternoon, Phil's jaw clenched. He'd only agreed to allow Julian in the house because Lina wanted to see Shiloh. The guy was a first class prick as far as Phil was concerned. He and Shiloh had broken up and got back together at least half-of-a-dozen times. Julian had left her in the middle of the night at parties with no way to get home, tossed her clothes onto their front lawn and told her to get out, and changed the locks to their house when she was at work. Each time, Shiloh had called Phil. Although Julian hadn't done anything unseemly in over a year, Phil couldn't trust or respect him.

He did, however, have a warm spot for Shiloh, who he thought of as a younger sister. With long curly brown hair and a youthful vibe, Shiloh sometimes seemed younger than her forty years. "Merry Christmas, Shi," he said as he greeted her with a hug.

"Merry Christmas to you too." She kissed his cheek. "And now I need alcohol," she announced before slipping away.

When Julian moved to follow her, Phil stepped in his path. He had no idea what Shiloh saw in him. Katie had once said that he looked like a rat with his small eyes and narrow face. Phil agreed.

"I don't want any trouble, Phil," Julian said nervously. "I—"

"I don't either," Phil interrupted, his voice low enough not to be overheard. "But last time you were in my house you screamed at your wife in front of my children. If you so much as raise your voice while you're in my home, I will personally deliver you to the curb. Understood?"

"Yeah." Julian answered, nodding vigorously.

"Good." Phil stared into his eyes until Julian dropped his gaze.

"Everything okay?" Lina asked, joining them. "Merry Christmas, Julian."

"Merry Christmas," he mumbled before stepping around her and hurrying away from them.

"You promised to be nice," Lina whispered to Phil.

"I was. I just told him the ground rules."

"That wasn't being nice. It's Christmas. The family is together. Let's be thankful and forgiving. Just like the priest said during the homily last night. You were listening, right?"

"I let him in our home, didn't I?"

"Be nice." Lina stood on her tiptoes and kissed his cheek. "I'll be watching you," she said before walking off.

Lina was peering into the oven several hours later to see how her Cornish hens were faring when Megan asked if there was anything she could do to help. "Remind me never to make Cornish hens again," Lina answered.

"Why? They're so good."

"Making five is slightly less complicated than making fifteen. It wasn't the smartest choice for a crowd. And in answer to your question, yes. Could you run down to the basement and grab some more ice? I think we're running low." As Megan headed off, Lina realized it was the first time she could remember Megan offering to help with dinner preparations. Normally only Logan offered, and even that was rare.

"Where do we keep the fancy plates?" Katie asked, coming into the kitchen from the dining room.

"The china? Why? Did I count wrong? There should be nine at the adult table and five at the kids'."

"Matt and his grandma are coming. We need two more plates."

"What?" She'd never even met Matt's grandmother. "Katie, why are you telling me this right now? Dinner is in less than an hour, and I only made fifteen Cornish hens. That will make sixteen people."

"I'll share with Matt. Where are they?" She began opening cabinets, standing on her tiptoes to compensate for her height.

"You don't just invite someone to Christmas dinner without asking."

"I thought Dad would say no. Where are the plates?"

If the memory of her hangover weren't so fresh, Lina knew she'd be pouring herself a glass of wine, and even with the memory the thought was tempting. "This isn't okay." She couldn't imagine Phil's reaction. Katie was right. He would have said no. Christmas was about family. He would never have allowed a boyfriend—any boyfriend—to come.

"I can't uninvite them," Katie said. "They're supposed to be here in five minutes."

"They are in the bottom drawer of the hutch in the dining room," Lina said, resigning herself to the reality that they were coming.

"Where do you want it?" Megan asked, returning with the ice.

"The counter is fine. I need you to do me a favor. Go tell your father that Matt and his grandmother are coming for dinner."

Megan frowned. "I thought we weren't allowed to invite anyone until we're engaged."

"Please just tell your father."

"But it's not fair. When I was dating Brian you—"

"Megan, I know," Lina said, cutting her off midsentence. "Just go tell him."

Megan was gone less than thirty seconds when Phil came into the kitchen, his jaw set. "Lina, what in the hell?"

"Calm down," Lina said, laying her hand on his chest. "This is news to me, too. She just told me."

275

"She's just going to have to uninvite them," he said a second before the doorbell rang.

"They're innocent in this," Lina said, clasping his hand so he couldn't walk away. "This was all Katie. There's nothing we can do about it now, so we'll just make the best of it."

"He'd better have his tattoos covered," Phil bit out before heading toward the door.

Lina made a point of not feeling sorry for people who came from different socioeconomic backgrounds. It seemed disrespectful. But when she saw Matt standing in the foyer of her home with his grandmother, her heart ached. Matt was dressed in the slacks and dress shirt that were part of the suit Lina had bought him for Alice's wedding. He looked handsome but uncomfortable out of his normal uniform of faded jeans and a black T-shirt. His grandmother, who looked to be in her seventies, was short and plump and clearly more uncomfortable than her grandson, clutching a bouquet of flowers. She was wearing a faded green dress that had seen better days and a worn pair of black pumps.

"Merry Christmas," Phil said, his voice relaying none of the displeasure he had voiced seconds earlier. He turned on his full charm offensive, as if she were a jury he was trying to sway instead of the grandmother of a boy he didn't want in his house on Christmas. Lina had known he wouldn't be rude, but he was going out of his way to make Matt's grandmother feel welcome, and Lina knew it was because he could feel the other woman's unease. She looked like a fish out of water in their palatial home.

***

Phil took another large helping of mashed potatoes. The carcass of his Cornish hen was completely stripped of meat, and he was still hungry. He watched his brother poking at his equally picked over hen and had to stifle a laugh. The meal may have been picture worthy, but it certainly wasn't meant for a man, not one their size anyway.

He could hear the drone of Drew Rayburn's voice from the far side of the table. It was basically in the background the entire day. He doubted they'd have to worry about Matt joining them again, at least not with his grandmother, who had made the unfortunate blunder of choosing the seat directly beside Drew's. With the exception of the short time it took Phil to bless their meal, Drew had been talking to her nonstop.

His gaze shifted across the table to Lina, who was laughing at something Adele was saying. She'd always had the best laugh. The tone was higher than her voice, but not too high. As a teenager he'd try to think of funny things to say, just to hear that laugh.

She pushed back her chair and picked up her dish, coming around the table and silently exchanging hers for his. She pressed her lips into his cheek before returning to her seat. He looked down at the half-eaten Cornish hen before him. When he raised his eyes to hers, she mouthed *I love you*.

After the dessert dishes were cleared away, Phil followed his brother and father out onto the back deck to enjoy a cigar around the firepit. "Did either of you invite Drew?" Bruce asked.

"No," Phil and Mike said in unison.

"The only reason I came out here was to get away from him," Mike added.

"We can't not invite him," Bruce said, getting to his feet. "I'll go see if he wants to join us."

"This will help," Phil said before pouring some more scotch into Mike's glass.

"How does he not know how boring he is?" Mike asked. "He's an astrophysicist. His IQ is probably above one fifty. Why isn't he smart enough to figure what his audience finds interesting? I tried to steer the conversation away from molecular dynamics and asked him if he was a Ravens fan. Apparently, he is. Did you know there are eight subspecies of ravens and they live about twenty-one years?"

Phil laughed aloud. "Are you making that up?"

"No." Mike continued. "They weigh about two and a half pounds. Maybe Lina should serve them for dinner next year instead of that tiny hen."

Phil continued to chuckle.

"You think it's funny because you basically ate two. Jeanie would have stabbed me with her fork if I tried to share hers. Speaking of which, do you think Lina could talk to her, maybe encourage her to go to the gym or wherever she goes to exercise? I swear she's put on at least fifteen pounds in the past year."

"How much have you put on?" Phil asked dryly.

"We're talking about my wife."

"You want a fit wife? Get *your* ass to the gym. Maybe she'll join you. You have a gut, Mike."

"True." Mike patted his belly. "Maybe I should do a triathlon with you. The training will force me to get in shape."

"You should do one," Phil agreed, "but I think my triathlon days are over for a while. I have Liam every other weekend. There's no time to train."

"Mom and Dad were disappointed they didn't get to meet him."

"Me too. You should meet him."

"I should," Mike agreed. "Bring him by sometime."

A feeling of unease again tugged at Phil when he thought of Liam.

Chapter Twenty-eight

"Y ou can't do that," Katie was saying when Lina entered the kitchen the following morning. "Mom, tell him he can't take the car from me." Lina looked from Katie, who was standing beside the kitchen table with her fists clenched, to Phil, who was looking down at the newspaper appearing completely relaxed. "I'm not sure what we're talking about."

"I'm trying to go to the store to return all the stupid gifts people gave me so I can get what I want and Dad took my keys."

"Oh." Lina's gaze shifted to her in-laws, who were pretending not to be listening to the conversation as they ate their breakfast. "Maybe we shouldn't discuss this in front of your grandparents."

"There's nothing to discuss," Phil said, pausing to shake out the newspaper before turning pages. "Her punishment for inviting Matt and his grandmother over without permission is the loss of the car for the remainder of winter break."

"I'm seventeen years old," Katie fumed, stomping her foot. "I'm too old to be punished."

"Keep it up and I'll make you spend the entire winter break with me."

"Mom!"

"Sorry. I'm with your dad on this. You shouldn't have invited them without discussing it with us first." She gave Phil's shoulder a squeeze as she passed him on the way to the coffee.

"Matt's grandmother doesn't cook. They were going to go to Ruby Tuesday for dinner. I love him! I didn't want him eating at Ruby Tuesday on Christmas."

"That's a discussion we should have had, then. But we didn't. Instead you decided on your own to invite them to dinner."

"Because Dad is so unreasonable! He would have said no!"

"Lower your voice," Phil said, annoyance creeping into his.

"Other kids have their boyfriends and girlfriends over on Christmas."

"Other kids have different parents," Phil said.

"I wish I did!" She stormed from the room only to return seconds later. "May I borrow your car, Mom?"

"Unless your mother or I send you out on an errand, you have lost your driving privilege for the remainder of your winter break," Phil said.

"Why?" Katie put her hands on her hips.

"Katie," Lina warned, knowing she was on the verge of pushing Phil too far. "You knew when you invited them there would be repercussions."

"I bet you two had Christmas together when you were my age." She turned to her grandmother. "Did Mom—"

"Enough," Phil interrupted, snapping his newspaper closed. "Do you hear me?" he asked, frowning at Katie. "Another word and you'll lose the car for the month of January as well."

Katie crossed her arms over her chest and marched across the kitchen to where Lina was stirring her coffee. "I need you to take me to the store."

"Right now I'm going to have coffee and breakfast, and then I'm—"

"Will you take me to the store?" Katie asked, cutting Lina off midsentence as Megan came into the room.

"Me?" Megan raised her eyebrows, clearly surprised by the request.

"I need to return some things, and Dad is being...Dad won't let me drive."

"Is that okay?" Megan asked Phil.

"It's up to you."

Megan shrugged. "Okay. I needed to go anyway. Let me just get a yogurt."

"Something positive came from that," Lina said as soon as Megan and Katie left. "They're finally starting to act like sisters." She smiled as Logan, still sporting elf pajamas, came into the kitchen. "Good morning."

Phil frowned at him. "It's been three days. Don't they need to be washed?"

"Mom gave me another pair." Logan smirked.

"Should I be concerned?" Phil asked dryly.

"Phil, stop," Lina cautioned.

"What?" His eyes widened. "If he prefers feminine pajamas to normal clothes, I'd like to know."

"Well, maybe your son is more comfortable in his masculinity than you," Lina said. "Have you thought of that?"

"No." Phil met her eyes across the table. "I've never thought of that."

"Mom?" Katie said late that afternoon, stopping behind Lina, who was in the process of putting clothes in the washing machine. "I was thinking that taking my car away punishes you more than me because you're having to take me where I want to go now."

"I'll survive," Lina said dryly.

"It's not really fair to you, though. Maybe you should tell Dad that."

"He's not going to change his mind and neither am I, so you may as well accept your fate and next time think about the repercussions of your actions."

"God, I hate it when you do that."

"What?"

"Sound like Dad. It's annoying. If it were up to you, you would have let them come for Christmas. Grandma's right. Dad is a dictator. He sucks everyone's freedom away. You're not even a kid and you let him do it to you. And considering you're supposed to be our role model, you're not setting a good example. You should try standing up to him every once in a while."

"I'm sorry you see it that way, but I don't agree with you or Grandma. A marriage is a partnership and—"

"Forget it," Katie interrupted. "I need you to take me to yoga. You can come if you want. I mean, stay and do the class with me."

"That sounds good." She'd planned to take the day off and had already showered, but it was rare for Katie to actually invite her to do something and she wasn't going to pass on the opportunity. "I just need a few minutes to finish this."

***

Phil dropped his parents at the airport Friday morning for an early flight back to Florida. It had been three days since he'd received the last communication from Kim. The days of receiving picture updates were clearly a thing of the past. He was still experiencing the underlayer of unease regarding Liam, but knowing he'd be seeing him later that day abated the feeling for the most part.

He was in his study catching up on some work e-mails when Lina poked her head in the door at about three thirty. "Can you take Logan to Will's, or do you want me to get one of the girls to drive him?"

"Is he going to be gone all weekend?" Logan disappearing every time he had Liam was getting old.

"He'll be gone until the first. He's going skiing in Vermont, remember?"

"Now I do. I can take him."

"You're starting to remind me of Katie with all the texting," Phil said halfway to Will's house, when Logan had barely looked up from his phone. "Is it the girl that you cut your hair for?"

"Tiffany," Logan supplied.

"Tiffany, right. Tell me about her."

"She's cool. She isn't in to drama like a lot of other girls."

"Any sports?"

"She used to play soccer. Now she just goes to the gym."

"Do you have a picture?" Phil asked as they came to a stop at a red light.

In an instant Logan held out his phone. "I gave her that necklace for Christmas."

Phil smiled as he looked at the cute girl with big green eyes, not seeing any of the red flags her image had elicited in Lina. "She's pretty."

"She's beautiful," Logan corrected. He pulled his phone back, tapped on the display, and presented Phil with another picture. In this one she was standing on a beach in a black bikini.

"How serious is this?"

"I don't know. Serious, I guess. I asked her to be my girlfriend."

"You're being careful?"

"Yeah."

"Condoms?"

"Yes. We're careful."

"Always, Logan. One mistake would change the entire trajectory of your life."

"I know, Dad." He began to pat his knees in beat to the music streaming from the stereo.

Phil shook his head. His elf-pajama-wearing son was having sex. Lina would be crushed when she found out.

Ten minutes later, Phil was standing on Kim's front porch. The house was dark, no light visible from the inside. He banged on the door and pressed the button for the doorbell to no avail. He felt a mixture of fear and annoyance. He took out his phone. It rang several times before switching to voice mail.

"Where are you?" he bit out. "I'm standing outside your place. It's five o'clock on Friday and it's my weekend. Call me as soon as you get this. I want Liam." He ended the call before jogging back toward his car, the side of his jaw clenching and unclenching.

"Where's Liam?" Lina asked when Phil arrived home ten minutes later.

"I don't know." He didn't pause, continuing through the kitchen to the front of the house.

She turned off the sauce simmering on the stove and followed him back to his study, where he was sitting at his desk, typing away on his keyboard. His jaw was set, and she could feel the anger rolling off of him "What's going on?"

"Liam wasn't home. I need to look at our custody agreement." His eyes were narrowed in concentration as he stared at the screen.

"Where is he?" She crossed her arms over her chest

"I have no idea." He reached into his coat pocket and pulled out his cell phone, immediately bringing it to his ear. "Where is he? What...? Why are you waiting until now to tell me this...? No...I didn't say that. I said I would see him Friday—today. According to our agreement he's mine this weekend. Where are you...? You took him out of the country without telling me...? Where is Liam?" He came to his feet. "Give me the address. I'll go pick him up." He scribbled something on a piece of paper. "Who is it...? Who...? So you don't know them...? Why didn't you tell me?" He was brushing past Lina as he headed back toward the kitchen. "That's bullshit. You didn't tell me you were planning to leave him...Let her know I'm on my way." He shoved the phone back into his pocket.

"Phil, wait." Lina caught up to him in the mudroom.

"I have to get Liam." He continued into the garage.

"What's going on? Where is he?"

"I have to go. We'll talk when I get back." He lowered himself into his car.

"No!" She grasped the top of the car door before he could close it, wedging herself into the space between the door and the car. "You're not leaving without talking to me."

"Lina." He was gripping the steering wheel so tightly his knuckles were turning white. "There's something wrong. I can feel it."

"What are you talking about?"

"With Liam. I need to get to him."

Lina could see the distress on his face. "Let me get my coat. I'm coming with you."

"Slow down," Lina said a few minutes later. "You're going thirty miles over the speed limit. It's going to take a lot longer to get to him if you're pulled over for speeding."

"I knew there was something wrong. I've been feeling it off and on for days. I just thought I was imagining it."

"Where is he?"

"She arranged to have someone watch him while she vacationed in Mexico. But apparently the woman came down with the flu, so she gave her the name of a friend of a friend. She left him there on his birthday."

"His birthday?" Lina repeated, her stomach dropping. That meant she'd left him over Christmas.

"Like he's a fucking dog," he bit out.

"I'm sure he's fine." She rubbed his shoulder.

"When she offered to let me have him for Christmas, she didn't tell me it was because she was planning to leave him."

"I know." She began to knead the back of his neck. "How far do we have to go?"

"East Baltimore. Another thirty minutes."

"Is that near Hopkins?"

"Yes."

It wasn't the worst section of Baltimore, but it certainly wasn't one of the better areas. She felt her first jitters of unease. "I'm sure he's fine."

***

The blood began pumping harder in Phil's veins as he reached the assigned street. He was only forty minutes from his home, but he may as well have been in a different world. Even in the dark he could see the decay of most of the homes. Lina's nails were biting into the skin of his forearm through his coat.

"That one looks cute." Lina nodded to a house that looked like a flower among a field of weeds, with a brick front and freshly painted shutters. A nativity scene, complete with a lit-up manger, covered most of the small front yard.

"This is it." He slowed next to a white mailbox beside a gravel driveway.

"How do you know? I don't see an address."

"That's three six eight," he said, nodding back at the house they'd just passed. "This has to be three six nine." He turned into the driveway, his headlights illuminating a pickup truck and a small white ranch.

Phil noticed a man sitting on top of a picnic table in front of the house smoking a cigarette when he began to exit his car. "Come on," he said to Lina. "You're not waiting for me."

He took Lina's hand as they walked up the driveway toward the house, the sound of the gravel under their feet piercing the night air. "Is this the Bailer residence?" he asked the man who was watching his approach.

"Who's asking?"

"Phil Hunter. I believe my son, Liam, is here."

"Who's she?" His gaze had shifted to Lina.

"My wife, not that it's relevant to my question. Is my son inside?"

"If she's your wife, who's the woman who dropped him here?"

Phil ignored him, pressing his hand into the small of Lina's back and leading her past the picnic table and up the stairs to the front porch.

His knock was answered by a heavyset woman with bleached-blonde hair badly in need of a touch-up. "May I help you?" Her hand was immediately at her hair, as if trying to make it presentable.

"I came for my son," Phil said.

"Liam?" She frowned.

"Yes."

"I'm supposed to watch him until the first."

"His mother should have texted you. I have him for the weekend."

"Let me just check my phone," she said before walking away from the door.

"Christ." He plowed his fingers back through his hair.

"Relax." Lina ran her hand down his back. "We'll have him in a second."

The woman returned within moments holding her cell phone. "You're Phil?"

"Yes," he answered shortly. "Where's my son?"

"I was just fixin' to feed him, but—"

"We'll feed him. Would you just take me to him?"

Phil followed Lina into a small foyer and then down a narrow hallway to the kitchen in the back of the house. His heart constricted when he saw Liam lying on his back on the dirty linoleum floor in only a diaper, sucking on a bottle.

Another boy, who looked to be about two, also clad only in a diaper, was strapped into a high chair, eating Goldfish from the tray.

"Hey, buddy." Phil kneeled down beside Liam.

Liam's eyes widened, the bottle slipping from his mouth as he scrambled up. "Dadda!"

Phil smiled. "Hey there."

"Dadda!" He threw himself into his father, burying his face in his chest as he began to cry.

"It's okay." Phil rose to his feet, cradling Liam in his arms. "Shhh," he whispered, his mouth against Liam's head. He smelled like a mixture of sour milk and cheese.

Liam reared back his head, pointing his small hand at the other boy as he babbled something incoherent through his tears. There was a small bruise and a scratch beneath one of his eyes, and his hair was crusty on one side with some type of dried food.

"He's probably trying to tell you that they had a few scuffles. Adam here isn't real keen on sharin' his toys, especially considering he just got them for Christmas. Liam wouldn't stop taking them. I finally had to hide them all. They been getting on better since."

"Scuffle?" Phil repeated, looking at the other boy, who was watching him curiously as he stuffed the crackers in his mouth.

"Just kid stuff. Nothin' too serious. Henri said we should let them work it out—that they needed to establish who was alpha. It was fine when they were just hittin' and pullin' hair, but once Adam would start bitin' him, I'd make Henri pull them apart."

"Biting him?" Lina gasped. She was beside Phil, looking at Liam's back. "Oh my God."

"He's twice his size," Phil bit out. The blood rushed to Phil's head as he saw at least three bite marks on Liam's back. The worst was on his right shoulder. There was a perfect imprint of a set of little teeth, the skin around it bruised.

"Henri called Adam the heavyweight and Liam the welterweight. He loves boxing."

"Let's go," Phil said to Lina as he headed out of the kitchen. He needed to leave before he took his frustration out on the demon in the high chair or the moronic woman who'd been watching his son.

"It didn't break the skin or nothin', but I put Bactine on it just in case and some Neosporin," the woman said, hurrying after them. "Adam's always been a bit of a biter, but there's never any lastin' damage."

"Phil, wait," Lina said. "We need his things. He isn't even dressed."

Phil shrugged out of his coat as they reached the foyer and bundled it around Liam, who was still crying. He pushed open the door, waiting for Lina to precede him out before following.

"So, he'll be back Sunday?" the woman called out after them.

"Are you fucking crazy? No, we won't be back!" Phil exploded.

"Stop," Lina whispered.

"But I've only been paid half. Who's going to pay me the rest?"

"What's goin' on?" the man sitting on the picnic table asked.

Energy surged through Phil when he saw the sadistic bastard who'd taken pleasure in his son's abuse. He turned to Lina, pressing Liam into her chest. "Take him," he bit out.

"Phil, no. Think of Liam. He's upset enough."

"Lina—"

"No." She clutched his arm, propelling him forward. "Leave it. Just keep walking. Don't even look at him."

They drove directly to the hospital. Liam became so hysterical when the nurse tried to take him from Phil, the doctor let Phil continue to hold him while he performed his examination.

"There's just one spot that penetrated his skin," the doctor said several minutes later, after cleaning the area around the three bite marks on his back. "It's rare for an infection to ensue, but you should keep your eye on it. I'll prescribe an antibiotic cream as a precaution. You can apply it to the spot on his shoulder as well as the superficial scratch on his face. I'm also prescribing a mild hydrocortisone cream for his diaper rash. Do your best to keep his skin as clean and as dry as possible. If it gets worse, take him to his regular pediatrician." He took off his rubber gloves. "And I would recommend finding a new babysitter."

It was almost eleven when they finally arrived home, complete with Liam's prescriptions and a fresh package of diapers. Katie, who was stretched out on the couch with Matt, jumped up and met them as they came out of the mudroom.

"Liam!"

"No!" he cried, fisting Phil's shirt. "No, Ay. No, Ay."

"It's okay." Phil pressed his lips to the top of Liam's head. "Daddy isn't letting you go."

Katie took a step back, her brows pulled together in concern. "What's wrong with him? And why is he wearing that weird thing?"

"It's a hospital gown," Lina said before briefly telling her and Matt, who had joined them from the family room, what happened.

"Jesus," Matt said.

"Would you make him a bottle?" Phil asked Lina. "I'm going to take him upstairs." Liam's face was buried in his chest and he was continuing to fist Phil's shirt, clearly afraid Phil was going to hand him off to someone.

When Phil dropped down onto the couch in the master bedroom, Liam relaxed a bit, releasing the material of Phil's sweater and looking around. "You're safe," Phil whispered. "Daddy is never going to let anyone hurt you again. I promise." He felt another surge of anger. He'd been experiencing them off and on all evening. This time it was toward Kim.

The sound of the door opening preceded Lina's arrival. "One bottle," she said in a soothing voice as she approached.

"No!" Liam once again gripped Phil's shirt, turning his face away from her.

"I didn't even know until ten minutes ago he could say 'no,'" Phil said. "Thank you."

"Do you think I should leave you alone?" Lina asked. "He only seems to want you near him."

"No. I need you. I'm so fucking angry. How could she have left him there?"

"Don't think about that right now, not while you're holding him. He needs you to be calm for him."

He took a deep breath. Liam took the bottle from him and leaned against his chest as he brought it to his mouth. "He needs a bath. He smells like spoiled milk."

"Do you want me to get it ready?" She stroked her hand over his knee.

"You don't mind?"

293

"Of course not."

Liam, who normally loved baths, began to cry as soon as Phil tried to set him in the water, once again fisting his shirt. "Come on, buddy, you smell. Let me just give you a bath." He forcibly pried him loose and placed him in the tub.

"Dadda! Dadda!" Liam howled, reaching for him.

"I'm right here," he said, kneeling beside the tub. "I'm not going anywhere."

Liam's cries only grew louder as he refused to stay still, attempting to climb out of the tub and back to Phil. "Dadda!"

"Just take a shower with him," Lina said from behind him.

"A shower?" He pulled Liam from the tub, cradling his slippery, wet body against his side. When he turned to Lina, he could see tears in her eyes.

The shower worked. Phil was able to clean Liam's body and hair, and when he was done Lina helped dry him off and then they were dressing him in elf-patterned pajamas that matched the ones Logan had been wearing all week. Liam stood in the center of the bathroom, his dark hair slicked back, staring down at the elves on his shirt.

Phil felt himself relaxing. "Now those I get." He took Lina's hand, lifting it to his mouth. "Thanks, baby." He kissed the inside of her wrist.

***

When Lina woke up, she was alone in bed. She squinted at the alarm clock. It was two thirty. She found Phil exactly where she expected to, standing beside Liam's crib, peering down at him. He hadn't even bothered to get dressed, wearing only his boxer briefs.

She stepped up beside him, stroking her hand over the smooth skin of his muscled back. "He's fine," she whispered, looking at Liam, who was lying on his back sound asleep with his little arms curved above his head. "Come back to bed."

"His life isn't going to be as easy as our kids', Lina."

She knew he was right. "He still has you."

"How did that work out for him this week?"

"You didn't know. It's not your fault."

"That's no consolation to me. I'm his father. It's my responsibility to protect him, and I didn't. What kind of life is he going to have with a mother like her?"

"My mom would say he chose this path, this life."

"God." He sighed. "If only I could believe what Alice believes. Wouldn't that make life easier? Our children have never spent a minute in the care of a stranger. They probably don't even know people live the way those people do. How many times would that kid have bitten him?"

"Don't." She wrapped her arms around his middle, leaning into his warmth as he curved his arm around her shoulders. "You got him out of there."

"How could she have left him there?"

"I don't know." It was beyond her comprehension. "Come on," she whispered, taking his hand. "We don't want to wake him."

Lina thought she'd heard a baby. She opened her eyes and looked around her bedroom. Another cry interrupted the still morning, and she remembered Liam. She untangled herself from Phil's warm body, slipped on her robe, and quietly left the room.

Liam was standing in the crib, his little hands gripping the sides of the rail, when Lina opened the door to the nursery. "Dadda," he called out.

"No. Daddy's sleeping."

"Mama."

Lina sucked in her breath. "No, but I'm someone's mommy." She crossed to the crib. "Hi," she whispered. Her heart tugged as she looked into eyes so similar to Phil's. "How long have you been awake? Do we have our happy boy back?"

He was staring at her intently, like he was again trying to memorize her face. "Mama."

She felt a lump forming in her throat. "No," she whispered. "I'm Lina."

"Mama," he repeated. He touched her mouth with his hand.

She brushed away a lone tear that slipped from her eye. If only it were true and Kim had never happened. "I think someone needs his diaper changed."

***

Phil slowly became conscious of a tap on his face. He swiped at it with his hand, coming into contact with something hard and plastic.

A high-pitched "Dadda!" preceded a hard smack to the center of his face.

"Oww." He groaned, opening his eyes.

"Don't hurt Daddy," Lina said, laughing softly. She took the bottle from Liam before he could strike again.

"Dadda!" Liam shrieked, a wide smile lighting his face when he realized his father was awake.

"Hey, buddy." Relief flooded through him, knowing the upset from the previous day was gone from Liam's mind.

"Dadda." Liam crawled onto his chest. "Dadda," he said again before giving him an openmouthed kiss on his cheek.

"That was so sweet," Lina said. "He kissed you."

"He needs a little work on the delivery." Phil wiped the slobber from his cheek with the back of his hand. "You should have woken me. You didn't have to take care of him."

"I wanted to." She was lying on her side, propped up on her elbow. "He's eaten and read a book and done a puzzle." She leaned forward and brushed her lips over Phil's. "Good morning." She kissed him again.

"Mama," Liam said, pointing at Lina. He began to bounce up and down on Phil's chest.

"I can't get him to stop calling me that."

"He knows a good thing when he sees it. Don't you?" he asked Liam as he lifted him in the air, the muscles in his arms and shoulders straining beneath his skin. "I'm going to show you a proper kiss, okay?" He brought him down and gave him a kiss on the cheek. "Now kiss Mommy." He held him out toward Lina.

"Phil, don't call me that."

He smiled when Liam gave her an openmouthed kiss. "Why not?"

"Because I'm not."

He caught a flicker of sadness in her eyes and felt bad for teasing her. "I'm sorry."

"I think his diaper rash is already getting better. I applied all of his ointments."

He let Liam fall toward his chest before immediately thrusting him back up into the air, eliciting deep chuckles from his delighted son.

"Thanks, baby." He brought him down and kissed his nose before launching him up again.

"I'm going to run out to the mall and buy him some clothes. He doesn't even have a coat."

Chapter Twenty-nine

"You know the connection that Phil has with me?" Lina asked Adele a couple of hours later when she met her at the mall. "Do you remember?"

"The one that woke him up out of a sound sleep and had him running to our house in the middle of the night when you were a teenager and you and Shiloh were in trouble? Or had him beelining to the hot tub when you were drunk and almost drowning last year?"

"I was not drunk," Lina said. "I had fallen asleep."

"Whatever. No, I don't remember," Adele said glibly. "That's not something that really sticks in someone's mind, a connection between people that transcends space."

"Well, he has it with Liam, too," Lina said, choosing to ignore her sarcasm. "He sensed something was wrong before we found him."

"It's his son. That makes sense. I think a lot of parents have that with their kids." She lifted up a faux-leather jacket, an exact replica of Matt's. "You should totally get this for Liam. Phil would hate it."

"I already have two coats," Lina said, looking down at the full cart of baby clothes she'd picked for Liam. "I think I went a little crazy here. I came to get a few outfits. We only have him through the first."

"Look at the little Ravens jersey."

"That's adorable," Lina gushed, taking the jersey. "Why is everything cuter when it's small? That's seriously enough." She tossed the shirt into her basket. "He's going to outgrow half of these clothes before he even gets to wear them. Let's get out of here before I find something else."

Twenty minutes later they were sitting across from each other in a café sharing a pastry. "You should come by and meet him tonight," Lina said. "We're going to celebrate his birthday and Christmas. I've already invited Mom and Drew and Mike and Jeanie."

"I would, but I have a thing with William tonight."

"Oh." Lina took a sip of her coffee.

"Oh," Adele mimicked. "You need to get over this aversion you have to me fucking your boss."

"I don't have an aversion to you doing it with him," Lina said. "I have an aversion to you telling me about it. If you could just talk in general terms about him it would be better. Nothing referring to his anatomy or your sexual escapades."

"I've never met a man who was better with his—"

"No," Lina interrupted. "Whatever you're going to say, don't. I have to see him twice a week. I don't want it in my head."

"Tongue."

"Oh my God. You're unbelievable. Why do you do that?"

"Because I love your reaction. You're too uptight."

"I like myself just the way I am, thank you. Let's talk about something else. I have enough stress in my life right now. You shouldn't be trying to add to it."

"I was trying to lighten it."

"It's like a nightmare, thinking of Liam there. He's such a sweet little guy." A vision of him kissing Phil that morning came to her mind.

"You should have let Phil beat the crap out of that sicko. Watching little babies fight." Adele pulled her lips back in disgust.

"When we were picking him up, I had this realization that just keeps coming back to me. I know Liam is Phil's son, but when we walked into that kitchen and Liam saw him, he looked at Phil with the most intense love in his eyes—like Phil was the most important person in his world."

"Are you crying?"

Lina wiped at her eyes. "It just makes me sad. Phil only sees him every other weekend and a couple of hours during the week. How can he be the most important person in Liam's world?"

"Who else would be? The mother who left him at some stranger's house on his first real Christmas so she could vacation in Mexico?"

"I'll stay home with him," Lina told Phil the following morning as he got ready for church.

Phil was standing just outside his wardrobe, buttoning his shirt, while Liam sat on the carpet nearby patting Knight, who'd been acting like Liam was part of the pack since the previous day, following him around the house and letting Liam pull his tail and ears without complaint.

"He's a year old. He hasn't been baptized. He's never been in the inside of a church. I want to start taking him."

"We will." Lina replaced his hands with hers, finishing the last few buttons of his shirt. "We just need to give it a little more time. Another month or two." It wasn't about her. She didn't relish it, but she could handle the petty gossip which was sure to ensue when her neighbors realized Phil had an affair. It was Logan she was worried about.

"I don't want him to feel different."

"He's a year old. He's not going to remember any of this. We'll take him soon." Lina brushed her lips over Phil's. "I promise."

Chapter Thirty

L ina awoke with a knot in her stomach. It was New Year's Day. Liam was going home. She closed her eyes and took a deep breath. The days of not thinking about him when he wasn't in their home were forever gone. She loved him as if he were her own son.

The realization had hit her two nights prior. He'd woken in the middle of the night. Instead of waking Phil, she'd gone to him. As she'd held him in her arms, feeding him his bottle, they'd stared into each other's eyes and she'd felt as if there were an invisible string connecting them and he was reeling her in. It was in that moment that she realized she loved him unconditionally, not because he was Phil's or because she was supposed to but because she could feel a oneness with him.

***

Phil watched Lina zip up Liam's coat and put a black beanie—a miniature replica of the one he normally wore—onto his head. "You know the car's in the garage, right? He's going to be outside for less than thirty seconds, if that."

"The windchill today is in the teens again." She carefully pulled the hat down over his ears. She was fussing over him just like she used to fuss over their children. "Perfect." She kissed him for what seemed to Phil like the tenth time in the past minute.

"I thought you were coming with me."

"I am."

Katie came into the room and took Liam from Lina. "Are you going to miss me?" She kissed his neck. "I'm going to miss you. Give me a kiss." She turned her cheek to him, and he put his open mouth against her cheek. "Do you want to say goodbye to Megan?" Katie asked before carrying him into the family room, where Megan was stretched out on the couch watching television.

Megan kissed him goodbye. She wasn't as effusive as Katie with her attention, but over the past few days she seemed to be warming to him, reading him a couple of books the day before and helping Phil give him a bath that morning after he'd wiped applesauce all over his hair.

As Phil watched Katie walk toward them, Liam smiling adoringly at her, he felt a stab of unease at the thought of returning him to Kim. "Come on, Liam," he said. "We have to go."

"You're not going to get angry," Lina said for the third time that day as he pulled out of their driveway.

"Are you telling me or asking me?" Despite the promises he'd been making to himself and Lina, he could feel the adrenaline in his system picking up as he drove toward Kim's.

"Think of Liam. You don't want to scare him." She was leaning into the back seat as she talked, pulling Liam's hat, which had crept up, down around his ears.

"I know." His grip tightened and untightened on the steering wheel. He needed to keep it together.

"Tell her to never leave him with strangers again. We'll watch him. And tell her you're going to start taking him two nights a week, just like the custody agreement says."

They hadn't discussed it, but her words didn't surprise him. Her bond with Liam seemed to expand more each day. He shifted one of his hands from the steering wheel to her thigh, and she immediately covered it with hers. They made the rest of the drive in silence.

"There he is!" Kim, looking healthy and tan, greeted Liam with a smile. "How's my favorite man?" Her eyes lifted to Phil's.

Phil returned her gaze with a cold stare.

"Mama!" Liam smiled, and then buried his face against Phil's neck, suddenly shy.

"Why didn't you tell me you'd kept him?" She stepped back so Phil could come into the foyer. "I felt ridiculous showing up to pick him up."

"You didn't call to check on him?" Anger bloomed within him. "I had him for five days."

"Mama," Liam said, peeking out at her before once again burying his face against his father's neck.

"She had my number. It wasn't like he would know if I was calling."

Phil bent down to a knee. "Let's take your coat off."

"How was he? You kept him at your house?"

"Mama!" Liam waved at her, something Katie had taught him to do over the course of the past few days.

"Hi, handsome." She crouched down beside Phil. "Are those clothes new?"

"Do you care about him?" he asked coolly, not looking away from Liam as he removed his hat and jacket.

"Of course I care about him. What kind of question is that?"

"A serious one. Wait a second, buddy." Phil balanced him against his thigh as he pulled his pants down and undid his onesie.

"You're going to change him right here?"

Phil lifted his shirt and then the onesie over his head. "My wife would never have let this happen to one of our children." He shifted Liam so she could see the teeth imprints clearly visible on his back. "What kind of woman leaves her son with a complete stranger over Christmas so she can go on a vacation?"

Her face paled beneath her tan. "Who did that?"

"Suddenly you care?"

"Of course I care." She narrowed her eyes as she looked at his back. "That woman was a licensed day-care provider. She watches children every day. And he doesn't even know what Christmas is. How much do you remember from when you were one?"

"Next time you plan to go away overnight without him, you tell me," he bit out.

"Dadda." Liam's brows were pulled together in a frown, and his lower lip began to tremble.

"It's okay." He smiled at Liam, his anger diffusing in response to his son's reaction. "Daddy is just telling Mommy not to be so selfish." He ran the back of his knuckles down Liam's cheek. "Okay?"

"Mama," Liam said, turning to Kim as if to make sure she was okay.

"Hi, baby." She pulled him into her arms.

"I'll see him tomorrow." Phil came to his feet.

"What do you mean 'tomorrow'?"

"Tuesdays and Thursdays. Starting now."

"So, do you think this is permanent? Dad bringing Liam here?" Megan asked later that evening as she sat at the kitchen island watching Lina clean up the remnants of dinner.

"Yes. Where else would he take him? He's part of our family now."

"But he's not yours."

"No, but he's your father's. He's also my children's brother."

"He's not the same as a real brother or sister, though. Or a real son to Dad. He doesn't live with him. Dad doesn't even like his mother. He regrets ever knowing her."

Megan was jealous of him, Lina realized. She hadn't expected it. But it made sense. He was competition for her father, whom she adored.

"He's his son, Megan. Your father will love him as much as he loves the rest of you. It's just how it is when you have children. You love them all."

"I don't believe that." Megan looked into the family room, where Phil, Katie, and Logan were watching television. "It's going to be a little annoying having him around if everyone always has to act so goo-goo over him. It was all about him. Everyone just wanted to make him laugh or smile."

"He's a baby, a baby who has had a pretty traumatic few days. Have a heart."

"What happens if something happens to Dad?"

"What do you mean?"

307

"You know. With his money," she whispered. "Would Liam get any of it?"

"If something happened to your father, I would get all the money."

"All of it?" Megan frowned. "That doesn't seem fair. We're his kids. You're not even a blood relation."

"I'm his wife, Megan," Lina said, narrowing her eyes at her oldest child, whose ability to say insensitive things seemed boundless. "Everything he has is mine and vice versa."

"But you don't have anything," Megan said. "You've barely worked."

"I maintained the home and raised our children so he could make a living and support all of us. It's a partnership."

"I get that, but it doesn't seem fair that it would be fifty-fifty. The mothering part is so much easier than the working part. It's not like you have to go to school to be a mom. I could see ninety-ten or something like that."

"Well, lucky for me the law isn't on my daughter's side." Lina continued to wipe the counter.

"What if something happens to both of you?" Megan continued. "Would Liam get anything then?"

"Nothing is going to happen to us," Lina said.

"But in the unlikely scenario it does, I just want to know."

"Well, considering he is a blood relation, don't you think he should?" Lina asked.

"No." Megan shook her head. "Because then his mom would get it, and she doesn't deserve anything."

"I see." Lina slowly nodded. "So, you deserve it because you're my daughter."

"Right," Megan agreed.

"But I don't deserve anything."

Megan sighed. "You know what I mean."

"No, actually, I don't. But if something happened to me and your father, your uncle Mike would have all the answers to your questions." The truth was the estate would be put into a trust and ultimately split equally between Megan, Logan, and Katie, and Liam would be the beneficiary of a generous life insurance policy, but Lina had no desire to share that information with Megan.

Lina watched Phil swipe through the pictures she'd taken with her phone during the birthday party. There were at least fifty, and a dozen were of Liam smiling as he sat on Phil's lap in front of his birthday cake. Unlike Logan and Katie, who hadn't liked the attention a party garnered during their younger years, Liam, like Megan, seemed to draw energy from them. He had been "on" the entire afternoon, charming every adult in the room with his contagious smile and sparkling blue eyes.

"I wish we had more, you know, from the last year, but it's a good start."

"I have a lot."

"You do?" Lina was surprised. He was never the picture-taking type of parent. She couldn't remember him ever taking pictures of the kids.

"From Kim. She used to send me one every couple of days. It stopped after the yoga studio incident."

"You texted with her every day?"

"No. I rarely texted her." He shifted to the side as he took his cell phone from his pocket. He tapped on the display a couple of times before passing her the phone. "She just sent me pictures."

Lina tapped away from the pictures and began to scan through old text messages. Most of the messages were from Kim to Phil, with very few going the other way. She'd sent him random updates about Liam, telling him about words he said or whether or not he'd slept through the night, mostly just general information. She sent him a new picture of Liam almost daily. Phil rarely responded unless it was a direct question and then only if it pertained to Liam. There was one text asking him if he'd gotten caught on the backup going into Baltimore after a tractor trailer capsized, spilling its contents all over 95N. There was no reply from Phil. On another couple of occasions, she'd asked him specific questions about his work, whether or not he was working on a particular case she'd heard his firm won. Again, there was no response from Phil. On a few occasions she asked him how his day had been. He handled every occurrence of a non-Liam-related text the same. He hadn't responded. Even without a response Kim continued to ask questions, not quite daily but at least a few per week. It was as if she was having a one-way conversation, and Lina had no doubt she had been doing it to stay connected to him.

"She is so manipulative."

"What? What happened?" Phil reached for the phone.

"I was just reading all the messages she sent you."

"What did she say?"

"They're your messages. It's what she said over the past year."

"Oh." He relaxed back into the couch. "I didn't pay attention unless it was about Liam."

"She was trying to have a relationship with you. That's what all this communication is."

"It doesn't matter what she was trying to do. I wasn't interested."

"It's still wrong. She's a terrible, terrible person." A vision of Liam on the dirty linoleum floor flashed in her mind. "Poor Liam."

"I gave you my phone so you could look at his pictures. Not to upset you. Let me see it." He took the phone and tapped on the display, bringing up a picture of Liam sitting in front of a birthday cake with one burning candle. "Here." He placed the phone back in her hand and curved his arm around her. "Flip back through them."

Lina's heart constricted as she stared at the photo of Liam with his hair neatly parted on the side. He looked so much like Phil. It had been only a few hours and she already missed him. She began to swipe back through the pictures. There were well over one hundred. There were pictures of him as a newborn, crawling, and standing, smiling, even crying and taking a bath. It was an amazing catalog of Liam's first year of life.

Lina blinked back tears when she came to the end. "How come you never showed me any of those? It's his whole life."

"I don't know. You never asked."

"I'm sorry," Lina whispered later that night. She was lying in bed beside Phil in their darkened bedroom, trying without success to fall asleep.

"Why? What did you do this time?" he teased.

"I haven't been letting you share him with me."

"Lina, you don't have—"

"No. Let me just say this. It makes me sad that you didn't have anyone to share him with. His first step, his first tooth, his first word."

"We shared his first 'no' together."

"Stop. I'm being serious."

"I am, too. He's a year old. We have the rest of our lives to watch him grow. You've been the selfless one in this relationship, Lina. You're not going to apologize to me. I don't accept it. Now, come here and kiss me."

Chapter Thirty-one

The following afternoon Lina was logging off her computer and preparing to leave for the day when William stepped into her office. "Do you have time to make a few mods to the kitchen you sent over earlier? I want to see how it looks with the kitchen island a foot wider and a few more lights above the cabinets."

"Sure." So much for getting a head start to beat traffic.

"Also, it's not urgent, but the stone you want for the fireplace—would you figure out if any of the suppliers we have on account carry them?"

"Okay."

"You're doing a fantastic job, if I haven't told you." He paused in the doorway.

"Thank you and you have. More than once."

"Good." He continued to hesitate in the doorway. He was running his tongue over the edge of his lower lip.

Lina averted her gaze, cursing Adele in her mind for telling her about his special talent with his tongue. "I'll get right on the kitchen."

"Would you do me a favor?" he asked. "Tell Adele I said hello."

"Bastard," Adele fumed as soon as Lina passed on his message. She'd called her as soon as she was in her car and headed home.

"Wha—what happened?"

"What happened? The prick cheated on me. That's what happened."

Lina's stomach dropped. "I'm sorry. I didn't even know you were exclusive."

"Clearly we weren't. He went out with someone else."

"After you'd agreed not to see others?"

"No, not officially. But I wasn't seeing anyone else. I liked the asshole."

"But if you didn't agree to be exclusive, how can you—"

"I don't want to talk about it," Adele said. "Just tell him to go fuck himself."

Lina was still reeling from her conversation with Adele when she arrived home. It had been years since Adele had sounded so upset about a guy. Not even the breakups of her marriages had seemed to faze her, though of course she was the one who'd ended them.

"Is he coming this weekend?" Logan asked when he saw her. He was standing in front of the open refrigerator.

"He" was Logan's code word for Liam. "Liam? No, not this weekend. But he's going to be here tonight."

He frowned. "Why doesn't Dad just take him out to a restaurant or whatever he used to do?"

"Because he's a baby and it's hard to entertain him in a restaurant. It's just a couple of hours."

"I hate when he's here."

"Liam?" Katie asked, coming into the kitchen from the family room. "I love when he's here."

"How long until dinner?" Logan asked, ignoring Katie, which Lina saw as progress, considering he normally snapped at her when she talked about Liam.

"Half an hour." Lina waited until Logan left the room to address Katie. "Why do you have to do that? You know talking about Liam upsets him. Why do you insist on baiting him?"

"I'm not. I'm just trying to desensitize him to the idea of a brother. I read that if you're afraid of something, slowly exposing yourself to it breaks down the fear."

"He isn't afraid of Liam."

"I still think it will work." She peered into the oven. "What are you making? There's nothing cooking."

"I ordered in from that new Italian place down the street. Why don't you set the table?"

"Why don't you ask Megan?"

"Because I asked you, and it's Megan's last night here. She's going back to Charlottesville tomorrow."

"I thought she was going back on Saturday," Katie said.

"It's supposed to snow, so she's leaving early."

The sound of the garage door opening alerted them to Phil's arrival. A minute later Liam ambled into the room, saw Katie, and threw his arms around her legs.

"Liam!" Katie lifted him into the air and planted a kiss on his cheek. "Let's go find Knight."

"May I say hello to him?" Lina called out as Katie began to leave the room.

"Sorry." Katie crossed the kitchen to Lina.

"Hi, handsome." She kissed his cheek.

"Mama." He smiled and held out his arms.

"Lina," she corrected.

As soon as she took him, Knight trotted into the room, tail wagging. Liam struggled to get down. "Daw!" he yelled. "Daw!"

Lina set him on his feet, and he instantly went to Knight, blinking his eyes as he averted his face from Knight's licking tongue while still attempting to pet him.

"Down, Knight," Phil ordered as he came in from the mudroom. Knight immediately complied, dropping to his haunches and ceasing his licking.

"Liam likes to be licked," Katie said.

"It's dirty." Phil set his briefcase just inside the door, dropped a kiss on Katie's head, and crossed to Lina. "How was your day?"

"A little longer than I expected." She touched the side of his face when he leaned in and pressed his lips to hers. "William has a terrible habit of giving me assignments at the end of the day. I had to order takeout again."

"Tell him to stop, that you have a family to take care of."

"No, I'm not going to do that. It's my job. Balancing that with my family isn't his responsibility. How would you react if one of your lawyers blew off something you wanted them to do so they could get home earlier? And don't say it's different because it's me."

"It is different. You don't need this job."

"But I like working." Before he could walk away, Lina hooked her finger into the waist of his suit pants. "I think we can suffer through takeout occasionally."

"It's fine." He kissed her again. "I'm going to change. Do you have him?" he asked Katie, nodding at Liam, who was touching Knight's nose.

"Yep."

"I thought Dad would be in a bad mood because of Logan's history grade," Katie said as soon as Phil was out of hearing distance.

Lina's stomach sank. "Did he get his report card?"

"I don't know," Katie answered, avoiding her eyes. "Come on, Liam."

"Katie? What do you know?"

"Nothing." She left the room with Liam in her arms.

Lina ran her hand over her forehead. Logan had told her he'd pulled his history grade up. "Oh, Logan," she whispered aloud moments later as she sat behind the computer in Phil's study, scanning the report card that had been e-mailed to her that afternoon. He'd received a D in history. Phil was going to be furious.

***

Two hours later, the sound of Liam wailing greeted Phil when he joined Katie in the kitchen. "What happened?"

"Nothing," Katie answered, continuing to help Liam into his coat. "I think he's sad to be leaving."

He continued to cry when Phil lifted him into his arms. "Don't cry." He kissed Liam's forehead. "You'll be back in two days."

"Maybe he knows I'm leaving," Megan said. "Are you sad because you aren't going to see me for a few months?"

Liam responded by burying his face against Phil's chest.

"What's all the crying?" Lina asked, coming from the front of the house.

"He started as soon as he saw his coat," Katie said. "He doesn't want to leave."

"Aw." Lina's lips turned down. "Come here, Liam." She held out her arms.

Phil was surprised when Liam willingly went to Lina, resting his head on her shoulder as he continued crying. As he watched Lina consoling him, he thought of the time Kim left him crying hysterically, opting to go for a run instead of comforting her son.

"I'll come with you," Lina said. She pressed her lips against Liam's head before following Phil to the car.

Ten minutes later, Phil was pulling into an empty spot in front of Kim's town house. Liam had cried himself to sleep on the drive over. "She isn't home," Phil said, noting that Kim's car was missing.

"You're a couple of minutes early. It's not quite eight thirty."

As if on cue, headlights preceded Kim's car sliding into the spot beside them. Phil reached for the door handle.

"Perfect timing," Kim said, climbing out of the driver's seat. She was wearing a business suit, her skirt a couple of inches above her knees. "It was one of those days where the time moved too fast. I didn't even stop for lunch. Please tell me he fell asleep. I have another three hours of work."

"He's asleep." Phil opened the back door of his car.

"Do you mind carrying him to the door? I've got my briefcase and…" She trailed off when she saw Lina. "What is she doing here?"

"My wife?" Phil raised his eyebrows.

"If I'm not allowed near your house, I don't want her near mine."

"I don't care what you want." He leaned into the car and unbuckled Liam. "I'll be right back, baby," he said to Lina.

"I'm serious," Kim hissed, following him up the walk. "You came in here threatening me and telling me never to go near her and then a month later you bring her here. How is that okay?" She unlocked the front door and stood back so he could enter with Liam.

"Put down your things and take him." Phil remained outside.

"Are you just going to ignore my question?" she asked, standing in the open door.

"Are you trying to wake him up?" Phil asked shortly.

"I want you to answer me. If you don't want me anywhere near her, why would you bring her to my home?"

"Because she's my wife and I like her with me," he said coldly. "It's not about you. You're insignificant in my decision making. If you don't want her near your house, arrange a different location for pickup or drop off."

***

Lina could tell even from a distance Phil was angry. He was holding himself too rigid. She feared he would awaken Liam. Kim's arms were crossed over her chest. She looked upset. As Lina observed her, she felt nothing but disgust. Any lingering jealousy had evaporated when she'd seen Liam on the dirty linoleum floor. Kim didn't even look attractive to her anymore. She looked like the woman who'd left her own son alone on Christmas.

"Jesus, I can't stand her," Phil said after returning to the car.

"She wanted him to be asleep. She was gone for a week and had only yesterday evening with him and she's hoping he's already asleep. How could she not want to interact with him?"

"She isn't you."

"She isn't even a bad mother. She's awful."

"You'll get no argument from me." They drove on in silence for a few minutes before he spoke again. "I noticed Logan barely came out of his room again. I'm not sure how this is just going to take care of itself. We're going on three months."

Lina's stomach turned at the mention of Logan. "There's something we need to talk about."

Chapter Thirty-two

"No learner's permit next week," Phil told Logan after they called him down to the kitchen shortly after returning home. "And the gaming system is gone until I see an A instead of a D. Is that clear?"

"Can't I just take the test?" Logan asked. "I don't have to drive."

"No," Phil said. "We'll talk about it again after your next report card."

"What?" Logan's gaze swung to Lina. "That's, like, three months away."

Lina gave him a sympathetic smile, hating his downtrodden expression. "If you raise your grade, you'll still be able to get your license on time."

"But what about the driving school? I'm already signed up."

"Mom will call them in the morning and hopefully be able to postpone enrollment. If we lose our money, you'll be paying for the next class. You're better than that D and you know it."

"Why can't I just take the class? It's not like I'll be driving by myself."

"That class is the first step to gaining your driver's license. Driving is a privilege," Phil said. "You haven't earned it."

"I got an A on my last history test. I can show you the—"

"It's too late. We'll talk again when you receive your next report card. Any questions?"

"If I get As on my next few tests can I have my games—"

"No," Phil interrupted. "This isn't a negotiation. We've had this discussion once already. Your gaming is done until your grade is up. Understood?"

Logan dropped his eyes. His hands were clenched together in his lap.

Phil's gaze shifted to Lina. "Did I cover everything?"

"I think so."

"Good." Phil pressed his hands into his thighs as he pushed himself to his feet. "Let's go get the games."

"Why?" Logan frowned. "I'm not going to use them."

"I know you're not, because you aren't going to have them."

"But they're mine."

"Hopefully you'll get them back in three months. Let's go." He nodded toward the front of the house.

"Maybe Liam will make you prouder," Logan fumed, suddenly angry. "Maybe he'll be a star athlete and student."

"Stop trying to deflect. This isn't about anyone but you, Logan. You were neglecting your schoolwork. And now you're suffering the consequences."

"How come you don't have to suffer consequences? How come you can have a baby with someone else and nothing happens to you?" He slammed back his chair and came to his feet.

"Logan," Lina warned, standing up herself. "Stop it!"

"It's okay," Phil said, touching Lina's arm, his eyes remaining focused on Logan. "Let him talk. You don't think I've suffered consequences?"

"No," Logan answered. His face was red and his hands were clenched in fists at his side. "You shouldn't even be here. Mom shouldn't have taken you back."

"Maybe not," Phil said. "But she did. And even if she hadn't, we'd still be having this conversation because I'm your father."

"I wish you weren't."

"Logan." Lina gasped.

"Everyone knows what you did. The kids at school. The kids in the neighborhood—everyone!"

"I don't care about *everyone*." Phil stepped in front of Logan when he attempted to leave the room, blocking his path. "The only person *I* have to answer to is your mother. Not you, not your sisters, and definitely not our neighbors. And you can wish I weren't your father, but I am and I'm not going anywhere. And as long as you live in *my house*, you live by my rules. Is that clear?" His voice was level, but his eyes were narrowed and his jaw clenched.

"Whatever," Logan mumbled, his eyes downcast.

"Look at me," Phil ordered. "'Whatever' is not the proper response. I provide the roof over your head, the food on the table, and the thirty-thousand-dollars-a-year school you attend. When you're on your own, supporting yourself, you can talk to me any way you choose. You don't even have to talk to me. But while you live in *my house* you will talk to me with respect regardless of what you may feel. Is that clear?"

Lina's heart began to beat harder as Logan continued to meet Phil's eyes. "Logan—"

"Stay out of this, Lina," Phil growled. "Is that clear?" he again asked Logan.

"Yes," Logan finally answered. His chin had begun to shake, and Lina could tell he was about to cry.

"Good. And now I want your gaming equipment."

When Logan preceded Phil from the room, Lina slumped down into her chair, letting out the breath she hadn't realized she was holding.

Even after a glass and a half of wine Lina was still feeling shaky when she went upstairs to take a bath. She was submerged up to her neck in rose-scented bubbles when Phil joined her in the bathroom, lowering himself to the edge of the tub.

He dipped a sponge into the water and began to run it over her leg. "Megan wants us to watch a movie with her."

"He didn't mean it. You know that." She clasped his hand beneath the water. "He was angry."

"I don't know whether he meant it or not. It's irrelevant, though, because I am his father."

"He didn't mean it," she repeated.

"Will you join us? It's her last night."

"Phil, he—"

"I'm fine, baby. I promise. Katie desensitized me to cruel words from my children. Stop worrying about me."

"I know his words hurt you. You don't always have to put on this tough-man exterior."

"But I am a tough man." He winked at her.

She sighed, giving up discussing it with him. "I'll be down soon. Just start without me."

When he tried to stand, she held on to his hand. "I love you."

He leaned in and met her lips for a long kiss. "I count on it."

Lina found Logan in his room, sitting on the edge of his bed, staring down at his phone. "What was that about? You don't hate your father."

"I don't want to talk."

"Well, we're going to." She sat beside him on the bed.

"Why did he have to do it? I hate that kids know he had a baby with someone else. It's embarrassing. Will's mom told his dad that she would never have taken him back if he did what Dad did."

"She said that in front of you?" She couldn't believe it.

"No. Will told me. But she said it just the same."

"I'm sorry. It was wrong for them to talk about us, especially when Will could hear them. I know this hasn't been easy for you, having people gossip about us. But I'm not going to let other people's opinions dictate our lives. I have loved your father since I was your age, and I chose to forgive him. I don't regret that decision. Your words today hurt him. You can never take those back. He'll probably remember them for the rest of his life. I know I would if you said them to me."

"Okay, sorry. I was mad."

"You're apologizing to the wrong person. And being mad is not an acceptable excuse. You're always responsible for the words that come out of your mouth. I was upset with you when I saw your grades. So was your dad. We didn't say things we didn't mean to you."

"Sorry," he repeated.

325

"I know you continued to play video games on school nights despite the fact you knew you weren't supposed to. I didn't tell your dad because I assumed you were doing your work. That was the wrong decision on my part. And today's punishment—not letting you get your learner's permit—that was my decision, not your father's. He thought that was too harsh." She came to her feet. "So, if you want to be mad at someone, it should be me."

***

The next evening, the first snowstorm of the season blanketed the Baltimore area with a foot and a half of snow. Phil was up early, using the snowblower to clear the driveway. He was half finished when Logan joined him, holding out a travel cup. Phil turned off the snowblower.

"Mom made you coffee."

Phil took the cup, immediately bringing it to his lips and taking a sip of the warm liquid. "Thank you."

"It's supposed to snow another six inches, according to the weather guy."

Phil took another swallow of coffee. "At least it's cold. The snow is light."

"Are we going to go to Grandma's when we're done here?"

"I was planning to." He doubted Drew had ever shoveled snow. "I'm going to wait for the snow to stop. Give them a chance to clear the main roads."

"Cool." Logan looked down at his feet.

Phil took another swallow of coffee, waiting to see what else Logan would say. It was the first real conversation they'd shared since Logan had lost his temper, and he could tell he was trying to gather the nerve to say more.

"I'm sorry for what I said," Logan rushed out. "I didn't mean it. I'm glad you're my father. I don't know why I said it. I was mad, and it just came out. I'm sorry." There were tears swimming in his eyes when he raised his head.

"I know you didn't." Phil clasped his shoulders.

"I like having you as a father," Logan said, his chin quivering. "I wouldn't want a different one."

"It's okay, buddy." Phil squeezed his shoulders. "I'm sorry you're having to listen to people gossip about your family because of me."

"It's not so much anymore. It was more when school first started." He blew out a stream of air. It was clear he was trying not to cry. "Should I start shoveling off the back deck?"

It was normally Logan's job to clear off the deck and patio while Phil used the snowblower to clear the driveway and front walk. "Why don't you take over for me instead?"

"Really?" Logan's eyes widened. "You're going to let me use the snowblower?"

"Do you think you can handle it? It's not a toy."

"I can definitely handle it."

"All right. Let me show you how to use it."

Phil spent most of the day with Logan. After clearing their property, they took Lina's four-wheel drive to her parents' and cleared off the driveway and sidewalks. Like Phil suspected, Drew had no interest in helping. He did have an interest in teaching though. He'd donned his winter coat, hat, and boots and joined them outside. The day's lessons centered around snow, something he had endless experience with after his years in Chicago.

"Now, lake-effect snow is created when a cold-air mass moves across a long expanse of warmer lake water," he explained to Logan. "The warming lower layer of air picks up water vapor from the lake and—"

That was all Phil heard before he started up the snowblower, effectively drowning Drew out.

"Grandpa talks a lot," Logan said when they were in the SUV and headed home.

"He does," Phil agreed. "He has a lot to say."

"He's kind of boring."

Phil smiled. "Maybe you'll appreciate him more as you get older."

"She's calling you," Logan said softly. He was looking at Phil's phone on the center console.

"Who's call…?" Phil trailed off when he saw Kim's name was on the display. "I'll just let it go to voice mail."

Logan turned to look out the window.

"How would you like to go skiing for a weekend—just the two of us?"

"Really?" Logan swung his gaze back to Phil.

"Sure. You have a three-day weekend coming up for the Martin Luther King holiday. We can fly to Utah."

Phil checked his phone when they arrived home. Kim had left two voice messages and sent three texts. She was out of milk and diapers, was snowed in, and didn't own a shovel. Phil found Lina in the sunroom flipping through a magazine.

"I have to go to Kim's."

"Now? Why?"

"She's out of diapers and milk and has no way of getting to the store."

"They've been predicting this storm for three days," Lina said.

"I know. And I'm sure she's manipulating me, but what in the hell am I supposed to do? I don't want Liam to suffer."

Lina closed her magazine and held out her hand. "Let me see your phone."

"Why?" Phil frowned as he handed it to her.

Lina tapped in his passcode. "Because I'm calling her." She brought the phone to her ear. "No, this is his wife. My husband is busy. I'm sure with a computer and a little money you can hire someone to assist you." She ended the call and handed the phone back to Phil. "She'll figure it out."

***

"Logan, you're going to burn yourself," Lina warned when he tried to take a cookie off the baking pan she'd just removed from the oven. "You can wait another five minutes."

"No, I can't," he said, scooping up a cookie. "Ahh, it's hot," he yelped, tossing the cookie from one hand to the other.

"Of course it's hot. It just came out of the oven. Don't put it in your mouth or you'll burn your—Logan," she scolded when he plopped the entire cookie into his mouth.

"So good," he said over a mouthful of cookie.

"You're as bad as your father."

Logan poured himself a glass of milk before snatching two more cookies and dropping down at the kitchen island. "Dr. Drayton is dating a supermodel. Well, an ex-supermodel. Her name is Kathy Paige. Have you heard of her?"

"I have." An image of a blonde with cat-like green eyes and flawless skin flashed in her mind.

"Brian said she's almost as tall as his dad. He thinks she's the one."

329

Lina paused in the process of placing rolled balls of cookie dough onto a baking sheet. "Brian thinks or Dr. Drayton thinks?"

"Both, I guess. He met her in a gallery. He told Brian as soon as he saw her, he forgot all about the painting he was there to see. They're moving in together."

"Wow." Lina turned back to her cookies, a warm feeling filling her chest. Nick was in love. Despite Phil's belief otherwise, she knew Nick was a good man and she wanted him to be happy.

"How long did you date Dad before you knew you loved him?"

"I thought I loved him the moment I saw him. And I never stopped thinking it."

"Did you feel like you almost couldn't breathe for a second? Like all you could see was him and the world stopped?"

The warmth Lina was experiencing at the memory of meeting Phil disappeared in an instant. Logan was talking about himself. He thought he was in love. "Not exactly. And I think these feeling of insta-love aren't even real," she said, carefully choosing her words. "They're more infatuation. Real love takes time to grow."

Logan's eyes narrowed in confusion. "But you just said you always loved Dad."

"I know, but it could easily have fizzled out. In the beginning it was infatuation, which feels very similar to love, and then it transitioned to real love. But that's only because we both felt the same and continually nurtured the relationship."

"And you were my age when you met him, right?"

"I was."

"Cool." Logan tossed another cookie into his mouth.

"You need to talk to him and tell him he doesn't love her," Lina told Phil later that evening. "He's going to get hurt."

"He's fifteen years old. If he gets hurt, he gets hurt. He'll survive." Phil reached around her and turned out her bedside lamp.

"He isn't tough like you. He's sensitive and introspective."

"I'm sensitive and introspective."

"No, you're not. I can't recall you ever having your feelings hurt. You just don't care what other people think."

"I care what you think."

"I'm talking about people in general."

"Why should I care what other people think?"

"That's exactly my point. Logan's different. Remember the time in first grade when Erin Reiner told him he was a loser?"

"No."

"I remember how his eyes filled with tears when he told me. That's when I first realized how sensitive he was."

"You baby him too much. It isn't okay for him to cry because someone says a cross word to him."

"He was in the first grade."

"Yeah, and you should have told him to suck it up. I wish I had been home. Your reaction probably taught him that crying about other people's words was acceptable."

"Oh, forget it. It's impossible to discuss things with you when you get like this."

"Like what?"

"Disagreeable."

He laughed. "Because I don't agree with you I'm disagreeable?"

"You think the way you think and act is the way all men should think and act."

"No, just my son."

"Good night," she sighed.

"I'm teasing you, baby." He kissed her forehead. "Don't get mad."

"It's not funny. I was trying to have a serious conversation with you. I'm worried about him."

"I know you see him as this fragile boy, but that's not who he is. He has the same kind of blood pumping through his veins that I do."

Chapter Thirty-three

Lina was finishing up a meeting with her assistant a few days later when the receptionist called to tell her Adele was there to see her. "What are you doing here?" Lina asked after meeting her in the lobby.

"Nice place. Very modern," Adele said, looking around the open space with its hardwood floors, high ceilings, and exposed brick walls. She slipped off her coat, revealing a black dress which looked more appropriate for an evening out. "I was in the area, so I thought I'd stop by to see where you work."

"There's not that much to see." Lina proceeded to take Adele on a tour, showing her the kitchen, where Adele helped herself to a water, the large conference room, and finally her office.

"Nice." Adele ran her fingers over Lina's rustic desk. "Very chic. And a leather chair." She dropped down into the chair behind Lina's desk. "I like it."

"I'm glad."

"You're so fucking neat." Adele looked around the room with its sparsely filled bookcases and small round table with four chairs set in the corner. "Are those their properties?" She nodded to the black-and-white photos of buildings gracing the walls.

"Yes."

"Lina," William began, stepping into her office. "Do you...?" He trailed off when he saw Adele instead of Lina sitting behind the desk. "Well, well, well, what do we have here?" He smiled, revealing his dimples.

"I'm here to visit with my sister," Adele said. "Kindly go back to wherever you came from. I have no desire to see you."

"And yet you're in my office."

"I'm in my sister's office. Did you give him my message, Lina?" Adele asked. She hadn't looked at William since he'd entered the room.

"What?"

"You know, my response to his 'hello.'"

"Oh no." Lina suddenly realized the only point to Adele's visit was to run into William. "I'm not going to do that."

"Fine. I will." Adele rounded the desk.

Lina's stomach sank. "Please don't. This is my—"

"Go fuck yourself," Adele said, poking him in the chest with her finger. "That was my response."

He grasped her wrist when she attempted to walk around him.

"Let me go."

"Not until we talk."

"I'm mad at you."

"I kind of got that from the 'fuck you' response to all my texts and the fact that you won't return my calls."

"I don't give second chances to anyone."

"The plans were made months ago. She was a friend of the family. I didn't even know you wanted to be exclusive."

Adele gripped the lapels of his suit jacket. "Did you fuck her?"

Lina wanted to leave, hating to witness such a personal conversation, but they were blocking the door and seemed to have completely forgotten about her presence.

"No." He framed Adele's face with his hands. "You're the only one I want to fuck."

"Take me to your office," Adele whispered, tugging on his tie.

Lina couldn't do it. She couldn't sit at her desk, knowing Adele was on the other side of the wall being fucked by her boss. She gathered her things, told the receptionist she had a headache, which was actually true, and headed out.

There was an unfamiliar car in the driveway when Lina arrived home. School had been canceled for the second day due to the remnants from the weekend snowstorm. She assumed it belonged to one of Katie's friends.

Knight greeted her enthusiastically when she came into the kitchen. Katie came from the family room, frowning at her in confusion. "What time is it?"

"Early. I took a half day. Whose car?"

"Tiffany's."

"Tiffany's? She's here?" Lina walked toward the family room.

"They're upstairs," Katie said, crossing toward the pantry.

Lina set her purse and laptop on the kitchen island. "You know you're not supposed to have friends of the opposite sex upstairs when your father and I aren't home."

"I'm right here."

"Well, he's not supposed to be up there either."

"I'm not his babysitter. What do I look like, Megan?"

"No, but you are his older sister. It wouldn't hurt you to remind him of the rules," Lina said over her shoulder as she headed toward the front of the house.

She ascended the stairs, hoping Logan had simply chosen to go upstairs to watch television in the upstairs den. Those hopes were dashed when she walked down the quiet hall toward the children's bedrooms. The den was empty, and Logan's door was shut. She could hear the muted sound of music.

She knocked on the door. When there was no immediate response, she knocked harder.

"What?" The door opened a crack to reveal Logan shirtless and in a pair of shorts. His eyes widened when he saw Lina. "Mom."

"You have five minutes to join me downstairs."

Lina paced the kitchen, trying to calm her nerves. She wished Phil were home. She didn't want to deal with this by herself.

"What are you doing?" Katie asked.

"I'm waiting for your brother."

"Why do you look so stressed?"

"Because I am stressed. And would you please just go upstairs so I can deal with this?"

"He's fifteen. You had sex at fifteen."

Lina closed her eyes. She would never forgive her mother for sharing that information with Katie. "Go. Upstairs. Now."

"You are so being Dad right now."

"Go!" She pointed toward the hall.

As soon as Katie left the room a dejected-looking Logan, now dressed in sweats, and an exceptionally beautiful girl in jeans and a sweater arrived in the kitchen. The girl looked as embarrassed as Logan, her eyes downcast.

"Please have a seat," Lina said, waiting for them to be seated before sitting down at the head of the table. "This is going to be quick. Logan knows the rules, but I'm going to repeat them because he seems to have forgotten them, and you haven't heard them. This is a Catholic household. Unless there is an adult present in the house, you are not allowed to have opposite-sex guests upstairs. Okay?" Her gaze shifted between them.

The girl nodded.

"I'm sorry," Logan said. "It isn't Tiffany's fault. It was my idea."

Tiffany blushed.

"I know you're both uncomfortable, but I'd be remiss if I didn't ask if you used protection."

"Mom!" Logan groaned, heat going up his neck to his face. "We're not stupid."

"Good, because I have no desire to be a grandmother yet."

"Please stop," Logan pleaded.

"Maybe you should introduce me to your girlfriend," Lina said.

Logan quickly introduced Tiffany.

"I'm sorry, Mrs. Hunter," Tiffany said, sincerity in her green eyes. "It won't happen again."

***

Logan was at the kitchen island eating a bowl of cereal when Phil arrived home from work. "Isn't that going to ruin dinner? Where's your mom?"

"I'm not sure if she's making dinner. She's been in her room all afternoon." He avoided Phil's eyes.

"What's going on?"

"She kind of caught me and Tiffany in my room."

"Kind of?" Phil repeated. He set his briefcase on the counter. "What are you talking about?"

"She came home early from work and Tiffany was here. I know it was wrong."

"Oh, Jesus." Phil headed toward the front of the house.

The master suite was dark when Phil entered. He could just make out Lina's form curled under the comforter on the bed. He should have warned her. He'd just wanted to let her believe Logan was her baby a little longer. He sat down on the edge of the mattress beside her. "Hey." He stroked his hand down her back. "Logan told me what happened. You okay?"

"I know I'm being ridiculous, but I just need one night. Would you take the kids out? I want to be alone."

He stood up to take off his suit jacket and kick off his shoes, and then he was stretching out behind her and pulling her into his arms. "You're not being ridiculous," he said against her ear.

"He's too young to have sex," she whispered, choking on a sob. "He's only fifteen. I don't want him to grow up."

"I know." He tightened his hold on her. "But we don't have any control over these things."

"I'm going to be fine. I just need to take tonight to mourn the loss of him."

"You haven't lost him."

"I have," she cried. "He's a man now."

Phil chuckled despite his attempts not to. "No, baby. He is not a man. He's just a boy who's having sex."

"Well, tell him to stop. I hate the thought of it."

"I will."

"He isn't going to listen, is he?"

"No."

After sending Katie out to pick up dinner, Phil sat down with Logan at the kitchen table. "What were you thinking? You know the rules."

"Sorry." Logan dropped his eyes.

"Was your sister home?"

Logan's face heated. "Sorry," he repeated.

"You've lost the privilege of having females on the second level, even when we're home. Do you understand me?"

"Yes." Logan lifted his eyes. "I know I was wrong. I'm sorry."

"I remember what it feels like to be your age. And I know you're going to continue having sex regardless of what I say, but you're not allowed to have it in this house. Is that clear?"

"Yes." Logan nodded.

"Having it here today, while Katie was home was disrespectful to both the girl and your sister. I have taught you better than that. You brought her over here and had sex with her before you even introduced her to me and your mother. That too was disrespectful. If you're going to try to act like a man, I expect for you to behave like one. You need to treat her and every female you come in contact with like you want males to treat your own sisters."

The following day Phil was checking his messages during a short break from a day-long deposition when he saw a missed call and text from Kim. Liam's babysitter had come down with the stomach flu and couldn't watch him. Kim was in court and couldn't get away.

Phil cupped the back of his neck, his mind racing. He couldn't leave his client. He lifted the phone to his ear and called Lina. After briefly telling her what was going on, he asked her if she could pick up Liam. "If there was any way I could get out of here, I would," he said.

"Don't worry," Lina said. "I'll go get him now. I'll be there in ten minutes."

Two days later he was about to go into a meeting when Kim again contacted him. The babysitter, who thought she'd recovered, was once again vomiting. Phil called Lina. "It's just a bad week for me," he explained, "or I would do it."

***

Lina was thankful to see her mother's car in the driveway when she arrived home with Liam. She'd called her as soon she'd hung up with Phil.

"Thank you. You're a lifesaver." She immediately passed Liam to Alice. "I have a conference call in three minutes."

Lina almost forgot Liam and her mother were in the house. After the conference call she'd worked on a kitchen design, not leaving Phil's study, which now served as her office as well, until her stomach reminded her it was lunchtime.

Lina found her mom and Liam in the family room. He was sitting beside Alice on the couch, patiently watching her as she examined his palm. "Please tell me you aren't reading his palm."

"Mama!" Liam smiled.

"You should see his intuition line. I think it rivals Phil's. Do you know what time he was born? I have to do his chart."

"No idea." Lina lifted him up and kissed his cheek. "How was he?"

"Perfect."

"Has he eaten?" Lina headed toward the kitchen with her mom following.

"Of course he's eaten. It's after two."

"Wow." Lina looked down at her watch, finding it hard to believe how fast the day was going. "There don't seem to be enough hours in the day. Do you want something to drink?"

"Your auras are merged right now. I used to see that with you and Logan when he was a baby."

"Our auras? You always said everyone has a separate aura."

"Everyone does have a separate aura, but they merge at times when you're spiritually connected. When you're with Phil I can't tell where one ends and the other begins. It's less with Liam. They aren't completely merged but there's a definite overlap."

Lina normally made a point of not listening to her mother when she talked about anything occult related, but she found herself curious today, probably because she wanted to believe what she was saying, that she had some type of special bond with Liam.

***

Friday night Phil arrived home from work to find he and Lina had the house to themselves. Logan was out on a date with Tiffany, and Katie had gone to Baltimore with Matt to watch his band perform.

"I'm taking you out," he said when he saw Lina pulling things from the refrigerator. "You've worked too hard this week."

"But you prefer my cooking to restaurant food."

"Doesn't matter. You're getting the night off."

341

He took her to a Mexican restaurant a few miles from the house, known for the best margaritas and salsa in the area.

"To the end of a long week." Phil tapped his beer bottle to Lina's margarita glass.

Lina smiled. "Yes, but rewarding. And don't thank me again for watching him. I love having him around. I'm not just saying that."

"I'll thank you with my tongue later."

"No." Lina cringed. "I wish you hadn't said that. It makes me think of William."

"What?" Heat rushed to Phil's head. "What does—"

"No. Not like that. It's something Adele said. I can't get it out of my head."

"Something sexual?" His eyes were narrowed.

"Stop. He's Adele's boyfriend. It makes me think of them, not him."

He relaxed back into his chair. "Great," he said sarcastically. "Remind me to thank Adele next time I see her. Just what I need. Adele and William in my wife's head when I'm making love to her."

"I'm sure given a little effort on your part you can make me forget them," she teased.

"You think?" He pressed his foot against hers beneath the table.

"I do."

"How long do you think it will take me?"

"Not long." She pressed her foot back against his.

He suddenly regretted taking her out. What in the fuck had he been thinking? If they'd stayed home, he'd already be inside her. "Let's get out of here."

"I haven't finished my drink."

"I'll make you another one at home."

"I like this one." She ran her tongue along the salt on the rim of the glass before taking a sip, never letting her gaze break from his.

He was hard in an instant. "Keep it up."

"I will." She did it again.

"Let's go." He pulled out his wallet as he came to his feet.

"No." She laughed, and he felt his chest expand with love. She had the best fucking laugh. "I'll be good. I promise," she said.

He reluctantly sat back down. "That was your last warning."

"I promise."

He was hard for the remainder of the meal, unable to think past what he was going to do to her as soon as they got home. He noted the appreciative stares she received from men as he led her toward the front of the restaurant, his hand pressed to the small of her back.

"Daddy!"

Chapter Thirty-four

Phil stopped in his tracks, grasping Lina's waist as he pulled her more firmly into his side. Liam, Kim, and Randall Bryce, an attorney at Kim's law firm, were standing in the crowded lobby, waiting to be seated.

"Daddy!" Liam, who was being held by Randall, reached for him.

"Hey, buddy." Phil released Lina to take Liam, not noticing the curious glances from other patrons. He'd had no idea Kim was involved with Randall Bryce. He didn't know him well but had always thought highly of him. "Bryce." He shook the other man's hand. "My wife, Lina," he said when Bryce's gaze shifted to her.

"Hello." Lina returned his greeting, her voice sounding cool and composed.

"Mama." Liam reached for her.

"Hi, sweetie." Lina squeezed his little hand.

"No, Liam," Kim said, laughing softly. "She's way too old to be your mommy." She plucked Liam from Phil's arms.

"What did you just say?" Phil said through clenched teeth.

"It's okay." Lina laughed aloud. She curved her arm through his. "It takes a lot more than biology to make a mother. It was nice meeting you," she said to Bryce. "She isn't worth it, Phil," Lina said when Phil continued to glare at Kim. "Let's just go."

Phil was still fuming when they reached the car. He looked back at the restaurant, wanting to go confront Kim for what she'd said to Lina. "I just—"

"No," Lina interrupted. "If you're concerned with me, you'll get in the car and take me home."

"I don't want her to get away with that."

"With what—saying I'm too old to have a baby? It may be true. I don't care. I'm not insulted. She has no power to hurt me anymore. I know who she is. And if you go back there and upset her, two things will happen. She'll know she got to you, and Liam will suffer, because I have no doubt you'll manage to upset her. And if she's upset, she'll be a worse mother than she already is."

Phil was quiet on the drive home. His hands were gripping the steering wheel hard enough to whiten his knuckles. "I hate that I opened you up to her. That I brought her into our fucking lives."

"Do you know what I hate? I hate that you're letting her ruin our evening. I hate that instead of being present with me, you're living in your head, obsessing about words that didn't even bother me. That's what I hate."

"I can't help it. Protecting you is second nature to me." He dropped one of his hands on her thigh. "That's why I'm never going to be able to forgive myself for bringing her into our lives."

"You need to stop. I'm a big girl. I don't need protecting."

Phil got his days mixed up, not realizing until he received a text from Kim asking if he could keep Liam for the entirety of the three-day Martin Luther King weekend that he'd scheduled his ski trip to Utah on one of his Liam weekends.

"That's this coming weekend? No." Lina was putting away groceries when he told her. "I should have caught it, too."

"I'll just reschedule for the next weekend," Phil said.

"No. No. That would require him to miss a day of school, and he's been too excited. I'll just watch Liam."

"You?"

Lina laughed. "You don't think I'm capable of watching a one-year-old for a weekend?"

"I don't want to put you out."

"Watching Liam is not putting me out. And I have Katie. As long as I don't ask her to help, she'll basically watch him all weekend."

Lina smiled as she watched Liam trying to pull her mother's hair. He seemed almost as enamored with Alice as Katie, following her around and wanting her constant attention. Drew, who was trying his best to bond with Liam, was having no luck. It was as if Phil's low opinion of him had been passed to his son.

"Ma!" Liam screamed before covering his eyes with his hands, mistakenly believing he couldn't be seen by others if his eyes were closed.

"Where's Liam?" Alice asked. "There he is," she said when he dropped his hands, eliciting gurgles of laughter from him before he again covered his eyes and shouted her name.

It was Sunday afternoon and the third day in a row Alice had made an unannounced visit, seemingly delighted in who she referred to as her newest grandchild.

"I finally met Adele's William last night," Alice announced. "The sexual energy between the two of them is off the charts."

"Okay. Please no more." Lina covered her ears. She'd finally gotten to the point where they didn't sneak into her mind when she was having sex with Phil. "Don't say one word about their chemistry, sex life, or anything else. It's bad enough when Adele does it."

"I think they had sex in my bathroom."

"Mom. What did I just say?" Lina frowned at her.

"It's a small bathroom. It had to have taken some creativity. Do you even think the sink would hold her?"

"I'm sure they didn't have sex in your bathroom."

"Oh, I'm sure they did. They were in there for at least ten minutes."

"Okay, well, thank you for the new visual."

***

Phil and Logan arrived home from Utah late Monday afternoon. Lina had just strapped Liam into his car seat when Phil pulled into the garage.

"I was just going to the grocery store," Lina explained after greeting them.

"I'll come with you," Phil said.

"You're coming grocery shopping with me?" Lina's eyes widened in disbelief.

"I haven't seen you in three days. I'll take what I can get." He framed her face between his hands before kissing her deeply. "I missed you."

"You must have if you're actually coming to a store with me." She fisted his jacket. "I missed you too." She brushed her lips over his.

"Daddy!" Liam yelled. "Me. Me, Daddy."

"To be continued," Phil said before reluctantly lifting his head. "Hey, buddy." He leaned into the back seat and kissed Liam's cheek,

Ten minutes later, Phil was following Lina through the grocery store, Liam perched against his side.

"Hi." Jodie Redding, a woman who lived in their neighborhood stopped when she saw them. "I didn't know you had a baby." Her eyes were on Liam. "He's adorable." She squeezed Liam's hand. He rewarded her with a smile. "He looks just like you."

"So I've heard." Phil returned her smile.

"And you," Jodie began, turning her attention to Lina. "You look incredible. I don't remember seeing you pregnant. It hasn't been that long, has it?"

"I'm not his biological mother," Lina said.

"What?" Jodie frowned. "He looks just like Phil."

"He is Phil's. We had a bit of a rough patch and Phil and I were separated for a while. This is his son, Liam."

"Oh." Jodie's eyes widened. "I'm sorry. I didn't—I had no idea." Her gaze darted briefly to Phil.

"That's okay. How would you have known?" Lina said before giving the woman a forced smile.

"Well he is beautiful," Jodie said. "It was great seeing you both."

Phil didn't say anything about the conversation with Jodie until they were in the car. "I'm sorry," he said. He'd seen the embarrassment in her eyes and hated that he was responsible.

"It was only a matter of time."

He cupped the side of her cheek. "I'm sorry," he repeated.

"I know." She covered his hand with hers. "It wasn't as bad as I expected."

He felt a rush of regret for what he'd put her through and continued to put her through. "I love you," he said deeply.

It was after midnight when Phil delivered Liam to Kim. She was supposed to be home by eight but had texted him at seven thirty telling him she'd been held up and wouldn't be home until ten. Shortly before ten, the time changed to midnight.

"He's a baby," he said after handing a sleeping Liam to Kim.

"Believe me, I know. Every time he wakes up crying in the middle of the night, I'm reminded."

"Why don't you dig down deep and try to find some maternal instincts?" Phil bit out. "You're his mother, for fuck's sake."

***

Lina could feel the anger rolling off Phil when he stretched out in the bed beside her a short time later. "She acts like he's a burden. I drop him off at midnight, which means she's barely seen him in five days. After I left, she texted asking me if I could keep him until ten tomorrow night."

"She's selfish. Good mothers are selfless with their children. I doubt she has the ability to put anyone before herself." Lina curved her body into the side of his. She could feel the tenseness in his body. "It's late. Just go to sleep."

"I feel guilty every time I drop him there. It's like I'm letting him down."

"Don't," Lina whispered, aching at the pain she heard in his voice. "You're doing everything you can."

"What if it isn't enough?"

"It is. He knows how much you love him. He'll always know. That's what's important. We'll always be here for him."

He released a breath. "I hope you're right."

"I am." She slipped one of her legs between his, burrowing deeper against him. She turned her face into his neck, breathing in his familiar scent. "I'm glad you're home. I missed you."

"I missed you, too." He brushed his lips over the top of her head. "Thanks for watching him."

"Please stop thanking me. I love him. He's a little piece of you. I see you in him." She felt disloyal to Logan as she voiced it aloud for the first time, but it was true. And it wasn't only his physical attributes. Even though he was still a baby, she could see flashes of Phil's personality in Liam. He had Phil's confidence and charisma. Even at one, he walked into a room like he owned it, charming every person he met.

"How tired are you?" Phil asked as he stroked his hand down her back.

Lina slid her body over his. "Not too tired," she whispered against his lips.

***

A week later, Phil was standing at the kitchen island flipping through the mail when Lina told him she was going to New York for training. He stilled with a letter in his hand, his gaze shifting to Lina who was pouring herself a glass of wine. "Why am I just hearing about this?"

"I just found out myself today. It's for the SketchUp Layout course. I told you about it when they hired me." She took a sip of wine before crossing to the refrigerator. "Are you planning to run before—."

"Isn't there a class you could take around here?" He'd set down the mail and was watching her with a frown on his face.

"The course is only offered in New York, Chicago, and LA. I thought New York was the best option." She took a salmon filet from the refrigerator. "It's only going to take twenty minutes for me to prepare this. Are you exercising?"

"We're almost at the end of the month.".

"And?" Her eyes narrowed. "What does that have to do with anything?"

"This was a trial. We were going to reassess after three months."

"That isn't going to be necessary because it's working."

"You agreed we would discuss it," he said, annoyance flaring in his chest.

"There's nothing to discuss." She turned her back to him as she placed the salmon on a baking sheet.

"That isn't a decision you get to make unilaterally."

"I'm not quitting if that's where you're going." She began to season the salmon.

Phil cupped the back of his neck, watching her roughly shake some spices onto the salmon. "Baby—"

"I'm not quitting, Phil. I love what I'm doing."

"You loved staging, and that didn't require travel."

"I liked staging," she corrected. "I didn't love it, not like this."

He needed to tread lightly. "What if you keep the job but don't travel?"

"What?" She spun around, her hands on her hips. "I have to travel. We have properties in other places."

"And you can coordinate over the phone." He could feel his pulse increasing and struggled to stay calm.

"You're being ridiculous."

"I'm balancing the needs of our family."

"Our family is fine."

"Is it?" He raised his eyebrows. "Logan has a D in History. Do you think Logan would have taken his girlfriend to his room if you were home?"

"That's not fair! Neither of those things are my fault. I can't believe you!"

"Calm down."

"No," Lina fumed. "I'm not going to calm down. I'm mad. I've found something I love to do. You should be happy for me and instead you're trying to take it away from me."

"I'm not taking anything away from you."

"I know you're not because I'm not quitting. Dinner will be ready in thirty minutes. This discussion is over."

The conversation weighed on Phil's mind through dinner and later as he helped Logan with his chemistry homework. When he came into the master bedroom after locking up the house and setting the alarm, Lina was coming out of the bathroom. She was completely naked.

His body stirred in response. "God you're beautiful."

"I'm still mad at you." She walked past him with her chin tilted up slightly, pulled back the comforter, and crawled beneath the sheets.

"I'm just trying to protect you."

"No. You're trying to control me."

"No." He slowly shook his head as he made his way to her. The mattress shifted as he sat down beside her. He used his fingers to brush her hair back from her forehead. "It would kill me if something happened to you."

She took his hand. "Nothing is going to happen to me."

"I don't like you traveling without me. It's not safe. There are a lot of fucking crazy people in the world."

"Plenty of women travel alone. I think I can handle myself. Why can't you have a little faith in me?"

"I do have faith in you, baby. It's everyone else I don't trust."

"I'll get Adele to come again. Would that make you feel better?"

"You not going would make me feel better." He hated the thought of her walking around in that city of millions of people without him.

"I'm going."

"Saturday? I thought you were done tomorrow." Phil was shrugging into his suit jacket as he came out of his wardrobe.

"I am, but Adele's coming again, and we thought it would be fun to go shopping and explore a little more." She zipped her garment bag closed.

"Since when is Adele going?" he asked, his brows pulled together in a frown.

"I told you I was going to invite her. You didn't want me going alone, remember?" Her eyes widened. "Why are you upset?"

"I'm upset because I thought you were going to be home tomorrow, and now, five minutes before I have to leave for work, you're telling me you aren't going to be back until Saturday night. Why didn't you tell me last night?"

"Liam was here. It just slipped my mind."

"So I'm going to be alone on Friday night?"

"Yes. We didn't have plans, did we? You have Liam this weekend."

"I know, and I thought you'd be here, too."

"I'll be home Saturday night."

"Do the kids know?"

"Yes." She nodded. "Logan's spending the night with Brian, and Katie has a concert. You'll have the house to yourself."

"I guess I'll see you Saturday, then."

"Don't be like that." She gripped his hand before he could walk away.

"How do you expect me to be? You knew I didn't want you to go away one night. And now you're telling me you're going away for two."

"I just thought it would be fun to have an extra day in New York City with Adele. Last time it was more stressful because I was interviewing."

"I've got to go. I have a meeting with a client this morning." He tried to pull his hand back, but she wouldn't release it.

"You're not going to wish me luck or kiss me goodbye?"

He leaned in and pressed his lips to hers. "Good luck. I love you. Call me tonight."

Phil opened his third beer of the evening before dropping down onto the couch in front of the television. It was eleven thirty. He'd put Liam down a couple of hours earlier, answered a few e-mails he hadn't gotten to at work, and then he worked on a brief for Monday. The time alone was giving him flashbacks to all the lonely nights he'd experienced at the house in Farside. He took a long drag from his beer bottle. Over the course of those six months, he'd never gotten used to being by himself. It was different when he traveled for business. His mind was in work mode. Now, as he stared at the television screen, he felt a similar loneliness to when he'd feared he'd lost Lina.

He lifted his cell phone from the coffee table and looked at the display. Nothing. "Fuck." He leaned back into the couch, spreading his knees wide. He'd talked to her briefly at seven. She and Adele were getting ready to go to dinner. It had been four hours. They should have been back in their room. Instead they were twenty blocks from their hotel at a place called Oliver's, according to the tracking app they shared on their phones. The app had been the only reason he'd been able to sleep at night during their separation. It was the last thing he'd done before going to bed each night, checking to make sure she was safe at home. She always had been. But she wasn't now. She was off at some nightclub with Adele. There was absolutely nothing he could do to keep her safe.

His phone lit up with a new text message. He was disappointed when instead of being from Lina it was from Kim. *How was he?* He tossed the phone back onto the coffee table.

Katie arrived home at midnight. After locking up the house, he went up to the master suite, turned on the television in the sitting room, and stretched out on the couch. Lina finally texted at 1:15. *Are you still up?*

Yes, he typed back. His phone immediately began to ring. "Are you in your room?" he asked.

"No. We're at a club. It's small, and they have a great band. Did you know the clubs stay open until four a.m. here?"

"How much have you had to drink?" He thought he heard a slight slur to her words.

"I'm not drunk." She laughed. "I'm having fun. You don't have to worry. We're just dancing."

"Who are you dancing with?" He sat up.

"No one. I'm just dancing."

His hand tightened on the phone, imagining her in the middle of a dance floor surrounded by leering men. "It's late, baby. Why don't you go back to the hotel?"

"It's not late here. Just go to sleep. I'll be fine, and I'll see you tomorrow."

"Don't hang up. Where's Adele?"

"Out there waiting for me. I'm in the bathroom, holding up the line. I have to go."

"Wait—how much have you had to drink?"

She laughed softly. "I'm fine, Phil. I promise. I had two glasses of wine with dinner and two drinks here. I'm done drinking. I'm just dancing and enjoying the band."

"You're twenty blocks from your hotel. I don't want you walking this late at night."

"Oh my God. You tracked us?"

"Of course I tracked you. It's late, and I hadn't heard from you for hours."

"Don't worry. We'll take a cab. I have to go. Love you." She was gone before he could respond.

"Fuck." He sighed, bringing the phone down from his ear. He drafted a quick text: *Text me when you're back at the hotel*

He was surprised when he received an immediate reply. *Stop worrying,* she texted, followed by an emoji blowing a kiss.

When Liam's cry came over the baby monitor an hour later Phil was in bed but awake. He slipped on a pair of sweatpants and made his way to the nursery only to find Katie struggling to lift Liam out of his crib. "What's the matter?" she cooed as she pulled him into her side. "Are you scared?"

Phil's worry over Lina was temporarily overshadowed by his awe of Katie's absolute devotion to Liam. Liam was a

356

big baby, and Katie's petite size made him look even bigger, but that didn't stop her from cradling him in her arms.

He crossed his arms over his bare chest, propping his shoulder against the doorframe as he watched her comfort her little brother. "Does he need a diaper change?"

Katie spun around at the sound of his voice. "Why are you sneaking up on me?"

"I wasn't." He pushed off the wall. "You just beat me here." He stopped beside her, looking down at Liam, whose eyes were almost closed. "Shh." He pressed his index finger against his lips. "He's almost asleep," he whispered, carefully removing him from Katie's arms and placing him back in the crib.

They watched him for several seconds, ensuring his eyes remained closed, before leaving the room. Phil heard the soft sound of voices as he pulled the nursery door closed and realized the television in the second-floor rec room was on. "You were still up?"

"I'm watching a movie."

"It's late. You should go to bed. You need to get up early and work on your college apps."

She frowned at him. "I'm seventeen. You need to stop trying to father me."

He wrapped his arm around her and kissed the top of her head. "I'm your father. I can't stop fathering you. Good night."

As soon as he entered his bedroom, his phone buzzed with a new text message from Lina.

Safe and sound in my hotel room. Love you.

He let out a relieved sigh as he stretched out on his mattress. He was asleep in less than a minute.

Lina arrived home a little after eight on Saturday evening and was disappointed when Katie told her Liam was already down for the night. "He was like a crazy man all day, and then he just fell asleep while Dad was feeding him his dinner. Like literally. His face just dropped forward onto the tray, right?" Katie asked Matt, who was sitting beside her on the family-room couch.

"He did a face-plant into a bowl of yogurt," Matt answered.

"He didn't even wake up when Dad was cleaning him off," Katie added.

"Where is Dad?" Lina asked.

"Exercising," Katie answered. "We're going outside to use the firepit. You're responsible if Liam wakes up."

Lina was in the master bathroom putting her toiletries away an hour later when she felt a presence in the doorway. She looked up to find Phil in shorts and a sweat-drenched T-shirt, leaning a shoulder against the doorframe. "How long have you been there?"

"Not long." His eyes traveled over her. "Did you have fun?"

"Yes. Did you?"

"No." He slowly crossed to where she was standing, pressing her back against the vanity. "Did you dance with anyone?"

"Adele."

"Anyone else?" He gripped the bottom of her shirt and began to lift it up.

"What are you doing?"

"Answer my question."

"No, only Adele." She lifted her arms up as he removed her shirt. "It's only nine."

"Why didn't you tell me you wanted to go dancing?" He was reaching behind her as he spoke and unclasping her bra.

"I didn't know I wanted to until I heard the music." She felt the chill of the cool air against her breasts as her bra fell to the floor. "Did you lock the bedroom door?"

He yanked his T-shirt over his head, tossing it on the vanity behind her. "How many men came onto you?"

"You're being silly," she whispered.

"How many?" He grasped the sides of her hips, easily lifting her and placing her on the vanity.

"Everyone was just having fun. It wasn't like that."

"It's always like that." He dropped his mouth to her neck, biting and licking his way to her ear. "You're mine," he growled. "I don't want other men watching you, wanting you, if I'm not there to protect you."

"I was fine," she said breathlessly, gripping his upper arms as he dragged his mouth down her neck to her shoulder, his scruff rough against her skin.

"I've seen the way men look at you. Promise me you won't go out to a place like that again without me." He sank his fingers into her hips as he pressed his lower body into the juncture between her legs.

"Phil—"

"Promise me. I was out of my fucking mind last night. I'll take you dancing. I'll take you clubbing. Whatever you want. But I don't want you in those places without me."

"You're talking too much." She reached between them, stroking her hand over his erection.

He pulled back long enough to strip off the rest of his clothes, and then he was kissing her, his tongue stroking over hers as he unclasped her jeans. He reached into the shower to turn on the water while she finished undressing, and then he lifted her off the floor. She wrapped her legs around his hips as he took her into the shower.

"Do you think it's odd that Phil has such a negative reaction to my traveling?" Lina asked Adele the following weekend when they met for lunch.

"Odd for Phil? No," Adele answered. "Odd for a normal person? Yes, it would be very odd."

"He seems to genuinely fear that something is going to happen to me."

"He just likes to have complete control of you. When you're traveling, you're not under his thumb. He can't stand it."

"That is not true."

"How many times over the years have I tried to get you to go away for a girls weekend? Phil wouldn't let you."

"It wasn't Phil. It was me." The idea of going away with her sister had appealed to her, but when it came to the execution, she'd never been able to go through with it, not able to leave Phil. The thought of being without him overnight would bring out a feeling of panic. It was a lingering effect of the trauma she'd experienced as a teenager, feeling unsafe at night unless she was with Phil. The one positive outcome of their six months apart was finally learning to feel safe alone.

"Maybe it was you, too," Adele conceded. "But Phil didn't want you to leave either. He thinks of himself as your protector."

Adele's words, *he thinks of himself as your protector,* replayed in Lina's mind long after their lunch was over. She finally realized it was striking a chord in her because it was the exact phrasing her mother-in-law used to describe Phil over Christmas.

"I have a question," Lina said to Susan Hunter over the phone later that day. "Do you remember how you said Phil thought of himself as my protector? You were in my room looking at that picture of us as teenagers."

"Of course."

"What did you mean exactly? I mean, I know a husband protects his wife, but was there a deeper meaning? Were you implying that Phil takes that role more seriously than other men?"

Several seconds passed before Susan responded. "I don't think he can help himself, not after what he witnessed happening that night to you and Shiloh. It changed him. I think it would have changed any man. Phil couldn't stand to have you apart from him after that."

"I thought that was me. I thought I couldn't stand to be apart from him."

"It was mutual. Phil couldn't leave you any more than you could leave him. Why are you asking about this now?"

"He doesn't like me traveling overnight," Lina admitted. "It upsets him. He thinks something is going to happen to me. But he has no problem leaving me. He goes away on business. A couple of weeks ago he took Logan skiing for the weekend."

"He leaves you in your home, which has the most elaborate security system of anyone I know. Bruce said he spent thirty thousand dollars on it."

"I've never really paid attention," Lina admitted. She recalled the number of times Phil had called while on trips to remind her to set the alarms. He could see remotely from his phone whether or not the alarm was set. "What am I supposed to do?" Lina asked. "I have to travel for my job."

"You've gone away twice already, and he survived. Just have patience with him. It's still new. He'll adapt."

***

"I think I figured out why you hate me traveling without you," Lina told Phil as they were preparing for bed. "It's because of that night."

"What night?" He frowned across the bed at her.

"When Shiloh was attacked."

His entire body tensed up. Even after twenty-six years the memory of seeing Shiloh raped and a man restraining Lina had his pulse increasing. "I don't see the correlation."

"You saved me that night so you feel like you have to continue to protect me."

"I do have to continue to protect you. I'm your husband." He stretched out on the bed. "Come here," he said patting the mattress.

"I'm not a sixteen-year-old girl anymore," Lina said as she laid down beside him, curling her body into the side of his. "I'm a woman who is careful. You don't have to worry. I can take care of myself."

"Taking care of you is part of who I am," he said against her ear. "You're my girl."

Lina lifted her head so she could see his face. "I'm going to have to travel occasionally. I don't want you to get upset every time."

He shook his head. "I can't help it. I don't like you apart from me. Maybe it's because of that night. I don't know. But if this job makes you happy, I'll deal with it. I won't like it, but I'll deal with it."

"I love you," Lina said.

"Yeah?"

"You'll always be the boy I want to swim naked with," she whispered.

Chapter Thirty-five

Phil was late to pick up Liam and then forgot to pick up food on the way home. "Just order a pizza," he told Katie, handing off Liam to her. "I think he needs a diaper change."

"No way."

"I'll give you ten dollars."

"Twenty."

"Fifteen and make sure he's completely clean and dry."

Phil continued upstairs, pausing beside Logan, who was on his way down. "How was your history test?"

"Good. I think I got an A. Is Mom home?"

"She has a late meeting. Katie's ordering a pizza."

Logan's lips turned down. "I liked it better when Mom didn't work. We're always ordering in."

"We need to support Mom. She's happy." Phil touched his shoulder as he continued by him and up the stairs.

When he returned to the kitchen Katie was feeding Liam. "Where's Logan?"

Katie inclined her head. "Where do you think?"

"Daddy!" Liam banged his tray.

"Hey, buddy." Phil patted the top of his head. "Where is he?" he again asked Katie.

"In his room, hiding from Liam. Liam waved at him and he just turned around and left. It's starting to hurt Liam's feelings. His little lips turned down."

Phil looked toward the front of the house, debating whether or not to talk to him. He'd thought after their three days together on the slopes Logan might be a little warmer to the idea of Liam, knowing he was still getting quality time with his father. That clearly wasn't the case.

"I can talk to him later if you want," Katie said. "Or maybe I'll have Matt talk to him and tell him how much it sucks to have a dad that doesn't care about him."

"What are you talking about?" Phil frowned at her. "Don't compare me to Matt's deadbeat father."

"I was comparing Logan to him. Obviously you care about him."

Phil didn't see the correlation, but he was too tired to verbally tangle with Katie. Instead he pulled a beer out of the refrigerator.

"Daddy." Liam waved at him.

Phil smiled, taking a chair beside Liam's high chair on the opposite side as Katie. He stole a Cheerio from Liam's tray, making an exaggerated motion with his mouth as he chewed it. Liam took a cheerio and imitated his father.

"I think he's smart like me," Katie said. "You know, not just IQ smart but wise, too. I can see it in his eyes."

"Speaking of smart, how are the college apps going?"

"Done. I'm going to Maryland."

"What do you mean you're going to Maryland? With your grades and SAT score, you're going to have a lot of options."

"I don't need options. I already got into Maryland. I did the early admissions thing."

"Who said you could do that?"

"I did. It's my life. I get to decide where I go to college."

"Does your mother know?" Annoyance flared in his chest that this had been kept from him. He'd wanted her to go out of state and get away from Matt.

"Daddy!"

"Just a second, buddy." Phil continued to stare at Katie.

"I'm not like Megan. I don't have a need to share every little detail of my life."

"Deciding on a college is not a little detail," he said through clenched teeth.

"To me it is. Why are you getting so upset?" She put a spoonful of rice cereal into Liam's mouth.

"Because I think you chose your college based on your boyfriend, and that's the wrong reason."

"You gave up a scholarship to Duke and went to Maryland so you could stay with Mom. What's the difference?"

"You aren't your mother and me. That's the difference."

"It wouldn't have mattered what we said," Lina said when Phil told her about Katie a few hours later. "Did you really think she was going to leave him?"

"I hoped." He was sitting on the edge of his bed, leaning forward with his elbows braced on his knees. "Logan ignored Liam again."

"You didn't say anything to him, did—"

"No," he interrupted. "I didn't want my wife to get mad at me."

"Thank you."

***

Phil was leaving his office on a Friday in the middle of February when he received a text message from Kim asking if he wanted Liam for the weekend.

"Do you think you could give me a little more than an hour notice next time?" he asked when he arrived at her house.

"Something came up." She stepped back from the door. "He's in the family room."

There were a couple of small suitcases and a pair of ski boots to the left of the door when he came into the foyer. "You're going skiing?"

"Something came up," she repeated.

"And something came up Wednesday night and something came up Monday. You'd rather go skiing than spend a fucking weekend with your son."

"How would you like to try being a single working parent with full custody of a one-year-old? It's not exactly *fun*. You get to waltz in and out of his life while I do all the work. I have an idea. How about if you have him all the time, and I visit him twice a week and every other weekend? How about that?" She raised her eyebrows. "Exactly," she continued when he didn't respond. "Easy to criticize me when the truth is you don't want to deal with him full time any more than I do."

Phil was still upset about his run-in with Kim when he arrived home with Liam.

"Would you run Logan to Will's?" Lina asked as soon as she saw him. "I need to shower if we're still going out to dinner. Katie said you're paying her and Matt to babysit."

"Is he ready?" he asked, handing Liam over to her.

"Yes, he's just watching television. Is everything okay?"

"Fine. Logan, let's go," he called out.

Logan came from the family room. "Bye, Mom," he said, completely ignoring Liam as he disappeared into the mudroom.

"I'll be back." Phil kissed Lina and stroked his hand down Liam's head before following Logan out into the garage.

"What are your plans?" Phil asked Logan as he drove toward Will's neighborhood.

Logan shrugged. "I don't know. Just hang out, I guess." He was patting his hands on his thighs in beat with the music streaming from the stereo.

"How about Tiffany?"

"I'll probably see her."

"You should invite her over. I still haven't met her."

Logan nodded, continuing to slap his thighs. "I will."

"How about tomorrow night?"

Logan's hands stilled. "I'm going to still be at Will's."

He was avoiding Liam. How had he missed that? "Isn't one night enough with him?"

"I already told him I'm staying until Sunday."

"How about if I pick you up in the late afternoon tomorrow? That way you'll have the day. I don't like you missing church. You've been away on a lot of Sundays."

"I'm going with his family. And I already told him," Logan repeated. "We have plans to go to a movie tomorrow night."

"Avoiding him isn't going to make him go away, Logan."

In an instant Logan's entire demeanor shifted from relaxed to tense. He crossed his arms over his chest and turned his head toward the window. "I don't want to talk about it."

"What are you afraid of?"

"I'm not afraid of anything. If you hadn't cheated on Mom, he wouldn't be here. Which means he shouldn't be here because you shouldn't have cheated on her."

Phil's hands tightened on the steering wheel. "You're right. I shouldn't have cheated on her. There's also no way I can go back and not have done it. You have a brother whether—"

"He's not my brother," Logan snapped. "Stop calling him that."

"Don't use that tone when you talk to me."

"You don't want to hear what I have to say. You only want me to agree with you."

"That isn't true, Logan. I'm trying to have a conversation with you right now. Why don't you talk to me instead of the goddamn window?"

Logan turned his head from the window, staring at his father. "The only siblings I have are the ones you had with Mom. He isn't Mom's son and he isn't my brother, so I wish you would stop trying to convince me he is."

"You share DNA. He *is* your brother," Phil said, managing to keep his voice level.

"Not if I don't want him to be," Logan said stubbornly.

"That isn't how it works. You can't just wish things away. This is life. Things happen."

"He happened to you, not to me," Logan said.

"You're acting juvenile. Your behavior, running away from your family, is juvenile."

"Katie's right. You're always trying to tell us what to think. You can't make me care about him. I don't care about him. I wish he had never been born," he fumed.

Phil took a deep breath, trying to maintain his temper. "He's innocent. If you want to be angry at someone, be angry at me."

"I am angry at you," Logan bit out.

"What do you expect me to do, abandon him? What kind of man would I be if I didn't acknowledge him?"

"The same kind of man that would have him in the first place," Logan mumbled, again looking out the window.

"What did you just say to me?" Phil snarled. They'd arrived at Will's, and he threw the car in park. "What did you say?"

"Nothing." Logan opened the passenger door.

"Look at me, Logan!" he exploded.

"What?" Logan paused with one foot out of the car, clutching his backpack against his chest.

"You think you're in a position to judge me?" He was livid. "You're holding an innocent little boy responsible for my actions. Whether you like it or not, he's your flesh and blood. He's *your* brother."

"No, he isn't," Logan said, shaking his head, tears shimmering in his eyes. "He's your bastard." He was out of the car.

"Logan!" Phil threw open his car door, struggling with his seat belt as he scrambled out of the car. "Logan, get back here!"

Logan ignored him, running up the front walk and into Will's house.

***

Lina was humming while she dressed for dinner. She was happy. She'd spent the better part of the day playing with bathroom ideas for the Columbia property. After weeks of struggling, she was finally mastering the software program, giving her the ability to quickly see her ideas unfold in virtual reality.

The sound of her cell phone buzzing caught her attention. She was surprised to see Will's home number.

"Lina, it's Joan Ellis. I debated whether or not to call and then thought I would want to hear from you if Will showed up at your house distraught."

Lina dropped down into a chair. "Logan," she whispered.

"He was crying when he arrived. He seems better now. He wouldn't share what was wrong, but I thought I should let you know."

"Did something happen with Logan?" Lina met Phil in the garage before he was even out of his car.

"Yeah. He said some awful things to me. He reached a new low." He slammed his car door closed.

Lina's heart sank. "You promised me you wouldn't talk to him."

"I didn't intend to. It just happened."

"Wait." Lina fisted the lapel of his coat when he tried to walk past her. "What did you say to him?"

"I just wanted him to come home. It escalated from there. I should have exercised more restraint. Then I wouldn't have his fucking words in my head." He continued around her and into the house.

Lina rubbed her hand on her forehead, releasing her breath.

***

A fierce protectiveness gripped Phil when he saw Liam sitting beside Katie and Matt on the rug in the family room watching a ball roll down a spiral tower. He kneeled down beside him. "Hey, sweetie."

"Daddy!" Liam lost interest in the tower, throwing himself at Phil.

Phil felt Liam's warm face press against the side of his neck. He breathed him in, taking in his powdery scent. He rose to his feet with Liam in his arms.

"We need food. That shouldn't come out of the fifty you're paying me to watch him," Katie called after him.

"I can get us food," Matt said.

"No. You shouldn't have to pay. We're doing them the favor. We had to cancel our plans. Dad, do you hear me?"

"I'll pay for your dinner." Phil pressed his lips against Liam's head as he headed toward the front of the house, swallowing down the lump in his throat.

"Daddy, Daddy, Daddy," Liam chimed between slobbery openmouthed kisses to the side of Phil's jaw as they ascended the stairs.

Phil was stretched out on his side on the floor in Liam's nursery, helping him build a block tower, when he saw Lina pause in the doorway. "I just need a few minutes with him."

"Mama!" Liam smiled.

"Hi, little man." She came farther into the room, pulling her legs under her as she sat down on the floor with them despite wearing a dress. "You're messing up your suit."

Phil placed a block on the top of the stack Liam was building.

"He didn't mean it. Whatever Logan said to you. I just texted with him. He's upset. He asked if you're mad."

"I'm not mad. I'm disappointed in him."

"That's not fair. This is a complicated situation for him."

"It is, but he's fifteen, not five. He's responsible for the words that come out of his mouth."

Phil hesitated outside Logan's partially closed door. He'd just returned from dropping Liam at Kim's. Logan had arrived home an hour earlier, just after seven p.m. and immediately went to his room, offering only a mumbled "hello" on his way past the family room, where Phil had been stretched out on the floor building a soft block tower with Liam.

Phil tapped on Logan's door before stepping into his room. Logan was lying on his bed with his eyes closed, earbuds in his ears, and his cell phone resting on his stomach.

"Logan?"

Logan's eyes immediately opened, and he scrambled to sit up. "Hey."

"Let's take a walk."

As they headed down the driveway toward the road a few minutes later, Phil asked, "Are you warm enough?"

"I'm good," Logan answered. "I'm used to it from walking him." He nodded at Knight, who was trotting along several yards ahead of them. "Do you think he'd be good to run with?"

"Sure. It may be difficult at first, training him to stay at your side and not follow scents, but that probably wouldn't take long."

They walked on in silence for a few minutes before Phil began to talk.

"Do you remember the time you fell at recess and had to get stitches in your chin?"

"Mom wouldn't let the doctor stitch me up because she didn't want me to have a scar. She made them get a plastic surgeon."

"That's right." Phil had forgotten that part. They'd ended up having to wait another two hours for the surgeon to arrive. Phil had tried to convince her that it didn't matter if a boy had a little scar on his chin, but there was no reasoning with Lina. Logan's face was not going to be marred.

"How about Megan's appendicitis? Do you remember that? You and Katie came to the hospital with us."

"In our pajamas. And then Grandma came and picked us up."

"Do you know why we did that?"

"Because you had to take her to the hospital and you couldn't leave us alone. We were too little."

"But why did both Mom and I have to go? Why didn't one of us stay home with you?"

"I guess you both wanted to be there."

"That's right," Phil said. "It's the same reason I came to the hospital when you cut your chin. I didn't want you to go through that without me there to support you."

"Why are you bringing all this up?" Logan asked.

"The night before Thanksgiving, Liam's mother took him to the hospital with a high fever. She didn't know what was wrong with him. She asked me to come, but I didn't because I didn't want to leave your mom and you kids.

"A month later she offered to let me have Liam for Christmas. I said no because I didn't want to bring him into our house during our family holiday. Because of that decision, he woke up on Christmas morning in a stranger's home. When I picked him up several days later, he had the imprints of another kid's teeth on his back. His mother had left him in the care of a person who wasn't fit to watch him.

"Do you know where I was when that was happening? I was with you, your sisters, and your mother in our nice house while he was frightened and away from everyone he knew." He paused, taking a moment so he could keep the emotion from his voice. "He's a one-year-old, Logan. Twice over the course of one month, I wasn't there for him. How many times have I not been there for you?"

"I don't know," Logan mumbled.

"Zero," Phil answered. "I have *always* been there for you. The answer is the same for your sisters. You have always been my priority. Protecting you and keeping you safe is my responsibility as your father."

"We weren't your priority when you were with that woman."

The words were like a punch to his stomach.

"I'm sorry," Logan mumbled. "I shouldn't—"

"No. Don't apologize. You're right. I failed your mom. I failed you. I failed your sisters. I brought pain and shame to my parents. I didn't behave like the man they raised me to be. There is one other person I failed, and besides your mother, I think I failed him most of all. And that's Liam."

"Can we just not talk about this?"

"No. We're going to talk about this. When I'm done, we never have to discuss Liam again if that's what you'd like. That little guy who had teeth marks on his back is my responsibility. He's as much my son as you are. I know you don't like hearing that, but he is. And because of my transgressions, he's going to have a much more difficult life than you. He doesn't have me full time like you do, and he has a mother who left him with a stranger so she could go on a vacation without him—that's his reality. And as wrong as it is, people will look down at him because of the circumstances surrounding his birth, circumstances he had no control over. They may even use derogatory words to describe him."

"I'm sorry," Logan said. "I shouldn't have said it."

"No, you shouldn't have. You don't have to have anything to do with him, Logan. I'm not going to pressure you to accept him into our family—that's your choice—but I will not allow you to disrespect him, *ever*. Is that clear?"

"Yes," he said, dropping his chin. "I'm sorry."

"And you're not disappearing on weekends anymore. This is your home. It's where you belong. Your mother and I only have two and a half more years with you before you leave home, maybe permanently. I'm not losing you any more than I have to. We have a large house. You can figure out how to coexist with him."

***

Two days later Phil was staring into the mirror above his bureau, tightening the knot on his tie, when the doorbell rang. He frowned as he looked at his watch. It was only seven.

"Was that the doorbell?" Lina called out from the bathroom.

"I've got it," Phil answered. He was halfway down the stairs when he heard Kim's voice.

"Could you get your father?"

"You shouldn't be here," Logan said. "You need to leave."

"Tell your father that the nanny didn't show up, and I have court. He can deal with this."

When Phil reached the foyer, he found Liam and Logan standing about five feet apart, staring at each other. He strode past them, yanked open the front door, and caught up with Kim as she reached her car. "What in the fuck are you doing? You can't just leave him here."

"I have court," she said as she dropped down into the driver's seat. "I can't very well take him with me."

"This isn't my problem." He gripped the top of the door so she couldn't close it. "I can't watch him today."

"Then get your wife to. Because I can't do it." She pulled on the door. "Let go."

"You need a live-in."

"Fine. But I don't have one right now, and I have to get to court."

Phil reluctantly released the door, stepping back as she sped away. "Fuck!" He dragged his hand down his face. As he headed back up the walk, he saw Liam, dressed in his pajamas, standing in the open doorway watching him, a smile lighting up his features.

"Hey, buddy." He lifted him up, noting there was no sign of Logan. He felt a swell of annoyance that Logan had left him unsupervised until he saw him watching them from halfway up the stairs.

"What's going on?" Lina asked as she passed Logan. "Was Kim here?"

"Yes."

"Mama." Liam smiled.

"Hi, sweetie." She stroked her hand down his back. "What are you going to do?" she asked Phil.

"I need you to watch him. I know you're supposed to go to Bethesda today, but—"

"I have a nine o'clock meeting. I'm presenting. I can't just call in."

"I have client meetings all day," Phil said, attempting to keep his voice level. "I have to be there. I'm sure you can reschedule."

"No, I can't." She shook her head. "It's an important meeting."

"It's not as important as my meeting," Phil bit out.

"I can't believe you just said that."

"My meetings feed our family."

"My job is important to me. I'm not calling in." She continued down the hall.

"Lina," Phil called out, following. "Would you at least call your mom?"

"They're in Florida."

"I need your help right now. I wouldn't be asking you if there was any other way."

"I took care of him the last two times this happened. It's your turn."

An hour later Phil arrived at Hurte, Dunlop, and Smith with Liam in tow. As soon as he stepped off the elevator, every female in the vicinity was surrounding him, *coo*ing and *aaw*ing at Liam. Within moments he was passing his son off to a female associate and making his way to his office.

"Good morning." Anne smiled as soon as she saw him.

"I have my son with me today," he said. "He was just dropped in my lap. I have—"

"I'll take care of him," Anne interrupted. "Where is he?"

"In the lobby probably." He handed her Liam's diaper bag. "Maybe you can call a service and they can send someone out to watch him or…" He trailed off, not sure what to say.

"I've got it," Anne reassured him. "Don't worry about him."

"Thank you. Remind me to give you a raise," he said over his shoulder as he went into his office.

***

Lina was too busy worrying about her presentation to think about Phil and Liam, but as soon she returned to her office after a successful meeting, guilt set in for leaving Phil to deal with Liam on his own. It was a little before noon. She stared at her cell phone, debating whether or not to call him and see if he needed her to come home. She knew William wouldn't care if she left, but she did have a lot to do and doubted she'd get much done with Liam underfoot.

After a few minutes of pondering, she sent Phil a text. *Everything okay?*

It took him five minutes to reply. *Yes. Under control. I'll see you tonight.*

Deciding to take him at his word, she pushed Liam and Phil out of her mind for the remainder of her workday, concentrating instead on a new bathroom design. When she arrived home at five, she was surprised to find Phil's car missing from the garage.

"Where's Dad?" she asked Katie, who was lying on the couch in the family room reading.

"I don't know," Katie answered, not looking up from her book. "I'm not his babysitter."

Lina took her cell phone from her purse and called him as she walked back into the kitchen. "Where are you?"

"Just leaving the office."

"Where's Liam?"

"With me."

"You took him in with you?"

"I didn't have much of a choice, Lina. I'll see you soon."

"Mom?" Logan had come up beside her.

"Hi." She ran her hand down his arm. "How was your day?"

His hands were pushed deep into his pants pockets, and he was looking down at his feet. "I wanted to tell her what a bad person she is."

He was talking about Kim. She cupped the side of his cheek, lifting his chin up so she could see his eyes. "I prefer that you just ignore her."

"I'd thought about it for a while. What I'd say if I ever saw her. But then my mind just went blank."

"It's okay. I don't want you talking to her."

"You're ten times prettier than she is."

"Thank you." She brushed her lips over his cheek. "I love you."

It wasn't until they were in bed and lying in the dark that Lina brought up the morning's events to Phil. "That wasn't fair. You expected me to drop everything this morning. I may not make as much money as you, but I have responsibilities. I have people counting on me, people who think what I'm doing is important even if you don't." She'd been thinking about it all day, vacillating between guilt for leaving him and anger that he'd expected her to stay home. At the moment she was feeling anger.

"I didn't say it wasn't important."

"Yes, you did. You said your meeting was more important."

"My job is what supports us," he said after a few seconds. "We couldn't live on your pay alone."

"This isn't about money. My career is important to me. I was a stay-at-home mother for more than eighteen years. I'm not doing it again." She rolled away from him.

"I'm not asking you to." He molded his body into the back of hers. "Don't be mad. Today was an extraordinary situation. There was no warning. I was scrambling."

"No, you weren't. You were trying to get me to scramble—to change my schedule. You made me feel guilty, and I didn't like it. It ruined my day."

379

"I'm sorry. The last two times you managed to handle it, so I just—I just assumed you could again." He brushed his lips over her shoulder. "I wasn't trying to make you feel guilty."

"I love Liam. I do. But I don't want to be a stay-at-home mom again. I like working. It's important to me."

"I understand." He wrapped his arms around her. "I'm sorry I made you feel bad. It wasn't my intention. In the future I'll just ask and not make any assumptions, okay? I know he isn't your responsibility."

Her anger diffused in response to his words. "It's not about that. I love him, and when I'm available I like to spend time with him. It's just today wasn't a good day."

"I know, baby. I'm sorry I made you feel bad."

Chapter Thirty-six

When Phil arrived home the following evening, a young girl was sitting with Logan at the kitchen table. His gaze shifted from them to Lina, who had turned from the stove at the sound of his entrance.

"Was traffic bad?" Lina asked, joining him. "I expected you half an hour ago."

"I was held up." He met her lips for a soft kiss.

"We have a dinner guest." She took his hand and led him toward the table, introducing him to Logan's girlfriend.

"You look like Logan," Tiffany said. "I mean he looks like you," she corrected, smiling.

Phil exchanged a few pleasantries with the girl who had clearly captured his son's heart. Logan hadn't looked away from her once since Phil entered the kitchen, staring at her with a doe-eyed expression.

She was poised and confident as she responded to Phil's questions, telling him about her family and her college plans.

She was the oldest of three children, and she hoped to attend Penn in the fall.

"I'd like to be a pediatric surgeon one day," she said. "That's my goal. I love children and I want to be a surgeon, so it fits." She smiled.

"I love her," Lina whispered to Phil as she followed him out of the kitchen. "She seemed so different last time we met after, after…" She trailed off.

"The circumstances were a little different," Phil said. "I'm sure she was uncomfortable." He continued up the stairs with Lina on his heels.

"She doesn't seem like the type of girl who would have sex at her boyfriend's house," she said when they were in the privacy of their bedroom.

"And how does a girl look who has sex at her boyfriend's house?" Phil took her hand, tugging her toward him.

"I don't know. Less wholesome."

"You had sex with me at my parents' house."

"I know, but that was different."

"How was it different?" he asked against her lips.

"It was us."

As soon as Phil took out Liam's jacket Sunday evening and tried to take him from Katie, who was helping him build a tower of blocks, Liam began to cry. It was the third time over the course of the weekend Phil had attempted to take Liam out. He'd taken him to visit Mike and Jeanie Saturday afternoon and then to a local Italian restaurant with Lina the same evening. Both times Liam had been happy to go. Late Sunday was a different story. He seemed to have an uncanny ability to know if the outing Phil planned was to take him home. It had become a recurring scenario on Tuesday and Thursday nights as well. Lina said it was because he was tired, but Phil knew otherwise. Liam wanted to stay with them.

Liam cried the entire drive to Kim's, not falling asleep as was normally his habit. Phil's nerves were shot by the time he reached Kim's front porch. He felt a mixture of guilt for upsetting Liam and anger at Kim for being such an awful mother that her son didn't want to go home to her.

When Kim opened the door, Liam fisted Phil's shirt, shouting, "No, Mommy," as he buried his face against his father's neck and continued to sob.

"Why didn't you drive him around until he was asleep?" Kim asked.

"I don't know. Maybe I thought his mother would want to visit with him since she hasn't seen him in three days," Phil bit out. "Come on, buddy," he said in a much gentler tone as he peeled Liam from his chest. "It's okay."

"Your house is more fun because of your kids," Kim said. "I can't entertain him like that."

"Take. Him," Phil ordered. He pushed Liam into her arms.

"Daddy!" Liam cried, reaching for him, tears streaming from his eyes.

"I'll see you Tuesday." He turned away from them, guilt rocketing through him as the sound of Liam's cries followed him to the car.

***

Two weeks later, Lina was surprised when Logan asked if it was okay if Tiffany came for dinner on a Thursday. "She's going on a college visit, so I won't be able to see her this weekend. Please?"

"She's welcome here, honey. I just wasn't sure if you remembered that Liam was coming over." She could tell by the clench of his jaw that he hadn't.

"I already invited her," he said.

"Does she know about him?"

He nodded. "Can you call Dad and ask him to take him to a restaurant or something?"

"Logan. No. I'm not going to do that to your father or to Liam. He likes coming here."

"It's a Liam night," Katie announced, coming into the kitchen. "Look what I bought him." She held up a book of poems by Rumi.

"Don't you think he's a little young for that?"

"No." Katie frowned. "His brain will absorb it. It's better than all those silly books you and Dad fill his head with."

"We'll eat upstairs," Logan mumbled.

"Where's Liam?" Lina asked when Katie came into the kitchen alone. She'd taken Liam out of Phil's arms as soon as they'd arrived home thirty minutes earlier, whisking him away to the family room to read to him from the Rumi book.

"I thought he came in here to show you the book."

"He probably followed your father upstairs. I'll check."

She was climbing the stairs when she heard Logan's raised voice. "Go away!"

"Logan!" Tiffany scolded. "What is wrong with you? You hurt his feelings."

"I want him to go away."

Lina's heart dropped when she heard Liam begin to cry. She continued up the stairs.

"It's okay," Tiffany said in a soothing voice. "Come here. He's like a miniature you. How can you be mean to him? He's a baby."

"I don't want him here," Logan said.

"He's trying to give you his book. Take it. Logan, take it."

Lina gripped the banister, continuing to listen, unobserved, to the conversation unfolding in the upstairs den.

"Now what am I supposed to do?" Logan asked.

"Read it to him."

"I'm not going to read it to him. It's a stupid book of poetry."

"He's watching you. He has your nose and lips. He's so cute."

Lina touched her finger to her lips when Phil approached from their bedroom, nodding toward the den. "Logan is with Liam," she whispered.

Phil's eyes narrowed, his attention immediately shifting in the direction of the den.

"Ball," Liam said.

"Yes, that's a ball," Tiffany said. "He's trying to give you the ball, Logan."

"Ball!" Liam yelled excitedly.

"Now he wants you to give it back to him," Tiffany said. "He's trying to bond with you."

"I don't want to bond with him," Logan said stubbornly.

"Just give him the ball back." Tiffany laughed. "Now take it again."

"This is stupid," Logan said. "How long do I have to do this?"

"As long as he wants," Tiffany said.

Lina squeezed Phil's arm. Tears sprang to her eyes.

Chapter Thirty-seven

A couple of Saturdays later, Lina was finishing putting the last of the breakfast dishes into the dishwasher when Logan appeared with Liam perched on his hip. Lina's eyes widened.

"Would you take him? He won't stop getting in front of the television."

"Lo Lo," Liam said, patting Logan's arm.

"And saying that," Logan continued, clearly annoyed. "Katie is supposed to be watching him, but every time I put him in her room he comes right back out and blocks the television. He's ruining the game." After pulling his history grade up, Logan had earned back his gaming system and had been playing nonstop with Brian, who had spent the night.

"I'll take him. Come here." She held her hands out to Liam.

"No!" Liam tucked his face into Logan's neck.

"What's going..." Phil trailed off as he came into the room.

"Lo Lo," Liam said, patting Logan's face.

"Yes, that's Logan," Phil said.

"He won't let me put his down," Logan complained.

Lina fought hard to keep from smiling as she watched Logan try unsuccessfully to dislodge Liam from his side. "I'll get him a cookie," she said, crossing to the pantry.

As soon as he saw the cookie, Liam stopped fighting, and Logan lowered him to the floor. "Stay down here and eat cookies," Logan told him before leaving the room.

"Lo Lo," Liam said as soon as Lina handed him a cookie.

"No. Logan's busy." She lifted him up. "Maybe Daddy will take a walk with us. It's a beautiful day." She kissed the side of his cheek.

"He was holding him," Phil said, a look of disbelief in his eyes.

"I know." Lina smiled. "It's a beautiful day."

***

Three days later Phil had just returned to his office after a lunch meeting when Anne came in and set a letter on his desk. "It says 'personal' across the top, so I didn't open it. It was couriered over this morning."

"Thank you." He absently opened the envelope as he read through an e-mail, pulling out a single sheet of paper. He pulled his gaze from the computer screen and looked down at the letter, frowning when he saw Kim's name and address across the top. The subject line read, "Intent to move out of state."

Phil had no memory of the drive to the law offices of Hendrix, Wolff, and Pearson. When he stepped off the elevator and into the lush lobby, he almost collided with Tom Hendrix.

"Phil, what—"

"Is Kim in?" he interrupted.

"I don't know—"

Phil brushed past him. "Is Kim Ryan in?" he asked the receptionist.

"Yes, but—"

Phil continued past her desk, not hearing anything else she said as his long strides carried him toward Kim's office. When he reached her closed office door, he rapped on it twice before pushing it open.

Kim, who was sitting at a round table in the corner of her office with a man and another woman, came to her feet. "Phil?"

"Would you excuse us?" he asked the other two, not taking his eyes from Kim.

"I'm in the middle of a meeting," Kim said.

"We'll just wait outside," the woman said before hurriedly following the man from the office.

"You need to reread our custody agreement," he said, his voice level. "You can't move to New York. I've already called my attorney. We're filing an objection in the morning."

"Good. Now, if that's all, I'd like to get back to my meeting. I'm trying to wrap everything up. I'm moving in two weeks."

"You aren't taking *my son* out of the state."

"I'm done living in suburbia. You can't dictate where I live."

"The fuck I can't. We have a legally binding agreement that states you can't take him more than fifty miles from me."

"That agreement is going to change because I'm moving to New York."

"You're not. I won't allow it."

"What are you going to do?" She smiled smugly. "Sue me for custody? We both know you don't want him."

When Phil left Kim's office, he found himself driving the familiar route to his church. The subtle smell of candle wafted in the air when he opened the doors a short time later. He made his way to the wrought iron votive stand in the back corner, lowered himself to his knees, and lit a candle.

He prayed for Liam. He prayed for his family. He prayed for strength. Minutes passed.

When he was finished and coming to his feet, the door opened and Father Mathew entered. "Phil."

"Good evening, father."

"I didn't expect to find anyone here tonight," the older priest said.

"I didn't expect to be here."

"Is everything okay?"

"No."

Father Mathew lowered himself down onto a pew, leaving space for Phil to sit beside him. "What are you struggling with?"

"You know I have a son that isn't Lina's?"

"I do."

"His mother plans to move to New York with him. I've been trying to convince myself that it will be okay, that a baby is better off with their mother but I know that isn't true, not in this case."

"Is she abusing him in some way?"

"No, not physically. But she doesn't spend enough time with him. He isn't her priority. I know he's happier with me. I see it in his eyes when I pick him up or drop him off. He wants to be with me. I'm afraid she isn't capable of nurturing him. She's too selfish." Phil clasped his hands together in his lap. "But I can't take him. I know he's an innocent baby and I'm the reason he's here but I can't be a full-time father to him. I can't do that to Lina."

"Have you spoken to Lina?"

"I won't ask her to raise him. She has already sacrificed enough for me. And I can't leave her and my other children – I won't leave them. I was lost without her. There's no solution."

"There's always a solution. God doesn't present us situations we can't handle. You need to control what you can control and leave the rest in God's hands. Be the best father you can be to Liam. That's all God expects of you. That's all you should expect from yourself."

**

Lina was in the produce section of the grocery store when she had an overwhelming feeling that Phil needed her. There was no cell service in the store so she abandoned her cart and went outside to call him. There was no answer on his cell or office phone.

Her anxiety went up a level when she arrived home and Phil's car wasn't in the garage. He should have picked up Liam more than an hour earlier.

"Have you heard from Dad?" she asked Katie who was in the family room watching television.

"No."

"Logan?" She ran up the stairs. She found him at his desk on his computer. "Do you know where your father is?"

"No." He frowned. "What's wrong?"

"Nothing, I just. I—I can't find him." She left his room, hurrying to her bedroom, hoping to find something, anything to relieve the fear consuming her. "

"Mom?"

She spun around at the sound of Logan's voice. "Is he home?"

"No. What's going on? Why are you so upset?"

"I don't know." She put her fist to her mouth. "I just—I need to find him." He needed her. She could feel it with every pore of her being.

"Do you have him on your phone? You know, the tracking app?"

Lina parked beside Phil's BMW. The church was dark, but the door was unlocked. She saw him as soon as she stepped inside. Relief surged through her, knowing he was at least physically okay. He was kneeling in one of the pews, his head bent in prayer. She hesitated, not sure whether to interrupt him.

Her heels tapped on the worn hardwood floors as she approached but he didn't seem to hear her as he continued to pray. When she stopped within feet of him, she realized he was crying, his shoulders shaking. She'd never seen him cry.

"Phil?" She sat down beside him, clutching his arm. "What's wrong? What happened?"

"I need to be alone, baby," he said, his voice raw with emotion. "Please."

"No." She stroked her hand over his back. "You have to tell me what's going on." Tears came to her own eyes. "Did something happen to your parents?"

"No." He shook his head. He covered his eyes with one of his hands.

"What? You have to tell me," she whispered. "Please."

"She's taking him. She's taking Liam. They're moving to New York."

Her heart dropped. "No." She shook her head. "She can't do that. Call your lawyer. Make them stop her."

"I can't stop her."

"What do you mean you can't stop her? You're his father. He needs you."

"The judge almost always sides with the custodial parent in cases like these."

"She isn't a fit mother. We can prove it—show the judge how many hours she leaves him with the nanny. We'll tell them about the way she left him over Christmas. The bite marks—there are medical records. We can beat her."

"Those arguments only come into play if I'm fighting her for custody."

"Then fight her for custody. She isn't taking him away from us. He needs you. He needs you too much."

"I can't make you do that."

"Make me do what?" She shook her head. "I love him. She isn't taking him away from us."

Lina met Adele for breakfast the following morning. Phil was gathering evidence for the temporary custody order his attorney planned to file first thing Monday morning, so Lina had offered to take Liam with her.

"You can't be surprised," Adele said after Lina told her the events of the previous day. "The only reason she was here was to get Phil. She's finally accepting that will never happen."

"She's not taking him," Lina said emphatically. "Whatever it takes. We're going to get him." She felt a lump in her throat as she looked at Liam, whose eyebrows were pulled together in concentration as he tried to zip up the jacket of the teddy bear he was holding. Losing him wasn't an option.

"What about Logan? What did he say?"

"Nothing yet." She pulled her gaze back to Adele. "We haven't told the kids. There's nothing to tell them yet. But Logan is starting to come around. It may be an adjustment, but he'll be okay. Phil thinks we have a good chance of being granted joint custody. With that she can't leave."

"Who's going to watch him while you work?"

"Probably a nanny. I'm not going to worry about that yet." She'd do whatever it took, even if it meant switching to interior decorating full time so she could be home with him, if that's what the judge required.

"Is he always this good?" Adele asked.

"He's good at entertaining himself if that's what you mean. I think he's been forced to."

"I'm pregnant," Adele calmly announced.

"What?" Lina's eyes flew to Adele. "By—by William?"

"Yes, by William," Adele said, frowning at her. "He's my boyfriend."

"I know. I just—why didn't you tell me?"

"I just did."

"Does he know?"

"Of course he knows. It was his idea. I'm forty-three years old. I didn't even think I'd be able to get pregnant. I was just trying to humor him. It only took him a month to knock me up—asshole."

"Oh my God, Adele." Lina came around the table and gave her a hug. "You're going to be a mom."

***

As Lina preceded Phil and his attorney into the courtroom two weeks later, nerves churned in her stomach. She sat in the first row behind Phil and his attorney. A few minutes later she heard the sound of the door opening as Kim and her lawyer appeared. Lina didn't acknowledge her, staring straight ahead as Kim took a seat at a table beside her attorney.

A door in the back of the room opened, and a bailiff ordered everyone to stand as the judge entered the room. The next hour was a blur. Phil's attorney spoke first, outlining their case and what they were seeking, full custody of Liam. Phil didn't expect to get it, but he thought it would give him a better chance at gaining joint custody.

Kim's attorney stayed mostly silent as Phil's attorney claimed Kim didn't spend enough time with Liam, providing fifteen months of invoices from seven different babysitters. Liam spent an average of sixty-five hours a week away from Kim, not including his time with his father. Next, the Christmas incident was outlined. This time Kim's attorney did object, stating his client had offered Liam to his father and that the caregiver in question was licensed in the state. Finally, Phil's attorney listed the number of extra weekends Kim had given Liam to Phil over the past six months. It amounted to an extra weekend each month. The attorney ended by saying that it was more in Liam's interest to be a member of a two-parent household.

When Kim's attorney spoke, he argued that it was unreasonable to make Kim stay in Maryland when her extended family all resided in New York. She had secured a position offering a substantial pay increase at a firm with more potential for personal growth. He argued that she was trying to build a career, and as a single working mother, the hours she spent away from Liam shouldn't be held against her.

When the lawyers were done speaking, the judge announced he would have a decision by the following week. Lina released a breath as she watched him leave the room. She had no idea how he was going to rule.

"I'm not staying here," Kim announced, addressing Phil directly as they all came to their feet. "We can end this all right here. If you agree to no child support, you can have full custody."

"He agrees," Lina said.

Kim continued to look at Phil. "Good. You can pick him up later today."

"Again?" Katie asked when Lina told her they were having a family meeting in the living room. "This is getting ridiculous."

Moments later Lina was beside Phil on the couch. Logan was in the club chair, and Katie was kitty-corner to them with Liam on her lap.

"Lo Lo," Liam announced, pointing at Logan.

"Why does he constantly say my name?" Logan asked.

"Because he loves you," Katie said. "Don't you, Liam?"

"Your mother and I went to court today to keep Kim from moving with Liam to New York," Phil began. "We left court with full custody. This is his home now. With us."

"All the time?" Logan asked. His gaze swung between his parents.

"Lo Lo!" Liam shouted.

"You hear that, Liam?" Katie asked. "You're going to live here all the time. No more crying because you have to leave."

"Yes, all the time," Phil answered Logan. "It's going to be an adjustment for all of us. But it was the only way we could keep her from taking him. We're going to have a nanny come to the house to watch him while your mom and I are working."

"What about his mom?" Logan asked.

"He's a Hunter," Lina said. "He belongs with us."

Epilogue

Four years later...

"Liam Michael Hunter," said the announcer.

Phil watched Liam confidently stroll across the stage to receive his diploma for completing kindergarten. As soon as he had the certificate in hand, he dropped down to one knee, pumping his fist in the air. The audience roared with laughter.

"Logan," Lina whispered. "Did you tell him to do that?"

"No." Logan laughed. "Matt did."

"No, I didn't." Matt laughed.

"Did you get it?" Lina asked Phil. "Did you get a picture?"

"Yeah, baby," Phil answered. "I videotaped him."

"I can't believe it," she whispered. "He's growing up."

"I don't know if five is growing up." He stroked his hand down her back when he realized she was crying.

"You know what I mean." She clutched Phil's arm as she leaned against him. "And now he's leaving." He was spending the next month with Kim's parents at their cabin in upstate New York.

"You have me and Logan." Logan had just arrived home after completing his sophomore year at Duke where he was studying architecture. Although he'd been heavily recruited for lacrosse, he'd decided he didn't love it enough to play in college. He'd ended his relationship with Tiffany the year before, breaking not only Tiffany's heart but Lina's as well. He'd told Phil he was too young to tie himself to one girl.

"It's not the same. The house is going to be too quiet without him."

"I'm sure Adele and William will let you borrow Elijah," he teased. Adele's son, who was now three, was notoriously energetic. He had only two speeds, tornado level and off.

"Be nice," Lina said.

"I was serious." He looked past Lina to where William was standing with Adele, holding a sleeping Elijah. It had taken a full two years, but Adele had finally forgiven him. She'd even asked him to give a toast at her wedding reception when she'd married William.

"I can't believe she didn't show," Lina whispered.

"I can." She was talking about Kim. Kim's parents, who were standing in the row directly behind them, had said she'd planned to come. In the four years since Kim moved to New York she'd visited only twice, and on both occasions she'd had meetings in Washington. She had no real interest in Liam. Her parents came down regularly. Lina insisted they stay at the house so they could have quality time with Liam. They'd taken him to Disney World the year before for a week, but this would be the longest period of time Liam would be away from home.

Phil's gaze shifted to Katie, who was staring down at her phone, no doubt responding to a tweet about Matt. She'd graduated a week earlier from the University of Maryland with a degree in philosophy. There had been times over the past couple of years when he'd wondered if she'd finish. Matt's career had begun to take off. Katie handled all of his social media, which had become a full-time job. She'd persevered, though, managing to graduate with honors. They were leaving the following week for Europe, where Matt was playing to sold-out venues across Scotland and Ireland. They'd been dating six years. Katie had informed Phil a few days earlier that if she believed in marriage, she'd marry Matt. Of course, she didn't believe in marriage because it was a man-made institution.

Phil's gaze traveled over his family. He figured Liam was the only graduate with three pairs of grandparents in attendance. To Alice's delight, she was Liam's favorite. He spent a weekend a month with Lina's parents, and Alice served as their on-call babysitter.

Megan, who was standing directly in front of them with her boyfriend, a medical student at the University of Chicago, had just completed her second year of law school at Northwestern.

Phil pressed his lips into the side of Lina's head, tightening his arm around her. He was truly blessed.

After the final graduate walked across the stage, the guests filed out of the auditorium and into the main lobby, where refreshments were being served. Lina smiled when she saw Liam making a beeline to Logan, confirming her suspicion that he was the one who'd told Liam to drop to one knee when Logan gave him a high five.

He came to her next, pausing just long enough to let her kiss him before shoving his certificate at her. "Look, Mommy. It says my name."

"It does. Why don't I hold it for you? I'll keep it safe."

"I'm going to go play with Alex," he said.

"Wait." Phil clasped the lapel of his jacket before he could run off. "You need to thank everyone for coming."

"Thank you for coming!" Liam yelled excitedly before bouncing away.

"*Interior Design* magazine is featuring your kitchen on the cover," William said, stepping up to Lina.

"My kitchen?" Lina's eyes widened.

"I just got the e-mail. The New York property. This is huge, Lina."

"Oh my God." She turned to Phil. "Did you hear that? My design." Her heart felt like it was beating out of her chest.

"I heard." He framed her face with his hands. "And I'm not surprised. Congratulations, baby," he said before kissing her softly.

SWIMMING NAKED

www.ingramcontent.com/pod-product-compliance
Lightning Source LLC
Chambersburg PA
CBHW030649120726
47905CB00001B/127